Ruin, Reins and Redemption

A Teapot Cottage Tale (#4)

Annie Cook

www.Anniecookwriter.com

*For my dearest friend Vicki Finlay, who started my
love of horses when we were in our teens,
too many moons ago to count.*

Chapter One

Without a scrap of warning, Stuart Thomson jolted wide awake, and realised he'd woken up in a different bed, in someone else's house.

Through the thick, confused fog of a heavy Chivas Regal hangover, he remembered that he was in the Lake District, on holiday with his eternally belligerent fourteen-year-old daughter Meghan. They were in a holiday house called Teapot Cottage on Ravensdown Farm, on the edge of a town called Torley. He was a very long way, both geographically and metaphorically, from his life as he used to know it.

He winced a little, and squinted, as the early morning sun bounced brightly into the bedroom through the four-inch gap between the curtains. He vaguely remembered dragging them together last night before he'd fallen into bed, but he clearly hadn't done it very well. His bleary eyes struggled to cope with the brutally cheerful light. He wasn't much of a morning person at the best of times, but this awakening felt like someone had smacked him across the top of his head with something blunt and heavy, and thrown shards of glass into his eyes.

He hadn't been drunk when he'd collapsed on top of the multi-coloured crocheted bedspread and passed out. At least, he didn't *think* he'd been drunk. It had been a very long time since he'd been on any kind of alcoholic bender.

No; last night's 'blowout' had consisted of a mere two glasses of brandy, admittedly liberal in portion-size, and with only a smattering of soda. Adrienne Raven, the owner of Teapot Cottage, had briefly dropped in to welcome him and Meghan, not long after they'd arrived, and she'd told him there were a few inches left in the bottom of a bottle under the kitchen sink. It had been left by the previous tenant, apparently, and she said he was welcome to it if he wanted it. The one small can of soda that had been left behind as well was the size you'd normally get on a long-haul flight to somewhere, or in a particularly stingy hotel mini-bar.

It hadn't gone far at all, and Stuart had reasoned (rightly or wrongly – he still couldn't decide) that a couple of very strong drinks were better than just one weak one, and there was no point in leaving half an inch of brandy in the bottle by itself. It would have ended up looking lonely and pathetic, after the soda ran out, and he wasn't a fan of it 'neat.' *Almost* neat, as an eighty-twenty ratio, wasn't quite so bad. As a totally bizarre twist on the Pareto Principle, it was hardly enough to add up to getting roaring drunk, but it was all a matter of tolerance, he supposed, as he rolled over and stretched his legs.

His capacity for alcohol used to be pretty high, although it had never been quite as high as he'd once kidded himself, or anyone else who would listen. Nowadays, it seemed that two generous drinks were enough to turn him into a morning-after basket case of desert-dry mouth and thumping headache.

He shouldn't have had the brandies at all, really. He should have known better. The last six years of having too much time to stare at four straight, too-close walls, with everything in the world to think about, had taught him a lot. The top thing on his list of eviscerating revelations was that having a bit too much to drink, even at a level where you assumed you could still function, could quite literally put you on a one-way road to hell.

For Stuart, the worst of circumstances had well and truly taken the shine off getting drunk or even pleasantly merry. He wasn't really interested in drinking, anymore. The brandies had been a token gesture; a kind of 'welcoming himself back to life,' in some vague way, and celebrating his freedom with a drink. It was never intended to be more than that. Even if there had been more brandy in the bottle, he doubted if he'd have drunk any more of it. It wasn't exactly his favourite poison. He'd been a gin and tonic man, once, and nothing like as self-aware as he'd thought himself to be, to gauge when he'd had enough or a bit too much of it.

Gin was fairly fashionable again these days, thanks to carefully executed marketing. It was now available in a dizzying array of colours and infusions too, designed to appeal to the younger crowd and to anyone like the man he used to be; keen to make some kind of misguided impression on colleagues, clients and friends. Stuart had loved to be the life of the party, always ready with a joke or a funny story, and alcohol had always helped to give him confidence. But many people still called gin 'Mother's Ruin,' and the closeness of that to the truth was as near to unbearable as anything could ever be for Stuart, without driving him clinically insane.

One mother in particular had been ruined forever by his desire to impress; a pregnant mother, innocently crossing the street, who wouldn't have been expecting a car to come around the corner at breakneck speed, driven by a man much drunker than he thought he was, who was late for a post-lunch meeting. That poor woman wouldn't have anticipated being flung forward and sent hurtling through the air at a frightening speed, to end up in a grotesque, twisted heap, a heartbeat later. And nobody in her world would ever have expected her and the baby she was carrying to end up dead.

But that's what had happened, and that poor young mother and her unborn baby were gone forever, in the blurry blink of a drunk-driver's eye. Stuart wondered when – or *if* – his nightmares would ever end. Would the day ever come when he'd be able to enjoy life again without the crippling guilt of still being alive after robbing another man of his wife and child? Would he ever be able to get behind the wheel of his car again without hearing or feeling that gut-wrenching thump, as his car hit poor pregnant Karen Balik and sent her flying for a hundred yards?

It was bad enough, that he'd hit her. She might have survived if that was 'all' it had been. But she'd landed on the opposite side of the road, in front of an oncoming truck that didn't have a hope of stopping or even slowing down, before she went under its wheels. Everything had happened *way* too fast and for that desperately unfortunate mother, and her child still waiting to be born, the ruin was crushing and complete.

Stuart remembered again now, how the screams of passing pedestrians had pierced the afternoon, along with the sirens that quickly followed. He'd sat in his car with his face in his shaking hands, as blood gushed into the gutter on the opposite side of the road.

Say nothing, do nothing, look at no-one. Wait for the police to arrive.

Somewhere within his shattered mind, he'd known they'd smell the alcohol on him, and he'd known his career as a high-flying corporate lawyer was over, in that instant flash of mother's ruin, almost unbelievable in how quickly it had all come to pass. Conversely, the minutes that had followed had felt like hours, as he'd sat there in his car, as solid as a statue, waiting for the consequences to unfold.

He'd pleaded guilty in an open and shut case, where there was nowhere to go but prison, and he'd found himself with plenty of time for self-recrimination. When Karen Balik's husband Nengah had found out his prison number and written to him, telling him he'd forgiven him for what he'd done because that's what God would want him to do, Stuart had no idea how to feel.

Simple, stark, straightforward script on white lined paper in a brown, unembellished envelope. Forgiveness, from the one person who should, by rights, have had the entitlement to hang his wife's killer in gibbet irons in the street, and leave him there to rot.

Stuart had served six years. He'd originally been sentenced to nine, without eligibility for parole for the first six. Model behaviour, supplying free legal advice to anyone who asked for it, and a long stint as a trained 'Listener' offering support to other prisoners in emotional crisis, had not only helped keep him safe and respected on the inside. It had all helped his parole application too, which had been granted at his very first hearing. Nobody stood up and howled at the injustice of his early release, and when he walked out of the prison gates with his suit hanging off him, thanks to the stone and a half he'd lost in the exercise yard, nobody was there to throw anything at him, verbally or otherwise. Nobody was there at all, in fact, which was exactly what he'd wanted.

There was a bus stop not far from the prison gates, but he'd decided to walk into town. It wasn't far, and he relished the freedom of finally being able again, to walk to *wherever* he wanted, and for as *long* as he wanted.

A 'greasy spoon' cafe near to the bus station (a place he'd once have turned up his nose at the mere sight of) made good on its promises of bottomless coffee and 'the best breakfast in town,' and it had felt like a guilty pleasure. It hadn't been a pretentious and over-priced bistro like the kind of place he used to frequent, and it hadn't offered a pavement, al-fresco option with a crisp white tablecloth, gleaming glasses and pitchers of bucks fizz to order. But it had been a lot better than the standard prison fare he'd become accustomed to. Luxury took different forms, he'd supposed, depending on where you were in life.

Stuart had then got on a bus for Taunton. On that hour's ride, which he'd also relished, he'd managed to see a lot more of life than he'd seen from his tiny, barred window for the previous six years. Even if most of it was inane and boring to most people, it wasn't at all, to him. It was real, everyday life that he hadn't been a part of, for way too long. As tragic as it was to admit, the banality of someone else's washing blowing on a clothesline, or a tramp rifling through a dustbin, was entertaining. It was affirming, somehow, that life really did roll on.

The time he'd spent in his hometown on that first day of freedom had been both terrifying and fascinating in equal measure. Things had certainly moved on apace from when he'd last been on the streets, and a lot of the shops had changed. His beloved Rising Moon Chinese restaurant was gone, replaced by a dodgy-looking dive called 'the Chook Shed,' that looked more like a not-so-subtle advertisement for salmonella than a worthwhile place to eat.

Comfortingly, some places were still where they'd always been. At least nobody had hijacked his favourite department store and turned it into an amusement arcade, and a shoe shop he'd once been very fond of was still trading successfully.

He had gone into the bank first, to pick up the new card that his prison social worker had arranged for him to collect. His mother had transferred some money into this account from one of his others.

His next stop had been the department store, where he'd bought three pairs of dark-denim jeans, half a dozen shirts, and a dark blue, lightweight blazer. He'd added a pair of funky trainers to the pile, along with some underwear and a couple of bundles of socks.

The baggy suit that had once fitted him like a glove and cost an absolute fortune had somehow felt incongruent with who he was, post-sentence. He'd resisted his initial urge to just bin it, and had asked the shop assistant to bag it up instead. He'd walked out of the store in a new outfit, carrying his old one in a separate bag under one arm, and from the minute he'd hit the streets again he'd felt a lot more 'normal.' No more did he feel like the disgraced, dishevelled, disbarred solicitor with guilt and shame written all over him. He was finally able to shake the feeling that he had no right to return to society.

'Clothes make the man,' someone once had said, and a lot of people laughed at the notion. He'd once thought it ridiculous himself, that a man could be so easily transformed simply by what he might choose to wear. But, having donned a far more casual set of clothing, Stuart had finally understood that in some cases, how you felt really *did* depend on how you were dressed.

In any case, he wasn't a confident, practising solicitor anymore, so why would he want to look like one? He was officially unemployed; one of the 'great unwashed' he used to sneer at, and the pretence of looking otherwise, as he wandered the streets in an effort to feel like part of the world again, had actually started getting on his nerves. There was no-one to impress anymore, with his over-priced and now less-than-fashionable suit and natty tie, or his obscenely expensive shoes. The man who had once been so driven by his own desire to stand out from the crowd was now overwhelmed by the need to conform; to not be obvious at all, to anyone.

That particular reality had been as new to Stuart as the outfit he was wearing. He'd handed the carrier bag of suit, shirt, tie and shoes into the first charity shop he could find, not caring that the only remaining testaments to his old sartorial self were his boxer shorts and his pair of dark grey diamond-patterned socks.

The next things on his list that day had been getting a good shave and a decent haircut, then calling into the High Street phone shop. He replaced his impossibly outdated i-phone with a new one that was eight times more capable, according to the shop assistant who'd been unusually kind and patient in explaining its different functions.

At the end of that first free day, he'd collapsed into a cab for the journey home from town to his mum's. Travelling by taxi was something he'd always taken for granted, in his past life, but that day it had felt like a true luxury, as he'd sat back and marvelled at how well the day had gone.

Nobody had spat in his breakfast, and the bus driver had been friendly. The shop assistants he'd interacted with had all been kind and polite. The barber hadn't tried to slit one of his carotids with his cut-throat razor, the woman in the charity shop had been absurdly grateful for his little gift of clothing and shoes, and the taxi driver had been inanely, cheerfully chatty. What's more, Stuart's money had appeared to be as good as anyone else's.

Yes, his first day on the streets had been a better start than he'd expected. He'd come to the conclusion that since he didn't have 'killer' tattooed on his forehead, nobody was any the wiser about who he was, where he'd been, or what he'd done to an innocent bystander in a flash of drunk complacency and smug self-absorption.

He blinked hard now, and dragged himself back to the present. It was probably time to get up.

Welcome to the first day of the rest of your life.

Stuart yawned, stretched again, and hauled himself out of bed, trying to ignore his pounding head. It was time to get the kettle on. Some good strong coffee was in order, not to mention a bacon sandwich, and it was possible that when those heavenly smells permeated the upstairs bedrooms, Meghan might be tempted out of her self-imposed exile. Her bedroom door was firmly shut, as he padded past it in his stocking feet, and headed down the stairs. He wasn't sure she'd even roll out of bed much before midday. From what he knew about teenagers, which admittedly was woefully little, he imagined they generally stayed stuck in their beds until someone went in with a crowbar and levered them out.

Yesterday's long trip up here hadn't exactly been laden with scintillating conversation, as he'd somehow foolishly hoped. Instead, his daughter had sat in resentful silence for most of the way, only perking up slightly when they stopped at a motorway services so she could demolish a plate of chips with some hideous form of plastic cheese poured all over them. All attempts at conversation had been met with sighs, monosyllabic grunts and rolls of the eyes.

More than once on the journey, he wondered why the hell he'd bothered to try and instigate a 'bonding holiday' with his only child. After so much time inside, he'd felt he owed it to Meghan to spend some quality time with her, without the normal day-to-day pressure of the home environment. As cramped as it was, they'd bumbled along together at his mum's little house ok for a couple of weeks, but he'd realised that some time away with Meghan wouldn't just give his poor old mum some much-needed breathing space. It might also lay the groundwork, for getting to know his daughter properly again and enabling her to learn a few things about the dad who should have been present but wasn't, during the most important developmental years of her life.

Rebuilding his relationship with Meghan was Stuart's top priority now, and he wanted their time away together to be meaningful and positive. It occurred to him that as far as his daughter was concerned, being taken away from her friends and familiarity for most of the summer break would probably feel less like a holiday and more like an abduction. But he wanted to make this work. He wasn't about to turn around and go home. Admitting defeat wasn't an option – at least not yet.

Downstairs, he frowned at the bright red Aga that dominated Teapot Cottage's cosy little kitchen. He knew nothing about how to use one, but it was switched on, and its hotplates were working. A whistling kettle sat on the bench, so he filled it from the tap, opened the chrome lid of the right hotplate, and sat it on to boil. So far, so good.

It was Saturday and there was, apparently, a fairly decent Farmers Market in the church hall, which acted as the town's community centre. Mrs Raven had mentioned it yesterday, when she'd popped in. She said it was worth a visit, to get a few provisions and he seemed to remember that it started at ten o'clock. He checked his watch. It was just after eight-thirty, so there was plenty of time to get a shower, a much-needed shave, and a bit of breakfast. But nothing ever happened before his first, all-important caffeine fix.

He found a packet of ground coffee in a cupboard next to the Aga, nestled next to a good-sized cafetiere. Just after His and Meghan's arrival, he'd also found half a dozen eggs in the fridge, along with a small block each of cheddar cheese and butter, a bottle of milk, and a packet of bacon. A loaf of home-made bread, a bowl of fresh tomatoes, and a bottle of red wine sat on the table, with a 'welcome' note propped up against it.

Considering holiday cottages didn't usually provide anything at all, Stuart thought the offerings were incredibly kind. It felt unusually generous, and that in itself was humbling. In prison, life had been anything *but* generous. It was a hard, uncompromising place, where kindness was pretty thin on the ground in all directions, and generally something to be suspicious of when it did rear its head.

He'd come out from his six years in 'the can' to find that he'd lost pretty much everything. His career was gone, of course, and so was his marriage. It had been an unpleasant revelation, how shallow his second wife had been. Annabel had very quickly decided that being associated with a banged-up killer was never going to help *her* career as a solicitor. She'd divorced him, sold the house from under him, and abandoned his daughter Meghan; all within the first year of his sentence.

Meghan had gone to live with her nan; his mother. She'd been just nine when Stuart had gone inside, and the transformation she had undergone in the six years he'd been absent was awesome yet terrifying to him. She was a young woman now, and she felt more like a stranger than his own flesh and blood. Aside from knowing nothing about teenage girls, he was all at sea to pinpoint even a small commonality between himself and his daughter, other than the shared loss of her mother, his first wife Willa, who'd died from a brain haemorrhage when Meghan was four.

Stuart appreciated how challenging life had been for Meghan. She was angry at the world, and in many ways her hostility was predictable. But he was very concerned that she'd started directing her anger towards people who *hadn't* abandoned her or let her down, as well as the ones who had. People like her teachers, the school psychologist, her nan, and a lot of the kids at school had suffered a backlash from her. Her belligerence hadn't won her many friends. A lot of people had started actively avoiding her, which only made her even more isolated and upset.

Meghan was 'remote,' her teachers said. She had a few friends that she spent her time with but to everyone else she was mostly uncommunicative, and especially unwilling to talk to anyone in authority, about anything that mattered to her. When pressed, she became hostile and abusive. The school counsellor hadn't been able to get very far with her, other than to simply confirm what Stuart and everyone else already suspected; she had 'abandonment issues' (*no shit, Sherlock!*) and was carrying a lot of rage and resentment, some of which appeared to be non-specific. It was hard to tell for sure, because she wouldn't talk about anything.

She was messing up her grades at school, too, and Stuart was conscious that her GCSE's were coming around in another year. The reality was that if she didn't pull her socks up, she wasn't going to get anywhere near the marks she was capable of achieving. Unless he could get her to change her attitude, it was going to be almost impossible for her to pass those all-important exams.

The last thing Stuart wanted to do was nag, or make like the whining parent, but he knew how important it was that Meghan do well at school. At some point in the near future, they were going to have to talk about it, and he hoped the holiday would put them on a better footing, so that when he did voice his concerns, they might be more amicably received. She might not yet fully understand the importance of her GCSE grades, but she needed to, one way or the other. Failing her exams (and shortening her prospects) wasn't the way he wanted her to appreciate how critical they really were.

He knew that Meghan had been heartbroken when he'd gone to prison, leaving her without the most important person in her life. She'd been forced to live – initially at least – with the stepmother she hadn't really warmed to, and he knew she was pretty pissed off with him for that. It was something they could and *would* talk about soon, and he'd brace himself for however hard she might rage at him over it, because it needed to come out, and he probably deserved every last lacerating word she had, to slash him with. But he still wasn't sure how she felt now about what he'd actually *done*. That conversation might be even more difficult, on both sides.

He'd written to her, all the way through his sentence, and she'd written back for a long time, but it all changed when she hit puberty and suddenly decided she was too angry with him to keep in contact. She'd written a blistering letter, just before she'd turned thirteen, telling him what an embarrassing, murdering asshole he was, and that she never wanted to write to or see him ever again. The letter had broken his heart, and although he'd continued to write to her after that, she'd never responded.

The prison psychologist had helped Stuart to appreciate that the angry rantings of a bewildered adolescent girl who was trying to make sense of herself and her messed-up life, with only her gran to guide her, were entirely understandable. He got it; he just wasn't entirely sure what he could do about it. But he resolved to do his damnedest to keep plugging away, in every way he could think of, to get things on an even keel.

He was under no illusions at all about how much rebuilding he had to do. Getting a job and achieving a measure of independence again was only part of it. He did have a decent amount of money in the bank, though, which was a pretty fair start. For all her faults, Annabel hadn't fleeced him during the divorce. She hadn't left him a single stick of furniture, but she'd consolidated the joint assets and made sure he got exactly half of what everything was worth. In typical lawyer-fashion, she saw to it that the money was meticulously and evenly split, with no loose ends to be tripped over or challenged. And she'd kept his car for him; a top-of-the-range Audi A8 coupe, that she'd had repaired after the accident and put into storage, along with his other personal possessions. The cost of it all had been paid out of his half of the settlement, of course; Annabel was fair, but she wasn't overly generous. She'd left his pension fund intact too, but probably mostly in the interests of preserving her own!

Stuart thought she probably should have sold the car, even with depreciation hitting it hard. But, to be fair to *her*, she knew how much he liked it. Keeping his car for him was the only real kindness she'd shown. It meant something, although it was hard to see it as much of a positive, given the fact that the Audi was now nearly seven years old and worth less than half of what he'd paid for it. It still stung, that he'd only got to drive and enjoy it as a brand-new car, for a few months before the accident.

Annabel absconding with eye-watering speed had left him reeling for a long time. They'd never even got to the point where they'd sat across from one another in the prison visitors' room, and he'd told her to get on with her life. She'd simply made her choice and gone ahead and acted on it without *any* conversation. She'd told him in a letter, that she was leaving. It felt cowardly to him, at first, but later he wondered if maybe it was all she was capable of doing, under the circumstances. After all, she hadn't asked for her own life to be upended. She never saw that coming, and she had to do what was right for herself, in response. She had a good reputation as a family law solicitor with the legal firm she was working for. They'd been talking about eventually offering her a partnership, even before Stuart had screwed up their lives.

Annabel had worked her socks off to get to where she was, and having her career tarnished over something that was none of her own fault was a terribly unfair prospect. She needed to salvage what she could before she lost all the traction she had gained. She'd only been thirty-six, when Stuart's accident had happened, and she was still at the stage in life where establishing herself careerwise was more important than love.

It would have been nice if she'd thought otherwise, but that wasn't realistic. She was still too young, and still had too far to go, and deep in his heart Stuart knew it. He had no choice but to sign the divorce papers and take her desertion on the chin.

He was a big boy; he'd bounce back. But Annabel dumping his daughter so completely, at the most vulnerable time of her young life, was a hard one to forgive. Would it have been so damned hard to maintain at least *some* form of contact, or at least ease herself out of Meghan's life a little more gently, in a way that made it less traumatic for the poor kid?

Although Stuart had lost his career, his marriage, and a lot of other things besides, none of that was as important anymore as re-establishing a good relationship with his daughter. Meghan had already lost so much herself, and still had so much to grieve for at such a tender age, and the fact that he'd been the cause of so much of it tore him apart. He made a promise to himself, that no matter what happened in his own life, even if it never recovered, he had to make sure hers would, and she would have the opportunities she fully deserved.

Killing Karen Balik and her unborn child had been the worst kind of accident, and he'd never forgotten for a single second that it had been the result of decisions that hadn't been accidental at all. He'd *chosen* to drink as much as he did, and he'd *chosen* to get behind the wheel of his car after the fact. He'd *chosen* to believe he was capable of driving responsibly. Every arrogant course of action he'd taken before that accident had been an active, conscious choice. He still grappled, more than most people would ever know, with his guilt and remorse.

Maybe most people with an ounce of compassion would acknowledge that while it didn't exactly compensate for the loss of two lives, or the devastation for two families, Stuart Thomson had paid his debt to society in judicial terms. They might also believe that maybe, condemned forevermore as he was to regretting his actions on that fateful day, he'd already suffered enough. Maybe most people would feel that he'd accepted and dealt with his punishment; that he'd paid a high enough penalty already without being further condemned by others whose own selfish, catastrophic errors of judgement and terrible mistakes in life mercifully fell short of ending someone else's life. Maybe his daughter, with enough time and maturing perspective, might eventually forgive him for the mess he'd made of *her* life, and maybe he would, at some time in the future, get to rebuild his own.

That was a hell of a bunch of big maybes, but they were all he had to hang his hopes on, for now.

One of Stuart's biggest revelations, in the aftermath of everything, was seeing who'd stuck around and who hadn't. A surprising number of people did, which continued to surprise and humble him, but many had drifted off, consistently failing to respond to his messages, or crossing the street or suddenly disappearing into shops or offices on 'urgent errands,' when they saw him coming and wanted to pretend they hadn't.

It wasn't so much the statistic *itself* that upset him, because he'd been prepared for some fallout. He knew some of the people in the crowd he used to hang out with would bail on him. What got to him the most was who had made which choice. Some of the people he thought would turn their backs on him had done quite the opposite, while others; people he'd once thought of as good friends, had melted away like ice on a hotplate.

Nothing like the small matter of manslaughter, to sort the wheat from the chaff.

Meghan had endured a similar experience; not so much when it first happened, but later, with certain friends who came and went. She too had felt the support of some who had matured enough to understand that her father's life-robbing error of judgement wasn't her fault. She'd also felt the pain when the more vacuous and shallow of her so-called friends found out what had happened in her past and backed off and fell out of contact.

Of Stuart's friends who'd stayed, most had reasoned that it could have been any one of *them* instead of him, especially those who'd been just like him; cocky enough to believe their own half-drunk, slurred self-assurances that they were fit to drive after three pints of ale (or three gin and tonics) too many. Stuart's experience had compelled some of his friends to question themselves, and he was glad about that. If, after witnessing his experience, just one of them made the choice not to get behind the wheel under the influence, then more good had ensued than expected. Every cloud has a silver lining, even if it was for someone else.

Some of Stuart's friends had also openly observed, from various points along the spectrum between benevolence and frustration, that he'd managed to turn self-flagellation into an art form and, at some point, he had to stop beating himself up about the past. He knew they were right. But it was a lot easier to say, from the benefit of distanced perspective, that everyone made mistakes and at some point they had to forgive themselves, try to be a more mindful person than they were before it happened, and get on with living their lives.

The friends all meant well. Everything had been said with the best of intentions, with real commitment to helping Stuart and Meghan in whatever way they could, to build new lives. The support was wonderful, and it helped a lot, both practically and psychologically. He was profoundly grateful to the people who cared enough to want to be a part of that long and difficult process of reconstruction.

Stuart didn't volunteer much information about himself anymore, to people he didn't know. It wasn't through shame, although there was of course still plenty of that. His decision to be circumspect was borne of concern for his daughter, and the fact that it wasn't just he who need to rebuild his life. Meghan's life had been decimated too. She had lost her mother to a brain haemorrhage, her grandfather to a stroke, her father to the courts and prison, and her stepmother to abandonment. Her home had been sold from beneath her, and friends who she'd trusted had rounded it all off for her by dumping her like a hot brick. She needed time to allow her boat to stop rocking too. There was a very real need for them both to deflect as much attention as possible away from themselves while they figured out a new way forward.

The less outsiders knew, the better.

The kettle started whistling on the Aga, which punctured Stuart's bubble of thought. He grimaced at the empty glass from last night, sitting on the bench and still stinking of brandy, with a little still sitting at the bottom that he'd somehow managed to miss. As he rinsed it out, he was glad that the only thing left to drink in the place was Adrienne Raven's gifted bottle of wine. He was fairly sure she wouldn't be offended if he returned it to her with a kind 'thanks anyway.' He was pretty much done with drinking.

He set about making the coffee and melted a knob of butter in the frying pan to cook the bacon. He also threw in a couple of eggs, for good measure, and broke the yolks. May as well have a bacon sandwich with an egg in it. A bit of extra protein never went amiss.

This morning's breakfast offering; the fail-safe Cholesterol Special.

As the smell of frying bacon filled his nostrils, Stuart cut a four slices of bread and slathered them with butter. He also sliced a couple of tomatoes. He had just finished making the coffee and was sitting down to his breakfast when he heard Meghan's bedroom door open. He looked up to see her coming down the stairs in her scruffy tartan pyjamas with a pair of bright blue bed socks on her feet. Her hair was rumpled. She was fourteen-going-on-fifteen but this morning she looked more like twelve.

He girded his loins for the usual contemptuous stare and condescending attitude, and was astonished when she just blinked distractedly instead. She didn't really look at him at all, and she spoke with something that actually verged on politeness.

'Can I have some coffee?' she looked hopefully at the cafetiere on the table.

'Sure. Grab yourself a mug from the cupboard and help yourself. There's an extra sandwich too, if you want it.'

Stuart tried not to sound too keen or insistent. Meghan was going through a fussy phase with food; changing her mind every other day about what she would or wouldn't eat. He was worried about her getting enough nutrition, so he always made a point of making a variety of things available, and he mostly let help herself to whatever she wanted to munch on. If some of what she chose for herself wasn't high on the healthy list, it was at least still sustaining in some form, which was better than having to deal with an eating disorder and a flat-out refusal to eat what was put in front of her, no matter how much trouble he or his mother might have taken, to prepare it.

He'd decided that stocking up on fruit, low-fat cheeses and yoghurts and low-sugar rice puddings was the way to go, along with a variety of cooked foods that could be eaten cold from the fridge, such as ham, roast beef, cooked prawns, or chicken slices, so she always had choices. His mum did most of the cooking but whenever Stuart did it he always made an extra helping of whatever he cooked, so Meghan could simply reheat it if she was in the mood for something more substantial than a few slices of salami. He'd learned, through bitter experience, that trying to insist on her eating anything specific that he deemed to be important usually just prompted her to refuse point blank to eat it.

Last weekend, he'd clearly been too enthusiastic with his offering to make Meghan a 'bacon butty.' She'd screwed up her face in response and said 'Eew! Dead pig? No thanks.' This morning though, she seemed perfectly and inexplicably happy to fill her face with an egg and bacon sandwich and was eating it with something approaching real delight. He quietly acknowledged the small but important victory, but wisely chose not to comment on it. If he seemed half-hearted about food, she would be interested. If he seemed keen, she wouldn't be, at all. He'd long since given up trying to figure that out, but he had learned how to manipulate her into eating. All he had to do was pretend he didn't care.

'How did you sleep?'

Meghan nodded. 'Pretty good,' she mumbled, through a mouthful of breakfast. 'You?'

Stuart pulled a face. 'Okay I guess, although that Chivas brandy I drank last night bit me royally on the arse this morning.'

Meghan grimaced. 'Yeah, you kind of look more shit than royal, Dad.'

Stuart pulled another face. 'Thanks, brat.'

'What're we going to do today?'

Stuart talked about the need to get some groceries and mentioned the Farmers Market. Meghan just shrugged, half-heartedly. While she wasn't exactly hard to please, very little seemed to impress her these days. It was that horrible, seemingly unavoidable fourteen-ness he'd been warned about.

On bad days, she was a monster; belligerent, critical, and virtually impossible to engage in any kind of constructive conversation. Stuart prayed for the 'good' days, when she didn't deign to speak to him or look at him at all.

He had to concede though, that a trip to a local produce venue to look at lettuces and hocks of ham was hardly the thing to set the interests of a teenage girl on fire. He wondered if there was a bowling alley or a cinema close by, where they could go sometimes while they were up here. He couldn't expect his daughter to sit at home every night for seven weeks of summer with no interaction of interest.

What was there, around here, to go and do? He admitted to himself that he hadn't really done much research into that, before they came. He'd been more concerned with them spending quality time together and getting to know one another properly again. He was hopeful that they could become close again, like they were before he'd so successfully and thoroughly ruined their lives.

An hour later, after showers and another pot of coffee, they were ready to leave the cottage. Meghan surprised him, by stopping to gaze out through one of Teapot Cottage's panoramic windows and remarking on how stunning the view was, of Torley Valley.

'Yeah, it's something, alright. There are worse places to hang out for a while, I guess.'

As they left the cottage through the front door, Meghan gasped, and pointed to the lush green field that flanked the cottage. A large pale brown horse with an almost-white mane and tail was standing stock still at the fence line, quietly gazing at them both with the most exquisite brown eyes.

Meghan immediately walked over to the horse and began talking to it in a gentle, quiet voice. Stuart swiftly swallowed down the instinctive parental warning to be careful, and stood silently watching her as she interacted with the horse. His heart was in his mouth. Next to his slight slip of a daughter, the animal seemed huge. She continued to speak to it, in low tones. She stroked its nose and let it nuzzle her hand. All of a sudden, she put her arms around its neck and drew closer to it.

The horse rubbed its nose against her shoulder and stood quietly as she hugged it. Stuart hoped she wasn't hugging it too hard; that it wouldn't bite or kick out at her in protest.

She released it and turned to him. He eyes were shining.

'Oh, Dad! Isn't she beautiful? She must belong to the farm.'

'Yeah, probably. Maybe you can ask up there about her later, find out what her name is, and all that.'

'Carrots, Dad. We'll have to get a bag of carrots at the market, maybe some apples too, so we can feed her.'

'You'll need to ask the owners, sweetheart, if it's ok to feed her. It's manners to ask, and she may not be allowed certain things.'

Stuart knew a fair bit about horses, having ridden when he was young. Friends of his parents had run a local stables, taking care of people's horses and offering lessons. He'd learned to ride when he was about ten, and when he was old enough, he'd worked there at weekends and in the school holidays, mucking out and exercising the horses from time to time. Once he'd got a bit older and more interested in hanging out with his friends instead of shovelling dung and sweeping stables, he'd given up the riding and hadn't given much thought to it since.

They would definitely need to find out if it was okay to feed this horse. Most people were very particular about the welfare of their animals, and rightly so. But, Stuart reasoned, it wouldn't hurt to buy a bag each of apples or carrots; things they could eat themselves if it turned out they weren't appropriate for someone else's horse! At worst, they'd end up eating a lot of apple crumble and carrot cake for a week or two.

They drove into the town, which was busy. The car park at the back of the church hall where the Farmers Market was being held was already full, with cars queued waiting for spaces to free up. He managed to find a spot just off the pretty High Street, in a road called Amble Walk, directly outside a cafe called Ye Olde Torley Tea Shoppe, which he recalled had been mentioned by Adrienne Raven. The owner was a friend of hers, apparently, although Stuart had forgotten what Adrienne had said the woman's name was.

The place didn't look particularly special, although the food in there was reportedly very good. Stuart thought he might treat

Meghan to a pot of tea and a cream cake once their errands were done, before they set off for home.

The Farmer's Market was bigger and much busier than he expected. There were about thirty stalls in total, crammed into the space, selling everything from rustic wooden bird houses and columns of netted nuts to hang in trees, to blocks of delicious-looking home-made fudge and sumptuous rounds of cheese. There were plenty of people milling around, browsing, buying and chatting. He assumed that most of these traders were local cottage-industrialists, who made their own lemon curd and cushion covers at their kitchen tables and sold them to friends, family, and the occasional passing tourist.

Meghan wandered off more or less immediately. A few minutes later, he spotted her hovering over a small stand that offered fresh flowers and bits of cheap and cheerful jewellery. She was talking with the girl who was manning the stand. They were of similar age, he noted with pleasure. Maybe his daughter was already making a friend.

The food at the fruit and vegetable stands looked colourful and fresh. Stuart bought a few things, including a bag of apples and another of carrots, and stowed everything away in his backpack. Meghan had moved on from the jewellery stand and after casting an eye around, he noticed that she was now over at the other side of the room, talking to Adrienne Raven, who was selling jams, jellies and boxes of free-range eggs. He was suddenly very glad he hadn't bought eggs from another stand that was selling them. It would have felt vaguely disloyal to his new landlady, particularly since she'd already given them their first half dozen as a gift when they'd arrived.

'Hello again,' he ventured as he got closer to the stand. He smiled briefly.

Adrienne looked almost excited to see him.

'Oh Mr Thomson! Hi! You made it! I hope you've been able to get a few provisions? It's a bit more expensive in here than the town's little supermarket, if you could call it that. But everything's organic and absolutely fresh, and it all tastes like it's supposed to. I think it's worth the extra few pennies most things might cost, but that's just me.'

She smiled, a little self-consciously. Clearly, the market was something she felt passionate about. He didn't blame her one bit. The place was fantastic. It looked to be just as much of a catch-up and gossip point as a place to buy bread and cheese, he noted, looking at the handful of crowded tables in one busy corner of the hall where people could buy a cup of tea or coffee and a slice of homemade cake from a selection on offer. People were chattering their heads off. Coming here every Saturday was probably the highlight of everyone's week.

He turned his attention back to Adrienne, who was speaking to him again.

'Meghan was asking me about Astro, the horse in the field by the cottage. I've just been explaining. We took her in, about three months ago. She'd been abandoned on the edge of the village, just tied up and left at the side of the road, of all things! She'd been very neglected. A local resident reported it to one of our local vets, and he rescued her and treated her for cracked hooves, parasites and various other problems. He's looking for a home for her but in the meantime she needs a safe place to stay while he rehabilitates her, so we've got her at Ravensdown for the time being.

'We don't take in strays, as a rule,' she added. 'Our farm's not really equipped to support that, but our vet's a very good friend and Astro is beautiful, so of course we wouldn't dream of saying no. She's part Palomino, we think. She seems happy to share the field with the sheep, and they don't seem to mind her.'

Adrienne's eyes were dancing. She was an attractive, slim, fifty-something woman. When she'd popped in at Teapot Cottage last night to welcome Stuart and Meghan, not long after they'd arrived, she'd seemed like a very merry sort and today she was no different. Stuart decided that he liked her. So, apparently, did Meghan, who had a fairly hard and fast rule not to offer so much as the time of day to anyone she hadn't immediately fallen in love with.

It seemed that carrots and apples, in moderation, would be perfectly acceptable for Astro, as would the occasional polo mint in the absence of the better alternative of fresh mint, which horses did love, and which acted as an effective aid to digestion. He did remember that much from his own days of hanging around at stables. Adrienne added that there was a little mint in the herb garden at the back of the cottage, and they might also find some growing in the hedgerows along the driveway to the main road if they were prepared to look for it. Her stepdaughter had apparently sowed a lot of stuff that grew quite well in hedgerows, and everyone knew how rampant mint could be, if it decided it liked where it was planted.

'Astro's lovely,' Meghan spoke up. 'She's far too nice to not be loved or wanted by someone.'

'Oh, I agree,' Adrienne nodded. 'A few people have already expressed some interest, but she's had a really rough old time of things and Darren, the vet, is very particular about who she goes to. He'll be picky to a fault about that, so we may have her for a good while yet, but I don't mind at all because I feel exactly the same. She's a special girl, and she needs an equally special owner, bless her. She's no trouble. Darren comes to check on her every few days, and he's happy with her progress. She seems to be enjoying her life at the farm.'

'Why is she called Astro?' Meghan asked.

Adrienne smiled and shook her head. 'That's a very good question. And the answer is, I don't really know. My step-daughter Feen named her, and I'm sure she'll be happy to explain it, if you ever get chance to ask her. But she suits it, don't you think? Astro? Kind of ethereal and planetary?'

Meghan nodded and gently smiled. 'Yeah, I think it's perfect.'

As they were leaving, Stuart had a good look at the community notice board in the foyer, to see if there was anything interesting happening in the area. There was a notice inviting people to audition for an up-coming play at the local amateur dramatics club. He mentioned it to Meghan, who grimaced at him.

'I can't think of anything worse. But you should go for it, Dad!' She smirked mischievously. 'Actually, all joking aside, that could be a bit of a laugh. I heard that a lot of solicitors end up in am-dram. All that posturing in court, I suppose. It's probably good training!'

Despite himself, Stuart laughed out loud. Who was this mellow, humorous person, and what had she done with his moody, sulky, waspish teenage daughter?

As they were loading their stuff into the car, he remembered about tea and cake.

'D'you fancy it?' he enquired.

Meghan shook her head. 'Nah. I'm still full of that bacon sandwich. Maybe we can come down another time for a cream tea. Make it a special treat, or even have a proper lunch? I bought a couple of books at the market, off that second hand stall. I'm keen to get started on them.'

Stuart started the car. 'Didn't you bring a whole box full of books?'

'Yeah, but these are a bit special.' She rummaged around in her voluminous canvas bag, pulled out two books, and waved them at him. To his astonishment, they were craft books. One was about making jewellery and the other was writing calligraphy.

'Wow! They look interesting. You planning on learning a few new skills?'

Meghan shrugged. 'We did a bit of calligraphy at school, and I really liked it. And the jewellery book? I was talking to the girl on that flower stand at the market. Her name's Jayde, and she told me she makes a bit of her own jewellery that she sells on there. Some of it was nice, what she made. Earrings and stuff. I think I'd like to give it a go myself. Maybe I could sell some too, or get her to do it for me, for commission or something.'

'Good for you! Might teach you another art too; the art of sitting still.'

Meghan poked her tongue out at him. 'Yeah well, the books were only a quid each, although I might have to get some pens and blank paper. You know, to practice my calligraphy?'

Stuart frowned at her. 'Well, why didn't you say, when we were in town? We're halfway back to the bloody cottage now! We could have picked some stuff up for you before we left. There was a stationery shop, wasn't there? Not far from the hall?'

'For God's sake Dad, just chill the hell out, would you?' Meghan snapped, her impatience returning with full force. 'It can wait, and this place isn't exactly a heaving metropolis of choice, in case you hadn't noticed. It's a bit pathetic, don't you think? We should go over to Carlisle in the week, find a *good* shop, and get some proper stuff.'

Stuart shrugged again, resisting the urge to point out that until Meghan decided whether she actually was serious about either of her new projects, it might be wiser to buy just a few things, which almost certainly could be bought locally. But, as they approached Teapot Cottage, he could see that what she was more concerned about right now was talking to that horse again; Astro. The car was barely stopped before she was out of it and over at the fence. The horse wasn't there, so Meghan called to her.

'Astro? Come on, gorgeous girl. I have apples for you!'

Stuart rummaged in the backpack, found two apples, and tossed them over to his daughter, who caught them expertly.

'Come on, girl. Come and get these. Yum, yum!'

Astro ambled over slowly from the other side of the field, her eyes slightly wary until she recognised Meghan and her gait became more decisive as she walked towards her.

'That's it. Come on. Here!' Meghan held out an apple.

Like every other protective father whose imagination was wretchedly graphic when it came to the harm that might befall his offspring, Stuart held his breath and waited for the bloodcurdling shriek that indicated Astro had bitten Meghan's fingers off.

Mercifully, it never came. Instead, the horse took the apple gently and crunched it slowly to a pulp, never taking her eyes off Meghan as she did so. As Stuart watched, in awe, horse and teenage girl looked deep into one another's eyes and held their gaze. It really did seem to be a true bonding of souls.

Stuart felt his skin prickle. He could hardly breathe. Even the hard-bitten lawyer in him could see the most profound connection taking place between this horse and his daughter. But it was too late to intervene, even if he'd wanted to. Meghan had clearly lost her heart already, and it looked very much as if Astro had lost hers too. These two damaged, delicate, lost little souls had found and given balm to one another through a connection Stuart could categorically feel, even if he didn't understand it. The lump in his throat was huge.

Meghan reached up slowly and placed her arms gently around the horse's neck again, as she'd done earlier that morning. She laid her cheek against Astro's, murmuring to her softly. Again, Astro rubbed her nose against Meghan's shoulder. The horse snorted gently, and stood stock still, simply absorbing the young woman's love for her that even Stuart could feel. It was a magical thing to witness. Meghan stood with her eyes closed as Astro then placed her nose into the side of Meghan's neck. Somewhere in Stuart's chest, something moved.

He eventually shook himself out of the strange little bubble, and picked his and Meghan's backpacks out of the car. His hands were shaking as he unloaded his shopping onto the kitchen table.

What the hell was that? What just happened there?

He made them both a cup of tea and went to sit in the window seat, staring down at Torley valley. Was that some kind of magic, that he'd just witnessed? The very question made him want to laugh out loud. It seemed that he had seen and felt a true meeting of the minds between a horse and a human being.

People talked about those kind of connections all the time, but Stuart largely believed them to be a little fanciful. Loving someone was real, of course, and having them love you back, if you were lucky, well – that was real, too. He'd experienced that. His love for his first wife Willa, Meghan's mother, had been deep, real, and meaningful. His love for Annabel had been nothing like it, but Stuart believed it had been real, nonetheless, in its own way. His love for Meghan was also very deep and real. He truly believed it was the only reason his heart kept beating at all.

But as to the whole soul-connection thing between a horse and a human, it was a bit of a stretch to imagine *that* being real, even though enough people had professed to have found it. Having never experienced it for himself, he simply had to believe – or not – those who said it was real for them.

He'd always been on the fence about the idea of 'soulmates' but this connection between Meghan and Astro had felt almost surreal. It unsettled him, although he couldn't articulate why. Maybe it was the subtle challenge to his own belief system that prompted him to question the reality he'd always felt so sure of, and so comfortable with. Was he jealous, on some level, that his daughter had experienced something verging on the transcendental, that he'd never had the chance to realise for himself? Or maybe it was more basic; that he'd like to take the place of the horse, and know that she loved him more than anyone or anything else.

Meghan came into the house, and he pointed to her cup of tea, which he'd placed on the coffee table by the sofa.

'Thanks, Dad.'

'So, you've made a new friend then?'

His daughter allowed a slight smile. 'Yeah, I have. Well, two actually. There's Astro of course, and there's Jayde, the girl at the jewellery stand at the Farmer's Market. She's a year older than me. She lives in town, and she told me there's a youth club that meets every Friday night in the same hall.'

Stuart looked at his daughter, again baffled by the transformation she seemed to have undergone in less than 24 hours. Maybe all this child had needed was a change of scenery. When they'd arrived Meghan had been as bad-tempered and sulky as usual. He'd been wondering how to keep her amused, but if today was anything to judge by, he might not have that much to worry about after all.

'So, is it something you'd want to go to, this youth club?' Again, he was careful not to appear too enthusiastic, not wanting her to dig her heels in and write off what might be a nice opportunity before she even properly found out what it was, just so she could have the upper hand.

Meghan shrugged. 'I dunno. Probably not. It sounds a bit lame, to be honest. You know, small-town people, small-town thinking, all that stuff.'

'Hmmm. Maybe.' As always, Stuart chose his words with great care. 'Did Jayde seem like a small-town thinker, though?'

Meghan thought for a moment then shook her head emphatically. 'No, not at all. She seemed kind of cool actually, you know, nice. Friendly, but not too much. I told her I was here for seven weeks and she suggested I go down sometime and see what it's all about, but she didn't make a big deal about it.'

'Well, I guess if she's cool, some of the other kids must be too. Cool kids don't hang out with losers, at least I don't think they do. They never did in my day, and some things don't change. Her friends might be nice people too.' Stuart kept his tone carefully casual.

Meghan shrugged again. 'Yeah, maybe.'

Stuart yawned and stretched his neck from side to side. 'Ah well, let me know if you decide you want to go. I can run you down there and pick you up again.'

He decided to go for a jog, and as he pulled on his running gear, he sent a silent prayer of gratitude into the ether, for whatever forces were at work to make his usually hostile and uncommunicative daughter not only civil, but verging on friendly towards him.

Chapter Two

Meghan was relieved that her Dad had taken off for a while. His runs were usually half an hour to forty-five minutes long, then he'd spend another ten minutes or so in the shower, so it was a decent block of time for her to relax and not feel like she was under a microscope. She loved him, she supposed, but she didn't know him that well anymore, and *Christ*, he could be a pain in the arse! He never left her alone for more than five minutes. She got that he was keen to establish a good relationship with her again, and she tried not to let his puppy-dog enthusiasm get on her nerves, but the truth was, she still wasn't sure how she really felt about him.

She was pretty embarrassed about the letter she'd sent him, a couple of years ago. It had been mean, and she knew she probably shouldn't have sent it. Ever since he'd come out, she'd been waiting for him to say something about it, but he hadn't. He was acting as if it hadn't even happened. She'd been surprised when he'd carried on writing to her after she'd sent it, and had never mentioned it in any of *his* letters. He'd also said, many times, that she could go and visit him if she wanted. She hadn't expected that, and she hadn't been sure how to write back.

At first, she wasn't ready to apologise for her letter, because her anger had been more than just a flash in the pan. It had lasted for many months, and as more time passed, even when she'd simmered down again, the prospect of responding to any of his overtures seemed to get harder, so it just became easier not to. She certainly hadn't wanted to visit him in prison! But later, when she started to realise how much her horrible words must have hurt him, she was too embarrassed to say sorry. She figured she could probably say it now, if he said something about it first, and she was waiting for that chance, but so far he hadn't said a word about it, and she wondered if he ever would. It wasn't a conversation she felt ready to initiate, herself.

She thought back to when she was nine, before her world had exploded for a second time. Her Mum had died when she was four and she and Stuart had been on their own for a couple of years, adjusting to life without her, until he'd met Annabel. She was a solicitor too, and they'd met at some fancy function somewhere. Annabel had been there with someone else, apparently, but it had only seemed like five minutes later that she'd ditched that dude and started seeing Stuart instead. Then she started staying over at weekends, then some nights during the week as well, until she more or less became a permanent fixture at the breakfast table.

A few months after that, Stuart had sat Meghan down and asked her whether or not she'd be okay about having a stepmother, who would never take the place of her own mother '*of course,*' but who would be a good mum to her, if Meghan was prepared to give her a chance. She had nothing against Annabel, and she'd shrugged her shoulders, and said 'okay.'

From the start, she'd been more or less indifferent about her stepmother. There was nothing, either specific or vague, to be unduly upset or overly enthusiastic about, and her father seemed to be happy, so she regarded Annabel as an inevitable but not unpleasant addition to the household.

It had lasted three years in total. The first two were what most people would have called normal, with the three of them living together in something approaching harmony. They weren't what you'd call a close unit, but they'd bumbled along like any other family. Day to day life had been okay, but Annabel always seemed to be preoccupied with other things, almost as if Meghan and her dad were a bit of an afterthought in her life that she had to keep remembering to engage with. Stuart was always pretty busy too, although he did manage to make more time. They had good holidays, and usually did nice things on the weekends. Life had felt pretty stable, all things considered.

And then Stuart's accident happened. That was when everything changed.

Him screwing up so badly and going to prison, well, that wasn't what Annabel had signed up for, was it? The lovely house, the flash cars, posh breaks abroad every few months, untold hours in five-star spas, *that* was what she'd signed up for.

Not long after Stuart had so thoroughly disgraced himself, Annabel's initial mortification had turned to anger. She ended up being as mad as a hornet for most of the time, and she barely spoke to Meghan at all. A few months after that, her self-preservation gene had kicked in, and she'd started divorce proceedings, loudly and publicly telling anyone who would listen that the marriage had been doomed from the start. Stuart had a drinking problem, he was verbally abusive when he was drunk, blah, blah, blah, and why should she be expected to wait around for someone like that and watch her personal and professional reputations become ever-more tarnished by association while she brought up someone else's 'snot'?

The man Annabel had described was a far cry from who Meghan understood Stuart to be, but maybe there was more going on than she'd seen for herself. At seven, eight or nine, how did you know if your dad really was as dysfunctional as someone else who was close to him in a different way said he was? By the time Annabel got around to saying all that, Stuart had already gone to jail, and the chance to observe her dad herself, to see what might be so 'wrong' with him, had gone.

Although Annabel's abandonment of her had stung for a while, it hadn't left Meghan feeling as bereft as everyone expected her to feel. It wasn't very nice, being labelled publicly as a 'snot' to people she didn't even know, but her ambivalence about her stepmother had acted as a kind of shield against being too hurt by it. She could also kind of appreciate now, as her own perspective on life was maturing, how difficult things might have looked or felt for the image-conscious, social-climbing second wife, once her husband had smashed his own credibility to pieces and ended up in jail. Who *would* want to be in that situation, picking up the pieces, trying to save face and preserve your own reputation, while being expected to start paying all the bills and single-handedly care for someone else's kid?

Meghan supposed that if Annabel had loved her father (or even Meghan herself) as much as she'd apparently loved their lifestyle, she might have stuck with it. Obviously, she hadn't. Her career clearly meant more to her than anything else, and on one level Meghan did understand that. After all, having slaved your guts out studying for a gazillion years, going into massive debt and sacrificing what ought to have been the craziest, most fun-filled years of your social life at uni, to pass your exams and get your dream career instead, wouldn't you fight as hard as you could to keep it after someone else had selfishly fucked everything up for you?

By the time she'd managed to work through the bewilderment and disappointment at how Annabel had spouted off, without a care for how hurtful it was to anyone else, Meghan had become fully aware that she and her stepmother had never felt, or even managed to fake, any real affinity with one another.

So what was the point in being angry, then, about the way the woman had behaved? Annabel had muttered, as she'd dropped Meghan at Nan's and driven away from the curb; 'it's nothing personal.' For her, it obviously wasn't. It was less about Meghan herself than it was about the circumstances. No love invested, so no love lost.

Meghan had tried to put it all behind her as best she could, and focus on the fact that that living with her nan had turned out to be the lesser of two evils. As Nan had put it, on the back of everything that had already happened, Meghan didn't need to grow up in an 'emotional vacuum,' which is all Annabel would have been capable of providing.

'I'd have stepped in anyway,' Nan had explained, 'so you may as well be with me all the time, love. I'm over the moon to have you.'

Meghan didn't miss her stepmother at all, but she did miss their old house, especially her old bedroom. The one she had at Nan's was really small and cramped. She loved Nan, and living with her wasn't hard. In fact, Meghan thought she was pretty cool, as old ladies went. Sometimes she could be really annoying, like when she took ages in the bathroom when Meghan needed to use it herself, or she fussed too much about what she'd wear to go out, and how important it always was that her shoes matched her handbag, of all weird things. But she was kind, generous, and loving, and she'd even tried to listen to Meghan's much-loved music. It was so funny though, how she'd shaken her head and confessed that no matter how hard or how often she tried, she just couldn't see what was good about it. Instead, she'd tried to get Meghan to listen to hers, which was all old seventies and eighties stuff, and when Meghan had shaken *her* head straight back, Nan had laughed and presented her with an expensive set of headphones.

It was a good compromise, and so typical of Nan, who had her own ideas and liked living her own way (which included sometimes playing that crappy old stuff so loud it literally rattled the windows), but she didn't want to spoil anyone else's fun.

When Stuart had first floated the idea of spending the summer away from Somerset, Meghan's stomach had clenched with dismay. The thought of spending seven weeks with him, in the confines of a small cottage in the middle of nowhere was the very last thing she wanted to do. She'd rather have stuck pins in her own eyes, but it wouldn't have helped to have said that, so she'd gritted her teeth and agreed to it. The only other choice available was to continue staying with Nan all summer. If Nan wasn't out and about all day every day with her silly old friends, she'd be having them over at the house, moaning and complaining about the state of the nation and their endless aches and pains. Meghan managed to miss most of that by being at school, but an entire summer of it, while she hung around the house, was more than she could face. Spending the time with her dad instead would hopefully be the less painful of the two cheerless choices, so she'd agreed to at least try to make it work with Stuart.

In any case, the only three friends she was interested in hanging out with were going to be busy or away for the summer themselves. Amy was going camping in Bordeaux with her extended family, which simply sounded boring, and Hayden had got himself a girlfriend and didn't really want to hang out much with anyone else, which suited Meghan just fine anyway, because who the hell wanted to be a gooseberry all summer?

Her other friend Elise had headed out to Queenstown in New Zealand, to visit her older brother who was out there working in a nightclub in the town. He'd bankrolled Elise's flights, and she was headed for a party-filled kiwi winter of skiing and après-ski, and maybe a bit of no-strings sex, if she found someone nice to have a fling with. That one, Meghan was seven shades of jealous about, and she didn't mind admitting it. Not that she'd had any sex yet, but it was quite an exciting prospect, and it didn't seem fair that Hayden and Elise were probably going to get the experience before Meghan could, herself. She had very little faith that she'd get the chance to lose her virginity way up here in a place nobody had ever heard of, miles from any kind of social scene, in 'the land the world had forgotten.'

Telling her friends she was off to spend the summer in the rainy old Lake District with her dad, in a place called Teapot Cottage, had made them laugh out loud, although their laughter wasn't mean. Hayden had wished her luck, saying he knew what a big deal it was, to be away just with her dad, who she had to get to know all over again in a new place, with nothing and nobody familiar around her to act as any kind of buffer.

What none of them got was the fact that for Meghan it wasn't just 'a big thing.' It was *shit-scary*. Being under her dad's microscope all summer was the worst thing that could ever happen. What if they discovered they hated one another? She had no idea what the next seven weeks would be like, but she was dreading it. There was always the possibility of running away, and hitch-hiking back to Nan's. Or Stuart could admit defeat and take her home early, himself. If she acted out enough, she could probably push him to it.

Today though, as a first day, had turned out surprisingly well. She had already met someone nice and been invited to a social function (if the youth club could be classed as such), and she had also managed to meet and fall in love with a horse, of all things.

Didn't see that one coming!

Until today, Megan had never touched a horse in her life. She remembered growing up with friends who were into horses. A couple of them had ponies and they'd spend hours and hours talking about them, but Meghan hadn't been interested. She couldn't see the attraction. But this horse, today, here in the field by the cottage, was something quite different. The experience wasn't just petting an animal in a field. There was something incredibly special about Astro. Meghan felt it as soon as the horse looked into her eyes. It was as if Astro could see right into her soul, and was telling her that everything was going to be okay. Even to herself, the explanation sounded corny but because she had no other way of describing it, it would have to do. She looked forward to spending more time with Astro. Smiling, she settled herself more comfortably into the window seat.

The sound of a car door slamming startled her. Blinking, she realised that she'd dozed off for a bit. The sun had moved around from the bay windows, leaving the room a little more in shadow than it had been before she'd fallen asleep, but not much. She could hear the shower upstairs, so her father was back, at least. That meant it was probably around lunch time. She checked her watch. It was twenty to two! She heard a man's voice outside and realised that whoever had driven up to the cottage had gone directly to the side of it and was talking gently to Astro. Curious, Meghan opened the front door and peered out.

An old but well-restored dark green Land Rover was parked in the driveway, behind her father's car. It had yellow signage on it, saying 'Lakeview Veterinary Practice.' Meghan remembered that Mrs Raven had said something about her vet checking up on Astro every week. She decided she wanted to meet him, to find out what she could about the horse.

When she got closer to the fence, she saw that he was on the other side of it, on his knees, with one of Astro's hooves in his hands. He was checking it closely.

'Hello.' Meghan volunteered. The vet looked up. He was in his late thirties, she supposed, and he had a kind face. He was well-built, with heavy tattoos all down his arms and across his chest and neck, and he had short dark hair, a well-trimmed moustache and goatee, and kind brown eyes. He was handsome, in a rough, careworn kind of way; way too old for Megan to have any real interest in, but she appreciated that a lot of women his own age might find him hot. He had a face that seemed to hold a lot of stories behind it.

'Hello yourself! He stood up and smiled, revealing a set of very nice teeth. 'Are you staying in the cottage?' Meghan nodded. She didn't know what else to say to him. But he kept smiling, and she decided he was probably quite nice.

He stood up and came towards her, offering his hand. 'I'm Darren Davies, local vet, and this is Astro.'

Meghan grinned. 'I'm Meghan Thomson, and I know her already. We made friends this morning.' As if to reinforce her comment, Astro came forward and immediately placed her nose into the side of Meghan's neck. Meghan hugged her gently.

'Wow! That's amazing!' Darren looked astonished. 'I've never seen her do that before. She's normally really shy with strangers.'

He seemed easy, relaxed and easy to talk to. Meghan found her confidence.

'Mrs Raven told me you found her abandoned. I can't believe anyone would do such a horrible thing.'

Darren shook his head. 'Ah, you'd be surprised what people are capable of. Ten years in the trade, and I still feel like ripping the heads off some of them, when I see how they treat their animals.'

He went on to describe how he'd found Astro tethered by a piece of fraying string to a barbed wire fence at the side of a busy road. It had been pouring with rain, but he'd abandoned his car to walk her a mile and a half to safety nonetheless, which wasn't easy as she had two cracked hooves and was malnourished with hardly any strength.

'The whole way, while I was walking her, I was just trying not to cry, I was so angry,' he admitted. 'But I got her to a safe field, and I'm gradually managing to rehabilitate her. She's in much better shape now, but it's taken months, and she's still very shy. She probably always will be, but she certainly seems to have taken a shine to you!' Darren was grinning now.

'How old is she?'

'By her teeth and her bones, I reckon her to be about five. But horses can live until they're around thirty, and sometimes a lot longer if they're well looked after, so she needs to go to a good forever-home. I won't let her go to just anyone. She's been through too much. She's had her trust shattered. Whoever she goes to will have to rebuild that trust over a long period of time, and it won't be easy. She'll need to be with someone who really understands horses and knows how to carry on with the work I've started.'

Meghan laughed as Astro nuzzled the side of her face.

'She's fab. I love her. She deserves the very best, don't you, sweet girl?'

At that moment, Stuart came out of the cottage. He held his hand out to Darren Davies.

'Hi. I'm Stuart Thomson, Meghan's dad. You must be the vet Mrs Raven was telling us about.'

Darren shook his hand warmly. Yeah, that's me. Darren Davies. I pop up every few days on my way home, after the practice shuts, just to give Astro the once-over.'

'How's she doing, really?' Meghan enquired, hoping that the beautiful animal really was as healthy as she looked. There was a sadness in the creature's eyes, though, that made her heart ache.

'Physically, she's doing really well. Mentally, she still has a way to go. She was abused, that much was evident, but I'm not sure in how many ways. She's very shy and if you make any sudden movements she tends to rear up a bit, so my guess is she was beaten as well. Whatever it was, it blew her trust.'

Darren's tone was matter of fact as he spoke, but he kept stroking Astro's mane. It was very clear that he liked her a lot. Meghan felt like crying. Poor Astro. So gentle and loving. How could anyone treat her so badly? Darren was still talking, and she turned her attention back to him.

'She has palomino in her, not sure how much, maybe a quarter. But it's given her this lovely colouring, and the gorgeous velvety brown eyes. She's a real beauty, aren't you, chicken?' He nuzzled Astro's cheek and kissed it. Here was a real vet with a real heart. A competent but compassionate man. *He's exactly the sort of guy you'd want, to be taking care of your pets,* she thought to herself.

Darren asked her if she'd had any experience with horses. Meghan told him that she hadn't but was interested in learning. Stuart piped up.

'I know a reasonable amount. I used to ride, back in the day. When I was at secondary school I worked a few summer holiday seasons in a riding school and stables, usually on the end of a pitchfork, or grooming and exercising the horses. I can do it all, but I'm not what you'd call an expert in any of it.'

Darren nodded. 'Astro needs a lot of exercise, but I don't think she's ready to be ridden, in fact I'm not sure she ever will be. I wonder if maybe the best we can do for her is find her a home where she can just live out her days in enough space to trot around on her own, and hopefully with at least one other nice horse for company, without fear or worry. Ah well,' he shrugged. 'Time will tell.'

Meghan was thinking. Suddenly she spoke up again.

'We're here for seven weeks; enough time for her to get used to us. I could exercise her, if you like? What does it involve?' She giggled as Astro snickered at her and nudged her gently in the back, causing her to stumble forward a little.

Darren grinned and then chewed his bottom lip, thinking. He explained that Astro would need a halter, and a rope. 'That might work. She clearly likes you. Just lunging, walking around with her like that, will help a lot. Keeping her moving, that's what's important, running her in a circle and maybe jumping her a bit, over small obstacles, to help keep important muscle groups in good shape. She could also do with a bit of grooming, if you'd be up for that? It's a nice thing to do. She enjoys that, when I have the time to do it. She might let you do it.'

Meghan started to get excited about the prospect of having more meaningful interaction with the horse. She eyed Stuart, and bit her lip apprehensively.

'What do you think, Dad? Would that be okay? Could you help me?'

Stuart shrugged. 'Yeah, if you like, why not? We can help out with that, sure. I've got *some* experience with it, although I'm a bit rusty, as I said.'

Darren grinned again. 'It's not something you really forget. You'd soon get back into the swing of it, if you've done it before.'

Stuart invited Darren into the cottage for a cup of coffee. The vet quickly checked his watch and grinned, proclaiming that he did indeed have time for a quick one before his wife was expecting him home. As the two men disappeared into the cottage, Meghan cuddled Astro again.

'We are gonna be good friends, Astro,' she whispered to the horse. 'You can trust me, I promise. I will never let anyone hurt you, ever again.'

As she joined her father and Darren in the cottage, she was surprised at how conversant Stuart actually was about horses. She had no idea he knew so much! It was hard to imagine him as he once was – a carefree boy, at work mucking out stables and exercising horses, to help pay for a new bike. She decided she probably should make more of an effort to get to know more about him.

Darren was asking him some questions, calculated ones, clearly trying to assess whether Stuart's level of experience was where he said it was. That was fair enough. As a committed professional, Darren needed to trust someone with an animal's welfare. Clearly, he took his own responsibilities very seriously. Meghan leaned forward.

'It's very good of you, to trust us. You don't even know us, do you? We could be anybody, really.'

Darren nodded. 'I know enough, I think. Your dad has some sound knowledge, and I'm not far away to keep an eye on things. I'd expect you to contact me if you had any worries, of course. And if Astro trusts you, which she seems to, who am I to tell her she's wrong? Horses are very intuitive. They know when someone's alright or not.'

Darren went on to say that he had a halter at the surgery that he'd drop by with on Monday after vet practice. He was sure there were a few old combs and brushes lying around too, that he could let them borrow, for grooming. Stuart said he would ask up at the farm if they had any old logs or fence posts they could let him have, to create a couple of small jumps in the field.

Darren drained his drink and stood to go. He turned to Meghan.

'I've seen how Astro's taken to you, Meghan. She already trusts you a little, so I'm happy to let you work with her, but just a bit, for starters. Don't expect too much at first, ok? Don't push her too hard. She may take a while to get used to the halter so if she won't take it, don't worry. You can still get in the field and wander around and let her follow you. It never needs to be for very long.'

His eyes met hers, and she knew what he was thinking. He was trusting her, and he needed her not to let him down. She just held his gaze for a moment and nodded. He nodded back, and that was it. All of a sudden, Meghan had a job to do, and it felt like the most important, most wonderful job in the world.

Darren promised to stop by on the following Monday evening, and drop off the halter and any brushes he might find. Stuart assured him that they could get some themselves, if he didn't manage to find any. Darren also said he'd have a word up at Ravensdown Farm, to let the Ravens know he was aware of any activity the holiday guests might get up to with Astro during the coming weeks, so they wouldn't worry.

Meghan was excited. All she wanted to do was spend time with Astro. She couldn't wait to get started. Over the rest of the weekend she spent as much time as she could with the horse, talking to her, stroking her, and feeding her apples and carrots which Darren had assured her were fine in small doses. Mrs Raven came down on Sunday morning to offer her some old brushes that were in the barn, admitting that she'd no idea where they might have come from, because they'd never had horses at Ravensdown. She told Meghan she was glad they were going to good use.

As promised, Darren turned up just before six o'clock on the Monday night with a halter for Astro, and he took the time to show Meghan how to put it on. Astro was a little wary at first, and resisted Darren's attempts to place the halter over her head, but when Meghan stepped forward and put her arms around Astro's neck and whispered to her gently, the horse settled enough for Darren to fasten the halter. He'd also brought a length of rope with a clip on one end and a leather loop-handle on the other. He handed it he then handed to Meghan, while her dad watched on.

'Walk with her. Give her plenty of rope, and see if she follows you.'

Nervously, Meghan stepped away from Astro with the rope. As it came out to full length, Astro still didn't move. Meghan coaxed her gently, producing a carrot from her pocket and waving it at her. Tempted, Astro started to walk towards her. Meghan's heart was in her mouth. Somehow, in all the times when she'd stood next to Astro and petted and cuddled her across the fence, the horse's size and power hadn't been as evident as it was now, as she was walking towards Meghan.

'Don't let her see you're nervous,' Darren called to her. 'She needs to know you're the boss.'

Meghan straightened her shoulders and called gently but decisively to Astro.

'Come on, girl. Let's go.' She began to walk, and to her immense relief, Astro started to walk alongside her.

'Lengthen the rope out a little again, let her walk at her chosen distance for now, till she gets more used to you.'

Meghan did as Darren suggested, and let the rope out from about eight feet away. She started to walk a little faster and Astro followed her lead. Then Meghan broke into a slow jog. The horse kept pace. Megan started to run and Astro broke into a light trot. They went around the field three times, before slowing down, and coming back to the fence. Meghan was out of breath.

Darren was beaming. 'That was *brilliant*. Well done! You're a natural with her.'

'I'm all out of puff!' Meghan panted. 'I have to get a bit fitter than this, I think.'

'Well you'll get one another fit, I guess, and that's a good benchmark. When you've had enough, that will be enough for her, at least until you both build up a bit of stamina. Once she's fitter herself, you can circle her, so you won't have to run as far anyway. And you can lead her over jumps quite slowly to begin with.'

He patted her on the shoulder. 'That was an excellent start, Meghan. You don't need to do too much. Remember she'll run and trot and jump about a bit by herself out here, when she feels like it, so it's not all down to you. But regular exercise like this will improve and maintain her strength in a structured way.'

He confessed to not being able to find any brushes, but Meghan assured him that she had something to be going on with, until she and Stuart could get to an equestrian store to buy what they needed.

As Darren was leaving, he turned to Stuart. 'My wife Debby wants to know if you two would like to come over to our place for supper one night this week? We never have anything too exciting, but you're welcome to come and have a meal with us. Debs suggested either Thursday or Friday night.'

Meghan could see that Stuart was slightly taken aback by such a kind offer from a stranger.

Say yes! She silently pleaded with her father. To her immense relief he accepted, hiding his surprise well. 'Thanks, Darren,' he nodded. 'That would be great. How about Thursday, then?'

Darren winked at them both and grinned broadly. 'Sounds good. I'll let her know.' He reached into his pocket and pulled out a business card. 'Here's my number. Send me a text, and I'll fire one back with the time and address, and we'll see you Thursday.'

As he was getting back into his Land Rover he added; 'You can contact me before then, if there's any issues with the horse, or you have any questions. Any concerns at all, don't leave it. Get in touch, right?'

Meghan nodded vigorously. 'I might have some questions, but if they're not urgent I'll just write them down and ask you on Thursday.'

Darren gave her the thumbs up, started his vehicle, and drove away, giving them a short beep on the horn as he left.

Meghan was impressed by Darren Davies. He was kind, that much was clear, and he was generous too, giving her the opportunity to work with Astro, teaching her what to do with the horse, and inviting her and her Dad to their home for dinner. She wondered what his wife was like, and whether they had any kids.

She hoped she wouldn't have to contact Darren before they went to dinner. She made up her mind to master her work with Astro. Then, the next time Darren saw them together, he'd feel happy about Astro's progress.

It was nice that someone had faith enough in her ability to handle some responsibility. Darren Davies was trusting her with his horse. It was a pretty big deal, and Meghan didn't want to mess it up. She would work diligently with Astro, and after Stuart suggested they take a few videos of the workouts to show Darren, she leapt at the chance.

She knew her Dad was keen to try out more of the capabilities on his new i-phone, and she'd already shown him how to understand and use a lot of its different functions. He'd already learned how to download music and podcasts onto it. He was still building up his contacts on it, because his old phone had been so outdated when he'd left prison, it wasn't possible to transfer them, and many of them had fallen by the wayside anyway, or they'd been business contacts that were no longer relevant.

Meghan was surprised at how keen Stuart was to work alongside her, with Astro. She'd initially wanted to work with the horse by herself, but her Dad did have good knowledge, and enough experience to help her stay on track. Stuart taught her how to wash and groom Astro, and how to plait her mane and tail.

Meghan understood that he needed something to do as well, so together they made Astro their project, spending many hours with her each day. Stuart took a video of Meghan doing Astro's plaits, and he asked her to help him set up his own video channel, thinking he might start a small series of instructional videos. He said he'd ask Darren's advice about that, and permission to put his horse on social media, before he loaded anything up. Meghan thought it was as good a project as any, for him to be getting involved with.

Darren had texted Stuart to let him know where he lived, and they set off for dinner on the Thursday night, stopping off at the little supermarket in Torley to pick up a bottle of wine and a larger one of lemonade for the table, and a small box of chocolates for Darren's wife. The couple lived on Turnbull

Lane, on the opposite side of the valley. Their gorgeous little house was called 'Appletree Cottage,' and it had a spectacular sunken front garden.

When Stuart remarked on how pretty the house and garden were, Darren grinned. 'The place looks pretty good now, but it was a right mess when we bought it. The house had been abandoned. It needed complete renovation, and the garden was a wilderness that only my father-in-law had the stomach to take on. He made into what it is now. If it had been left up to me, I'd still be trying to clear all the bloody bramble out of there. Evil stuff, there was a *ton* of it.'

Darren ushered them indoors and introduced them to his wife Debby, who came out of the kitchen wiping her hands on her apron. She shook hands with them both. She was fairly short, with twinkly blue eyes and light brown, shoulder-length hair infused with gleaming blonde and caramel highlights. She seemed like a smiley sort, and she was thrilled with the box of chocolates, proclaiming with a cheeky grin that she wasn't going to share them with her husband.

The couple had three dogs. One was a waggy-tailed springer spaniel called Dolly, who was very friendly and sweet, and another smaller dog of an indeterminate breed, called Jasper, who was a tad more shy and kept more out of the way. But their border collie, Badger, was very excitable and made a massive fuss of Meghan. She laughed at him and pulled his ears playfully. He was gorgeous; big and shaggy with trusting brown eyes. 'Oh, I love him!' she exclaimed, as she tried to deter him from licking her face.

Debby laughed. 'He's a handful, that's for sure. It's like there's no off-button. He's an old dog now but he's still got tons of energy, in random spurts. We've three cats as well, and they're around somewhere. Lindy-Lou is really old and grumpy, and we also have Denzel and Queenie, but they're not too fussed about strangers so you might not see them.'

Darren chimed in 'It's an occupational hazard of being a vet. You tend to collect animals along the way!'

Dinner was almost ready, so they didn't have long to wait. Debby had made a banquet of food – far too much for four people really but, as she said, she'd wanted to make sure they'd have something they liked and could eat, since Darren had 'annoyingly' kept forgetting to ask them about any food allergies or things they didn't like. She'd done a dish of fluffy rice, and a vegetarian curry, along with a bowl full of salad, another of jacket potatoes, a plate of grilled chicken breasts and another of hard-boiled eggs and slices of cheese. A jug of rich salad cream sat on the table also, with a spectacular pavlova, loaded with cream and strawberries.

'Wow! This looks amazing!' Meghan proclaimed. Her mouth watered, and she vowed to try some of everything. Stuart also gave her the nod to have half a glass of wine, so it was shaping up to be a very nice evening indeed.

In the lovely kitchen, a baby monitor sat at the side of a two-element dark green Aga virtually identical to the one at Teapot Cottage, except for the colour. When she asked Debby if there was a baby in the house, Debby blushed gently and nodded, smiling.

'Yes, A baby girl, Ruby. She's just three and a half months. She's sleeping right now, but she'll probably wake up soon for her next feed. I'll take you up to see her in a bit, if you like?'

'I'd love that, thank you. I love babies.'

Meghan pointed at the Aga. 'We've got one of those things at Teapot Cottage. A bright red one. It's a bit scary. Do you like them?'

Debby laughed. 'As a matter of fact, I love this little green gremlin! We stayed at Teapot Cottage ourselves, just over a year ago. In fact, staying there was what decided us on moving here! We're from Devonshire originally, but we wanted to get out of the rat-race. A job opportunity presented itself for Darren that was too good to say no to, and I'm a theatre nurse so I got a job pretty quickly too, at the hospital in Carlisle. We moved here, lock stock and barrel. I'm on maternity leave at the moment though, and not due to go back for another few months.'

She went on to confess how intimidated she had been by the Aga at Teapot Cottage too, at first, until she started using it. Then she promptly fell in love with it, and decided she wanted one of her own.

'So we splurged, and got Gremlin! He had to come in on a pallet truck, with three men lifting him in. You wouldn't believe how heavy Agas are! And once built, they don't come apart, so we had to take the front door out of its frame to get him in. He's here to stay, so it's just as well I love him!' Debby laughed.

'He heats the radiators in wintertime, and that's important because we've done our first winter here, and my *God*, was it cold! Very different from the South Coast! But as a baking oven, and instant hotplates, an Aga is hard to beat. I wouldn't go back to a conventional oven now. A lot of people told me I'd feel that way, and I couldn't imagine that at the time, but I understand it now. So, I've named him; Mr Gremlin Green. He's part of the family now.'

After dinner, Debby took Meghan upstairs to see baby Ruby, asleep in her bassinette. The infant had the softest skin, and the sweetest, most perfect rosebud mouth. Her tiny fingers were curled around small scruffy bear sat next to her pillow.

'Oh, she's perfect!' Meghan whispered. 'I hope she wakes up. I'd love to have a cuddle, if she does.'

Debby grinned at her. 'Of course you can. She should be waking up pretty soon now for her teatime feed, so you shouldn't have long to wait.'

Meghan watched as Debby smiled adoringly at her daughter, and gently stroked the baby's cheek. She whispered gently; 'we waited a long time for you, didn't we sweetheart?'

As they made their way back down the stairs, Debby briefly explained that Ruby had been a long time coming, and was all the more precious for it. 'We're hoping to have another baby, as a matter of fact,' she added. 'It'd be so nice for Ruby to have a little brother or a sister.

Meghan hoped, with all her heart, that Debby and Darren would get their wish.

Chapter Three

What nice people, Stuart thought to himself. So generous and hospitable. Dinner was delicious, especially the pavlova. He was a sucker for a dessert, and he said as much to Debby who declared that the Aga was perfect for such things. Stuart laughed.

'We'll have to get to grips with the one at Teapot Cottage then, won't we, Meghan? Here's to Gremlin! Salutations, Mr Green!' He raised his glass to the extra member of the Davies' household.

He noted that his daughter seemed very happy. She had a small smile playing around her lips, and had been upstairs to see Debby and Darren's new baby. She looked at him, trying to look imperious, then failed and started laughing. 'Yeah, I s'pose we could give it a go. Maybe we can get the pavlova recipe off you, Debby?'

Debby grinned back at her. 'Course you can! Most people think a pav's really complicated, but it's easy-peasy actually. All you need is egg whites and caster sugar, and a little bit of vinegar and vanilla essence, and Bob's your uncle! But I will give you the quantities. Although...' she mused, 'I'm not sure the cottage has a good electric beater. You'd definitely need one. If you were going to beat egg whites to stiff peaks with a hand beater, you'd be at it all day.'

Stuart made a mental note to check the cupboards at the cottage, and to get one if there wasn't one. He assumed that Annabel would have commandeered most of the household items that had existed in the home they'd once shared. It wouldn't hurt to add a beater to the long list of stuff they would need, as he did intend to make a home *somewhere* for himself and Meghan soon after their return to Taunton. He couldn't realistically live with his mother for much longer in her tiny house, and he definitely wanted Meghan to live with him.

They all moved into the living room with cups of coffee and got comfy on plush dark green velvet sofas. Stuart realised that Darren was speaking to him, and he turned his attention back to what the man was saying.

......out again?'

'Sorry, Darren, what was that? I was a bit distracted for a second there, thinking about home appliances, of all things.'

Darren spoke again. 'I asked what your plans are, going forward, now that you're out again.'

Stuart stared at him. He wasn't sure what to say. Darren smiled at him gently.

'I know who you are. You're the lawyer who did time for killing that pregnant mother. I remember it, it was in Taunton, right? We used to live in Exeter, next city south. The accident, the scandal, it was in all the papers. I recognised you straight away up at Teapot Cottage, as you were introducing yourself.'

Stuart felt his face flaming. Again, he was stuck for words. He continued to stare at Darren, holding his breath, waiting for some kind of axe to fall. The other man held up his hands and continued.

'Stuart, I'm not judging. Far from it, mate. I was in and out of prison all the bloody time myself, before I turned my life around. You'd have been in Exeter bang-up, right? I know the place well, Stu. At one time they had a revolving door especially for me. But I got a second chance, and I took it, made something decent of my life. You've got your second chance now, and I just wondered what you might want to do with it. I assume you can't go back into legal practice?' He put his feet up on the coffee table as he spoke.

Stuart shook his head. He still felt slightly dazed. 'No, I can't. I'm struck off. It's all done and dusted, that part of my life. Boozy lunches, thinking I was invincible and above the law. I was a twat. Arrogant son of a bitch, entitled smart-ass, whatever you'd have wanted to call me. I don't want to be that person anymore.'

Darren nodded. 'I know what you mean. I was the worst kind of bastard, robbing people. It took the deaths of two people to make *me* face reality too, Stuart, and I was lucky. Off the back of it all, I got the kind of chance most people could never even dream about. I took it, and I haven't looked back. You shouldn't either,' he added. 'You've got a cracker of an education and heaps of other skills. There'll be loads that you can do.'

Stuart nodded. 'Yeah, I'm sure. First job, though, is getting to know my daughter again. Meghan was only nine when I got locked up.'

He went on to describe his circumstances now, having lost his marriage and his home, as well as his career. He spoke in matter-of-fact terms though. He'd never been one for feeling unduly sorry for himself. Darren looked contemplatively at him.

'I know what it's like to feel you've got blood on your hands, believe me I do. My mate lost his life, which he wouldn't have done if he'd been somewhere else instead of on a thieving job with me. I didn't kill him, but I left him in a place where someone else did, so I might as well have. And the person who killed him ended up dying as well. That *wasn't* my fault, but my actions didn't help her. Ironically though, her dying is what gave me the chance to become a better person.'

Darren went on to say it was a complicated story, for another time, but he indicated that he wouldn't mind telling Stuart about it at some stage. 'I don't broadcast it, of course, but I'd never shy away from it either. It's a huge part of who I am, and who I've become, and if a shared story helps someone else, then it's worth telling. You can google it too, if you want. Like your story, it's no secret, but it was a while ago now.'

Debby piped up, 'We're all a product of our history, of our journey, and nobody's perfect. There isn't a person on the planet, as far as I'm concerned, who's got the right to judge anyone else's thoughts or actions. And I think everyone deserves a second chance. They just have to move on from their stuff-ups and commit to being the best person they can be, going forward. If the second-chancers all did that, it'd be a much happier world for everybody.'

Stuart considered this. What an extraordinary direction this evening was taking! Debby and Stuart Davies were clearly compassionate people, realists, who saw the world in pragmatic terms. They knew who Stuart was, and what he'd done, how royally he'd messed up, and they'd still invited him into their home, made him welcome, and told him they didn't judge him. They wanted to be his friends. It was a humbling thing.

He leaned forward. 'I live with the guilt of what I did, every day. I know that a lot of people have forgiven me, including Karen Balik's husband, and he's the last person who should. And I'm deeply grateful for all of it. The biggest stumbling block I've got now is fully forgiving *myself*. That's proving a bit harder!' He managed a brief smile. 'I'm getting there, but it's a journey,'

Darren smiled back and stuck his hand out. 'Oh, I know all about *that*. Shake my hand, man. You're among friends here. And one thing I know to be true – if you throw yourself into doing something for the greater good, the self-forgiveness will come. When you realise that you can make a *positive* difference, and you start doing it, you'll realise that there's a lot more to you than just the criminal act that put you behind bars.

'Trust me. Retraining as a vet saved me. I fix poorly animals, and that also helps to heal frightened people, in its own funny way. You can put a lot back. You just have to work out how.'

'You make it sound so simple.'

Darren sighed. 'Stu, it *is* simple. We all overcomplicate things in our own heads, but we shouldn't. We just have to look at what matters, look at what helps the world, and choose to be a part of it. The rest follows. If you'd known me before, you wouldn't believe how radically different my life is now. I was a drop-kick common thief, with no prospects. Now, I have a career, a wife, a child, a paid-for home, and my life's as different now as night is from day. I took my chance. You just have to do the same.'

'I don't know what my chance is, yet.' Stuart observed, almost distractedly.

'It'll come, and probably when you least expect it. What you're supposed to do next will reveal itself when it's ready. You just have to take each day as it comes, until the right opportunity shows up, then recognise it when it does.' Darren looked at Stuart, speculatively. 'I have a funny feeling it won't be long coming.'

Stuart shrugged. 'Well, I hope it does come soon, because I'm living on savings and that's not ideal, and I don't want to touch the invested money from the sale of my house, because I need it for a new place. I need to be busy again. I *want* to be.'

Debby nodded. 'Yeah, you do need to be. But Darren's right. And I think you're doing the right thing, coming up here to take that breather you need, and re-establish your relationship with Meghan, before going back to your life, because you do need one another, you two. It will be a *new* life, and you both have to be ready for it together, and rested, and back in the world, present, for what comes next; whatever it may be.'

It was good, solid advice, from people who'd been through the mill. Debby went on to talk about the challenges the two of them had faced, in trying to have a baby, and how they had to work hard *together*, to decide on the kind of life they would have without the family they'd longed to raise.

Stuart couldn't imagine the anguish they must have felt, failing time and time over for *years*, to conceive. It must have been pretty tough to have had those heavyweight conversations, about what their lives might look and feel like as a childless couple if they did decide to stay together, or how they'd face the heartbreak of splitting up because the pressure was just too great. He was glad they finally had the longed-for baby that had ultimately rendered those difficult discussions redundant. Debby and Darren were good people. They deserved every ounce of their happiness. He said as much, and Darren countered, 'Well, if you think an old jailbird like me deserves all this, then you must know that you deserve a second chance too.'

Stuart decided he really liked Darren. The man called a spade a spade, and he talked a lot of sense. Darren grabbed the bottle of wine from the table and waved it at Stuart. He declined.

'I don't drink anymore, Darren. Not much anyway, and I certainly don't drink and drive.'

Darren smiled self-consciously. 'Sorry, Stuart, I wasn't thinking. You don't mind being around others who drink though, do you?'

Stuart shook his head, grinning. 'Nah. I'm virtually teetotal these days, but I don't expect everyone else to be. You go ahead.'

Debby piped up. 'I'm not drinking either, at the moment. I'm breastfeeding, and I really miss my evening glass of wine, I must say! And, speaking of feeding, I better go get Ruby up. She's sleeping like a rock and its gone time for her feed. Please excuse me.'

Stuart suddenly remembered he had a couple of videos to show Darren, who was very complimentary about them.

'Yeah, course you can put them online, but please blur Astro's face, if you would, and don't say where she is. I don't want horse thieves, or anyone who recognises her – especially anyone connected to her previous owners – to come calling, not that they'd be able to have her back even if they did show up. I'm her legal owner now.'

'Of course, no problem. I'll use a nickname for the public too, to help keep the anonymity. I guess that was a bit of a process then, being allowed to assume ownership? Horses are registered as legal property of an owner, aren't they?'

'Yeah, they are. I had to go through the courts to be granted ownership. It was all based on proof of abandonment, but it was pretty cut and dried. It wasn't difficult to prove she'd been left, the state she was in. I took photos and one of my colleagues at the surgery backed me up with a witness statement. The fact that I'm a vet made it more or less a rubber stamp, to be awarded ownership, but it was quite a process nonetheless.'

Darren shook his head. 'Abandoned horses are a bigger problem than most people realise. Luckily, there are animal rescue centres dotted around that take most of them and eventually find them new homes. But Astro was in a really bad way, and I just wanted to heal her myself. It would have been an easy enough thing to pass her on, but I dunno, Stu. There was just something about her. I didn't want to let go of her, once I had her safe.'

The two men chatted about horses for a while, and Stuart occasionally glanced over at Meghan, hoping she wouldn't be too bored. But, to his delight, she appeared to be more than happy to listen. Stuart understood that she already cared a great deal about Astro, and would appreciate any information she could learn about how to look after the horse. Darren turned to include her in the conversation.

'Pole work is good for horses. You know, laying out poles in different configurations to help them step straight, and maintain good posture? As well as helping keep them physically fit, pole work gets them thinking as well. Horses need mental stimulation as much as physical exercise.

'They're incredibly intelligent animals, and they appreciate a challenge. But there's a fine line between a challenging exercise and a stressful one, so you need to have a lot of patience, and also plan out your poles to ensure the layouts are something a horse can learn to master without getting worried about it.' Meghan was still listening raptly, but nodded now.

'Yeah, so she has to figure out her steps, at her own pace?'

'Yes! That's exactly right. Nothing too complicated. Start with some easy ones, then make them slightly more complex, but never too much so. It's supposed to be enjoyable, not stressful, and horses don't do well under stress.'

Stuart chipped in. 'Some can be quite highly strung. I remember a few temperamental ones from the stables I worked at. One or two of them used to get upset without much warning.'

Darren agreed. 'The more skittish ones need a bit more patience, certainly. A horse can tell when you're impatient or stressed yourself, too, and they'll always respond to it. You need to be calm to work with horses. In a herd, one can be spooked, which can spook another, and then you've a bit of a job to get them all calmed down. Even one stressed horse can be a handful, if you don't know what you're doing.'

He went on to say that he thought Stuart might be onto something with his videos about horse management. 'You might want to take a course or something, get certified, if you want to carry on with that, because you need people to know you're coming from a place of experience, otherwise it probably won't go anywhere.'

'I dunno if I want it to go anywhere,' Stuart mused. 'It just seemed like a nice thing to do, helpful or inspiring to someone, maybe. It's as much about getting to know my new phone as much as anything else,' he admitted. Darren laughed.

'Well, if it goes viral, or anything like that, you'll need to be prepared to answer a few questions at least!'

At that moment Debby came back in with a tiny baby, who was asleep in the crook of her arm. Meghan immediately got up and went over to them both.

'Oh, she's asleep again!'

Debby pulled an apologetic face. 'She is, I'm afraid. She woke up just as I got up there to her, and she latched on, had her feed, and more or less went straight back to the land of nod. To be honest, I'm relieved,' she admitted, looking down at her sleeping infant.

'She's not long recovered from the sniffles and she wasn't sleeping at all, through that. She was all stuffed up and snotty, crying a lot, and none of us got much sleep. I think she's making up for lost time now, aren't you Ruby-shoes?'

Meghan asked if she could hold the baby, and Debby held her out with a smile. Stuart watched as his daughter's face broke into a huge grin. She took Ruby and sat cradling her gently. 'Oh! She smells so good!'

Debby laughed again. 'She didn't a few minutes ago! She had a really stinky bum! But she's all changed, clean and powdered, and yes she does smell divine.'

Stuart could tell that this new mother was very proud of her baby. He offered to help her with the washing up, but both Debby and Darren emphatically refused their offer. 'Guests don't do the washing up,' Debby declared. Darren joined in. 'But friends do, so next time you come, you can.'

Stuart felt quietly delighted that Darren assumed there would be a 'next time.'

After another half an hour's chat, which was mostly about horses, Stuart raised his eyes at Meghan, who took his cue and nodded. As they were leaving, Meghan astonished him by stepping forward and hugging Debby Davies. She had clearly enjoyed her evening. Debby handed her a piece of paper, on which she had scribbled the recipe and instructions for pavlova. 'Good luck with it,' she said, returning Meghan's hug. 'And get yourselves an electric beater! You'll never make a decent pav without one!'

Stuart and Darren shook hands. Stuart felt compelled to thank the other man for his understanding and offer of friendship. 'This has been great. Maybe you'd all like to come to us for something to eat next week? Let me know what night would suit, and we'll make it happen.'

'Sure,' Darren nodded, as Debby clapped her hands. 'That'd be awesome. We'll have to bring stinky-bum, of course, but she sleeps pretty well in her portable bassinette, and is it ok to bring Badger as well? The other dogs are fine but he fusses and frets if we leave him behind, so we take him with us wherever we can. It's his age, I think.'

Meghan spoke up first, before Stuart could respond. 'Ooh, yes, do bring him! I could take him across the fields, and also introduce him to Astro!'

'We could have a roast of lamb,' Stuart offered, 'and you could take the lamb bone home for him.'

His daughter looked at him enquiringly. 'And who's cooking this roast lamb, Dad?'

Stuart rolled his eyes. 'I am, you crazy mare. I do have a *few* clues, you know!'

She pulled a face at him, then turned to Darren and Debby, who were by now standing on their doorstep.

'Well, if he's making the roast dinner, I'd better make the pavlova, so I'd better go buy a beater!' Grinning, she held out her fingers in the form of a cross. 'Be afraid!'

She and Stuart got into their car to the sound of laughter.

'That was fun!' Meghan beamed at him. 'Aren't they a nice family? Amazing baby too, and amazing dogs.'

Stuart had to agree that the evening had gone a lot better than he'd first expected. In truth, he hadn't known what to expect at all, being invited to dinner at the home of complete strangers, only that it would've felt awkward and ill-mannered to have refused. He was glad now, that they'd accepted and gone, because he did feel like he'd made a new friend in Darren

Davies. And, he thought, maybe Darren was right. If he, as a 'regular jailbird' with only a basic formal education, could so spectacularly turn his life around by going back to school, retraining in a new profession and establishing a new career, surely it was well within Stuart's own capabilities as an academically educated man, to do the same?

Darren was an interesting guy. Stuart wondered what he'd been like in the past, when he was in and out of prison, doing burglaries for a living, and facing a life of no prospects. He was intelligent, but probably just lazy, as Annabel would have said, as disparaging as she always was about criminals. He wondered, idly, what his ex-wife would have made of Darren, as an example of how well rehabilitation could work for those given the chance who really wanted to take it. He shrugged the thought away. It didn't matter what Annabel thought anymore. She was history, just another part of the life he'd left behind.

Stuart's future now was Meghan, and – what else? What was he going to do now, for a job? He supposed that wherever they ended up living would have more to do with employment than anything else, but until he figured out what to do next, there wasn't much point in looking for a house. At least they had the booked time at the cottage; six weeks or so left. Maybe things would become clearer over time, as they relaxed, unwound a little more, and got to know one another better.

A conversation would eventually be needed with Meghan, about how important her exams were going to be, and what the future might hold, but he figured she'd probably want to stay at the same school. She had friends there, and since she'd already had more than enough disruption in her young life, he couldn't really expect her to tolerate any more. She was pretty attached to her Nan too, and Stuart recognised how important that contact was. Nan had been the only real representation of stability Meghan had known since she was nine years old. But, needing to find something locally that would enable her to keep her life as stable as it now was, limited *his* options a lot.

His hopes of making a new start in a new place seemed slim. It would be a tough call, starting again in the same town where he'd made such a mess of so many lives, but it wouldn't be the hardest thing he'd had to do, would it? Darren had done it, hadn't he? Somehow, he'd find a way through, like he'd found a way through everything else so far.

As they drove back towards Teapot Cottage, Meghan became absorbed with her mobile phone, so he used the quiet time to reflect on the conversations he'd had during the evening, with Darren.

The man talked sense, and he was right about everything he'd said. Stuart really did have to find a way to do something meaningful with his life. There was no sane reason why his crime and punishment should define him for the rest of his life, unlike a lot of the blokes he'd done time with, who saw their own cards as indelibly marked, and who never expected to have a better life than the crappy one they already had. Some believed they'd stuffed up so badly nobody would ever employ them again. Such self-fulfilling prophecies kept the revolving door Darren had talked about spinning at the speed of sound. Stuart had seen so many inmates repeatedly locked up for petty crimes they never managed to learn from. They became 'career criminals,' eternally bouncing around the system, like ping-pong balls that didn't know where else to land.

Stuart knew he could make something better than that for himself and his daughter. He had a lot of good years left, to make a meaningful career for himself, just like Darren Davies had done. He was intrigued to know more about Darren's story. Cleary, there had been a lot of trauma in his past, and a lot of misguided decisions and bad behaviour. The fact that he'd triumphed over his circumstances, whatever they'd been, was a testament to his character, and his inherent goodness of heart. The fact that he'd reached out to Stuart, shared at least some of his story, and encouraged Stuart to start rebuilding his own life, meant a lot. He didn't have to do that. He'd *chosen* to do it, which said a lot about him.

But what had got Stuart's creative juices flowing was the conversation they'd had about horses. He thought back to his early teenage years, and how much he'd enjoyed working at his parents' friends' stables in the weekends and school holidays. Something stirred softly in his chest now, as he remembered that.

There was nothing like the smell of a horse, or the feel of its warm, damp hair beneath the palm of your hand. A lot of his long-forgotten equine knowledge had come back to him while he and Darren had been talking, and he'd surprised himself about how easy the conversation was. They'd started off chatting about Astro and her history and needs, but talk had soon turned to horses in general. Darren ministered to quite a few, locally, and was easy to see that he liked them a lot. He'd described them as intelligent creatures, and Stuart knew that to be true.

As soon as they arrived back at Teapot Cottage, Meghan was out of the car and over at the fence line in a flash, and this time Stuart joined her. It was almost dark, and Astro was way over at the other side of the field. They could barely make her out in the deepening gloom.

'Astro?' Meghan called softly. 'Come on, girl. Come for a bedtime cuddle.'

The horse slowly ambled over. 'In your own time, Astro,' Meghan giggled. As the horse came to the fence and placed her nose squarely into the side of his daughter's neck, Stuart couldn't help laughing.

'You two are friends for life.'

He wondered how difficult it might be for Meghan, when it came their time to leave, to say goodbye to Astro. Quickly he pushed the thought out of his mind.

Let's not dwell on that tonight. It's been such a nice evening. Let's not allow thoughts like that to take away from it. Not tonight.

'Come on, brat,' he said. 'It's time to turn in.' He reached across and gently stroked Astro's soft, velvety nose. 'Night, girl. See you in the morning.'

Meghan buried her face in Astro's mane, then kissed her nose. 'Sleep tight, beautiful. See you tomorrow.'

'She won't sleep much, you know, sweetheart. Horses don't. And they mostly sleep standing up.'

'Yeah I think I've heard that before. Why don't they lie down to sleep, like a dog or a cat would, Dad?'

'They can't lie for very long because of their weight. A lying position compromises blood flow, and if they're down too long it can create a lot of problems for them when they try to get up again.'

Meghan frowned, so Stuart reassured her. 'Don't worry, they sleep absolutely fine standing up. That's normal for them. They don't need a snuggly duvet and a soft mattress like we do.'

She shrugged and grinned. 'I guess they're horses, not humans, right? But I dunno, Dad. There's something almost human-like about her. I can't put my finger on what it is, but there's something...'

'Yeah, I think I understand what you're trying to say. But you don't need to figure it out tonight, sweetheart. Come on. It's time *you* hit the soft mattress. Tomorrow's another day.' They both went into the cottage and closed the front door. Meghan turned to him.

'Dad, I'm glad we came up here. It's nice here. Everyone we've meet so far, Mrs Raven, and the Davies', and Astro, and Jayde, have all been so welcoming and lovely. This cottage is so peaceful, it feels like we were meant to come here. I know that sounds silly, because its less than a week since I couldn't make up my mind about whether I could even do this. But I'm glad we came.'

She punched Stuart playfully on the shoulder, and he touched his fist gently to her jaw. It was their thing. They weren't 'huggy,' which was perfectly understandable, given the circumstances, but Stuart was hopeful that in time the hugs would come. In the meantime, he was happy to take the playful would-be punch routines as his daughter's way of showing affection.

'Night, brat. Sleep tight.'

Meghan bounded off up the stairs, still with an unnerving amount of energy. She was a thousand-million miles from the surly, uncommunicative teen who'd dragged herself so unwillingly into the car with him in Taunton less than a week ago. Stuart was astonished at the change, but he wasn't going to mention it. He decided he'd much rather just hold onto what felt like a fragile, frothy soap bubble, imagining that at some point it would burst and the real, ten-headed, razor-fanged Meghan Thomson would re-emerge. The last thing he wanted to do was burst that bubble himself by being 'all verbal' and 'banging on about it,' as she would probably say.

As he got into bed, it suddenly occurred to him that he hadn't thought about the accident all day. Even in his conversation with Darren Davies, where they'd both referred to their time in prison, the actual details of the accident itself hadn't come up. Darren hadn't asked Stuart about it, and Stuart was profoundly grateful that his new friend had observed the unspoken but generally observed 'rule' that existed between inmates. Unless one really wanted to talk about their own crime, others didn't ask about it. He and Darren had automatically shown that respect and avoided posing any direct questions to each other about what they'd actually done.

But even in his quieter moments, throughout the day when he and Meghan had been working with Astro, or when he'd been reading his book, or making lunch, or washing his car, the wretched, self-recriminating thoughts that typically intruded – particularly at those times – hadn't popped up at all.

Maybe it's a turning point.

He thought about it some more, and was surprised to find that he wasn't feeling guilty about not having the *thoughts* either! It was as if something had shifted, ever so slightly, while his attention was elsewhere. The anguish was certainly still there, when he tapped into it, but he'd somehow managed to keep it all out of his mind for the entire day. If that wasn't progress, he didn't know what was.

Unsurprisingly, he found himself unable to sleep. He tossed and turned for what felt like hours, going over the conversations he'd had with Darren, and how much of an example the other man had proved to be. Thoughts whirled around in his head, about the past, the now, the future, possibilities and dead ends, regrets and hopes, and although he was mentally exhausted, for a fleeting moment Stuart seriously wondered if he'd get any sleep at all. But the next thing he knew, it was Friday morning, and time to get up and make coffee.

Chapter Four

Adie got out of bed, stretched, and went to pull back the bedroom curtains. The bay window offered a slight sliver of view, over the field alongside Teapot Cottage, although the cottage itself couldn't quite be seen from it. In fact, it couldn't be seen from *any* of the windows at Ravensdown House, thanks to the tall yew hedge that surrounded the back of it.

Adie liked it that way. She knew the tenants all liked it too, that sense of alone-ness, as if the cottage was in the middle of nowhere, instead of only a hundred yards or so from the farmhouse. She'd very much appreciated that sense of remoteness herself, when she'd stayed there before she bought it. Nobody wanted their landlords peering at them while they went about their business, did they?

But most of the adjacent field was visible, if she leaned out of the window far enough, and even at this fairly early hour Adie could see that Meghan Thomson, was already out there, working Darren Davies' horse with a rope and halter. Most kids her age would still be in bed at lunchtime, during the school holidays, but this young woman seemed very keen to spend time with Darren's rescued palomino-cross. The horse was beautiful but damaged, and she needed careful handling, although you wouldn't know it from the way she'd bonded with Meghan. The two had met only a week ago, and already they appeared to be inseparable. Darren had shown Meghan how to exercise Astro, and she'd mastered the training well, showing kindness and patience with the horse, who rewarded it with an almost enthusiastic compliance.

Adie had never ridden a horse, nor did she have any desire to. She and her husband Mark had agreed to let Darren use the field for Astro for a while, but neither wanted to get involved with her care. They didn't know anything about horses, and had enough to be going on with, dealing with the rest of the farm. Darren came and saw to Astro regularly, and now her latest tenant's daughter had taken a real shine to her. Adie was satisfied that the horse's welfare was well taken care of without any need for her to get involved.

She thought she should go and invite Meghan to the coffee morning she had planned at Ravensdown. Unsure whether the young woman would want to spend a couple of hours with 'old biddies' like herself, her sister-in-law Sheila, and her other best friends Peg and Trudie, Adie decided to ask her anyway. They had their Friday morning coffee three weeks a month at Peg's café down in Torley town, but once a month Adie hosted it at Ravensdown instead, just to offer the women a change of scene, and invite other friends who weren't invited to Peg's for the more intimate Friday morning meet-ups.

'Friday coffee' had turned into something of a tradition, an event that had evolved from the Friday-night takeaway ritual that had started when Mark had been in hospital after a bad accident in the barn. He and Adie hadn't been married then. They were still working their way towards even declaring their feelings to one another. But, when it was all hands to the pump around the farm while Mark was laid up, Peg had started bringing Friday night takeaways and a bottle of wine to round off the week. It gave Adie and her now step-daughter Feen some much-needed downtime from the relentless farm duties, and from cooking. Over time, Friday night takeaway had changed to Friday morning coffee, and it was always a fun couple of hours. She wondered if maybe young Meghan might appreciate a change from just talking to her dad or to Astro. She could only ask.

She quickly showered and got dressed, and dragged a comb through her hair, before scraping it up into a messy bun and tying it with a piece of elastic. She'd had it cut quite short when she'd first come to Torley, but it was now long enough again to be tied back off her face. She didn't think she'd let it get any longer, in fact it was well overdue for a decent cut, so she made a mental note to contact Maddy Murphy at Torley Tresses, to make an appointment to get herself tidied up a bit.

It was easy to let yourself go a little, way up here, miles from the bustle of big-town life. Adie did care about her appearance, but sometimes the temptation to let things slide was hard to resist. She didn't miss the days of feeling obliged or expected to look perfect all the time, with flawless make-up, spotless clothes and every hair in place. Thankfully, that part of her life was long gone, but she didn't like to feel scruffy or unkempt. Bimbling around like a badger in tights all winter was one thing but, when spring and summer came, it was nice to put on a pretty dress and look at least halfway decent. Dresses had become her go-to, after menopause had dispensed with her waist. Nowadays, the skirts she used to adore just ended up drifting somewhere north of where they were supposed to sit, and simply looked ridiculous.

After she'd applied some sunscreen, she made her way quickly down to Teapot Cottage. When she got there, she was treated to the sight of Meghan jogging alongside Astro, encouraging the horse to trot gently, around the field. Adie leaned on the fence, watching for a while, and then she called out. 'You'll be pretty fit after all this!'

Meghan looked over at her and grinned. She raised a hand and continued until they made it to the part of the fence line where Adie was standing. She was a little out of breath.

'Hi. Is everything ok? I thought I'd do the morning run with her before it got too hot. Today's meant to be the start of a four-day heatwave.'

Adie nodded. 'Yes, it is, I think the forecast said it'll get to 29 or 30 degrees over the next few days. Astro will be glad of the shade from the cottage, until the sun swings around, then she'll have to stand under that tree in the corner. You seem to be doing very well with her, from what I can see. Have you topped up her water?'

Meghan nodded. 'Yeah, that was the first job this morning.' She wiped the beads of sweat away from her brow. 'I think Dad's still in bed, if you're looking for him.'

Adie shook her head. 'No, it's you I wanted to see, actually.'

Meghan suddenly looked wary, as only fourteen-year-olds can when they're told that an adult wants to speak to them.

Adie laughed. 'Don't look so worried! I only wanted to know if you'd like to come up to the house for girly coffee and cake at ten o'clock this morning. Well,' she added, 'when I say girly coffee, I mean we're all about a hundred years old, but we always have a good laugh, and I thought you might like a bit of a change from just talking to a horse and your dear old dad.'

Meghan clearly wasn't sure what to say. Adie put a hand on her arm. 'Please don't feel obliged. I won't be at all offended if it's not your thing, but it's from ten till around noon. If you want to come up, please just come, and no problem if not. I mean it. I won't be insulted if you don't want to spend a couple of hours with a bunch of 'old fogeys,' although my daughter-in-law Feen will be there too and she was born in almost the same century as you.' She grinned at Meghan and made her way back to Ravensdown House.

Gosh, teens can be tricky, she thought to herself. *I remember when Teresa was that age. It was all I could do to get her interested in anything except boys and make-up.*

After breakfast, she set about making some savoury scones and a chocolate cake. The cake would just about have time to cool and be iced before everyone was due to arrive.

Peg was the first to turn up, and she brought a jelly cake, which was one of Adie's favourites. It had a bottom layer of sponge, a layer of raspberry jelly, a layer of cream, and another slab of sponge for the topping, complete with a dusting of icing sugar. It was one of the specialities she made for her cafe. It was a firm favourite, but Adie had never attempted to make it. She was content to let Peg have that one to herself, especially after Peg had told her what a 'faff and a half' it was to make, but she always appreciated a slice when it came her way. There looked to be enough of it this morning for everyone. Peg smirked and waved it at her, then laughed as Adie's eyes gleamed.

'Surprise! I know you've been hanging out for jelly cake. Do I smell savoury scones, too? They're *my* favourite!'

Adie peered over Peg's shoulder as another car drew up. Hazel and Carla Walton got out of it, and so did Fiona Frost, the local florist.

Hazel had become a good friend since Feen and Gavin's wedding, and her daughter Carla was Gavin's mother. Carla could be porcupine-prickly, and bitingly sarcastic and defensive, when it suited her. She still had a bit of a chip on her shoulder about long-past events that had put her offside with

Adie and the rest of the town for a while but, as Feen's mother-in-law, she was family, and Adie was always at pains to make her welcome. She genuinely liked Carla now, despite their initial rocky start, and was always glad when she came to coffee.

The women all came into the house together, and sat around the kitchen table. Adie placed her scones, a bowl of butter and some plates in the middle of the table, along with the freshly iced chocolate cake and Peg's jelly cake. Fiona handed her a new packet of ground coffee and Hazel produced a carton of fruit juice and a packet of pretzels. Carla set a gorgeous big box of Belgian chocolates on the table.

'Sorry Adie, it's a bit of a cop-out, but you know me. Always sitting on my arse with far too much time on my hands. I was going to bake a batch of blueberry muffins but…,' she let the sentence trail off, and looked a little embarrassed.

'Carla, no! I know how busy you've been lately. I don't know how you even do everything, and still find time to come up here, but I'm glad you have, and the chocolates are a lovely addition. They're perfect. It's something we never get enough of. For whatever reason, we're all too guilty to buy them for ourselves. All that nonsense we tell ourselves, about a lifetime on the hips.'

Carla gave Adie one her trademark lopsided grins. 'Jelly cake doesn't do that, of course.'

Adie grinned back, and found more plates and bowls for everything and put juice glasses out.

Everyone went ahead and helped themselves as usual. They were all chattering happily when Adie's sister-in-law Sheila arrived with Trudie, the owner of the town's boutique GladRagz, who handed her a bag of still-warm croissants. Adie was delighted to see that her friends were all wearing pretty sun frocks, ready for what promised to be a sweltering day.

'Where's Feen?' Sheila asked excitedly, as she gave Adie one of her gorgeous 'signature' Parkin cakes. 'She and Gavin are back 'ere at Ravensdown aren't they? I'm so looking forward to seeing them all! Especially my great-niece and nephew. They're such lovely kiddies. They'll be 'alf again as big as they were last time I saw them, no doubt!'

Adie nodded, smiling as she always did at the way Sheila dropped her 'aitches.' She and Mark were from Lancashire, but while Mark's accent was as broad as the day was long, Sheila's had been tempered after nearly thirty years with her husband Bob, who spoke like a true English gent. When she became excited, however, her 'Lanky twang' became a little more pronounced. Her 'aitches' fell by the wayside, and she was even funnier and broader when she was drunk, which Adie privately believed wasn't often enough.

Feen and Gavin were indeed here for the summer, with their twins, Alder and Willow. They'd arrived a fortnight earlier, decamping to Ravensdown from London as usual, before the city's summer heat became too oppressive.

'They've taken the twins down to the park in the town, for a quick play on the swings and a paddle in the stream before it gets too hot. Feen said they'd be back in time for coffee, so she shouldn't be long. The twins are just hitting the 'terrible two's', so be warned if you do see them. They're a bit snivelly with the heat, I'm afraid.'

A knock at the door made Adie look up, and she was delighted to see Meghan Thomson peering around the kitchen door. She was dressed in a pair of flared lime green mid-thigh shorts and a pretty white cotton top with lace around the sweetheart neckline. She wore a pair of strappy white sandals on her feet, set off nicely with bright pink polish on her toenails. She looked young, fresh and very pretty. She'd brushed her long hair until it gleamed, and she had applied just the barest hint of lip gloss and mascara. She seemed incredibly nervous.

'The front door was open. I knocked but I don't think anybody heard, so I just came in. I hope that's okay.'

'Oh, Meghan, of course it is! I'm *so* glad you came!' Adie was genuinely delighted that Meghan had decided to pop in. 'Come in, come in! There's a fresh pot of coffee, and a ton of cake!'

She quickly introduced Meghan to everyone. 'I don't expect you'll remember anyone's names, but they'll all remember yours!'

'Hi,' Meghan said shyly. 'Nice to meet you all.'

Everyone started talking at once, and offering Meghan cake, coffee, scones and pretzels. Adie found it funny, to see her friends all flapping about like mother hens, making the young newcomer welcome. Feen chose that moment to come in too, flushed from the hot sun, and after Sheila and a few of the others had leapt up to give her a welcome hug, Adie introduced her to Meghan.

Feen was as warm and welcoming to Meghan as she was to everyone she already knew, and she pulled out two chairs, one for herself and one for the new guest. Everyone else wailed with dismay that Meghan wasn't going to sit next to them instead! The excited chatter quickly increased until it became almost deafening. Adie banged on the table with the back of a spoon. 'Come on everyone, let's all tone it down a tad, so we can hear ourselves think!'

If Meghan was overwhelmed by the exuberance of everyone's welcome, she didn't show it. Instead, Sheila quickly had her talking quite animatedly about her work with Astro. Sheila had some knowledge of horses too, apparently, having ridden on a neighbour's farm in Lancashire when she and Mark were growing up. Feen was listening intently to their conversation, with a light smile playing around her lips, but she didn't contribute.

As usual, everyone was having a good time. During a brief lull in the chat, after Fiona, Trudie and Peg were talking about the overall state of business in the town, Meghan put her hand up. 'You all sound like businesswomen. Do you all close up for the morning, to come up here?'

Fiona piped up. 'Good God, no! Friday's usually one of the busiest days for most of us, but once a month I get my niece to cover for a couple of hours although she isn't far from useless, to be honest, Lord love her.' Fiona shook her head and sighed heavily.

'The poor girl tries her best, but she'll never be a florist. She knows how to put a bouquet together, as I've taught her, but there's no artistic flair. She's one of life's little plodders, and she's capable enough to hold the fort for a morning, but that's about it.'

Carla piped up then. 'I've shut the shop until noon. Mornings tend to be pretty slow. I don't usually open early, anyway. My bell has never once gone before ten. Nobody seems to look for furniture early in a morning, unless they need something specific or urgent. I tend to get all my admin done from eight till ten, most days. It works well.'

Carla ran a furniture restoration business in Torley and lived in a lovely renovated flat above it. If her shop was closed, people could still raise her, if she was home, by ringing the doorbell at the side of the building.

Trudie nodded. 'That seems fair. I've had to close for the morning too. My part time lady has put her back out *again* and is off for the foreseeable, so it was either close or not come. And since the vicious rumour started circulating about jelly cake, it turned out to be no contest. I'm working my butt off, and I really need this break today. If people want something badly enough, they'll come back for it. I've got the mobile number in the window anyway so if anything's urgent, like a party frock for tonight, or some other short-notice drama, they can always ring me.'

Adie was concerned. 'Kathleen's put her back out, *again*? What a nightmare for you *and* her! That's the third time, isn't it?'

Trudie nodded again and rolled her eyes. 'Yes, the third time in six months. And always at the busiest times, although,' she hastened to add, 'it *is* genuine, the poor thing. She's not scalping me, and she'll be fine after a bit of down time, according to her doctor. But she can't lift any boxes or stand over an ironing board. It doesn't help me much with all the summer stock I've got to unpack and get pressed and priced up. There's cartons and bloody cartons of the stuff. The nightmare is *very* real!'

Trudie ran a hand through her wavy dark hair; a habit which Adie knew was a sign of fatigue. 'I'm going to have to try and find someone else to give me a hand, or I'll never get anything on the rails in time for when silly season starts officially with tourists, which is of course any day now. The school holidays have started. I should be miles ahead of where I am, with it all.'

'Surely there's plenty of school kids you could rope in? They're all on 'oliday now, aren't they?' Sheila enquired. Trudie thought for a moment.

'That's a good point. I only need someone for a week, or two at most, to help me unpack and do a bit of ironing. I can manage the shop on my own, of course.'

Feen cleared her throat, and finally chipped in. 'Well, here's a thought... does Meghan want a bit of a job?' She smiled at Meghan. 'You're here for a few weeks, right?'

There was silence at the table. Nobody spoke. Meghan flushed. She looked quite pleased, Adie thought, but more than a little uncomfortable. Adie decided to come to the poor girl's rescue.

'Well, six more weeks, actually. And for what it's worth, I think that's a great idea, if you'd be up for it, Meghan? You could maybe do a few hours in between the time you're exercising Astro. A little holiday job! Might be useful, to earn a bit of dosh?'

Meghan considered this for a moment or two. 'Well, maybe I could. I'm not bad at ironing. I always do it for us all at my Nan's.'

'And money is always helpful,' Trudie observed, smiling. 'I could use you for, say, three hours a day for six days straight, at adult minimum wage but cash in hand. How would that be? Monday to Friday next week?'

Meghan was blushing again. 'That'd be *great*. But don't you want references or something? You don't know me.'

'True,' Trudie nodded. 'But you love horses, so you're an 'animals' girl, and anyone who likes animals is streets ahead, in my book. Besides, I know where you're staying, and Adie has the details of where you live. If you mess me around and then take off, I can hunt you down and kill you. But to be honest, I don't expect there's much that could go wrong. It's just a bit of unpacking and ironing, and putting security tags on things. I'm sure you couldn't make too much of a mess of that, and I'll be there too of course, to supervise you.'

Meghan giggled. 'I'll have to run it by my Dad, but I dunno why he'd moan, if it's just for a week. I'll text him now. He's still getting used to his new phone, but I think he knows how to text me back!'

The others laughed, while Meghan texted her father. Shortly after, she got a ping on her phone. She beamed and looked up. 'He says I can do it. He's a bit paranoid though; wants to bring me in and meet you, and pick me up again on Monday. I guess he wants to check you out.' She rolled her eyes, and looked apologetically at Trudie.

'Of course he does! I'd be concerned if he didn't.' Trudie laughed. 'And if you hate it, you don't have to stay, and no hard feelings. Deal?'

'Deal.' Meghan reached across and high-fived Trudie's hand. Everyone around the table collectively cried 'Yay!' and the conversation then rolled on to the centenary festival that was due to happen in Torley the following month.

Carla took advantage of a brief lull in the conversation, and piped up: 'By the way. Dave and I have fixed the wedding for the first Saturday in October, so… save the date?'

She sat back and grinned, self-consciously, as everyone congratulated her. She produced her left hand, and everyone cooed over her engagement ring; three pretty gold-set diamonds in a straight row, with the centre one being just a little bigger than the two that flanked it.

Adie was overjoyed. 'Carla! That's wonderful news! I'm so glad! You and Dave are *very* well suited. You have so much in common, I'm sure you'll be very happy!'

Carla grinned and muttered 'I'll finally be a married woman, but God help me if I ever become respectable.' She looked squarely at Sheila. 'You'll have me for a neighbour, Sheila. I'm sure you're thrilled at the prospect.'

Shiela just waved a hand at her, and grinned. 'Aw, I've no quarrel with you anymore, love! Dave's a good bloke, and 'e deserves a bit of 'appiness. 'Is wife leaving 'im for 'is best friend knocked 'im around a lot. I'm glad you've got together and I 'ope you'll both be very 'appy.'

'We just might be, if I can somehow manage to avoid burning his house down.' Carla looked sheepish, as everyone stared at her.

'I'm suffering from some kind of weird, throw-back menopausal madness,' she admitted. 'Earlier this week I made a batch of forty-eight meatballs, and popped them onto a plastic tray to stick in the freezer, for free-flow; you know, for later? Well, I didn't put them in the freezer, did I? I put the bloody things in the oven instead, in my absent-mindedness, then later I switched the oven on to start getting something else ready, popped back downstairs to the shop for a bit, and ended up wondering what the terrible smell was, coming down the stairs. You should've seen the state of the oven.'

Adie shouted with laughter. 'Oh my God! How hilarious! Well, I'm glad I'm not the only one who does these mad, mental things!'

Fiona Frost was laughing too. 'The smell of meatballs and melted plastic! Yummy! It's okay Carla, I don't know what *my* brain is doing lately, either. One night last week, I went home and forgot to lock the bloody shop! Anyone could've waltzed in there!'

Carla grimaced. 'Yikes! That's not good! Bit traumatic, showing up the following morning to find someone's pinched all your cactuses!' She looked around the table at everyone.

'It would probably be me that would've done it. Not being prickly enough already, and all that. But seriously; how are we supposed to get through this? I thought I was finished with it all, *years* ago! I went through really early, in my forties actually, and everything settled down, but lately I've been having these mad lapses of concentration and forgetfulness. I'm driving myself bat-shit with it all.'

'What does the doctor say?' Adie smiled at her sympathetically.

'The doc reckons it's not abnormal to have gone through and then still have this kind of 'overhang' popping back to say hello and remind me that I'm actually *not* in charge of my own body. I never knew that could even happen! I just hope it doesn't go on for too long. It'll teach me for being so smug, I suppose, thinking I was done and dusted.'

''ormones 'ang around in their tattered state for a long time after we think they've settled,' Sheila explained. 'I feel like I'm on a bloody seesaw, 'alf the time. One minute I'm fine, the next

I'm fantasizing about ways to kill me bloody 'usband and 'ide 'is body. If it weren't for Feen's potions I'd have bumped the silly sod off years ago, Lord love 'im.'

'Well, even as I'm doing bizarre things I shouldn't be doing, like putting Dave's pristine white t-shirts in the washing machine with the new crimson towels, and almost setting my oven on fire, the man still wants to marry me. Brave soul.' Carla's lopsided grin made Fiona laugh again.

'I have to put an alarm on my phone now, to go off at shop-shut time, because I'm so scared of doing it again! And what's with all the bloody top lip and eyebrow sprouting, for God's sake? If I didn't keep on top of that I'd have a face to rival my father's! I'm still in shock, at how haywire my hair is going! Thinning on my head, but going bonkers everywhere else!'

Adie giggled. 'I know. Face maintenance. Gardening on an epic scale. Who knew *that* would become such a thing? Yes; things our mothers never warned us about, and bloody-well should have! Well, you lot didn't see *me* when I first arrived in Torley. I was the best candidate you've probably ever seen, for Yeti of the Year Award! My hair was long enough to sit on, but nowhere near as nice as it sounds. It looked more like a hanging mass of straggly seaweed.'

She laughed to herself and shook her head. 'Not long after I got here, in the throes of a messy marriage break-up and family in-fighting, I woke up and actually noticed myself. I got the shock of my own life, at how much I'd let myself go! I threw myself on Maddie Murphy's mercy, at Torley Tresses, and treated myself to a decent haircut and my first ever lip wax. But oh my God – the lip wax! I thought my top lip *itself* had been ripped off my face, let alone the hair! I couldn't believe the pain of it! It gets easier, the more you do it, but holy *moly!*'

'I'm considering electrolysis,' Trudie piped up.

Hazel cocked her head to one side, and pulled a face. 'That's a long process, isn't it? And not without its risks? Lots of expensive sessions and the threat of permanent numbness?'

'Got a friend who gets it done, reckons it's the best thing she ever did. Trouble is, I'd have to keep going to Carlisle for it. That's the nearest place that has someone who does it.'

'Well, get them to come over here once a month instead,' Fiona smirked, 'or however often you need to have it done, and we can all do it! Electrolysis parties! Woohoo!'

'We'd need a *lot* of wine.' Adie remarked dryly, and Fiona rolled her eyes.

'Wine, we can do. Moustaches, sprouting chin hair and runaway eyebrows, we can't. Sorry, but I'm sick of looking like I have antenna sticking out above my eyes. I have to do *something!* These days I'm too afraid to even leave the house without a serious magnifying mirror and a pair of tweezers in my handbag!'

Meghan was laughing now too. 'You guys are so funny. But for what it's worth, I think you all look pretty good. You should see my nan! She used to be a hippy when she was young. She's never plucked her eyebrows in her whole life! She's never worn makeup either, and she's really proud of it. One time I lost one of my false eyelashes and it fell through my shirt and ended up on the kitchen floor. She jumped out of her skin! She thought it was a centipede. She said she was wondering how it had got into the house!'

Everyone giggled at that. Carla nodded at her. 'False eyelashes are not something I've ever had to think about. My lashes were always pretty good, but my eyebrows are something else. I'm amazed at how many *white* hairs I'm pulling out! And they're so much thicker; it's like dragging dead trees out of my face! It's the brain stuff that worries me more though, if I'm honest. Like will I *really* burn the house down one day?'

'You probably won't, but you're in good company, Carla,' Trudie remarked. 'Most of us are whizzing around the menopause maypole, hoping like hell that we don't lose our grip on the rope. As to how we get through it? Well, for me, its HRT, but that doesn't mean the symptoms are gone. They're a lot more manageable, but I still feel and think all kinds of weird stuff, here and there.'

Adie nodded. 'I was never tempted to take HRT, but I do know that it works well if you get the right preparation. I think there's a bit of trial and error involved, but your doctor should be able to guide you, Carla.' She winked at her. 'Anyway, all that aside, huge congratulations again! You and Dave must come for dinner soon, and we can open a couple of bottles of bubbly.'

Carla inclined her head. 'That sounds nice. Thank you.'

Within seconds, everyone reverted back to chatting about the wedding, and Trudie was asking Carla if she could help her to find an outfit for the day.

'Thanks, but I thought I might wear that trouser suit you got for me, for Feen and Gavin's wedding? It hasn't had an outing since, and it's far too nice to just sit there hanging in the wardrobe.'

Sheila piped up, 'Ooh, yeah! That was *gorgeous*. I wanted to rip that off you and put it on *myself!* Trouble is, with my figure, I'd probably just end up looking like an 'ippo wrapped in a curtain. But it was so elegant on you, with your slim frame! I think that's a perfect choice.'

'I do too,' Adie agreed, thinking back to Carla's beautiful powder-blue trouser suit with its huge white, yellow-centred flowers. 'You looked *stunning*. That wraparound kimono-top and the wide flared pants were so flattering. But maybe a slightly more flamboyant hat, for your own big day? And closed-in shoes? It will be October so maybe the sandals you wore with it last time might not be too practical for late autumn…'

Carla nodded. 'Yeah, different shoes, and a different hat. That's me sorted. We just now have to get Dave to look less like a vagrant. Quite a challenge, but he scrubs up okay when he puts his mind to it, and he does have a couple of rather fetching crimson t-shirts. Perhaps you could do a few flowers, Fiona?'

Fiona smiled gently. 'It would be my pleasure, Carla.'

'I'll make your wedding cake,' Peg declared.

'And I'll loan you my cream mohair shrug cardi, to wear over your suit.' Adie offered. 'For your something borrowed?'

She grinned as everyone chattered on. She was pleased that Meghan Thomson was going to work with Trudie for a week. Poor Trudie was utterly snowed under, and Adie could see how tired she was. The summer stock arrival was always a big deal, and she needed real help. But as overwhelmed as Trudie was, it was never an easy thing for her, to ask for it. That was a big deal too, and Adie was thrilled that such a ready solution had been found. By Monday, Trudie would have support, and Adie had no doubt that Meghan would be capable of doing what was asked of her, if her work with Astro was anything to judge by. It seemed that Teapot Cottage was still working its magic, providing much needed help via one of its tenants, to the local vet and the local clothing merchant!

Adie was tempted to ask Meghan about her dad, but something stopped her. Stuart Thomson had been quite reserved since their arrival. While his daughter was sociable enough in her own quiet way, Stuart himself seemed very reticent. He hadn't been the most forthcoming of people, and even in polite conversation, Adie hadn't been able to draw much out of him. Meghan didn't talk much about him either, even when Hazel had politely asked about him and what he did for a job. Meghan had neatly sidestepped the question, and someone else had quickly taken the conversation in a different direction. Ah well, some families were more private than others, and that's all there was to it, Adie supposed. Stuart Thomson had paid for his tenancy, so it was none of her business really, who he was or what he did for a living.

Noon was drawing closer, and once the third pot of coffee had been drained, and the jelly cake fully demolished, everyone stood up to leave. Fiona had a big wedding order to get ready for tomorrow. Peg's lunchtime rush was about to start and Trudie had to go back to her boxes. As usual, they were the first ones out the door, all hugging and air kissing Adie as they left. Hazel and Carla were right behind them.

Meghan was almost the last to leave. She was still sitting at the table with Feen, who was chatting to Sheila about her twins. As Adie began to clean up, all three women offered to help, but she shook her head, smiling. There wasn't much, and it wasn't like she had anything else to do for the afternoon. The cartons of eggs, and the jars of jam and packets of lavender shortbread, were already sitting in a cardboard box by the front door for tomorrow's Farmer's Market. For once, she was ahead of herself, and after she'd made Mark's lunch for twelve thirty, she could look forward to sitting in the sun for the afternoon and reading a book. If it got too hot, she could always jump in the pool and maybe give Feen a hand with the twins, as she'd already told Adie they would be swimming in the afternoon.

Feen took Sheila upstairs to see Gavin and the twins, and Meghan stood up to go. 'I'd better get back, Dad will be making lunch any minute, so if I go back before he *asks* me to, it'll be a brownie point.'

Adie grinned at her. 'I hope you're both enjoying the cottage.'

Meghan nodded. 'Yeah, it's great, thanks. It's such a peaceful place, and that view from the living room windows is really nice, isn't it?'

'Yes, it is. The cottage is a very special little place. Buying it was one of the best decisions I ever made. It brings a lot of joy and peace to people who stay there.'

Meghan thanked her for the coffee and cake. 'I like your friends,' she admitted. 'I thought they'd be a load of old fuddy-duddies, like you said, but they weren't. They were amazing, and really funny. Thanks for inviting me, I'm glad I came.'

'I'm glad you did too! You've got a little job out of it, for one thing, and I know how much Trudie will appreciate *anything* you can do to help her. You're welcome up here anytime, Meghan, and keep up the good work with Astro. She seems to like you very much.'

'I love her. She's just beautiful. It's so much fun spending time with her.'

Meghan said her goodbyes and left, and Adie left the front door open, in the vain hope that a breeze might materialise from somewhere and blow some cool air through the house.

Feen came back downstairs with Sheila, who kissed Aide on the cheek and promised to come over for Sunday lunch with her husband Bob.

'Ta-rah,' she sang as she waltzed out through the front door. She needed to get back to make Bob's lunch. They were farmers too, on the other side of Torley valley.

Feen turned to Adie. 'Right. Punch, then lool. Are you coming up?'

Adie nodded and grinned. Feen's quirky and natural use of Spoonerism always made her smile, even when she had to scramble her brain a bit to keep up with it.

'Sure. I'll just get Mark's food sorted and I'll see you up there. What did you think of young Meghan?'

Feen's mouth twitched. She seemed to be considering her words.

'Oh, come on, out with it!' Adie cajoled. 'I know you're itching to say something 'meep and deaningful' as you'd put it! Just say it!'

Feen laughed, and was thoughtful for a few seconds. 'Well, let's just say there's a lot going on in that young head. She hasn't had an easy ride, but her life is about to get a lot better, and soon. So is her father's.'

Adie couldn't get Feen to say any more. Her step-daughter had the uncanny ability to see into the future, and she was incredibly intuitive to people's suffering. There was something ethereal and magical about her. Her gift of insight unnerved a lot of people, but most of them knew that she didn't have a harmful bone in her tiny, size-six body. Feen was talented, gentle and unfailingly helpful. Adie adored her.

Feen also remarked on Carla's big announcement. 'So, October then, Adie! Best buy a new hat then, or at least dig one out from the wack of the bordrobe, for Darla and Cave's big day.'

'It's nice news, isn't it? I know you said last year that you saw them tying the knot. I'm surprised they've waited this long, although I suppose they were both pretty wary of getting involved, after their previous experiences.'

Feen nodded. 'Yes, absolutely. It took them a while to be sure, but now that they are, I think it's all going to be lovely for them. Carla popped up to see Gavin just before she left, to ask him if he'd act as Mest Ban for her. He said yes, of course. I think he's pretty excited.'

'I'm sure he is! I know he likes Dave, and he's in a much better place with Carla now too, after so long estranged. I'm glad they sorted everything out. Life's too short to be at loggerheads with your nearest and dearest.'

As Adie said the words, she knew them to be true. Her own journey, as painful and frustrating as it had been, falling out with her own family and then going through the long and excruciating process of repairing broken bridges, it had been worth it. Everyone was as close as they could be, given their geographical limitations, and their levels of recovery from past events that had rocked them to the core.

All in all, she couldn't be much happier with how her life had turned out. It wasn't that long since she'd been on the very edge of despair, with her life blown apart, and wondering if she'd ever be able to put it back together again. Coming up from Guildford to house-sit at Teapot Cottage, with its wonderful healing energy, had restored her, and enabled her to believe in herself again. It had brought such joy into her life, in the form of the people she was now surrounded and supported by.

Her own children were all grown up with relationships of their own. Matty and his wife Marie and their two kids, and Ruth and Gina with their daughter, were all down in Surrey and Teresa, her other daughter, lived in London. As scattered as they were, they were all in regular contact, and came for visits when time allowed. Adie often found it hard to believe that with Feen and Gavin's twins she was now a grandmother to five children!

Mark came in at twelve thirty, as he did every day, and she set a plate of corn and bacon fritters in front of him with a couple of thick wedges of buttered homemade bread.

'Thanks, lass. 'Ow did coffee mornin' go? Sounded like it were as rowdy as usual.'

Adie laughed. She didn't think she'd ever tire of hearing his accent. It always made her want to laugh out loud, and she frequently did. 'You weren't eavesdropping at the back door, were you?'

Her husband shook his head. 'Nay, lass! Even *I* know there's nowt good to be 'eard by any man, eavsedroppin' on a cluckin' band o' women, but I did 'ave to pop down to fetch tomahawk from be'ind back door. I needed it for a job in't barn. Yer sounded like a gaggle o' bloody barmy ducks, quackin' away in 'ere. Thought we might be 'avin' scrambled eggs for lunch!' He grinned at her cheekily.

'It's a *flock* of ducks, and a gaggle of *geese,* silly! But yes, we had a good time. The young girl staying with her Dad at the cottage came too. Meghan. I was surprised she turned up, but I'm glad she did. It worked out well for her, and for Trudie.'

Adie went on to tell him about Meghan working with Trudie at the GladRagz boutique in the coming week. She also told him how well Meghan was doing with Darren's horse. Mark carried on eating and nodded sagely.

'Aye; sounds like all that'll keep 'er out o' mischief for a bit. Teenage bloody girls; Lord knows 'y'ave to keep em busy wi' summat.' He finished his lunch, swilled his mug of tea and stood up again.

'Oh, and Carla and Dave are tying the knot at the beginning of October, so you'd better make sure your suit still fits, in plenty of time.'

Mark looked astonished. 'Are they? Ecky thump! That's a turn up fert book! I know they've been seein' each other fer a bit, but I didn't think it were that serious! Ah well, lass 'as a right to be 'appy, I suppose. Dave's a decent bloke, and good bloody luck to 'im, takin' on't queen of ice.'

Adie smirked at him. 'Don't be uncharitable! You know *perfectly* well that she's perfectly *nice,* under that gruff exterior. A bit like you! Bristly on the outside and soft as butter on the inside.'

Mark rolled his eyes and grinned. 'Whatever. Right, back to't grindstone.' He kissed Adie very soundly, gave her a quick pinch on the bum, and made for the kitchen door. Adie giggled and called to him as he left.

'Don't forget we'll all be up at the pool this afternoon, so if you get a bit hot and fed up, come and join us.'

Mark nodded, waved at her and left to go back to the barn. After she'd finished clearing up, she ran upstairs to gather her pool things and change into a swimsuit. On the landing, Feen and Gavin were bringing the twins downstairs, dressed in their little swimsuits and hats. Feen waved a bottle of sun block at Adie and she nodded. 'Good idea. Let's go out and get wet!'

The pool was blissful. Mark had already cleaned it early that morning. The sun was hot, so Adie swiftly pulled the sun umbrellas out of the pool shed and set them up beside the loungers. With the shade in place, it wasn't long before they were all relaxing gently in the heat of the day, the only sound being the occasional splash and giggle, as Gavin and Feen pulled the twins around in their little rubber rings. Both toddlers were slathered in sun block.

They'll need it today, she thought. She leaned back, closed her eyes and sighed contentedly. Tomorrow, the Farmer's Market would be busy. Today though, she had an afternoon of leisure and she planned to take full advantage of it. Dozing in the sun was the perfect way to relax.

Chapter Five

On Saturday morning, when Stuart came downstairs on his usual mission to brew a bucket of coffee and organise some breakfast, he was astonished to find his daughter on the phone. It was extraordinary that she was up this early at *all*, let alone actually having a civil conversation with someone. The best he could usually hope for, and only at around eight-thirty at the earliest, was a half-hearted, grudging grunt. But here was Meghan, sitting in the window seat, having what seemed to be a very cheerful chat, at a quarter to eight. Stuart wondered who she was talking to but held back from asking. He waved a coffee cup at her, and she nodded, but carried on with her conversation.

'Yeah, that's what I thought. But I'd need a laptop, because my phone is so small, the screen, you know? It would drive me crazy, to try and work through that. I'm sure Dad would agree to let me have one, but I guess we'd have to go to Carlisle for it, wouldn't we?'

Stuart tried not to listen, but the conversation, what he could hear of it anyway, seemed like it was potentially quite meaningful, unlike most of the chatter she engaged in whenever it rang or when she called someone. Most of her conversations generally tended to be about boys or hair, and it always left him seriously baffled, how long and involved a conversation could actually be, about the benefits of a pair of straighteners. As the kettle started to heat up on the Aga, he strained to hear over the top of it.

'Really? You'd do that for me? Why would you do that?'

Meghan's conversation continued and she sounded quite excited. Stuart couldn't wait until she got off the phone to find out what it was all about. For the first time since he'd come home from prison, his daughter's voice had real animation in it.

It wasn't that she wasn't capable of holding a decent conversation; she was actually very intelligent. She just never seemed to have much *enthusiasm* for anything. Even her excitement over working with Astro was muted and quieter than he would have liked. It was as if the stuffing had all been knocked out of her. Stuart supposed that it really had, in effect.

He felt a quick stab of anger towards the long-since departed Annabel, for simply giving up trying to parent Meghan, at the precise time when the poor kid had needed stability. Who really knew what damage had happened to his daughter? He had to be patient with her. It was going to take time, but given the change in Meghan's temperament since they'd come to Teapot Cottage and she'd started working with Astro, he did feel more positive than he had in a long time, that they'd eventually have a meaningful relationship. He was aware that he had to make big changes too, for that to work properly for them both. He just had to be very careful what they were.

Meghan clicked off her phone and bounced into the kitchen. 'Dad! Guess what?'

Stuart smiled and shook his head. There was no way in a million years he was going to guess what the conversation she'd just been having was all about. He held up his hands.

'Haven't the foggiest, brat, but it sounds pretty mega, whatever it is.'

She laughed delightedly. 'I've got the fabbest news *ever*, Dad! But I should start at the beginning, I suppose.'

She sat at the table and wrapped her hands around her mug of coffee. Stuart sat also, and what Meghan then went on to tell him left him speechless, in a peculiar mixture of disbelief and pride.

Apparently, she hadn't been able to sleep very well last night, with a jumble of thoughts bouncing around in her head, so she'd spent a lot of time on the internet. She'd googled a lot of information about horses, and had stumbled on a distance learning diploma course on Equine Management being offered by a very well-known online course provider. She read the course syllabus and decided she wanted to do the course, which encompassed everything from horse psychology and training to physiology and biology. She'd made a call this morning to Darren Davies, hoping to catch him before he went to work, to talk about it, explain what the course involved, and to ask him what he thought of her doing it.

Darren had seemingly thought it was an excellent idea. So much so, that he'd offered to buy her a basic laptop computer, as payment for the work she was doing with Astro. He'd also offered to pay for the course for her. It was heavily discounted, currently being offered at seventy-five percent off its usual rate because it was the summer holidays when significantly fewer people would be interested in studying. Meghan said the course total study time ran to a hundred and fifty hours, with a short exam at the end, and she worked out that if she studied for three and a half hours a day she could complete the course, and the exam, before she had to go back to school.

'That's a big commitment, sweetheart. Are you sure you'd be up for it? It wouldn't leave you much time for anything else. You've got Astro too, and all next week working at that boutique in town. This is meant to be a holiday, remember.'

Meghan looked at him thoughtfully. 'I know, and we're supposed to be spending time together, getting to know one another again. But maybe you could help me! You have good knowledge that could be of real help, Dad. What do you think? Darren wants you to call him, to talk about it. He said he wouldn't go ahead if you weren't happy about it. But you are, aren't you Dad? Please say you are!'

Stuart knew he *did* have to talk with Darren about the idea of him bankrolling a laptop for his daughter. It seemed like an unusually generous offer. He wasn't at all comfortable with it, given how little they all knew each other, but Meghan seemed so excited, he didn't want to burst her bubble. He could afford a laptop for her himself, so he decided he would thank Darren sincerely but politely refuse his kind offer. It was far too generous. He told Meghan to go upstairs and get dressed while he tried to contact Darren. There might just be time, before Saturday surgery started.

He dialled Darren's number, expecting to leave a message, and he was surprised when the vet answered his phone on the third ring, telling him he'd been expecting the call. He was even more surprised, after explaining why he thought the offer of the laptop was too generous, at the perspective Darren offered.

'Stu, it wouldn't be a gift. The laptop would be in lieu of wages. I know we haven't talked about me paying Meghan for working with Astro, but the truth is she's doing a fantastic job, and she fully deserves to be paid. I called in briefly this morning, really early, because I had to be down here to check on a dog that's recovering from surgery, in case I had to do more with him before we open this morning. It's a half-day and we're always busy,' he explained.

'Anyway, I drove up and quickly checked on Astro, and I have to say I'm thrilled with her progress, even just in the week Meghan's been working her.

'You see, I've worked it out, mate. If I had to pay someone to work two hours a day with the horse, seven days a week, at the rate I'd have to pay over seven weeks it would come to three times what a decent basic laptop would cost me. It's just economics, Stu, and it's still selling her short, to be honest, for all she's doing. I've no doubt that she'll keep it up.'

Darren went on to describe how much pressure Meghan's work had taken off him, which wasn't economically quantifiable at all, and he also said that if he paid her in wages, she might not spend it very wisely.

'This way, she'll get something worthwhile, and if the cost of the course is covered too, she might be more inclined to complete it.' Darren finished by saying that he understood Stuart's concerns but while he wanted to make it clear he wasn't indulging her, he wasn't going to exploit her either by not rewarding her for her efforts.

'Call it a well-earned reward for all her hard work. I once pulled a kid off the straight and narrow, dragged him into a life of crime, and he ended up dead. This would be my way of putting something back into the world to help *another* young life, and Tommy would be proud of me for doing it. I know he would. Debby and I would like to do this, if you'd let us, Stu.'

'I think you're already putting a lot back into the world, mate, but yeah, of course. If you really want to do this, I'll get behind you on it.'

'Great. D'you think she's committed to it?'

Stuart thought for a moment. Meghan could be about as stubborn as the day was long, but that wasn't always a bad thing. Flipped on its head, her 'fault' of stubbornness became a virtue of determination. If she set her mind to something, she didn't often waver from it. Getting her to make up her mind in the first place about something was more of a challenge than getting her to stick to it. He said as much to Darren but added that he wanted to pay for the course himself, so that it wasn't Darren's direct concern if she somehow ran out of enthusiasm and didn't finish it. Darren agreed that was fair enough. Then he said something else that made Stuart pull up.

'You know, Stu, maybe you should do that course as well. If it really is as cheap as chips, maybe you could enrol on it too, keep Meghan company, and build on your own existing skills. If nothing else, it's a bit of extra knowledge, and it might help, you know, with the whole father-daughter bonding thing?'

Stuart told him that Meghan had already suggested he help her with her course. This seemed like a natural way of doing that. It would potentially bring them closer. Darren said he'd get Debby to order a laptop online for delivery to Teapot Cottage, and Meghan could get started as soon as it suited.

As he sipped his coffee, Stuart pondered on what Darren Davies had said. There was no arguing over what a solid man he was. He seemed driven to keep doing good in the world. His demons had followed him too, from his past mistakes, and although he was in a much better and more well-adjusted place in his head than Stuart currently was himself, it was clear that Darren Davies was also never able to fully forget or forgive himself for the catastrophic damage he'd done in the past.

We're not too dissimilar, he mused. *Maybe I'll always be more committed to kindness and atonement too, now, and maybe I'll find a way to be more comfortable with myself through doing good things for other people. And why not start with my own daughter?*

Meghan came back downstairs again, with her eyebrows up around her hairline. Stuart briefly toyed with the idea of stringing her along for a bit, but he wasn't entirely sure they were truly out of the tantrum-woods yet, after only a week together, so he gave it to her straight.

'Darren's buying your laptop as payment for your work with Astro. Debby is ordering it for you, to be delivered here. I'm paying for your course though, and I'm going to do it too. We can study together, and we'll help one another to pass the exam at the end.'

Meghan jumped up and down clapping her hands. 'Oh Dad! That's amazing! Woohoo!' She did a little dance around the kitchen. 'Woohoo! I can't wait to get started! I can do mornings at the boutique, and afternoons studying, and work with Astro first thing, then again at lunchtime and after dinner.'

'You're taking a lot on, sweetheart. You must promise me that you'll tell me, the minute it all starts feeling like too much. I need you to be serious about that. You can't overload yourself.'

Meghan stopped dancing and beamed at him. 'I will, Dad. I promise. If I feel overloaded, I'll say. But you studied for a law degree and everything, so you're the master of swot. You can help me with techniques if I need it, can't you?'

'Of course I can. So we need to get *my* laptop fired up and get these courses bought, don't we?' He handed Meghan a plate of buttered toast and raspberry jam, which she took and more or less ate without even noticing, let alone moaning about the amount of fattening, cancer-feeding sugar that went into just one single pot of the 'evil' stuff.

'Can you enrol us both Dad? I need to get out with Astro. And then it's the Farmers Market. Can we go? I want to see Jayde. And you said we could have a cream tea sometime, and now I've met the lady who runs the tea shop I'd really like to go there. Her name is Peg and she makes the best cakes. Can we do that too?'

'Yeah, of course. We need some more stuff, so I'll get the courses set up, while you work the horse, and then we can head into town.'

As his daughter skipped happily out through the front door, Stuart checked the kitchen cupboards and made a list of what they needed. He might get a dozen of Adriene Raven's eggs this week, he thought. They were beautiful, with rich yellow yolks, a completely different taste sensation from the pale, watery offerings he'd been given in prison. For a couple of years he'd done a bit of cooking in the prison kitchen, and had enjoyed it, but the food that came in was only ever of average quality, so the offerings to inmates were correspondingly so.

One good thing about working in the kitchen was that you got first dibs on what was available, and he'd always managed to set a decent meal aside for himself before it became the overcooked and soggy mess that was often served up to the other inmates when the cooks had got the timings wrong. He'd stopped working in the kitchen when the Chief Cook left and the replacement had proved too belligerent and temperamental for Stuart to keep trying to get on with. Life was difficult enough without putting up with abuse from a jumped-up self-opinionated gobshyte who thought he was Gordon bloody Ramsey.

But his time in the prison kitchen had helped Stuart develop a few decent cooking skills. He was particularly fond of making puddings and desserts. He hadn't let on, at Darren and Debby's, that the pavlova she'd produced was something he'd be well able to make himself. He'd been known as the 'master of meringue,' in HMP Exeter.

Maybe he could start getting a bit creative here with the Aga. People who used them swore by them, although he'd had no experience with them himself. But, he reasoned, if his teenage daughter was willing to give it a go, with not much in the way of cooking skills herself, surely he could step up to the plate too! He decided to have a closer look at what was on offer at the Farmer's Market, and let his imagination work a little. There were a couple of very basic recipe books in the bookcase behind the front door, so he'd take a look at them, when he wasn't up to his eyeballs in Equine Management studies!

Meghan had sent him the link to the learning institute, so he switched on his laptop and quickly found what he was looking for. He enrolled Meghan first, and once she'd been set up with an account and password, he went through the process again and enrolled himself.

He had to smile at the thought of going back to studying. It had been a lot of years since he'd sweated away in the law school library at uni, cramming cases into his head before exams. He remembered sitting on the floor in one corner of his flat, with all two hundred criminal cases he had to be familiar with for his 'Crimes' exam, fanned out across the floor in front of him. He recalled the last-minute panic he'd felt, wondering if he really had a hope of remembering them all. Criminal law had been the most interesting of all his core subjects, but he didn't want to practice it. There wasn't enough money in it, for him. His speciality had been Contract Law, helping to protect the interests of large corporations. The payout was a lot better for that kind of work.

This course would be very lightweight, compared to what he'd once had to do. Meghan might find it a bit more challenging, but Stuart was confident that he could help her understand it and get through it all.

It was interesting, how one week with a horse after a chance encounter, when she'd never before expressed the slightest interest in anything of an equine nature, had led her to this. It was living proof that sometimes fate just had its hands all over something, guiding you in ways you might not be prepared for.

Stuart hadn't expected his daughter to fall in love with horses, or to totally transform her attitude in little more than a week. He hadn't expected to meet a new friend, a kindred spirit, in Darren Davies. Life was full of surprises, and sometimes, if you had enough trust to let life push you in a certain direction, you might just end up somewhere exponentially better. While the coming weeks at Teapot Cottage would certainly be taking a different turn from what he'd been anticipating, he allowed himself to believe that they may just be life-changing for them both, in some way.

The Farmer's Market was even busier this week. It was a lot more interesting for Stuart too, since he'd decided to look more closely at what was on offer, rather than just concentrating on covering the basics. Meghan had made a beeline straight for Jayde's jewellery and flower stand, and was deep in conversation about heaven-knew what.

Stuart spent some time at a wild-foods stand, talking to a very interesting guy who was selling various kinds of game, and who also had some interesting preserves to offer with his meats. On his recommendation, Stuart selected some venison medallions and a jar of gin and juniper jelly. He also bought leg of organic lamb and a small bottle of rosemary-mint sauce, and a fat chain of pork and leek sausages. He then moved on to a truly glorious cheese stand, and purchased an assortment of cheeses, including a locally produced goat's cheese, a lump of local mature cheddar and a creamy brie.

He found himself revelling in the food choices, and he was astonished to realise that he was enjoying himself immensely. Food had suddenly taken on a whole new fascination. A couple of loaves of home-baked bread joined his growing pile of goodies, as did a much bigger selection of vegetables than he'd bought the week before. He decided he'd make a cheddar and red onion quiche for dinner, with salad. A packet of fresh pasta joined his haul and a few other bits and pieces; some organic flour and freshly churned butter to make his pastry, and a block of dark chocolate and some kitchen spices. By the time he'd finished shopping, he'd had to buy a carrier bag to hold everything that wouldn't fit into his backpack.

Meghan was talking to an elegant, well-dressed old lady he hadn't seen before. As he caught his daughter's eye, she raised her eyes and motioned for him to come over. It would have looked rude to refuse, especially since the woman was also looking at him expectantly.

'Dad, this is Hazel. She's a good friend of Mrs Raven's. We met at the coffee morning yesterday up at the farmhouse.'

Hazel held out her hand. 'Pleased to meet you. Hazel Walton. My grandson Gavin is married to Adie's step-daughter Feen. Meghan tells me she is going to do a horse course while she's here. I was just telling her that I think it's a wonderful idea. I used to ride a little, when I was a girl. I was never very good, but I loved it.' Hazel had very blue eyes and a kind face. Stuart liked her immediately. He shook her hand then held up his carrier bag.

'I'm Stuart. I've just been availing myself of the magnificent offerings here. It's amazing, what there is! I'll be cooking for England with this lot.'

Hazel looked fondly around the Farmer's Market.

'The people of Torley love this market. We were in grave danger of losing it, until Adie came and breathed new life into it. The last organiser didn't care about it much, and it was dwindling away to nothing. It's the hub of the town now, on a Saturday morning. People come from far and wide, to sell and to buy.'

'It's far better than any other farmer's market I've ever been to, not that I've been to many.' Stuart didn't bother to mention that a farmer's market to him, at one time, would have been a complete non-starter, for something to do. He'd been with Annabel a couple of times, under protest, to a market attached to a garden centre when she was having one of her moments of following a trend for buying organic vegetables. It hadn't been at all interesting. This market, here in Torley town, was a different beast altogether.

Adrienne Raven was pleased to see him again. She introduced him to Trudie Sangster, who was standing nearby, chatting to another stallholder. She told him that Trudie was the owner of GladRagz, the boutique that Meghan was going to work in, for the coming week. Stuart greeted her and introduced himself, and asked her if she had time for a few minutes' chat. Trudie agreed.

'We can get a quick coffee over there, if you like?' She gestured over to the corner of the hall where the makeshift cafe was in operation. They found a rare vacant table and Stuart ordered couple of coffees. When he sat down with Trudie, she looked at him enquiringly, a smile playing around her lips. 'I don't want to presume anything, but let me just say, before you ask me anything, that I'm a happily married woman.'

She grinned broadly, and Stuart appreciated the ice breaker. He smiled back and cleared his throat.

'Trudie I wanted to talk to you about Meghan coming to work for you next week. I'm happy about it, so there's no issue there, but I'm thinking that you might have one with me.'

Trudie's eyebrows rose to her neat fringe as she continued to look at him. Stuart ploughed on. 'The thing is, I'm not long out of prison. If you google me you'll find all the depressing details, but basically I accidentally killed a pregnant mother while I was driving under the influence. I served six years of a nine-year sentence, and Meghan and I have come up here for the summer to try and rebuild our relationship. I've already lost my house, my marriage, and my career. I don't want to lose my daughter too, so that's why we're here.

'I want you to have the full facts. None of what happened with me was her fault. She's a good kid, and she won't let you down, but I fully understand if you'd rather not hire her.'

Trudie blinked a few times. Then she spoke, choosing her words carefully.

'Wow! I wasn't expecting to hear anything like that! Okay... so what was your career? What did you used to do for a living?'

'Solicitor. Corporate. I've been disbarred though, so I'm in transition. Figuring out what's next, all that.'

'You said you lost your marriage. Was that to Meghan's mother?'

Stuart shook his head. 'No. She died when Meghan was four. Brain haemorrhage. I brought Meghan up myself after that, with help from my parents, until my Dad died, the year before my accident. Mum carried on pitching in, but then I remarried, which turned out to be a very big mistake. My second wife abandoned Meghan, sold the house, a within a year of me getting locked up. Meghan went to live with Mum. And now I've been released, and I'm trying to figure out what to do with our lives in a way that will work for her too.'

Trudie chewed her bottom lip for almost a full minute, deep in thought. Eventually she spoke again. 'So she's lost two mothers, her grandfather and her home, and her dad's been away in prison for six years. Wow. What a doozy.'

'In a nutshell, yes. And a doozy, as an understatement, yes.'

Stuart sat back. He didn't know what else to say. Trudie leaned forward.

'How do you feel about what you did, looking back on it.' Her question was more curious than demanding.

To his horror, Stuart found himself fighting to swallow down the lump of sorrow in his throat. He shook his head, as if to clear it.

'I've done a lot of soul-searching, and in some ways I still struggle to believe I was that person, that catalyst for so much anguish. I was such an asshole back then. I'm not that guy anymore. Living with myself is still pretty hard, but I don't want anyone else to have to keep paying for my mistakes. Certainly not Meghan. She's been through enough. But, like I say, if you decide you'd rather not take her on for the week, I'll understand. I'd like to be the one to tell her though, if that's the case.'

Trudie shook her head resolutely. 'No, I'm happy to have her for the week. She seems very sweet. I had no idea she'd had such a rough ride, the poor kid. You wouldn't know that, from talking to her. And it took some courage, to tell me what you just have. It's a very big thing to take a chance on, telling a total stranger something like that.'

'Well, I don't make a habit of rocking up to strangers and saying 'hey, guess what...,' but you're employing my daughter, so you deserve to know the truth. But Meghan's not me, Trudie. She's a little messed up and troubled, but she does have good support. We both found out who our friends were, in this process, and some of them are solid.' Stuart rolled his neck and stretched.

'We're not exactly in a great place, her and me, but we're working on it. We're getting there. I think we'll be ok in the end.'

Stuart went on to tell Trudie about Astro, and the equestrian course Meghan had found, that they'd both committed to doing together.

Trudie nodded. 'She needs something to focus on, and it sounds like she has that, with the horse and everything.'

She drained her coffee cup and looked levelly at him. 'Thank you, Stuart, for telling me. You didn't have to, but it's good to have things like this out in the open. And we've all made mistakes, haven't we? We've all done it, at some stage, got behind the wheel of a car or done some other responsible thing when we weren't in a fit state to do it. Most of us were lucky enough to get away with it. There but for the grace of God, and all that. You weren't so lucky. But maybe there's been enough heartache. Maybe it's ok to leave it where it is now and look forward.'

She looked at him and shrugged. 'You've done your time, haven't you? Seems like you've paid a heavy price for it all, probably a bigger one than was fair, and that includes continuing to punish yourself for however long it will be. Let's hope it's not a lifetime. Meghan is certainly still welcome to work in my shop next week. I'm not one for dwelling on the past, and I believe everyone should have a second chance in life, especially when they've learned from their mistakes.' Trudie stuck her hand out and Stuart shook it gratefully. She got up to leave.

'Good luck, Stuart. You're an intelligent man, and you'll have another career. It seems like you've learned a bit about yourself in all this. Whatever you end up doing, I hope it will fulfil you, and I wish you well.'

She left without another word and didn't look back. Stuart was left with a vague feeling of anticlimax. He wasn't sure what he'd been expecting, some swinging sword of Damocles to sever his head, maybe an expression of outrage or condemnation. But Trudie Sangster had been pragmatic and unflinching in the face of his confession. That was encouraging. It made him wonder; if it was no insurmountable deal to the people he was going to meet in life, could he find a way to forgive *himself*?

He located Meghan and they set off for Ye Olde Torley Tea Shoppe. A cream tea was exactly what they both fancied and when Peg brought it over, Meghan introduced her to Stuart. She sat down with them for a minute or so, asking him how he and Meghan were both finding Teapot Cottage. With his mouth full of cream scone, all Stuart could do was nod at her. Peg laughed.

'Sorry, Stuart! It's an old bad habit I've got, waiting until folk have got their faces full and then asking them a question.'

Meghan mercifully bailed him out by saying how much they were enjoying the cottage. 'It has a great atmosphere, very peaceful and comfy. And the bed is gorgeous! It's the first time I've slept in a double bed. All the space; I want to take it home with me.'

Peg nodded. 'That cottage is a very special little place. Maybe Adie will one day tell you her own story about it. Anyway, I better get back to the kitchen. Lovely to meet you Stuart.' She winked at Meghan as she got up again.

Stuart remembered that they might need a couple of jotters to make notes on, as they worked their way through their course. They stopped off at the little stationery shop in Torley called 'Patchwork 'n' Pen.' When they went inside, Meghan exclaimed; 'Wow! Look at this place, Dad! Can you believe this?'

She had every right to be impressed. The little shop frontage belied what was, in fact, a veritable 'Tardis' inside. Although it was narrow, it extended back more than a hundred and fifty feet, and it wasn't just a stationery shop. It had a massive crafts section too, with eight sewing machines set up at the back in a square configuration. A massive patchwork quilt hung on the back wall behind them all. A well-worn, headless dressmaker's dummy with pins sticking out of the top of its neck was tucked into the recess below a set of stairs.

Clearly, someone gave sewing lessons here. One wall was racked in bolts of brightly coloured fabric and packets of 'fat quarters' although Stuart hadn't the faintest idea what that meant! One tall narrow stand held row upon row of embroidery threads of every imaginable colour, and another was bulging with paper patterns for knitting, cross stitch and embroidery. A basket on the floor was overflowing with an assortment of different colours and grades of wool.

The opposite wall contained a selection of sketch and paint pads, along with various tubes, palettes and boxes of different paints, colouring pencils and pastels. There were also about a dozen drawers set into the wall, and Stuart couldn't even begin to imagine what might be in them. Meghan pulled one open. It was full of crystal beads and jewellery fixings, partitioned into various colour and sizes by plastic inserts. A couple of large heavy pattern books sat propped up against the two biggest drawers. Stuart supposed they probably held a good choice of sewing patterns. It really was one of the most well-stocked shops he'd ever seen.

He selected a couple of A4 ring-bound notebooks and a few decent pens, along with a pack of post-it notes and a few other assorted bits and pieces. He also picked up a set of calligraphy pens and a traditional bottle of ink for Meghan, although he doubted if she would now have time to experiment with them, considering how much else she'd taken on in the last few days. His daughter had transitioned, more or less overnight, from a surly, sulky, unmotivated child to a young woman who was taking to responsibility like a duck to water. Stuart wouldn't have believed it, if he hadn't seen it with his own eyes.

As they pulled up at home, Meghan checked her watch. 'Right, I don't want any lunch, after that big cream tea, so I'm going to do an hour's work with Astro, then start my course.'

'It's Saturday. Don't you want to wait until Monday?'

Meghan stared at him, as if he was insane. 'What? No, Dad! I want to get started. Why wait for two more days? It's not like I've got much else to do, or anywhere else to go, is it?'

Stuart had to agree, there wasn't much point in hanging around, although he might see if he could get Meghan to relax a little later, with a decent movie if he could find one. He'd got some caramel popcorn at the Market, which he knew she enjoyed. The last thing he wanted was for her to not have any fun, and to burn out early because of it. He also thought he might give her a gentle nudge in the direction of next Friday night's Youth Club. She should spend at least a little time with people her own age.

But, having downloaded their courses, Stuart agreed they might as well make a start. He made a pot of tea and they both settled themselves at either end of the kitchen table and started to immerse themselves in their first course module; The Evolutionary History of the Horse. Meghan was still on her phone, until her laptop arrived, but she could read the module okay on it, and was happily taking notes.

Chapter Six

A knock at the front door startled Meghan. She'd been deep into her reading, and the last thing she and Stuart were expecting was company. She checked her watch. It was three o'clock already. Stuart got up to go and answer the door, and Meghan was surprised to hear Mrs Raven's voice. Stuart invited her in, which was also surprising. He wasn't usually that friendly towards people he didn't know well, and she understood why, but sometimes his brusqueness was embarrassing. Mrs Raven was the landlady though, so it would have been pretty rude not let her come in.

She had two half-dozen egg cartons in her hand. 'I saved these for you. I'm not sure if you wanted them, and no problem if not, but I wondered if you'd just forgotten. You scuttled off pretty quickly with Trudie for what looked like quite an intense chat, and then you didn't come back.'

Stuart clapped his hand to his forehead. 'Yes! I'd totally forgotten to get eggs! Thanks so much! I appreciate this. I'd have been kicking myself tonight, since I've planned to bake a quiche!'

Mrs Raven set the eggs on the table and smiled at Stuart's laptop and then at Meghan's notes. 'You guys look busy!'

Meghan grinned. 'Hi, Mrs Raven. Me and Dad are doing a course in Equine Management. We've just started.'

'Wow! Is this all to do with Astro?'

Meghan nodded. 'Yeah, I wanted to learn more about her, and how to work with her, and I found an online diploma course to do. Dad's doing it too so he can help me. I'm hoping to have it done before I go back to school.'

'Well, that's dedication, I must say! Doing that as well as working for Trudie and working with the horse doesn't sound like much of a relaxing summer holiday, though! I hope you'll have time to have some fun while you're up here, Meghan. There are some great walking trails, and a bit of entertainment over in Carlisle of course, if you felt like going over there.'

Meghan shrugged. 'I don't mind. Astro's amazing, the boutique will be fun, and the course seems really interesting.'

She found that she really meant it; she wasn't just trying to defend herself. Normally when an adult asked her if she was biting off more than she could chew, Meghan would feel defensive and snappy. Not today. She was surprised to find Mrs Raven's concern quite encouraging. The woman clearly seemed to really care that she and her dad enjoyed their time in the area.

'Well, I'll leave you to it.' Mrs Raven started to leave, and Stuart cleared his throat.

'Did your friend Trudie tell you what we'd been talking about?'

Mrs Raven shook her head. 'No. I didn't ask her, and she doesn't gossip. It's none of my business. I assumed it was to do with Meghan working in the shop next week.'

'Well it was, indirectly, but there was something behind it that I thought she needed to know. It's about me, actually. If you don't mind, I'd like to tell you too, so we can have everything out in the open, since we're going to be here for a while.'

Meghan was astonished. It seemed that Stuart had told Trudie about his past, as a precursor to Meghan going to work there. On the one hand it was nobody else's business, what they'd gone through but, on the other, Stuart was a convicted criminal. He'd served time in jail for killing somebody. It was an accident, certainly, but Meghan had found out for herself through bitter experience that not everybody viewed a mistake like that kindly – especially when the victims involved had been a mother and her unborn baby.

Meghan's heart was in her mouth. What if Mrs Raven was one of those people? What if she was so repulsed by what Stuart had done that she threw them both out of her cottage? What would happen about Astro? She'd have to stop working with the horse, and the thought of that broke her heart. Tears welled up in her eyes as she watched her father lead Mrs Raven to the sofa, and begin to tell her their story. Her cheeks burned as she heard him describe what had happened. She found herself unable to sit still any longer. She got up out of her chair and went outside to the fence line. She was crying properly, and she tried to catch her breath. Astro came to the fence and nickered gently into her face. Meghan threw her arms around the horse who stood, rock solid, while she cried into her mane for a long time. When she spoke, her voice was choked.

'Oh Astro! I'm not leaving you. I promise! Whatever happens, I'll find a way for us to stay together.' She wondered to herself, if they got thrown out of Teapot Cottage, maybe Darren Davies would let them take Astro back to Taunton with them. Maybe they could hire a field down there somewhere. 'I'll figure something out, girl. Don't worry. I won't leave you behind. I'll find a way to take you with us if we have to go.'

Meghan felt a lot less sure than she sounded, and the tears wouldn't stop. Eventually, she felt a gentle hand on her shoulder. It was Mrs Raven.

'Meghan, hush. It's alright. I know you're worried, but don't be.' Meghan looked up and saw her kind face, through her tears. Mrs Raven reached forward and pulled her into a firm, warm embrace. She murmured into Meghan's hair as she held her.

'Oh, darling! I don't know what you thought I was going to do, but I'm certainly not going to demand that you and your Dad pack up and leave! I want you to stay, very much! Both of you.'

Meghan's tears now turned to ones of relief. She realised she was shaking with it. Mrs Raven continued to hold her and stroke her hair. After a time, she released one arm and kept the other around Meghan, and led her gently back towards the cottage. Stuart was standing in the doorway. He punched her playfully, lightly, on one arm.

'Alright, brat? No need to be upset. We're allowed to stay!' He was trying to make light of the situation. Meghan wasn't sure how to respond, so she didn't at all. They all sat down, and Mrs Raven began to speak.

'Meghan, I've had a good chat with your dad, and he's told me everything that happened to you both, because although Trudie's not one for gossiping, he wanted me to hear it from *him*. I appreciate his honesty, darling. Let me first say how sorry I am, that you were all involved in such a terrible tragedy. That accident must have had a huge impact on you, and I can't even *pretend* to know how you feel about it, or anything else that's happened in your life.

'But I want you to know that I don't judge people for the mistakes they make, because everybody makes them! Some are just bigger than others, that's all. I respect your Dad very much for telling me what he did, even though it was none of my business, really. It can't be easy, admitting to something like that. I think you're both very brave.'

She crossed her legs and continued. 'Meghan, I respect you too. You're an amazing young woman, and I think you have a very bright future. I know Darren thinks that. He has faith in you, and so does Trudie. So that would have been good enough for me anyway, because I trust the judgement of those two completely, but what I've seen of you *myself* is that you are both very nice, very genuine people, looking to put the past behind you and start again. And everyone deserves to do that. I've had to do it myself, after screwing up my *own* life, and most of my family's too!

'That's a different story for a different day, but I will *gladly* be a part of you pulling your lives back together! If this time here at Teapot Cottage helps you to heal and consolidate your future, I'm all for it. You'll always be welcome here, and I mean that.'

Stuart spoke up. 'Thanks, Mrs Raven. That means a lot.'

'I think you'd better call me Adie, from now on. I can't stand on ceremony with people I know so much about! We've become friends, and that's what friends call me,' Adie laughed. Meghan spontaneously jumped up and gave her a hug.

As Adie was leaving, she suddenly jumped a little. 'Oh, I almost forgot the main reason I came down here, apart from the eggs, of course! I wanted to tell you about a horse-trekking place; Beaconsfield Stables. It's not that far from here, just on the other side of Carlisle. It's on Redemption Road, if my memory serves me correctly; the big road that runs for miles along the north side of the city. I wondered if you two might like to go riding, on one of the days you're here. I think they trek all across the back valleys, on different trails. The views from up there are probably amazing, and I think it's suitable for all levels of experience.'

Meghan looked at Stuart excitedly. Her eyes were shining. 'Ooh, Dad! That'd be a *great* idea! Can we? Can we do that?'

Her father shrugged. 'Sure, why not?'

Adie added, 'Might be less busy on a weekday too. Weekends tend to be busier everywhere, and its school holidays now. A lot of extra visitors flock to the region, especially for long weekends, so midweek might be a good time for you to go, as a suggestion.'

After Adie left, Meghan got straight on her phone and looked online for the stables she had mentioned. It was called, simply, Beaconsfield Stables and Trekking. It was closed on Mondays and Tuesdays, but was open every other day, with treks at ten in the morning, then at two in the afternoon. She showed her Dad, and he agreed to give them a call to book in for a trek. They decided to book for the Wednesday of the week following Meghan's week at GladRagz with Trudie. She was excited, when Stuart came off the phone having confirmed a morning trek. He grinned at her pleasure.

'Let's hope it's as much fun as it sounds. And let's hope it doesn't rain! It's a couple of hours, and we can be back in time for a late lunch, then we can study for the afternoon. Maybe you could think about going to that youth club next Friday night, too. You need to have some fun with kids your own age.'

Meghan rolled her eyes at him. 'Already sorted, Dad. I talked to Jayde at the Farmers' Market today. I'm meeting her outside the front doors on Friday night.'

*   *   *   *   *

Meghan was excited as Stuart turned onto Redemption Road, and then drove towards the Beaconsfield stables that were about halfway down. They'd probably never have found the place without satnav guidance, since there was no signage on the main road anywhere, to advertise the business, and it was located down an unmarked dirt track that was half a mile long and rutted with bumps and potholes.

As he drove into the yard, Meghan could see that although the place was laid out well enough, and the stable buildings themselves were solid and well-constructed, there was a vaguely depressing, neglected air about the place.

'This places looks a bit better-appointed than the one I worked at as a boy,' Stuart told her. 'But the atmosphere here seems a bit sad. I'm surprised. I dunno what I expected, but I thought there might've been more going on around here.'

They pulled up alongside two other cars in the carpark and got out, at the same time as a short, wiry, elderly man with grey hair and kind brown eyes came striding forward to meet him with his hand outstretched.

'Hello, and welcome to Beaconsfield. You must be Mr and Miss Thomson? I'm the owner here. My name's Warwick Ford.'

Stuart met his handshake. 'Yes. Stuart Thomson, and this is my daughter Meghan.'

Meghan shook his hand too, and then looked over at the horses. She couldn't wait to get started!

Warwick gestured for the two of them to follow him up to the stable block, where a young woman in her early twenties was getting the last of seven horses ready. Three other people were standing around chatting among themselves and holding hard-hats, and Warwick invited Meghan and Stuart to head into the annex and choose one each that fit, and complete the necessary paperwork required before they could ride. They had already been instructed to turn up in heeled boots and warm clothing. Warwick introduced the stable-hand as his granddaughter Lucy.

In line with Meghan having no experience, a solid older horse had been selected for her. His name was Finnegan and he was, as Lucy described, 'a bit of a plodder.' He was a solid, grey-dappled gelding, with soulful eyes. Meghan stroked his nose and he blinked at her quietly. She decided she liked him.

'You'll get no surprises with Finn,' Lucy explained to her. 'He's a more mature horse, but he's bomb-proof; great with beginners. He's a bit stubborn and he's unlikely to do much of what you tell him, but he won't scare you either. He'll just quietly follow the crowd, so it will be a nice sedate walk for your first trek.'

She showed Meghan how to mount Finnegan, how to keep her heels down in the stirrups, her knees into the sides of the horse, and how to hold the reins. She then moved on to ensure the others all had the same instructions. Stuart's horse was a beautiful brown bay, slightly more spirited than Finnegan, and her name was Sesame. She kept stepping sideways, but Stuart clearly knew how to handle her. It was fascinating to Meghan, to see her father on horseback, showing the kind of confidence and experience she never knew he had.

I wonder what else I'm going to learn about him, on this holiday, she thought to herself as everyone got in line. Lucy was to take the lead, with the other three people behind her. Then came Meghan, with her father behind her, and Warwick would bring up the rear.

Finnegan stepped forward, catching Meghan slightly off-guard. She grabbed the reins as her heart lurched. Luckily, she managed to stay upright in the saddle. She grinned nervously at her father. 'I wasn't expecting that!'

She found herself grinning again when Finnegan abruptly put his head down, disrupting her balance again, just a little.

'I thought you said he wasn't a handful!' she called to Lucy. She supposed her nervousness was common enough to the riding hands. They probably saw it all the time in people, but she still felt vulnerable and unsure what Finnegan might do next. She felt inordinately high off the ground, and she simply had to hope she could keep her balance and not fall off. That would be *beyond* embarrassing! Lucy flashed her a quick smile and a wink. Meghan decided that the key to not falling off the stables' most 'bomb-proof' horse, and maintaining some semblance of dignity, was not to panic every time Finnegan moved.

When Lucy had everyone mounted, she got on her own horse, waited for Warwick to do the same, then gave them all the thumbs up and started walking forward. They rode quietly to the end of the yard, and Meghan started to get used to Finnegan's odd-feeling gait as he ambled forward. As they turned left onto a narrow uphill track, she felt the horse gain his own confidence as he started walking a little more determinedly. He seemed to know where he was going. She reached down and patted his neck and spoke gently to him as they all made their way up a fairly steep slope. After about five minutes they reached a plateau on the hillside, and all the horses stopped. It seemed as if they all knew exactly what to do, and when to do it. Lucy turned her horse to face them all. 'Everyone ok?' she called.

Everyone assured her they were fine, including Meghan. Lucy called again. 'We're going to follow the track around this hillside now, and go up again, then along the ridge and down into the next valley. There's a stream at the bottom that we'll walk through, and then we'll take the track on the other side for about half an hour. Then we'll turn into the five-acre field, where those of you with a bit more experience can have a bit of a canter, if you like.

'Then we'll flank the stream for half a mile or so, cross it again, and pick up the track that will eventually bring us back around the other side of the stables from where we left. So, it's a loop.' She winked again at Meghan.

'Enjoy the views everyone, and remember this is meant to be fun, so sing out if you need or want to stop, for photos or anything, or if you have any worries. I'd rather you tell us if something's not right, than were unhappy and didn't say so, okay?'

Everyone gave the thumbs up, and Lucy turned her horse again and led the group along the track as promised. She'd told all the riders to enjoy the view and Meghan had to admit that from their vantage point, halfway up the hill, it was spectacular. A lake glittered in the distance as the sun bouncing brightly off it. From this far away, the surrounding hills dwarfed it to an almost puddle-like status.

She turned her face to the sun and let the warmth of it caress her skin. The air was fresh and clean, out here. It was a gorgeous day. There wasn't a scrap of traffic to be heard, and she was on horseback, looking at a view that few people in the world would ever see. It felt like a small slice of paradise to her, in that moment, there in the sunshine with her dad, with the smell of horses and gorse-flower in her nostrils. She felt profoundly at peace, and lucky too, for this opportunity she once couldn't have imagined. How wonderful of Adie Raven to have suggested this! Meghan knew she would never forget this day.

Finnegan continued to amble forwards and she found herself getting more used to sitting straight in the saddle and compensating for his slightly swaying gait. She wasn't confident enough to turn around to see how her Dad was doing, but he called to her a few times to ask her how she was getting on. She could also see the others in front of her, getting to grips with their horses. One woman was clearly well at home on her horse, and Meghan supposed she'd be one of the riders who might take advantage of the opportunity to do some cantering later.

As they eventually completed their walk around the hillside, with the views changing but remaining spectacular as the other side of the long deep valley came into sight, the track started to go down again, and Meghan could see the stream that Lucy had been talking about, in the distance. The track widened a little at this point and Meghan could hear her father talking to the owner, Warwick Ford. She couldn't really tell what they were saying, but the tone of the conversation seemed friendly. She was glad that he had someone to talk to. Mr Ford was a lot older, but she guessed they'd found something in common to talk about. Initially she's been worried that the riders would all be youngsters he wouldn't have much in common with, and that he'd just be bored out of his tree all day.

As they approached the stream, Meghan started to feel her nerves clawing at her stomach. She bit her bottom lip. They were supposed to cross here, but the water looked deep, and fast. It seemed like a bit more than just a 'stream,' as Lucy had described it. Would the horses really be able to cross this and not stumble and fall? Lucy turned her horse to face everyone, checking that they were all present and correct. As everyone draw into a circle around her, she spoke again.

'Ok, everyone. This is where we cross the stream. It's easier than it looks. I know one or two of you haven't done this before, but remember that the horses have, lots of times. They know exactly how to do this. They will all follow my lead like they always do. Warwick will be at the back, keeping an eye on you all, so just relax, take it slowly, and let them go at their own pace. We'll be at the other side in no time.'

She turned again and headed forward. In single file, the horses followed her. Meghan stifled a scream as Finnegan stepped into the rushing water. She looked down to find that the horse was already in it up to his knees. He ploughed on solidly though, behind the first four, and Meghan heard her Dad call to her. 'You alright, brat? You're doing great. Looks pretty good from here!'

She grinned, despite her nerves, appreciating Stuart's understanding of how nerve-wracking this part of the trek was proving to be. They were in the middle of the stream when Finnegan simply stopped without warning, and refused to go any further. Meghan leaned forward as far as she dared and said to him in a low voice, 'Come on, Finn. Keep going, that's a good boy.'

The horse wouldn't move. He stayed stock still, ignoring her efforts to move him forward. She shook the reins, and Finnegan continued to ignore her. She was terrified of digging a heel into him, in case he reacted badly and bucked her off or bolted. She pleaded with him to move, but to no avail. The other horses in front were now all out of the stream and moving on. She tried to call out, but a rising sense of panic stopped her voice from coming out. Stuart called out. 'Whoa, up front! Everyone, hold it!'

Lucy turned her horse to look back. She left the other riders and came back to the water's edge. She didn't appear to be worried at all, which Meghan found reassuring, but she was still very concerned about being stuck and wondering how she could resolve it with a horse that persistently continued to ignore her. She could hear the rushing water and felt it's momentum through Finnegan's body as the stream eddied and swirled beneath them. Lucy spoke up gently, but with authority.

'It's all good, Meghan. He's absolutely fine. He's just being Finnegan. Mr Contrary. Remember I told you he can be a bit stubborn? He likes to feel the water around his knees. He's just having a moment. It's nothing for you to be worried about.'

Meghan's breath came out in a hard rush. She was unaware that she'd been holding it. *He's having a 'moment'? Well, that's all fine, but what if he wants to stay here all day? What am I meant to do while he has his bloody moment, just sit here like a fucking freak show?* She fought back the urge to cry.

'Just keep your heels down, Meghan. Keep hold of the reins, but not too tightly, and give him just a very gentle nudge with your heel. Give him a click with your tongue, as well, and that should move him.'

Meghan did as Lucy advised her, and relief flooded through her as the horse did start to move forward again. He plodded onward through the stream and stumbled slightly on coming up the bank but quickly regained his balance after lurching forward to get all four feet on solid ground.

Meghan's heart was pounding. Her hands were shaking and she found herself fighting to control the tears that threatened to fall. Lucy came to her and touched her gently on the shoulder, smiling broadly.

'Well done! That was awesome! Finny very occasionally likes to stop mid-stream, but not often enough for me to actually remember that he does it, to warn his rider. I'm sorry, Meghan. That's my bad. But you did *so* well, you kept your nerve as a brand-new rider, which is amazing.'

Lucy seemed almost excited in her praise. 'You knew you weren't in any danger; you knew you were perfectly safe, and you handled it brilliantly. Finnegan can be a contrary old sod when you'd least expect it, but that's the worst you'll get from him. You've well and truly got him.' She gave Meghan another big smile. 'Ready to carry on?'

Meghan nodded, not quite ready to speak. She *hadn't* known she was safe, not at all! In fact, she'd never felt more vulnerable, but if Lucy thought she 'had' Finnegan, she wanted to continue to show that she did.

Lucy turned again and quickly trotted to the front of the line. As they moved off in the direction of a lush green field, she heard Stuart behind her. 'Very well done, kiddo! That was fantastic. You didn't panic. I'm impressed!'

Meghan rolled her eyes, and although she'd never let him know it, she was grateful again for the encouragement. *I was scared for a minute, but I don't want to be a baby, and it wasn't really that bad, I suppose,* she said to herself as they went forward.

As they arrived at a large field, Lucy leaned down and efficiently opened the gate, allowing all the horses to pass through. When everyone was in, she shut the gate again.

'Ok, everyone. You can dismount for a few minutes here if you want to, and have a bit of a leg stretch, and anyone who has the experience can take their horses for a trot or a gentle canter around the field. It's long and narrow, and well fenced, but please keep your horse under control, and no heroics please.'

She dismounted and came straight to Meghan, taking Finnegan's reins and allowing her to dismount. Meghan doubted if Finnegan would have moved much anyway but he did put his head down abruptly, to start munching grass, so she was grateful for the chance to stand on solid ground again for a few moments.

Lucy cocked her head to one side and looked at her. 'You okay?'

Meghan nodded. 'Sorry,' she mumbled, as she felt her face go hot. 'I panicked a bit, back there. I wasn't sure what to do.'

'Oh, no, you did great! The truth is, Finnegan doesn't trek as often as we'd like. Most of the people who come here these days are locals who are used to the horses, and they tend to find poor old Finny a bit too slow and dull. He doesn't get much chance to come out these days, and even when he does, he rarely pulls a stunt like that. But I still should have anticipated it and warned you. I'm sorry I didn't.'

'It's okay, really it is. Don't you get tourists, though? I thought you'd be really busy with it being school holidays and everything.'

Lucy pulled a face. 'I wish! But Grandad's just not up to dealing with big numbers anymore. He's getting too old to keep running it like it used to be. I'm only able to work here part time and we're not really making enough money to employ guides.' She looked sad.

'Nowadays we mostly just cater to locals and their kids, so weekends tend to be busier. We only take a smattering of weekday bookings now, just to keep the horses exercised as much as anything else.'

Meghan sensed that there was a lot more to the story, but Lucy cut the conversation short by excusing herself and going to talk to a couple of the others. Stuart came up to her on his horse. 'You okay? That was quite a moment back there, for you and Finnegan, wasn't it? For what it's worth I thought you handled it well.'

Meghan nodded. 'He just stopped so abruptly, like with no warning at all! I didn't know horses could even do that. I nearly went straight over his head, and then he just stood there, looking at nothing, like he was all zoned out. I thought he was having the horse equivalent of an epileptic fit or something!'

Stuart laughed so hard he nearly fell off his horse. 'Ah well, all good experience. I'm off for a bit of a ride out.'

With a twinkle in his eye, he turned and to Meghan's astonishment he set off at a full gallop. Within seconds he was a dot at the other end of the field. She was amazed. He then turned his horse and did a very impressive canter along the fence line, all the way back to where they were all standing. Then he took off again.

Meghan thought he looked fantastic in the saddle, moving fluidly, perfectly, in time with his horse. He was clearly an experienced rider. Lucy watched him for a minute or so, then evidently decided he was capable enough to be left to his own devices.

She turned her attention back to the rest of the group. One of the women who'd been on a horse in front of Meghan was also a very capable horsewoman, and quickly followed Stuart's lead. The two of them were having a lot of fun working their horses through trotting, cantering and the occasional field-length gallop. They were laughing together as they finished their workout and came back to the group. Stuart's eyes were shining.

'Did you enjoy that?' Lucy enquired, grinning. 'You both look like you lost sixpence and found a pound.'

Stuart laughed out loud again. Meghan felt a small glow in the pit of her stomach. Her dad had laughed today; *twice*, in the space of ten minutes, and it suddenly occurred to her that it was the first time she'd heard him laugh properly, openly, with real delight, since he came out of prison. He was having fun.

For the first time she felt a glimmer of something growing in her chest. Was it hope? Was it pride? Was it insight? She wasn't sure what it was, or why she was feeling it, but one thing she did know was that she wanted to hear more of Stuart's laughter. Her father was in his element, out here in the fresh air, on horseback. He was having the time of his life. It was amazing to watch him.

When Lucy had everyone mounted up again, she led them all back through the gate again, back onto the track, and then they carried on alongside the stream. Meghan knew they had to cross it again to head back, and she wasn't looking forward to it. She was still a little nervous about the incident last time. But, she reasoned, if Finnegan did the same thing next time, she now knew what to do.

Sure enough, as they crossed the stream again, the horse did exactly the same thing. He stopped dead, right in the middle. This time, although she still felt a lot of trepidation, Meghan allowed him to 'have his moment,' a full ten seconds of relishing the water around his knees, then she gently gave him a heel-nudge, and a tongue-click, and urged him forward.

He obeyed her perfectly, and left the stream without stumbling or slipping. If anyone noticed, nobody said anything, and Meghan felt a little surge of pride at mastering this aspect of Finnegan's behaviour.

When they arrived back at the stables yard, she checked her watch, and was amazed to find that two full hours had passed. As she dismounted, this time without assistance, she felt immensely sad that the adventure was over. She put her arms around Finnegan's wide, warm neck and laid her cheek against his.

'Thank you Finny. Thank you for a lovely ride.'

Finnegan didn't move. He merely sniffed, snorted, and blinked. Meghan felt his eyelashes brush her cheek. *He's just lovely*, she thought as she walked away. The horse were all beautiful, all shapes and sizes, and all glad, it seemed, to have been of service. They 'nickered' gently as their riders said goodbye to them.

Stuart had given his horse back to Lucy and was now deep in conversation again with Warwick Ford. As she got closer to them, she heard her father arranging to come and see Warwick again. She hoped that meant they'd be going for another ride. The two men shook hands, and Stuart then called over his thanks to Lucy, who raised a hand in return. Meghan also shouted her thanks and also that she hoped to be back. Lucy gave her the thumbs up and a smile in return.

As they drew away in the car, Meghan turned to her father. 'Oh, Dad! That was amazing, wasn't it? Can we come again?'

Stuart nodded and gave her a warm smile. 'Yes, I think we really should! What did you enjoy about it the most?'

Meghan thought for a minute, then answered, as honestly as she could. 'Well, actually ... that's a good question. You know, I don't think it was just one thing, Dad. The whole experience was amazing, almost surreal. The riding, the horse himself, Finnegan. Being up there above the world, overcoming my panic in the stream, the trail, the views, Lucy as a guide. All of it. I think it was a little bit of magic, Dad. That's what it all felt like. A little bit of magic.'

She felt her face flaming. Christ, how lame did that sound? 'Magic'? Like she was some five-year-old! But she'd been honest. A little bit of magic – that *was* how it had felt!

She looked at him, waiting for him to laugh at her. Instead, she was surprised to see him deep in thought. 'Penny for them, Dad? How did *you* find it?'

Stuart grinned at her. 'Me? I had a fantastic time. It was a little bit of magic for me too.'

'You're a great rider. You looked awesome today, riding hard out like that.'

Stuart grinned. 'Well, I dunno about a 'great rider.' I know how to ride of course, but it's been thirty years since I was last on a horse, so I'm pretty rusty, but it was really good to get back in the saddle. Literally.' He grinned again, at his own pertinent use of a well-hackneyed phrase. Meghan shook her head emphatically.

'Well, you looked like a great rider to me. If that's rusty, I'd love to see what you'd look like if you were up to full speed. *Can* we ride again, Dad, d'you think?'

Stuart had lapsed into his own thoughts again.

'Dad! Get with it! Can we go again? I've got the money I earned from working in the GladRagz boutique last week, I don't mind paying for us to go again.'

'Yes, brat. We can go again. We're going again tomorrow, in fact. I've arranged it with Warwick, the owner. I'm having a business meeting with him, and while we're doing that Lucy will take you out again.'

'Why are you having a business meeting with him?'

'I'm not sure yet. We just want to talk about a few things. But you'll have Lucy all to yourself, so that will be pretty cool. She can maybe teach you some riding skills, if you like, rather than trekking? Your choice.'

Meghan considered this for a moment. 'Yeah, maybe. Thanks,' she added. She supposed that Stuart would be talking to Warwick Ford about legal stuff. Just because he wasn't a practicing solicitor anymore, that didn't mean he'd lost his knowledge. People needed legal advice for all sorts of reasons. He could still help them somehow, she guessed. Maybe he was doing that in exchange for her next trekking session.

She put it out of her mind and instead concentrated on getting lunch out of the way so she could start her afternoon exercise session with Astro. As they drove back to Teapot Cottage she leaned back, closed her eyes, and drifted off into a happy daydream about riding Astro and discovering new trails together. Darren Davies had made it clear that riding Astro may never be a possibility, and Meghan knew that it certainly wasn't going to happen in the time they had left at Teapot Cottage, but it didn't hurt to dream a little, did it?

Chapter Seven

As he and Meghan steadily worked their way through the modules of their Equine Management course, Stuart was surprised at how much of his knowledge about horses had come back to him. The course was teaching him a lot more, though, and he was surprised at how much he'd enjoyed doing it. While Meghan had been working at GladRagz boutique, down in the town, he had almost completed his course modules. He only had one left to do, which he felt he could comfortably knock out in one morning, then once his modules had all been marked he would have a short exam to do.

He knew the Diploma was a given, as it had been a very easy course compared with the kind of academic study he'd had to do for his law and business degrees. But his prior knowledge of horses had been helpful in some parts of the course, allowing him to expand on his answers, which the tutors had encouraged him to do. Once he'd completed it he'd be able to devote his attention to helping his daughter complete hers.

Meghan was just under halfway through, but her other commitments meant she had less time. She also had no prior equestrian knowledge, but she hadn't let any of that intimidate her. As soon as the new laptop had arrived, she'd lost no time in making a start and working her way through the modules. She would be finished in another couple of weeks or so, now that she wasn't working at the boutique.

That week's work had been of enormous help to her confidence. For the first few days, Trudie had shown her how to unpack, steam-smooth or iron the new stock and price it, but on her last two days Meghan had learned how to work the till and had even sold a few items. She'd come back from her week's work walking on air, with a good amount of money in her pocket, a couple of nice tops (at a good 'staff' discount) and a real sense of achievement. Trudie had told her she would employ her in a heartbeat if the opportunity would ever come up, and she promised to act as a reference for her, if she ever wanted to go into another retail job, full or part time. It seemed that Meghan had really proved herself.

Stuart wondered if his daughter would be resentful of the job coming to an end before it had even really got started, but she'd known from the outset that it was only for a week and there seemed to be no fallout from her only having had that long. He was relieved about that, remembering how volatile she could often be, if things didn't go her way, and if her expectations weren't met. Clearly though, she hadn't any expectations that Trudie might keep her on. If there was a sense of disappointment, Stuart hadn't seen it.

The horse trekking this morning had been a complete revelation. He'd been fortunate that his position in the trekking line had put him next to Warwick Ford, the owner of the business, and their conversations had evolved into a discussion about the state of Beaconsfield's finances, and Warwick's personal circumstances. It had given Stuart a real feeling that there might be some kind of opportunity there.

It seemed that Beaconsfield Stables had been Warwick's late wife Susan's dream, and Warwick had got on board with it a hundred percent. They'd enjoyed many years of success with the stables, until Susan started to become ill with early-onset dementia, and could no longer participate fully in either riding or in running the business. It had fallen to Warwick to continue with things as best he could.

After Susan died, he'd employed a few guides, here and there, but they could only really offer part time positions, and the guides had all moved on to full time jobs or other things. Warwick's granddaughter Lucy was the only family member still interested, but she had other career plans, and as Warwick got progressively older, his energy and enthusiasm had started to wane. He'd wanted to keep the stables going, in Susan's name, but he was seventy-four now, and he was tired. He wanted to retire, and enjoy the years he had left.

Warwick didn't have much of a head for business, but he didn't want to disappoint his late wife by giving up. He soldiered on, but in his dwindling capacity he'd stopped advertising and had more or less shrunk the business to the level where he offered treks and lessons to locals and only the occasional tourist. It was pretty much all he could manage, and cash flow wouldn't allow him to employ anyone to do more of the running. The 'business' was now little more than a labour of love. It had long since stopped making any money, and it was quickly reaching a point where the logical thing would be to close it down. That explained the lack of signage on the roads, and the poorly constructed, outdated website that served to act as a bare-bones information guide to would-be trekkers.

The buildings and business certainly still had a value but, after years of dwindling, Beaconsfield wasn't worth as much as it might have been ten years ago. Warwick had confessed that he felt like he was between a rock and a hard place, because selling the business would also mean selling his home. The local council had confirmed he couldn't subdivide and retain the house as a separate parcel of land, and he didn't think he'd realise enough capital through the sale of the lot to get anywhere decent to live after the fact.

He wanted a house with a little bit of land attached, and that didn't come cheap. There had been talk, apparently, of turning the stables into accommodation and running it as some kind of retreat, but Warwick had no enthusiasm for the idea, and he felt that to do something like that would be sacrilege to Susan's memory, even if the council did approve the proposals. He thought the stables should be sold as what they were.

Stuart felt a real sense of conviction that maybe – just maybe – he could help. He was looking for a new job or career opportunity, but he wasn't sure what he could realistically do, working for anyone else in a role he'd be happy in. He had no clear idea of what he wanted to do going forward, and even if he decided on something, was there any guarantee that anyone would employ him?

Working for himself at something, or buying a business; they were the most logical solutions to his big dilemma. He'd thought about it a lot while he was in prison, and how his and

Meghan's future was going to shape up was pretty much *all* he'd thought about since his release, but when it came to deciding what he was interested in or might be good at, he kept drawing blanks.

Until today.

Until his conversations with Warwick Ford, before, during and after his belting ride around the five-acre field on a horse, with the wind in his hair, and the smell of the animal filling his nose.

Out there in that field, he'd experienced a rare moment of complete and utter bliss. He was also amazed to find that after thirty years out of a saddle, it really had been like riding a bike. The old posture instantly came back, the synchronisation of his body with the horse's movements; it all came flooding back like he'd done it all yesterday instead of three decades ago.

Was it outside the realms of possibility that he could make Warwick Ford an offer for his stables, and resurrect that dwindling business? Could he realistically make a living offering horse treks and riding lessons to tourists as well as locals? Warwick and his wife had done it successfully for decades, so maybe Stuart could too.

Yes, consumerism had changed significantly since the Fords had set up their business, but people still wanted to have a hands-on good time, didn't they? Could something be done to revitalize the stables, the trekking, and somehow add value so that Beaconsfield became a destination that could tick more boxes for people in search of a meaningful and happy experience that could extend beyond simply riding a horse for a couple of hours?

It would all depend on so many things. Firstly, there was Meghan to consider. Would she want to move? Leave her Nan, her friends and her life behind in Taunton? There were bound to be decent schools up here, and some kind of social scene had to exist, didn't it? Stuart couldn't have cared less about staying in Taunton, in fact it would suit him very well if they did find somewhere else, not because he wanted to run away, but surely a fresh start could mean a fresh place?

There was also the matter of how much it might cost to bankroll such a move, even if his daughter did agree to it. Did

Stuart even have that kind of money? He had a very respectable sum from the sale of his house, thanks to Annabel, but he had no idea how much Warwick Ford might have in mind, for his stables, even if he did want to sell. That would have to be the first discussion. Talk to Warwick first, then suss Meghan out if it turned out he could fund such a venture. No point in worrying her or getting her excited before he even knew whether it might be possible.

They were the two biggest stumbling blocks; his daughter and his bank balance. There were other considerations, too. Stuart would need a lot more than a simple online diploma in Equine Management to be a convincing host and operator. He'd have to do a lot more study, get a lot more in the way of qualifications, to be able to confidently run a riding school and trekking stables.

Then there was the issue of rebuilding the business. He had a couple of friends who were great with marketing and PR. One had his own small but successful PR business, and another was a senior manager at a bigger marketing firm. Stuart felt sure they would help him. They'd already said they would get behind him and support whatever career move he made, when the time came.

He also had to take a look around locally, find out what competition he might have and what they were doing, and do one of two things; either do something different, or do the same thing but ten times better.

He decided that he had to find out what Warwick Ford's real position was, both financially and emotionally, with Beaconsfield. Only then would he know whether there was a viable opportunity to take advantage of or not. His meeting with Warwick couldn't come soon enough.

*　*　*　*　*

As soon as Meghan had been set up again on Finnegan and had left the yard, Stuart accepted Warwick's invitation to coffee on the terrace at the back of his small house, which proved to be quite a sun trap. The man had very thoughtfully laid out a nice table, complete with cloth, with a silver coffee pot, sugar bowl and milk jug and two china mugs depicting the wedding of Prince Andrew and Sarah Fergusson. A slightly lopsided chocolate cake sat on a plate in the middle. It was iced in thick chocolate frosting, with fresh strawberries pressed into it. Warwick proudly told Stuart he'd baked it himself.

'I started baking after Susan died,' he announced. 'It gave me something to do, after dark. I found the nights the hardest. There's always plenty to do in the daytime around here, in fact the work never stops. But the nights were hard, at least at first. Sometimes I wouldn't sleep for almost a week. I got through it in the end, of course, the grief. But it made me a fairly decent baker, so do help yourself otherwise I'll end up eating the lot.' He patted his non-existent paunch.

As Stuart sat down, Warwick poured the coffee and handed him a cake slice and a plate, and told him to help himself. As soon as Stuart had cut himself a slice, Warwick did the same and as they settled into their seats, he also handed Stuart an envelope. Stuart raised his eyebrows. Warwick gestured to it.

'Open it and take a look.'

Stuart was stunned to find two sheets of paper, letter-headed, from two different estate agents. They were valuations for the Stables. They were dated yesterday. The figures on both weren't wildly dissimilar, but they were enough to make Stuart catch his breath. The numbers were bigger than he thought they'd be. He looked up at Warwick, who was grinning.

'I thought those might interest you. Not sure what it means for you, but if you did want to talk buying, I might want to talk selling, depending on what we might be able to agree on.'

Warwick went on to say that the conversations he'd had with Stuart on the trek had made him think a lot more seriously about what might be left of his future.

'I know you're not here for long, so as soon as you left yesterday I got straight on the phone and dragged a couple of valuers out here. They came up more or less straight away, and when I told them it was urgent they were both kind enough to come back with the paperwork at close of business.' He chuckled. 'One of the advantages of having lived here for decades, and knowing a few people in the trade. And the speed of the email system helps a lot too, of course.'

Warwick stretched his legs out in front of him. He sighed deeply. 'I know you're only sniffing around, and I might be assuming a bit much, off the back of one conversation, but I'm not getting any younger, Stuart, as I said, and I really do feel now that Susan would forgive me for moving away from all this. It's been ten years since she died, and I love this old place, but it's tiring. My heart's always been here, but I'm an old man now. I can't go on like this. I'm running the business into the ground, and she'd have hated that. I think the place needs new blood. Someone with enough energy to get it going again the way it was, and deserves to be again.'

Stuart leaned forward. 'It's a high value, Warwick. I know it's mostly to do with the price of the land, and I know a developer would pay that and probably more, for access to this place.'

'Yes,' Warwick snapped. 'And they'd probably put a hundred and fifty fucking horrible houses on it.'

Stuart jumped at the other man's vehemence. Clearly he'd touched a nerve by mentioning developers. Warwick shook his head.

'I know. I *could* sell out, very easily. I *could* take the money and run. But that just doesn't feel right. Susan would understand me giving up the business, but she wouldn't understand me selling it to some fat-cat developer for crowded housing. She wouldn't forgive me for being so selfish. I can't do it. I just can't.'

For a horrible moment, Stuart thought Warwick was going to burst into tears. But the man got hold of himself and continued.

'There has to be another way. There *has* to. We built this place from nothing, me and her. It was just a pile of dirt when we got here. I built this house, Stuart, and these stables, with my own two hands. To think of it all being demolished or turned into something unrecognisable, well, I think that would finish me off, and it would have poor Susan spinning in her grave. We built something *special* here. I know I'm probably just a sentimental old fool, but I'd like it to live on, after me.' Warwick was emotional but was managing to keep his stiff upper lip from wobbling too hard.

'We only have a daughter; Stephanie. She lives in Carlisle, and she was never very interested in horses. Lucy, my granddaughter; she likes the stables well enough, but she doesn't want to make a living at it. She has her sights set on moving to Oxford when she's finished her Arts degree. Her fiancé lives there and he doesn't want to move up here. I have a grandson too, Oliver, but he's not interested either. There's nobody to take this place over. It'll never be a family business, not like we wanted.'

Stuart could appreciate how Warwick's emotional ties to the stables had led to him getting into such a mess with them. It wasn't even a viable business, as he could see by the books Warwick produced. The turnover was tiny. It barely covered the horses' food and vet bills. But when Warwick showed him the accounts from the years before Susan had died, they told an entirely different story. Stuart was impressed by them.

'Wow! You really were quite successful at one time, weren't you?'

'At one time, yes. But I've let things slide. Susan was the brains behind all this. I was always the labourer around here. I could always do the manual stuff, like the building, take the treks, even giving some lessons to the uninitiated, to get them started. I know everything there is to know about horses, but Susan was the one who really made this place tick. When she died, the heart just fell out of the place. I've given it all I could, but I'm not her. Without her, it just hasn't been the same.'

Warwick also added that since he had no real head for technology either, he hadn't done anything with the website. He knew it was no longer fit for purpose, but he had no idea how to make things more attractive to tourists even if he wanted to. But he *didn't* want to; not anymore. Ageing and exhausted, he was all but giving up. Stuart felt a rush of compassion for him.

'My first wife died, Warwick, so I know how big a hole that punches in your life. But I was lucky. I was young, I had my daughter to think about, and I bounced back a lot quicker, probably because I had to. Meghan depended on me, and I had a demanding career as a solicitor too, which kept me busy. I don't practice anymore and, to be honest, I'm actually looking for a complete career change. I don't know whether this might be it, or not, but I'm open to talking about it. I do have to say though, right off the bat, that the numbers scare me shitless. I don't know if I can run to the valuation. I have to be honest about that, right here, before we talk about *anything.*'

Warwick shook his head. 'Forget the valuation. I don't want to sell for a song, but I do want this place to continue, so I think there's quite possibly a point at which we may be able to meet, if you are genuinely interested. Why don't I show you around properly? You can take a look at the yard, the buildings, the house and the old barn, see what you think.'

Stuart agreed, and as they wandered around the property Warwick explained that it ran to two and a half acres in total, with 99-year leases in place with the local council for the tracks he used for trekking.

The yard was clean, although a lot of the bushes and small trees that surrounded the large, circular walking pen had withered and died. The wooden railings, particularly those around the ring, were sturdy but in need of a new coat or two of paint, as did the stables themselves, Despite being well built and strong, they looked a little shabby. Stuart shrugged off the overall air of neglect. That could be fixed, of course.

He understood exactly how Warwick had got to this point. It was simply a combination of advancing age and retreating passion. The man simply didn't have the energy or the motivation to keep going, since his wife had died. While he'd shared her passion for it, up to a point, that had died with her. He was now almost crippled under the financial and emotional weight of carrying on when his heart just wasn't in it anymore. He'd also admitted being very concerned about the fate of the horses, if he sold up. They were like old friends to him.

The problems here, as far as Stuart could see – visually at least – were purely cosmetic. When they got to the old stone barn, he could see that despite a small corner of it crumbling, and being devoid of a roof, it too was solidly built, and had potential. The house itself was rather more modest than Stuart would have liked, and by Warwick's own admission, it hadn't been taken care of very well since his wife had died. It was scruffy, and dated, and it had gone past what Stuart called a 'tipping point;' where no matter how much you might scrub away at it until it was squeaky clean, it would never *look* like it was.

But that could be fixed too, and there was plenty of room around the place for extensions. He could immediately see, as one example, how quickly it would benefit from having a conservatory added alongside the kitchen, to provide a dining space that looked out across the yard, and over to the fells. It could be a real sun trap, and it would allow for the far wall of the existing dining room to be taken out to make the living space much bigger. The old log burner could be upgraded to something more modern, as could the outdated kitchen, and Stuart smiled to himself when he saw a small black Rayburn stove collecting dust in a forgotten corner of the kitchen. It was piled high with papers and kitchen utensils. It reminded Stuart of the Aga at Teapot Cottage. Warwick said that it hadn't been used for years. He couldn't remember if it even still worked properly. Stuart thought it was worth getting someone out to assess it, to see if they could get it working. It was gas-fired, so it was probably worth keeping, if so.

There were three bedrooms in total, and the biggest one was huge. It offered enough room to build an en suite with a small shower, toilet and basin.

The big old barn on the property was of great interest to Stuart. Might it be possible to convert it into holiday accommodation? It needed a lot of work, but it could eventually be a real asset to the business. To be able to offer lodge-style accommodation – he could go a long way with that. Maybe he could get schools interested, or other groups. Could he even keep Warwick on in the short-term as a part-time consultant, if the man could find somewhere local to live for a while? And how about offering a little more work to Lucy, whose expertise would be invaluable too, for the time she'd be here, as Stuart got started in rebuilding the business?

He started to feel excited about the prospects of the stables. As the two men wandered back to the patio where they'd had their cake and coffee, he closed his eyes, to try and consolidate his randomly firing thoughts, which were all over the place. Warwick stayed quiet, letting him think. Eventually he managed to get a clear picture on how he might proceed.

'Okay, let me ask you some questions. First, you say you built this place yourself?'

Warwick nodded. 'I used to build houses, when I was younger. I'm a carpenter by trade, although since I built this place I haven't done anything apart from put an extra bedroom extension on my daughter's place in Carlisle, about eight years ago. Old building methods probably, by today's standards, but still just as good. Everything got signed off, and nothing's fallen down.'

'Ok. You seem pretty fit for your age. Could you still do any building, d'you think, like maybe fit out the old barn and turn it into a lodge?' He gestured at the barn that sat within the western fence line of the property, about two hundred yards from the house. Warwick looked at the barn, and sucked in his top lip thoughtfully.

'Yeah, maybe. I might need some help, though! I'm not as strong as I used to be, you know; for hauling timber and the like. But yeah, it could certainly be done – and quite nicely too – if we got planning permission.'

'Would that be a problem?'

Warwick shrugged. 'I dunno. It's not listed, so maybe not. I wouldn't like to say what the council regulations might be on it. I know they can be a bit pedantic. Why? Are you thinking about providing accommodation?'

'Yeah, well, initially just for you, if you'd want it? I know you said you were worried about finding a place where you had some open space. If you sold to me you could rent somewhere cheap locally or maybe even stay with your daughter, until the barn was converted into a dwelling, and then you could move into it.

'It's just a thought, Warwick, but it would give you the opportunity to keep living here. Assuming we did get planning permission for the barn, and assuming you did want to stay on and live in it, we could draw up an appropriate tenancy contract.'

Warwick stared at him. 'You'd be prepared to do that for me? Are you serious?'

Stuart shrugged. 'Of course. Why not? It would all have to be reflected in the sale price of course. But if it meant I could get this place at a comfortable figure, I'd be happy to do it that way. A converted barn would be an asset to the stables eventually, as guest accommodation in the future, but it would be yours to rent until you decided you didn't want it, or couldn't live independently anymore and had to go into a care home or something. Until then, it would be your home.' He grinned at Warwick sheepishly.

'To be honest, I've another motive. I could really use an experienced pair of hands around here, even just on an ad hoc basis, until I got more established. I'd pay you for that, of course.' Stuart ran a hand across his mouth and chin, sighing heavily.

'I'm just kicking random thoughts around here, Warwick, thinking on the fly. I would have to talk very seriously to my daughter about all this, because it would affect her life dramatically, if I went ahead with it. If she wasn't on board, I couldn't take it any further. I'd also have to do some number-crunching to see if I could afford to do any of this at even the cheapest price we could agree on. At the current valuations, I almost certainly couldn't, but if you were negotiable...?'

He let the sentence hang in the air for a moment, allowing Warwick to consider negotiating on the price tag for the stables. He thought that if the man could continue to live on the property, (assuming they would be permitted to convert the barn), maybe that could be a persuasive factor in him lowering the price. Warwick cleared his throat and poured them both another coffee.

'What sort of rent would you be asking of me, if we did the barn conversion and I stayed on?'

Stuart shook his head. 'An attractive rent, Warwick. Below market value. The barn would remain the property of the stables. Is it as structurally sound as it looks?'

Warwick nodded. 'Yes, it's as solid as a rock. It's got foundations you could build a block of flats on. But what if you didn't get planning permission?'

'Well, I don't know why I wouldn't. It's private land, its well within the boundary and it will be an asset to the business, which will benefit the local area. That's something most councils support, don't they? I imagine that would make it fairly straightforward. I'd have to check, of course.'

Warwick tapped his fingers on the table for a minute.

'Well, as you say, you have to talk to your daughter. But if she's keen, and if the number crunching can come somewhere within this amount of the lower valuation on the basis that I can keep living here and have a paid part time job, I'd be willing to talk some more.' He scribbled a figure onto the bottom of the lower valuation and pushed it across to Stuart.

It made him take a hard swallow. The proposed drop was a massive hit for Warwick Ford to take, and his passion for what he'd built with his bare hands to continue was what drove him to it, but it was still tens of thousands shy of what he knew he could comfortably manage. He would have to scrabble around to try and raise the extra.

It was a tall order but maybe, among the more affluent of the people he was lucky enough to still count as friends from his old life, there might be the possibility of a bridging loan, or even an investment, of sorts. But first he had to talk to Meghan. If she didn't want this, it wouldn't happen. After everything she'd already gone through, there was no way Stuart could expect her to accept that kind of upheaval without being part of the decision. She would have to really want to move up here, and embrace a completely different way of life, if it even had a *chance* of working out.

Warwick talked a little more about the general area. There were a couple of good schools and as far as he could remember they were very highly rated. The University of Cumbria offered a lot of good degree courses, and Lancaster University wasn't much more than an hour away, so the educational prospects were certainly good for Meghan.

'You've already good skills to build on yourself, Stuart. Getting to grips with how things are run here wouldn't be difficult for you at all, but if you want to offer structured riding lessons you might want to take some kind of leadership training, and maybe a City and Guilds cert in adult learning, since a lot of the customers you might get could be adults who want to learn to ride.'

Stuart thought about that for a moment. Of course, he understood that adults responded to different teaching methods than children did. He didn't know a thing about teaching, or how to relate to learners but, again, it was something he could rectify fairly easily. Most learning institutions offered those types of courses.

Warwick looked at him keenly. 'If you don't mind my asking, why aren't you interested in practising law anymore?'

Oh, Christ. Here it comes. Stuart grappled with his conscience. Should he spill his guts to Warwick and risk losing this opportunity before he even had it within his grasp? Was Warwick Ford the kind of man who would judge? He didn't know him well enough to know, so he chose his words carefully.

'I love the law. It was all I ever wanted to do, right from being a boy. I was good at it too, contracts, corporate stuff. But I wasn't a very nice person. I made a selfish mistake, a very bad one, that cost someone their life and hurt a lot of other people too, including my daughter.

'I'm not allowed to practise anymore, and even if I was, I couldn't in all conscience carry on being the man I was back then.' He looked levelly at the old man.

'I'm at a crossroads, Warwick, both morally and practically. I need to find a new direction and rebuild my life doing something worthwhile to try and make life better in whatever way I can for Meghan, and for others too.'

Darren Davies' words echoed faintly in his head, about how putting something back into society became an important step towards absolution.

Warwick's breath came out through his teeth in a low whistle. 'But you have to make a living,' he observed.

'Correct. Luckily, I'm still young enough to retrain, go for something different. Until this week I had no idea what it might have been, but something about this opportunity lights me up, for want of a better description. I'm excited about this. I've felt dead inside for so long now, but this has definitely woken something up inside me again. If Meghan was happy about it, I'd love to do it, not just for myself but for her too.'

He went on to describe his daughter's growing attachment to Astro; the horse at Teapot Cottage. 'I dunno how she's going to bear it when we have to leave again. I'm really worried about that. It's like she's turned from a two-headed monster I barely recognised, back into my little girl again, while we've been up here. I don't want her to revert back, after we go home at the end of next month. She's been through a lot, and I certainly don't want her heart broken anymore. I don't know how to avoid that though, with this thing she's got going on with Astro.' He shook his head.

Warwick chortled. 'There's nothing more spectacular or terrifying than a teenage daughter, is there? Susan and I had our hands full with Stephanie through the early teens. She came right of course, as most of them do eventually, but it was a tough time for all of us. I still can't really say how we got through it. Sheer bloody-minded determination and ground-down teeth, I suppose, looking back.'

The sound of Lucy and Meghan coming back into the yard made them both look up. Stuart turned to Warwick. 'Well, I've several steps to take, in a certain order, before I can tell you whether I'm in a position to proceed. Let me talk to Meghan. If she's on board with it, the next step is to try and raise the capital, and if I can do that, then I need to find out if that barn can be converted, and at what cost, and we can take it from there.'

He put out his hand, and Warwick shook it. 'I'll come back to you within a week.'

Warwick nodded. 'Leave the barn enquiry to me. I'll phone the council and find out what's involved there. We'll know soon enough, I expect, if it can be done. There's no rush, but it would be good to know soonish, if we can make something work, because all this talking has galvanised me to take action. I have to get out, whichever way it all shakes down. Now that the seed's been planted, I mean.'

Stuart did know *exactly* what the old man meant. He felt the same way. Once you had a bit of clarity about where you were headed, you really just wanted to get on with it. As they walked over to where Meghan and Lucy were dismounting, he could see that Meghan was glowing with happiness. 'Hey, brat. Good time?'

She nodded excitedly. 'The best! We did a new trail and Lucy taught me all about posture.' She reached up and gently stroked Finnegan's nose. 'I think I've got it, that whole sitting upright thing, with the centre of your back in line with the centre of the back of the saddle, and it was a lot more comfy. We did well together today, didn't we Finny?' She padded the old gelding affectionately. 'No sudden stops!'

Lucy laughed. 'You did *very* well. You're a quick learner and you and Finnegan are nice together.' She smiled at Meghan and then at Stuart as she started taking the tack off her horse. 'Have you had a good meeting?'

Warwick and Stuart both spoke together, 'Yes, very good.' Everyone grinned, and Stuart and Meghan said their goodbyes and started their journey home, Darren and Debby Davies were coming over for dinner tonight, and Stuart was glad. He wanted to talk everything through with Darren, if there turned out to be anything to talk about at all. Now there definitely was, and Stuart was looking forward to that conversation. Darren's opinion would be valuable, one way or the other.

But first he had to have a very tricky conversation with Meghan.

Chapter Eight

'What? Are you kidding me? You can't be serious! Please tell me you're joking.'

Meghan stared at her father. She couldn't believe what she was hearing. He wanted to *what*? Move up here to the back of beyond, and start all over again in a place they didn't know, far away from all the people they did, and run a freaking *trekking stables*?

Stuart was sitting at the kitchen table looking at her, his face a mask of earnest. Meghan didn't know whether to laugh or cry. So that's what his and Warwick Ford's big business meeting had been about, this morning! Surely, he couldn't be serious, could he? But, judging by his face, he did seem to be. There wasn't even the vaguest hint of a practical joke here. She shook her head in disbelief.

'Really? I mean, seriously? It's one thing being here for a holiday Dad, but living up here? Why would we do that? We don't know anyone!'

'Does that really matter? We'll *get* to know people. We already have! Look at the Davies'. They're friends already, aren't they? You've said you love it up here.'

'I do! But we're here on holiday, Dad. It's not real life! It's like you've said yourself enough times, you love going to Tenerife, but would you actually want to *live* there? We've known the Davies' for five minutes. They're nice. But how do we know what sort of friends they'd be, if we were here all the time? They could decide they don't like us anymore, and who else do we know?'

Her father sighed heavily, and ran a hand down his mouth and chin; a habit she noticed he always reverted to whenever he was thinking hard or stressed.

'Look, Meghan, please don't go off on one, okay? Can I ask you to be mature enough to sit and listen, while I say my piece? Then, when you've thought about what I've said, you can say yours. This is just reactive behaviour, and it's not helping. I know it's a big thing to drop on you. I do. That's why I want us to really talk about it *properly*. I need you to be as mature as I know you can be, and really think about this instead of just having a childish tantrum and writing it off immediately as a no-go. I'd like you to really consider the possibilities up here – for both of us – before you make up your mind.'

Meghan felt stung at the implication that she was being immature. *How dare he say that? What the fuck does he know? He has no idea how I feel about anything!*

She bristled, but she but bit back her retort. Stuart was clearly losing his patience and she really didn't want to have a fight with him.

One thing she'd learned through living with Nan, was that when the woman set her mind to something there was no shifting her. You could argue till you were blue in the face and all you ever got for your effort was more angry and frustrated. Most battles with Nan were lost causes, so Meghan had given up on thinking she could make a difference to her. And, since Stuart was his mother's son, it stood to reason that trying to argue with *him* could be equally pointless. Apples didn't tend to fall far from their trees, and she knew how stubborn she could be at times herself, so maybe she *did* need to hear her father out.

They'd been getting on so well together up here. She'd hoped it was the start of something great, a real cementing of their relationship. She knew he wanted the same thing, so why did he have to go and ruin everything with some stupid, senseless, hare-brained idea of *moving* here? She hoped that Stuart also had his mother's ability to talk herself *out* of almost any idea she might have had, however good or bad, after giving it enough proper thought.

Hopefully, he would soon see reason and shelve the idea of moving to the middle of nowhere. Although it was lovely for a decent break from everyday life, and the perfect opportunity for them to start really getting to know one another again, it wasn't the kind of life she wanted, long-term. She wasn't sure *what* she wanted, but she *was* pretty sure it wasn't this! The Lake District was undeniably beautiful, but she was already looking forward to seeing her friends again.

She stared out through the bay window down into the valley, then took a deep breath to steady herself. In doing so, she realised he was right, she *was* being reactive. They *did* need to have a more even-tempered discussion about it all, and at least he hadn't just gone ahead and made the decision then told her she'd have to lump it. She knew a lot of parents would have done that, and then just presented the plan as a done deal. Like Annabel, when she'd said; 'I'm leaving,' and that was that. No discussion. She left. Done deal.

Stuart actually wanted to know what Meghan thought. He was inviting discussion about it, so that was showing respect, wasn't it? She figured that as outrageous as the idea was, of being uprooted yet again and this time dragged kicking and screaming out to the sticks, she maybe ought to try and respect him in return. She *could* at least listen and consider what he was saying. That *would* be the mature thing to do, and she wanted him to think she was mature enough to act like a grown-up, even if she felt more like a panicked little girl.

'Well, alright then. Speak!' She shrugged and sat down at the table. Stuart sucked in his breath and began to talk.

'Okay, here it goes. You might have noticed, or maybe you haven't, that I've been a bit stuck, trying to decide what to do with my life now, since I can't go back to my old career. I've been having a really hard time trying to figure out what to do next. In the run-up to my release, I talked a lot with the prison careers adviser, and we ran through lots of options – most of which I rejected, for various reasons. I either had to take a low-paid job, which would have put a lot of pressure on us, or work away, which I also didn't want to do, for *obvious* reasons. What we need is real stability, Meg. I know that.'

As Stuart started to open up and really talk about his feelings for the first time, Meghan found herself listening more intently. She was stunned to learn how anguished her father had been, and how much he'd struggled since even before he'd left prison, to work out how he could make a decent living for them both.

Lots of questions plagued him. Was he ever going to find someone willing to employ him in a job he might actually like, with his now vastly diminished professional prospects? And if he couldn't, what were the alternatives? Did he have the guts to start or buy a business and run it by himself? What did he really want to do? What would he *have* to do, to provide the kind of stability they both needed, to rebuild their broken lives? He'd been riddled with doubt and anxiety!

As he outlined the real-life challenges he was facing as a time-served criminal, she began to get a true understanding of how important it was that he find an opportunity that would fulfil him and provide them both with a relatively comfortable life. Stuart still had a lot of working life ahead of him. He was only forty-seven. He needed a job, something he could apply himself to, and take real pride in. Taking over the stables and resurrecting the stumbling business would give him the kind of challenge he thrived on. He would hate being in any kind of job that wasn't fulfilling or meaningful; that much she *did* know about him. She felt a surge of sympathy for him.

'Dad, I didn't know you were so worried. I dunno why, but I just somehow thought you had it all worked out, the future and all that. I guess I never really thought about how hard it might be, with your job and everything. I'm sorry. I've just been thinking about myself.'

She felt embarrassed by her own naiveté, taking it for granted that her father knew exactly what to do. She hadn't even *thought* to worry about the future; where they would live, or what their lives would actually look and feel like.

So much for being worldly wise! Where had she got the idea that Stuart already had everything figured out? She suddenly realised that she wasn't the only one who felt vulnerable and lost. Her father felt those things too, and it was up to him to try and rebuild their life. It wasn't up to Meghan. How could it be, as a fourteen-year-old girl, still at school, without the faintest idea yet what she wanted to do with her own life? She was already starting to consider her prospects, but she couldn't imagine how big a pressure it might be, to find something worthwhile to do with her life, if she had dependents to think about too!

Stuart was the responsible adult, but, he was asking her opinion about a really big, life-changing move. He was offering something she hadn't even considered as an option; staying up here in the Lake District and running a stables, of all things!

Nope. Never saw that one coming! But, as Stuart was trying to explain, meeting with Warwick Ford had apparently opened up the kind of opportunity that doesn't happen very often.

Meghan knew she had to try, at least, to appreciate that her dad had the chance to buy an existing business, build it up, and run it as a viable living. She could hear the excitement in his voice as he talked about the changes they could make, the services they could include, the fact that the schools and nearby universities were excellent. If she wanted to, she could work in the business after finishing her schooling, if she then decided that horses would be her thing. Stuart astonished her by telling her he thought she could become an excellent trainer of horses if she set her mind to it. She had no idea what to say to that.

Meghan suddenly had a sense that everything was shifting beneath her again, like it had so often since Stuart had gone to jail. Since the accident itself, in fact, which had changed the dynamics in their lives forever. That was the day when everything she'd previously thought of as safe and reliable had been abruptly taken from her. The future had suddenly looked a lot less secure, and then it just kept getting ever more so, until Nan stepped in and took Meghan in, to live with her. It had given her the stability she needed, but here she was, yet again, with everything potentially upended! She said as much, but Stuart shook his head and sat up in his chair.

'I appreciate it probably feels like that; but don't you see? This is a chance for *real* stability! A place of our own, a business you can be a part of too, if you choose to. It's a brand-new start. It's a far more solid option than me continuing to tear my hair out trying to figure out what I should be doing, and ending up in some dead-end job I'd hate.

'Meg, this is the only thing that's interested me since I first tried, too many months ago to count, to work out what I should be doing next. This opportunity's got me buzzing, in a way I've been genuinely scared I'd never feel again. I actually feel alive! It's like I've suddenly woken up from some kind of stupor. The future feels positive when I consider this, and it's the first time I've felt that way for a *very* long time.'

Stuart closed his eyes and massaged his temples. 'You know, Meghan, up here, riding that horse yesterday, it made me happy, in a way I haven't felt for years, since even before I made partner at my old law firm. Something clicked in my head, while I was riding that horse, and I think maybe, in some weird way, everything's coming together the way it's meant to, for me – for *us*.

'You met Astro, and Darren said you were a natural with her. Then we started doing the course, and I realised it was taking me completely out of my own head, and in a really good way. It gave me some distance for a bit, some time out, from everything that's been going on in my messed-up mind. Then I experienced that pure freedom, riding that horse, and then this opportunity came up, and I dunno, something clicked again. A career with horses. It feels like every step we've taken, since we first arrived here at Teapot Cottage, has started leading me towards that. Much as I hate to use the word, maybe it's some kind of fate.'

It certainly did feel as if something was converging, drawing them into its vortex. Meghan had to acknowledge that fate might indeed be playing some sort of part here. Someone had once said to her; 'there's no such thing as coincidence,' and maybe there really wasn't. Maybe all things really did happen for a reason. Was there a bigger message here than what they'd originally thought?

I'd have to be a fool to write that off without considering it at least. But do I have to be a part of some universe-driven grand plan too?

She sighed, deeply, and looked squarely at Stuart. 'Well, you could go ahead and do it, Dad. Of course you could, and I could carry on living with Nan, and come up for holidays and stuff.'

'Don't you want us to live together? When I came out, you said you did. I'm trying to work out something for both of us,

going forward. I don't want to be apart from you anymore.'
Stuart looked confused.

'Dad, I said I wanted to live with you because I didn't know what else to say! You're fresh out of jail, and I don't want to disappoint you. I *do* want things to work out, but all of a sudden everything feels like it's all up in the air *again*! I just keep thinking, here we go *again*, and it's not that I don't *want* to live with you. I think I do, but the truth is I'm still deciding! All I *do* know is that I don't want to have to give up everything that's important to *me*, just so you can have what *you* want! That's not fair. You left me! You did a stupid thing that was your own fault and I know you've paid a really big price for that, but *so have I!*'

'I know, and I'm trying to make up for that, Meggie! Can't you see? I don't want to let you down anymore. I want to give you the stability you need.'

'But you don't get to just come back into my life and pick up where you left off, Dad! A lot of things have changed! *I've* changed. I'm not a little kid anymore. I've had to figure out a lot of things on my own, with only Nan to help me. You have no idea how hard it's been for me.'

She was struggling to hold onto her temper now. It was so unfair, that everything had to change again! Didn't he get it? He kept saying he wanted stability, but he also kept saying things that just made her feel more *unstable*. She was starting to feel cornered and defensive again. She was aware that her voice was rising, and she made a huge effort to soften it a bit. She didn't want to keep yelling at him. That wasn't going to help *anything*. She took a deep breath and steadied her jangling nerves.

'I like my school, Dad. I like my friends, and I like where we live. I dunno if I want to give all that up! It's taken me *ages* to get into a good place.'

Stuart sighed heavily. 'Sweetheart, I know how many challenges you've faced, especially while I was gone. It took a big toll on you, I do know that. That's why I wonder if this might be a really good answer for us. I know its abrupt, and out of the blue. A week ago, I'd never have known either, that this might happen.'

He looked sadly at her. 'And I'm sorry Meggie, but you carrying on living with Mum isn't an option. Not now that I'm out. She took great care of you, and she loves you to bits, and she'd probably say yes to you if you asked her if you could stay, but it's not fair to her, Meghan.' Stuart passed his hand across his mouth and chin again.

'She's done her bit, don't you think? She's raised her own family; me and your uncle Colin, and then she stepped up again and looked after you brilliantly too. She's done a great job with you. You're amazing. But she needs to have her own life back now. She's not getting any younger. She's in her seventies now, and she should be enjoying her life on her own terms. She's more than earned that. It's only fair now, that we allow her to do it.'

As much as she hated to admit it, Meghan knew that her father was right. It *wasn't* fair to keep expecting Nan to carry on taking care of her. Poor Nan, she *did* deserve her own life, and the freedom to come and go as she pleased, without having to be responsible for a stubborn, stroppy granddaughter! Especially one who had a perfectly capable dad who had the parental right and the desire to take over. Who could say how many years Nan might have left? She'd more than earned the right to make the most of them.

'Well, if this is the kind of opportunity you want, can't you find something closer to where we already live?'

Stuart told her that he'd investigated, and the only other stables business for sale within a hundred miles of where they currently lived was a hundred and fifty thousand pounds more and did not come with a house.

'The reason this is so cheap – and it is still very expensive, let me say – is that it's up here in, as you describe it, the 'back of beyond.' That's why it's more within financial reach. The other one certainly isn't, considering there's no house with it either, and we can't live in a shed.'

'Can you even afford this one, though?' Surprisingly, Meghan's question made Stuart laugh out loud.

'On the face of it, no! But I have one or two ideas, to raise the balance between what Warwick's asking and what I do have. I think I can just about swing it, but I won't go ahead with it if you really don't want to. I would never force you into anything. Please believe that.

'I know how tough things have been for you, and I know that we have a long way to go. I don't want to be the bad guy, Meghan; bossing you around and telling you what's what. But will you at least think about it? Give it a day or two, to weigh everything up, and if you *really* don't want to move up here, I'll walk away from the deal, with no hard feelings. I promise.'

'Have you agreed to anything yet, Dad? With Warwick?'

'No. I told him it would be down to you. But in fairness I'd like to let him know one way or the other by the end of the weekend.'

That's a lot of pressure, she thought to herself. *It's all down to me, and what I decide? In just four fucking days?*

She nodded curtly at her dad, got up and grabbed an apple from the fruit bowl and took it out to Astro, who came to the fence enthusiastically. As Meghan fed the horse, her thoughts were in turmoil.

She'd not seen her dad so animated, so enthusiastic, before. This potential opportunity really did have him fizzing with hope and energy. It was a hard prospect to face, to deny him this, and she felt the heavy weight of responsibility. She felt grateful that her opinion mattered so much. It was good of Stuart to demonstrate how important she clearly was to him, in saying that he'd walk away from the deal if she said she couldn't face the prospect of moving away from everything she knew and was comfortable with. She had no doubt that he meant it. But if it did come to that, what would happen next?

Could she bear to be the one to throw the bucket of iced water all over his dreams? Meghan knew what it was like to have your dreams dashed. How could she live with the guilt of squashing her own dad's desire for a better life for them both, just because she wasn't prepared to make the adjustments?

Stuart definitely had his demons. He had to live every day with the hard knowledge that he had selfishly and cruelly robbed a young woman of her life and destroyed a lot of other lives in the process. Just because it had been an accident, that didn't mean it was an easy thing to square away. If this opportunity could help him to feel better about himself again, who was Meghan to stand in the way of that chance?

But what would the outcome be for *her*, if they moved up here? This was a very long way from everything that was familiar to her. It really was beautiful up here, and as Stuart said, there were good schools, and other things going on that she could get involved in. Lancaster University wasn't far away, and it was well-respected. She could read there and still live at home, once she figured out what she might want to study. But the thought of being so many miles away from Nan and her friends was horrible. Would everybody just forget her if she wasn't around? And what they hadn't touched on, as a very real fear she had, was whether she was even bright enough to go to university at all? Her grades were a mess, and she had no idea how to climb the mountain of clawing them back.

Astro nuzzled Meghan's neck. Meghan pulled head back and looked into the horse's eyes. 'Astro, what should I do?'

A small voice, barely audible, said 'hello' from behind her. Meghan turned around to see Feen Raven standing behind her. She jumped, startled.

'God you scared the crap out of me! I didn't hear you coming up behind me. I must have been miles away!'

'Sorry, Meghan! I didn't mean to give you a fright.' Feen pulled an apologetic face at her. She set down the basket she'd been holding, that appeared to have some ferns, a few wildflowers, and a couple of decidedly strange-looking plant roots in it. 'You really *were* theep in dought.' She stepped forward to touch Astro's nose.

'Hello beautiful girl!' She put her forehead against Astro's and stood quietly for a minute, then she whispered something quite long but completely unintelligible to the horse. She was then quiet again for a moment before stepping back and turning her attention back to Meghan.

'Forgive me for intruding. I was just walking by, and something prompted me to come over. I can see you've formed a beal rond with Astro. She's lovely, isn't she?'

Meghan nodded, remembering that Feen had a tendency to use Spoonerism; switching the first consonants on a pair of words. 'Yes, she is. We've made friends. I love her.'

Feen smiled enigmatically. 'How's the work going with her? Looks like a success. She was such a shy, timid creature when she first arrived, and she wasn't in good shape, but she's glorious now. I'll miss her when she moves on, although I do have the feeling that she won't be foing gar. And neither will you, perhaps.'

She looked closely at Meghan, a smile playing around her lips. Then she narrowed her eyes and frowned slightly. 'You know, whatever decisions you might have to make, this lovely horse wants to remind you not to forget that she's here.'

Meghan stared at her. There was something quite weird about Feen, but she couldn't really describe what it was. It was something that defied description, like the tiny woman was mostly in a world of her own, and only partially present in the real one. It was also as if she could see straight into people, and know what they were thinking.

For all that, as distracted and dreamy as she'd seemed when Meghan had first spoken to her at Adie's coffee morning (and still seemed to be even now), she was giving Meghan her undivided attention, as if she was the only other person in the world. It was the oddest feeling. Meghan suddenly thought that even if she lived to be a hundred and twenty, she wouldn't be able to find the words to describe the aura of this very lovely but utterly strange little woman, who constantly messed up her words, but seemed to be really smart, nonetheless.

Feen stood back, smiling. 'Anyway, I'd better get back to my work. I just went to gather some things I needed from the lower field. I make jewellery with flants and plowers,' she added as Meghan looked at her basket. 'I'm working on pieces for a designer, for an autumn theme, and they need to be ready in two weeks.'

'I met someone else who makes jewellery,' Meghan volunteered. 'Her name's Jayde. She sells her stuff at the Farmer's Market.'

Feen nodded. 'There's a lot of creative people in and around Torley. Lots of cottage industry goes on around here. There are worse places to live and work, that's for sure. Unfortunately, I only get to live for half of the year up here, now. My husband Gavin is a musician,' she explained. 'We live in London over the winter, and it's okay I guess, but I'd much rather be up here all the time.'

'Would you really? Why?' Meghan couldn't help herself. Here was someone who had the choice of where to be and would rather be here than in a vibrant, exciting city, and she was still so young! She simply had to ask.

Feen smiled gently. 'Well, it's home, for me. I grew up here.' She looked around her.

'I love this place. Up here, the sky is so big, and the grills are so heen. I can wake up listening to birds instead of honking horns and sirens. My children can creathe blean air, and my husband actually relaxes from time to time, which he *never* does in London. Our hife down there is lectic. It's okay for a while, but it never takes me long to start craving for the peace of this place. It's always so good to come home.'

She shrugged. 'Anyway, I need to get going, I've doads to loo.' She smiled again at Meghan. 'Enjoy your time at Teapot Cottage. Let it work its own special mand of bragic on you. Oh, and do come up to the house for the next coffee morning, won't you?'

Meghan nodded, smiling. 'I'd love to. Thanks.'

As Feen picked up her basket and walked away, Meghan had the strangest sensation of having been hugged, even though the little woman hadn't actually touched her. She watched Feen's retreating back until she was out of sight, but Feen didn't turn around again, and when she had disappeared around the side of Teapot Cottage, Meghan turned her attention back to Astro.

This lovely horse wants to remind you not to forget that she's here.

'As if I could forget!' she whispered into Astro's mane. All of a sudden, the impact hit her, of leaving again in a few weeks' time, and what it would mean for Astro. She'd feel abandoned all over again, by someone she trusted. Meghan swallowed down the lump in her throat. She pushed away the thought and concentrated instead on leading the horse around the field, gently and quietly around the perimeter and over a few rails in the centre, just by the halter. Astro walked beside her and stepped gently between the laid-out posts, uncomplaining, reflecting Meghan's quietude in her own soft movements. Meghan poured her heart out to the horse, who just listened, then nickered softly at her, as if to say, 'your secrets are safe with me.'

When she went back inside, she found Stuart cooking up a storm. He'd stuffed red and green peppers with rice, cheese and chopped porcini mushrooms and was now piercing holes in a leg of lamb with a metal kebab skewer and inserting small sprigs of fresh rosemary into them. He looked up as she came in.

'Look! Someone around here likes herbs – I found fresh rosemary in the garden, to go with the lamb. There's basil, chives, thyme, lemongrass, parsley and all sorts of other stuff all planted among rocks out there in the back garden. I don't suppose you'd peel the potatoes for us, would you?'

Meghan had forgotten that the Davies' were coming for dinner tonight. As she rummaged through the jumbled top drawer in the kitchen and located the peeler, she braced herself for more manipulation by her father, but was surprised when none came. Maybe he'd already decided it was a hare-brained idea and would say no more about it.

On the one hand, she was quite relieved to think that might be the case, but on the other she felt a slight pang of something – was it disappointment, that his dream might have been so easily shelved? And if so, was it *her* reluctance that had killed it? She didn't know what to think, or what to say, so she decided to talk about something completely different, and describe her meeting outside with the enigmatic Feen Raven. 'What kind of name is 'Feen?' she wondered aloud. She hadn't had chance to ask the little woman directly and in any case, it somehow seemed a bit rude, to just start a conversation about it. *Oh, by the way, why do they call you what they call you?*

Stuart shrugged. 'No idea. It's probably short for something. Josephine, maybe.'

He was happy to talk about other things too, it seemed, and by the time she'd described the funny but beautiful little woman to him and told him a little about the laps around the field with Astro, the meal was prepared and in the oven. He reminded her about her study, so she quietly set herself up in the living room, to work on the next module of her course.

Before she did, she Googled 'Gavin Black, musician.' She'd meant to do it after the coffee morning last week, when she'd heard his name mentioned, but she'd forgotten, with everything else going on. She wasn't holding out much hope of finding anything particularly interesting but, to her surprise, there was quite a lot of information about Gavin Black, also known as Gavin Raven-Black!

He was *incredibly* handsome, in a dark, 'rockish' kind of way, with long black wavy hair, startling green eyes and a dashing smile that showed the most perfect set of teeth Meghan had ever seen. In among the information she found about him was the fact that he had double-barrelled his name on marrying a Seraphine Raven, which explained where the name Feen had come from! The couple had twins – a boy and a girl that would by now be around two years old. Meghan was still amazed to think that such a tiny little woman, who must have been a size six at best, had managed to give birth to twins!

Gavin Raven-Black was a songwriter. He was the son of the late Martin Black, a world-renowned musician who had done session work for more than twenty years with some of the biggest rock bands in existence. That explained Gavin's rocker-like appearance; he was obviously heavily influenced in that direction. He was so good looking, it made her catch her breath.

Meghan didn't know much about rock music at all, but she'd heard of some of the bands Martin Black had played with, and knew a few that Gavin wrote music for. A couple of society magazines had posted pictures online of Gavin and his very glamorous-looking wife at London events, and she was amazed to know that Seraphine Raven-Black was indeed the woman she'd met at Adie's coffee morning, and again just now outside the door of Teapot Cottage. Feen was undeniably beautiful, but with her hair and make-up done, and wearing stunning frocks, she 'scrubbed up' to be absolutely stunning. They were a fantastic-looking couple.

Meghan was conscious that she only had a couple of hours before the Davies' were meant to arrive, and she really wanted to tell them that she'd started to make good headway on her course. If she could make a good start on this current module, before they showed up, she could report more up-to-date progress.

Darren was bound to ask, and she didn't want him to worry that he'd wasted his money on the laptop; that she wasn't serious about the course. She definitely was, and she'd learned a lot already, but this latest curveball that her Dad had thrown at her made keeping her mind on her studies a bit of a challenge. She also realised she was thinking too much about Feen and Gavin Raven-Black's glamorous lives in London. How amazing it must be, appearing in society magazines and having paparazzi chasing you for photos!

She dragged her attention back to her course module and soon she found herself immersed, only looking up again when she heard a car door outside. Coming back to the present, she was conscious of the delicious smell of roasting lamb, and her mouth watered. She looked at her watch and saw that it was seven o'clock already. Where had the last two hours gone?

Stuart was at the front door before the Davies' even had chance to ring the bell, and he welcomed them in enthusiastically. Darren came in first carrying Ruby in a car seat. The baby was sound asleep. Badger bounded in next, and came straight over to Meghan for a cuddle, and Debby came in last, holding a cake plate with another spectacular pavlova sitting in the middle of it, this time with slices of kiwi fruit and shavings of dark chocolate sitting on top of the cream. Everyone seemed jovial and very glad to be together. Meghan felt a quick stab of guilt that she hadn't made a pavlova as promised.

'Hi, Meghan!' After setting the gorgeous dessert down on the kitchen table, Debby greeted her with a warm hug. 'We've so been looking forward to tonight! How's everything going?'

Meghan grinned. 'Great, thanks. I'm doing well with Astro, and I'm onto my third module of the course already. I'm really enjoying it.'

She wasn't kidding. The course was thoroughly absorbing and interesting, and the questions weren't all that difficult. Meghan felt sure that she would finish the course and pass it well enough. 'Dad's already finished his. He whizzed through it while I was working down at GladRagz last week, but he can help me if I get stuck, not that I have yet. I'm managing it okay on my own so far.'

That's great news,' Debby beamed. Darren was settling Ruby at one end of the sofa. 'Look at her! She nods off in the Landy, as soon as we start it up. She'll hopefully sleep for a bit, at least until we're halfway through supper, which is usually the case. I always get to finish a cold meal, thanks to this little madam's internal feeding clock. I think she has radar, for when I want to relax and enjoy my own food.'

Stuart had laid the table while Meghan had been studying. She felt a little guilty that he'd done almost everything by himself, but she shook it off. He wanted her to study, and he was happy cooking, it seemed. Most cooks liked to be left alone to get on with it, Meghan knew that much. She'd probably done him a favour by staying out of the way.

Stuart poured everyone a drink while she saved her work, closed her laptop and put it away. They sat in the living room with their drinks and a bowl of crisps, as Stuart put the finishing touches to dinner. He'd made a butternut and sweet corn soup, which Meghan loved. Her stomach started growling. She was starving.

As they sat down to the meal, Stuart told Darren that he wanted to pick his brains, and he started telling him about the opportunity of buying Beaconsfield Stables. By the time he'd finished describing it, Darren's eyebrows were somewhere up near his hairline. The expression on his face was comical to Meghan. The he grinned widely.

'You know what? I think that's an offer worth considering. It would answer a few questions, wouldn't it? Like, what are you going to do with the rest of your life, as one example?'

Stuart nodded. 'Yeah, it's really grabbed my attention. Something in my gut is telling me to go for it....' he trailed off, clearly wanting to say more, but feeling unsure of exactly what.

'But ... what? What's holding you back?' Darren asked the question matter-of-factly, without inflection. He clearly wasn't judging or trying to influence Stuart at all.

'Well, there's a few things. It's a huge step geographically. It has big implications for both of us.' Stuart nodded across the table at Meghan. 'I'm also conscious that I don't know nearly enough about horses, to have much in the way of credibility with punters. I don't even know yet what I *need* to know, if that makes sense?'

Darren nodded. 'Yeah, I get that. Well, let's look at the bones of it all. Putting to one side the upheaval, and the ramifications of that, let's focus on the reality of what you'd be getting into, if you did buy the place as a going concern, to build back into a strong business.' He settled himself into his chair.

'Firstly, you'd want to make sure your horses are all in good shape. You'll never make it work if they're not in the best condition for what you'd be asking of them.' Darren chewed his bottom lip for a few seconds, thinking.

'I've not been up to Beaconsfield myself but I do know where it is, and I'm sure I know the vet who regularly goes. I have a feeling it's Ant Bretherton, who works for one of the practices in Carlisle. I can certainly give him a ring and ask his opinion of how the welfare's taken care of up there.'

Debby leaned forward. 'Meghan, what do you think of all this, as an idea? Is it something you'd like to do, as well?'

Meghan blushed, unsure of what to say. She didn't want to pour cold water over her dad's dream, but she couldn't say yes at this point. 'I'm still deciding,' she confessed, quietly. 'It's a really big thing.'

Debby nodded. 'Yes, it is. It's a huge, life-changing decision. I guess it comes down to whether or not you guys actually *want* your lives to change. We moved up here because it was what we both wanted. We were fed up with Exeter. Ruby came along unexpectedly, after we'd more or less accepted that we wouldn't be having any babies, and that was the deciding factor for us. We realised we wanted to bring a kid up in a less stressful environment. We wanted a fresh start, so the decision was easy for us, but it wouldn't be for everyone, I know.'

Darren also chimed in. 'It would have to be what you both want. Something like this, it's too big a deal to not be on the same page about.'

'It could be an expensive mistake,' Stuart observed quietly. Darren agreed.

'Yeah, it could. Or it could be the best move you ever made.'

Meghan turned to Debby. 'Was there anything hard for you about leaving Exeter?'

Debby thought for a minute. 'Yeah. It was what we wanted, but it was still hard leaving my friends; not that I had dozens or anything. Just a few, but they are important to me and I was worried about losing touch. In all honesty though, I don't miss them all as much as I expected to, because social media makes it so easy to stay in regular touch. We face-time, or phone, or text, all the time. Technology makes it so much easier to speak face to face in real-time.

'Our friends and family come up here a lot too, and we go down there as often as we can. We don't see everyone individually as much as we used to, but we do see different ones all the time so it's still regular contact.'

Darren piped up, then. 'To be honest, a baby cuts your social life to virtually zero anyway, so I honestly don't think we'd be any less home-focussed down there, unless of course you count the grandparents ability to pop over and babysit. That would be handy!'

'Yeah. Babysitters are pretty thin on the ground around here! But we've made some nice friends, so far,' Debby confirmed. 'That's important as well, to make the effort to be connected to the local community. Darren does that by default, as one of the local vets, but if it hadn't been a natural transition we'd definitely have made more of an effort. I'm quite a private person, but the people are good here, so making an effort wasn't as hard for me as it might've been if everyone hadn't been so welcoming.'

'D'you ever regret moving?' Stuart was watching them both closely.

Both said, in unison; 'Not at all.'

Darren went on to say that a couple of his friends from Exeter had moved away themselves. 'A lot of friendship networks get fragmented, at least in part. It might be because someone moves away physically, for a job or something, or maybe they take up with a partner people don't particularly like, or who lives elsewhere, or whatever. Some couples have kids, others don't, and that changes people's priorities, and friendship dynamics are affected, like when you can't spontaneously to do stuff together anymore like you used to, and all that.' He shrugged before continuing.

'There's always change and flux in friendships. And I do miss my mum, but she's got a good partner and she's happy in her own life. I don't have to worry about her. If I did, it might be different, I suppose.'

Meghan thought about Hayden, and his new girlfriend. Hayden was one of her closest friends, and the fact that he was a year older had never seemed to matter before, but that was already changing. She knew the dynamics of that friendship were shifting in a really significant way, with his attention switching to romantic encounters with girls. The writing was already on the wall. As soon as Hayden hooked up with a girl who had come to mean more to him than a one-night stand, Meghan and his other friends would very quickly be a lot less important. She could feel it already happening, even just through his texts. The tone of them was changing. What would it be like, going back to school, to find that Hayden wasn't going to be as big a part of her life as he'd always been, because his priorities had shifted?

And what about Elise, whooping it up in New Zealand with her brother and the posh ski-set? She would no doubt come home a lot more worldly-wise than she was when she went. If she had learned sophistication on the ski slopes, if she'd lost her virginity or fallen for a boy she would go on to moon over for months, would their friendship be the same? Elise hadn't even responded to Meghan's attempts at keeping in touch over the past couple of weeks. *Probably having way too much fun.* How good a friend was she in the first place, if she wasn't interested enough to find five minutes to say hello back, in response to any of Meghan's messages?

Amy was definitely the closer friend of the three. They were all great people, but Amy was the friend who was always *there*, though thick and thin, no matter what. She was staunch. But was one friend – just one person – enough to keep you anchored to a place, especially when everyone was so young, with endless possibilities coming up in their lives? Different universities or job options, meeting new boyfriends and finding new interests with them; all these and so many more opportunities would present themselves and Meghan already knew enough about change to realise that nothing was guaranteed to stay the same. Any one of her little group could simply get up and go wherever life took them, at the drop of a hat, maybe not straight away but eventually for sure. Would she be left behind? Maybe not. Maybe she'd be the first one to go. It occurred to her that she might turn out to be the trendsetter, the first one to be brave.

For the first time, she started wondering how much the events of this summer might change the friendships that meant so much to her. All four of them were doing very different things this year. Amy of course was merely camping with her family, which she did every summer, and she always came back the same; happy, bomb-proof, reliable and just, well, *Amy*. But Elise and Hayden were both having very different experiences this summer – as was Meghan herself. Would they be the same people they were, separately or together, by the time school went back? The more she thought about it, the more naive it felt, to expect that they'd all just pick up where they'd left off at the end of the last school year, that everything would still be like it was.

Debby cut into her thoughts. 'What might make it hard for you to leave Taunton? Is it your Nan? Your friends? Your school? I guess it must be a bigger decision for you than it is for your Dad, if you feel you have more to leave behind.'

Meghan was grateful for her insight. Yes, it was a relatively simple decision for her father, less so for herself. She spoke up.

'Leaving my nan. That's the biggest thing. I don't know if I could leave Nan.' Her voice wobbled a little, much to her embarrassment, but Darren looked at her sympathetically.

'Yeah, it's a lot to process, isn't it? A really big decision shoved at you that you hadn't seen coming, to leave everything you know, and people you love.'

Meghan nodded. As tears threatened, she suddenly felt unable to speak. Debby reached over and put a hand over hers. 'I know what it's like to feel overwhelmed. It's really important that you take the time you really need, to look at all the options, and decide what's really right for you, Meghan. Not just in the short term, but in the long term too.'

Stuart nodded. 'I don't want to put you under any pressure, sweetheart. As I've said before, whatever you decide, we'll go with. Pure and simple.'

He looked at her kindly. Debby squeezed her hand and let it go. Meghan suddenly felt that she needed to put some distance between herself and the adults. She excused herself politely and went outside and over to the fence line. Astro was already standing there, as if she'd been waiting, and Meghan hugged her quietly. Maybe this quiet, knowing horse would show her the answers she needed to find.

Chapter Nine

Darren scraped the last pieces of his dinner off his plate and sat back. He burped loudly and grinned. 'Oops! Sorry about that!'

Stuart grinned back, pleased. 'No you're not, but I'll take it as a compliment, I think!'

'You should! It was the best roast lamb I've ever tasted.' Darren ducked and grinned again as Debby took a good-natured swipe at him. 'Not that yours isn't lovely, Debs. But there was something a bit special about this one.' He started to tackle his piece of pavlova with real relish too.

Debby looked up as Meghan came back into the cottage, and smiled gently at her as she dished up another portion of pavlova. She set it down in front of Meghan, then turned her attention back to Stuart.

'So, big decisions! What do the books look like, if you don't mind me asking?'

Stuart cleared his throat. He was humbled that his new friends were taking such an interest.

'They look ok. It's not a catastrophe. As I said, the business has dwindled to not much more than a trickle, but that's been kind of deliberate.'

He went on to explain that Warwick Ford just didn't have the heart or the physical energy to put into keeping it at the level it was before his wife died. 'What he makes now just maintains the horses, more or less. But from what I can see there's no debt, the history is good, the property itself is freehold, and the business is registered, with everything you'd expect up to date. I can certainly have my own accountant look things over, to see if it all really is as sound as it looks.'

'The next step would be to get a property survey,' Darren observed. 'Our estate agent, Lance Martin, organised a local guy to come and survey Appletree Cottage before we bought it last year. We weren't going for a mortgage, but we wanted to know the place was sound before we threw all our money at it. We thought it might've been touch and go. It was a bit of a wreck, but he gave us a really honest appraisal. I can give you his number if you want?'

Stuart leaned forward. 'That would be great, yeah, thanks. If the business and house are sound and solid, that's a good starting platform. What really worries me is the fact that I just don't know what I feel I really need to, about horses. I've got the knowledge and the desire to build and run the business, but my equine prowess isn't where it should be. This little course I've just done has helped a bit, but I wouldn't say it's a good enough foundation to enable me to claim any real expertise.'

Darren shrugged. 'You could get more qualifications. You smashed the online diploma course in a week with a hundred percent on the exam. You could do more. I know there are a lot of courses out there. I did some in-depth equine stuff as part of my veterinary training, and I can help you with a few things.

'A lot of what Warwick Ford learned was probably just acquired through hands-on experience anyway, Stu. We could get you up to speed with the basics fairly quickly, such as horse husbandry and welfare, and you could do some distance learning stuff, maybe some meatier qualifications geared towards running an equine-centred business. It's not like you're a stranger to study, or academic work, is it?'

Stuart agreed. 'I managed to get some pretty good results at law school, and with the business degree. But it was all a long time ago. I hope I still have the head for it.' He looked up and smiled at his daughter, who had quietly eaten her dessert without saying a word. He then turned his attention back to Darren, who was sharing more of his own wisdom.

'It's a bit like riding a bike, mate. I went back to study in my late twenties, after someone took me on and trained me as a favour to someone else, and most of what I learned to start off with was hands-on, day to day. The academic stuff was daunting, but I really *did* have to do it if I wanted this career, so I knuckled down and got on with it.

'I hated school, you know? I was bright enough, but I never wanted to be there. For me, retraining was a choice, so it was easier. And, if a back-street no-hoper like me can get off his arse and do it in later life, anyone can. You're streets ahead of me, with the academic discipline, Stu.'

Debby nodded. 'Stuart, you could do any kind of equine-based degree standing on your head. You're already educated, and you really want this project. Darren's right, you'd hit the ground running on this. I imagine that compared to law school, something like this would be a doddle.'

It's probably a lot more science-based,' Stuart ventured. 'That's new for me.'

Darren shook his head. 'It's all facts though, and with the law you deal in facts, right? Something either is, or it isn't. Biology and chemistry are pretty much the same. Something is what it is, or it isn't; pure and simple. And you're not training to become a vet, are you? It's not like you'll need *masses* of science. Basic equine biology, really. Straightforward stuff.'

Stuart thought that was a very simplistic way of looking at things, but then he wondered if the other man was right to view it in such simple terms. Maybe Stuart himself was over-thinking everything, imagining hurdles to be bigger than what they really were. Fear, maybe?

He wondered if it might just be a case of looking at what courses were available and seeing if he thought he could manage what was expected. And after all, as Darren had pointed out, he wasn't going to train to be a vet. That was more medical, whereas what Stuart needed was more practical. Yes, he'd need to learn some equine medical knowledge and terms, but it wasn't the same thing as going for a medical degree. He didn't need to feel intimidated by the science, did he?

He looked at Darren directly. 'Would you be prepared to act as the official veterinary consultant for the business?'

Darren nodded shortly. 'Of course I would, mate. Goes without saying. And if you wanted to, I could spend some extra time teaching you a bit about horse health and medicine. Not that I think you'd need much of that knowledge for direct relevance, just enough to know what to watch out for and keep on top of, health wise, within the herd, but it would also help your confidence to have a good handle on that side of things.' He looked at Stuart thoughtfully. 'And you'd need to start as you meant to carry on.'

'Assuming the horses that are already there will come with the business and are in good condition, it would be wise to keep them, because they're experienced and they'll be of real help in setting an example for new ones. Building the business back up means you'll need to buy more horses in, too, but you don't want to acquire any in poor condition, or not fit for the job. You'll need robust animals, and you'll to get them checked out.' Darren chewed his lower lip for a moment, thinking.

'A professional opinion would be crucial. I could take a preliminary look myself, if you want, to assess what shape the existing ones are in, and I could advise you when getting new ones. The practice has a full range of portable x-ray, ultrasound, endoscopy and other diagnostic equipment, so I can look at the horses in their own environment and investigate anything that didn't look or feel right.' Darren went on to explain that after that initial check, if Stuart decided he did want to go ahead, he'd need a deeper vetting of the existing ones, and if he got new ones his vetting check would need to be very thorough.

'Vetting doesn't pass or fail a horse for purchase,' he expanded. 'It's effectively an in-depth assessment of its current and likely future robustness by identifying any pre-existing conditions, current health status and fitness for use. Any risks found or even hinted at would be discussed with you.

'You'll need a solid bio-security plan too, because where you're introducing new horses into a place where you've got existing ones, you have to protect them against the spread of any disease that any of the new ones might bring in. They'll be vulnerable to that.' Darren grinned at him.

Stuart pulled a face at him. 'I'd love you to help me with that, because I really don't want to end up with the yard locked down because of illness.' He didn't need Darren to tell him that if such a thing were to happen, he wouldn't be able to trade, or take any of the horses off the yard again. 'What kind of diseases can be transmitted?'

Darren rolled his eyes. 'You'd be surprised. There's a heap of stuff, and it's all transmitted differently. There's a thing called strangles, also known as equine distemper. That's a nasty respiratory airborne infection transmitted through bodily fluids like mucus. Similar contagious problems include horse flu and herpes. Then you've got ringworm, that's spread through infected hair or skin flakes.' He shrugged his shoulders, noncommittally.

'There are other less common ones, but you do have to be prepared for a potential raft of stuff coming in, and identify it before it goes through your entire string. You really can't be too careful. But that's not a big thing to sort out, to be honest. Get the horses you want to keep checked over, sell the ones you don't, get any new ones checked before you bring them in, and make sure you get them regularly monitored for health and hygiene.'

Stuart nodded slowly. 'There's eight horses there at present, but they had about twenty, at one time. The place is set up for at least twenty. I think they overbuilt it a bit, maybe they had bigger ideas at the start. I'd like to build it back up to twenty, eventually. It would take some time, though, because even if I can stretch to the asking price, there'll be little if any funds left for a good while to buy any more livestock. I'll need a clever marketing plan that will bring in custom at a rate I can manage, and enable everything to grow, but at a pace I can control.'

Stuart explained about revamping the old barn into a dwelling, to be able to offer accommodation, but admitted that it would also be a stretch. Buying the property, even if he could knock Warwick Ford down by the necessary tens of thousands of pounds, would leave nothing for such work.

Darren looked at him thoughtfully, chewing his bottom lip. He said nothing for a while, but Debby jumped in.

'Actually, if you could run to the cost of the materials, you might be able to get the labour for next to nothing under the WOOF scheme. Have you heard of that?'

Stuart frowned as he racked his brains. 'I think I have, actually. Isn't that some kind of work-for-food scheme, where people work on farms to support themselves as travellers?'

Debby nodded. 'Yes, in a nutshell. It's a world-wide organisation where someone who needs to have work done on a farm can offer temporary lodging and food to a worker with the expertise they need, and allow that person to learn about what they do on the farm. It's not just about crops and bee-keeping.'

She looked at Stuart, a smile playing around her lips. 'An equestrian establishment would probably qualify as a host, if you wanted, say, a carpenter for four hours' daily work, in exchange for room and board and a handful of free riding treks. It might be worth a shot, if you *could* put them up and feed them?'

Stuart beamed at her. 'That definitely sounds worth investigating. I can look into it, certainly. That would be doable, I think, and potentially very worthwhile.'

'You might get someone who would stay for a month, and five days' carpentry a week for a month could translate to a lot of progress on a barn conversion, by someone who knew what they were doing.'

Stuart felt like hugging Debby. Darren had remained quiet for a minute or two, deep in thought. He spoke up again now. 'How short are you, on what Ford wants, money-wise?'

'Thirty grand.'

Darren whistled. 'Do you have the rest sitting ready?'

Stuart nodded. 'Mostly, yeah. My half of the sale of the marital home's been sweating away in an investment account for the last five years. The interest has been minimal but it's better than a kick up the arse, and I can get access to my agreed quarter of Mum's house through the equity release scheme. She and I already talked about that before we left to come up here, when we were discussing how best to make Meghan's future secure.

'With that, it still leaves me thirty grand short, though. I might be able to get some kind of business development loan, if the criminal record doesn't put the brakes on it.'

'It might, especially if you're buying a business that can't demonstrate a profit. I think you'd be dead in the water.' Darren's reply was bald and flat, but at least it was honest. Stuart appreciated that. As a realist, Darren Davies was worth his weight in gold. If anyone could keep Stuart's feet on the ground it was his new friend.

He grinned ruefully. 'Thirty thousand isn't much, in the overall scheme of things, but it may as well be thirty million, if you don't have it. I have friends who might lend, but it's a question of how quickly I could pay them back. I couldn't make any promises and the last thing I'd ever want would be to let them down.'

Darren was thoughtful again. Then he spoke slowly. 'What if you could offer Ford fifteen thousand less, instead of thirty. If you told him it was a cash purchase, d'you think he'd take it?'

Stuart thought about it for a moment. 'He might. But that still leaves me with fifteen to find. It's a lot less, certainly, but I'd still have to look for investment or a loan.'

'Ok. But what if someone could put in fifteen as an investment, in exchange for being able to run a service of their own from the premises? Would that be something you might be prepared to consider?'

'Like what, exactly?'

Darren looked into the middle distance, clearly still thinking as he was talking. 'What if someone wanted to use a bit of the space for a horse-related business that was independent of your operation. Like maybe a horse hospital?'

'A horse hospital? What, you mean like a rehabilitation centre?'

Darren nodded slowly, frowning slightly. He was thinking on the fly, that much was obvious. 'Yeah, sort of. I'm just thinking, and it *is* only a thought for now, but if I was to put in a slice, and let that act as a lease for enough space to have a couple of horses that need rehab, would that work for you, d'you think?'

Meghan piped up. 'What, you mean horses like Astro?'

Darren nodded. 'Yeah, like Astro. She was in bad shape, and I didn't have anywhere to put her. She had to go into a field, and I was just lucky the winter was a mild one. I have a local farmer who does let me have a bit of space in one of his barns when I need it, but it's not always available, depending on what time of year it is, and what else he needs it for. I hate asking him, especially when he has to say no, because we both feel bad about it. It's not an ideal set-up by any means, but it's all I've got, for now.'

'D'you get a lot of injured horses, then?' Meghan seemed curious.

'It varies. It can be a bit like buses, with them. You won't get any for months, then you'll get two in a week. Most owned horses can stay with their owners while they heal from whatever's wrong with them, but the critical ones that need a lot more monitoring, or the abandoned ones like Astro, they tend to be a bit more tricky to look after. I've had three in the last eight months.

'I *could* take more off the local RSPCA, if I had capacity. They do phone me sometimes to ask if I can take any, but most of the time I have to say no. I don't have the resources or the space to treat many, as it stands, so I can't take them on. It really pisses me off that I can't do more.'

Darren went on to say that he had a bit of money put by for a rainy day, and wondered if his fifteen thousand could perhaps lease him enough space to regularly care for a couple of rehabilitees, since wanting to do more would mean renting space somewhere anyway, and he might as well help a friend in need if he could do it at no extra cost.

Stuart was nonplussed. This was a completely unexpected offer, and all the more wonderful and extraordinary for being so. He wasn't sure what to say. The lump in his throat wouldn't quite go away right now. His daughter stepped in, unwittingly taking the spotlight off his need to reply, for the moment at least.

'What do you do with the abandoned ones when you've healed them?' Meghan was clearly very interested in this aspect of Darren's work. Presumably, it wasn't the kind of stuff that anyone paid him to do. Stuart wondered what made Darren so keen to do such altruistic work, but his answer came before he even had chance to ask.

'I pass them on to people in the equestrian world. Breeders, stable owners, families and the like, depending on the horse, and it's needs lining up with theirs. Some people are happy to just have a horse to look after and keep safe and loved for its life, if they have the room, and a surprising number do. It helps recoup some of the cost of treating them, but that's not the biggie for me, Meghan, if I'm honest. Being able to help them is enough for me, really. I do it for love.'

He laughed and shook his head self-deprecatingly. 'Sounds corny, right? But I've turned into a bit of a crusader for abused animals, I'm afraid. I've got a bit of a soap box for that sort of thing. Even a horse in good condition is still an abused horse if it's been abandoned, as far as I'm concerned.'

Debby chimed in, laughing. 'I have to put my foot down a lot, to avoid us being overrun by the world's unwanted critters. Otherwise we'd need a hundred acres and a *very* big lottery win.'

Stuart was now doubly impressed with Darren Davies. The man was no saint, that much was clear, and his past was still slightly murky, but he had a heart as big as the world, and he wasn't afraid to show it. He cared. He truly did. Stuart had the feeling that if he had to put his life in Darren Davies' hands, it'd be safer with him than with any other friend he might choose.

Meghan looked at him unhappily. 'By the way you're all talking, it sounds like this is already a done deal; that you're doing it, whether it's what I want or not.' She looked as if she were about to cry. Stuart was horrified.

'No, sweetheart! Not at all! I made a promise to you and I intend to keep it. If you really don't want this, we won't do it. All we're doing is talking over the options of how we *might* do it if we decide to, that's all.'

'But Darren's already talking about a horse hospital, a rehab option, Dad. It all sounds like a done deal to me.' She sounded upset, and she looked it. He shook his head emphatically.

'Absolutely not. I mean it, Meggie. We're just talking. If this opportunity is not what you want, we'll put the brakes on it. End of. I *promise*.' He looked at her speculatively.

'Talking of which, have you made any kind of decision about it, yet?' He waited with bated breath for her answer. In just one word she could dash his dreams.

Debby intervened swiftly, effectively halting Meghan's answer at the pass.

'I hope you don't mind my saying so, Stuart, but isn't that rather a lot of pressure to put on Meghan? On the one hand she doesn't want to disappoint you, especially over something that you're this excited about, but on the other she has her own life to think about, and what the changes or sacrifices might be for her if she did agree to it. I'm sorry, but I really think you're asking rather a lot of a fourteen-year-old girl.'

There was an uncomfortable silence at the table. Nobody really knew what to say. Stuart felt a sharp spike of defensiveness, and had to wrestle with himself not to snap at Debby. She meant well, of course, and he realised that she did have a very valid point. In trying to be fair to his daughter, and consult her instead of simply making life-changing decisions that would have a big impact on her, *was* he actually placing too much responsibility on her young shoulders, to make the final decision?

He looked at Meghan steadily. 'God, I'm sorry sweetheart, if I've put too much on you with all this! Debby's right. This is a really big thing. I was trying to be fair, but maybe I've gone about it the wrong way. I dunno what the right way is, though. It doesn't seem right to just do this without consulting you, because the impact on you will be profound. I know that. But asking you to decide for us probably *is* asking too much. I'm just not sure how else to make this decision fairly for us both. It's a really big one.'

He shrugged and looked over at Darren. *Help me out here,* he silently pleaded.

Darren looked shrewdly at Meghan. 'Meghan, what is it you want in your life. What do you need?'

Again there was silence. Meghan seemed unsure of how to answer. Stuart encouraged her gently. 'It's okay sweetheart, just go ahead and answer the question as honestly as you can. It's really important that you do.'

Meghan took a deep breath. When she spoke, her voice was quiet and pensive. 'Nobody's ever asked me that; what do I need? Everyone's always assumed they knew. They all just made decisions they *thought* were right for me, or maybe just more right for *them,* like Annabel. I've just had to go along with stuff, because it didn't seem to matter to anybody *what* I thought, and I wasn't important enough to change anything.'

Stuart felt appalled. 'That's why I wanted to consult you over this business about buying the stables, Meggie. I wanted it to be about what both of us want, because you *are* important in this decision.'

'No, Dad. You just want me to tell you it's okay for you to have what *you* want.'

'Is that how you see this? Me trying to railroad you?'

She shook her head at him. 'No; I know you're not trying to railroad me. But unless I decide for myself, that everything I want and need is here, I can't say yes without making the sort of compromises that don't feel fair. And if I want to say no, I'll be letting you down, like stabbing your balloon or something.'

'So, to answer Darren's question then, what is it you want and need?'

Meghan looked around the table at all of them, and Debby smiled encouragingly at her.

'I need friends. I need good education options, so I can fix my messed-up school marks, and take my time to decide what I really want to do with my life. I need support to help me do that. I need my nan. And what I need most is to feel settled, like I *belong* somewhere, instead of everything being up in the air all the time.'

She shifted uncomfortably in her seat, as all three adults looked expectantly at her. She clearly wasn't used to this much attention. Stuart could only imagine how weird it must feel, but she doggedly ploughed on.

'I always knew that staying with Nan was temporary, but it went on for years, and I got used to it. I never knew what was coming next, after Dad got out, and I still don't! And I've got my GCSE's next year, and I know how important they are, and I know I need to do a lot more work to pass them.'

She suddenly ran out of steam, as if she couldn't find the words to continue. Red-faced, she sat back in her chair. 'I don't want it all to be down to me, what happens next, because if I make the wrong decision, I'll be the bad guy.' The last bit was mumbled, as if she was saying it half to herself, but Stuart, Debby and Darren couldn't fail to hear it.

No, you won't be, Stuart thought, quietly. *I'll just have to find something else, and I'm sure I will.* But the pang of potential loss was hard to ignore.

Darren shifted his weight in his own chair. 'Okay, that's a really good start. So can you now tell me, is there anything you *don't* like about living in Taunton?'

Meghan thought for a minute. 'Well, there's a few things, actually. Since I'm being honest about everything else, I may as well say. I hate that the people are so unfriendly, the neighbours and stuff. They look at us young people like they're waiting for us to mug them, or throw a brick through someone's window, or something. People are so suspicious of every move we make. And they're so rude sometimes. They think *we're* the rude ones, but even when you've done nothing wrong they still think you have, or are going to, and they decide they hate you.

'And everywhere is crowded, and busy, and noisy all the time. And there's no space to have a dog, and I really want a dog, I've wanted one for ages. But Nan is there, and my friends are there, so I guess I just deal with it. I dunno, I never really thought about it before, what I hate about it. But there it is, I guess.'

Darren smiled broadly. 'I get that, totally. I hated Exeter, for the same reasons. It's why I moved to the South coast, first chance I could get, even *before* I realised how much I hated the city. When my circumstances weren't so great, when my life felt like shit, which it did quite a lot back then, sometimes the noise of the city and all the people in it would just get completely on my tits and I'd have to get out. I'd jump on a train and head for the coast just to walk along the beach and clear my head.

'Open spaces helped me a lot, so I eventually moved down there. I had to keep working in Exeter, though, and that's where I met Debs, but the two of us couldn't really live in my poky little one-person flat, with Badger. We sold the flat, and Debby's house, and bought a bigger one back in the city, but I had to force myself to move back there. When we made the decision to move up here last year, I knew it was the right thing.'

Debby looked at Meghan levelly. Her voice was serious. 'We see people more regularly now than we used to when they lived in the same town! They come and visit. Who wouldn't want to come here for a visit, right? I bet your Nan would, and maybe your friends too. And we go back to Exeter as often as we can. We've built a life here, and it's a *good* life. People are kind and genuine, there's plenty of open space for Ruby, and whoever else might come along to join the family. I think I might've said all this before, but I'm saying it again.'

Debby went on to explain how living in a smaller community was so much nicer. She felt more connected to other people. It was she felt life should be.

'I have my work, at the hospital in Carlisle. It's really busy, and I commute, when I'm not on maternity leave, so I still get a daily dose of rat-race,' she said with a grin. 'But that's only one part of my life now, whereas I used to feel it was most of it, and I never realised how much being on that hamster wheel got me down, until I was out of it.'

Darren cleared his throat. 'I feel the same. I can get pretty busy at work, but when I leave again, it's not to sit in queues of traffic or on an overcrowded train. I'm home within ten minutes, and I get to sit and look at fells and listen to wildlife. It's not the ocean, but it's the next best thing.'

He stretched his neck. 'I guess what I'm saying is that what *we* want and need is all here. All I miss are the people; family and friends, but not as much as I thought I might, with the technology, and the fact that everyone wants to come up here to visit. I get that it might be a harder choice for you though, because you're still so young, and living in the city works for you, because it provides more infrastructure for young people than small villages do, and the city is all you've ever known.'

Meghan was thoughtful for a moment. 'So; if you had a horse rehabilitation centre at the stables, would I be able to help with that?'

'God, yes! Absolutely!' Darren exclaimed. 'It goes without saying. You'd be a *great* help! I could give you proper training, if you wanted it.'

'And are the schools okay up here? Would I still be okay if I changed, with my exams coming up next year? They're important ones. It really is the worst time to think about changing schools. What if nobody at the new school even likes me?'

Debby leaned forward. 'I don't think being liked is something you'd have to worry about, chick. You're lovely, and any kid with half a brain would want to be your friend. And yes, on the one hand you're absolutely right, about changing schools in the run up to critical exams. Your GCSE's *are* important, and disruption on the scale we're talking about is far from ideal, especially if you're already struggling a bit.

'But I believe the school you'd be going to up here is very good. We have friends here whose kids go to Lakes Academy, and then there's Tarndale College, where there are a lot of options to take, depending on what you want to carry on with or aim for, either a practical-based career or university. I have no doubt that they would guide you in the right direction.'

She went on to say that she knew about all of it, because she'd done her own research in determining what the educational framework would look like for the future her own child.

'If you felt you needed extra help, we could always get you some extra tuition,' Stuart offered.

'One of the nurses at work has a couple of kids enrolled at Lakes Academy,' Debby added. 'They've always had a very good Ofsted rating. Put it this way, we're not even remotely worried about the quality of education Ruby will get up here. In fact, I'm hoping she'll do better, with a lower pupil-teacher ratio. In my book, that has to help.'

'I met a nice girl at the Farmer's Market last week,' Meghan volunteered. 'She invited me to the local youth group. It's tomorrow night. I wasn't going to go. I thought it might be a bit pathetic, but now I'm thinking I might go and see. She's at Lakes, I think. I could pick her brains a bit.'

Darren grinned. 'I went to talk to that youth club, about six months ago, about wildlife preservation. It was mainly about feeding foxes through the winter, and what to do with hedgehogs and squirrels when they come out of hibernation at the end of winter. They actually seemed like a decent bunch of kids, for what it's worth. They had the odd piss-taker trying to be a smart-ass, of course, but after ten minutes I had their full attention. They asked some really good questions, too.'

Debby piped up, 'Stuart, why don't you take Meghan back over to Beaconsfield and let her have a really good look at everything, before you guys make your decision? Take a good look at the house, the yard, the horses, take a wander around the school, head into Carlisle city centre and look at what's on offer there for shops, recreation, and stuff, and see if you can get a bit of a vibe, about what it might be like to live there.'

'That's an excellent suggestion, Debby. Thank you. Of course, we can do that. Would you like to do that, brat? Take a decent look around?'

To Stuart's relief, Meghan nodded. 'Sure. Maybe Saturday we could do Carlisle? That's when I'd normally be able to go there, on a Saturday, right?'

'I can also tell you that if you did move up here, you'd be welcome to hitch a ride down and back with us on any weekend we were going, if you wanted to see your Nan,' Debby offered. 'We'd drop you at hers and pick you back up again. It wouldn't cost you anything. We go back about once every six weeks or so, on average.'

Darren chimed in; 'Yeah, and if we had the situation where we had to go down two weekends in a row, which we do occasionally for birthdays and stuff, we could always bring your Nan up here for the week in between, and take them back again.'

Stuart was speechless yet again, at the generosity of these amazing people. They'd known him and Meghan for all of five minutes, and they were already offering investment money, rides and untold other suggestions for what might help them to make a decision about moving to the area. He turned his attention back to Darren.

'Your offer of investment is incredible, Darren. I dunno what to say, other than it being a ball completely out of left field!'

Darren shrugged. 'It's an offer for a mutually beneficial arrangement, and as I said, it's only a thought. I'd have to take a good look at the place myself, to see what's possible there, if anything. And, even if there is, you're not obliged to take me up on the offer, and I wouldn't take offence if you didn't, but it could be as useful for me as it would be for you.

'I deffo want to do more rehab work,' he continued, 'but I need a facility and I'd just as soon help you out as pay the same amount of money or more to someone else. And, of course, Debs and I have to talk about it. I'm probably already in the doghouse for not talking to her about it *first*.' He smirked anxiously at Debby. She smiled, closed her eyes and gently shook her head.

As ever, Stuart's new friend had managed to simplify a potentially complicated proposal in a few sentences. It was a great skill, showing a lot of insight. Stuart supposed he himself was probably an over-thinker because so much of what had people eternally hamstrung in the world of contracts was the missed attention to detail. The small print.

He suggested that Darren visit Beaconsfield for himself, to see if the facilities there would satisfy his requirements. Darren agreed and arranged to meet him and Meghan on Saturday afternoon at Beaconsfield, to take a look at the stables.

'I don't think Warwick would mind in the least,' Stuart agreed. 'He's keen to get moving, now the seed's been planted. I'll contact him in the morning to arrange it.

At that moment, a shriek was heard from the living room. 'That's my cue,' Debby sighed. 'Feeding time!'

She excused herself and Meghan invited Darren out to the fence line, to show him what she'd been doing with Astro this week.

'She's jumping over small hurdles now. We've progressed past the stepping. She's really nimble on her feet. Come and see.'

As they went outside, Stuart started clearing the table. He put the coffee pot on, sensing that his guests would soon be excusing themselves and leaving for home. The evening together had been every bit as much fun as the previous one, and very productive. Stuart now felt, more than ever, that buying Beaconsfield Stables might be the right thing to do. Maybe if Meghan could be guided to see herself living up here happily, they'd have a real chance.

He wanted his daughter to be happy, and he would stop at nothing to ensure that. But he was allowed to hope, wasn't he, that his plan would be a supportive part of that, rather than a cross she would feel she had to bear?

As he stacked the dishwasher, he thought again about how big a burden it might be, for his daughter to feel forced to make the final decision. Her choice might be to return to Taunton and building a life closer to the people she knew and loved. As much as it hurt him, he resolved to be as positive and supportive as he humanly could, of whatever decision she made.

Chapter Ten

Once he'd got the baby and the dog safely into his Land Rover, Darren stepped forward to give Stuart and Meghan a hug each. Debby hugged them both too.

They were nice people, he thought to himself, as they drove away with everyone waving wildly. It had been an interesting evening, to say the least, and the food had been fabulous. He turned to his wife, smiling nervously.

'Debs, I'm gonna get in first, over this fifteen grand thing. I know it was unexpected for you to hear me offer him that, and it was for me too, to be honest. I never went there tonight planning to offer money to a virtual stranger. But I dunno, babe, it just seemed like the right thing to do, as the conversation went.

'What he wants to do, it got me thinking a lot more about what I've had in the back of my own mind for a long time. Maybe this is my chance, to realise that bit of my dream, and help someone else out with theirs in the process. It just seemed to make sense.'

He looked over at Debby, who was staring straight ahead, deep in thought. 'Debs, I'll withdraw if you want me to. I should have run it by you first, I know that. I'm really sorry I didn't. It's a lot of money to offer without consulting you. I did tell him it was just an idea, though, more than once.'

'I know you did. And I don't mind as much as I feel I should, because we've talked about it a lot, you wanting to do horse rehab work. I know it's important to you. I know it's a dream you've got. But fifteen thousand pounds *is* a lot of money. You have to make sure you get a contract from Stuart that will support *you* as much as it supports *him*, so you don't end up losing it all if he goes bust or something.'

'I will. Don't fret. But I honestly don't think we need to worry about him. I've been doing a lot of research into Stuart Thomson, and believe me, before he fell from grace he was a shit-hot contracts lawyer. He had a really good reputation for integrity, fairness and attention to detail. His clients loved him, Debs. They bloody *loved* him. He's not gonna give us a bum-steer on this. I just feel it in my bones.'

'Well I hope your bones turn out to be right,' Debby sighed, 'because if he does go ahead with this venture and he fails, you'll lose your money if you haven't got a watertight contract that promises to repay you as first-in-line creditor. You'd have to get our own solicitor to check out any contact of Stuart's before you signed anything.'

Darren nodded. 'And I would, you know that.'

He reached across and took Debby's hand. 'I have a good feeling about the guy, babe, and this is my way of paying it forward to a bloke in need of a second chance in life, like I got myself.'

Debby grinned. 'At some point you're going to have to pull yourself out of this pay-it-forward rut you're stuck in, and realise you've more than paid your dues in that regard.'

'Do I, though? If it feels good to keep helping someone else, and it doesn't hurt my heart or my pocket, Debs, why should I stop doing it?'

'That's a fair question, I guess,' Debby conceded. 'Just don't end up giving too much of yourself away. We need a decent sized chunk of your heart too, remember.'

She gestured to Ruby and Badger, sharing the back seat, both sound asleep. Badger had played stick-chase with Meghan outside, as the sun was going down, until he literally collapsed in a heap. Tiring that dog out was no mean feat, but Meghan had managed it.

Darren chuckled. 'My heart isn't divided. It just happens to be big enough to offer to other deserving individuals as well as the loves of my life.'

Debby stretched and yawned. 'The atmosphere at Teapot Cottage always makes me feel lazy and sleepy. There's something truly magical about that place.'

'There is. That little pile of bricks and mortar brought us back together, remember, and it gave us Ruby.'

A soft smile played around his wife's lips. He knew she was remembering their own time at Teapot Cottage, and finding one another again, where their sexual relationship had become once again more about being in love than simply wanting to create the baby they'd longed for, as it had been in the very beginning before the spectre of ongoing infertility had all but shattered their marriage. Having managed to reach a certain level of acceptance that they would never become biological parents, the discovery that followed, that Debby was pregnant, had been the single best moment of both their lives. Even Ruby's arrival, as beautiful and profound as that had been, couldn't eclipse that one, single, life-changing, miraculous moment when they first learned about the tiny kernel of her, growing gently inside Debby.

'Maybe the cottage is working its magic on those two as well,' Debby murmured. She yawned again. 'I know Stuart did a really stupid and tragic thing, but who *hasn't* got behind the wheel of a car at some point in their lives when they've had too much to drink? I know I did it when I was younger. Most of my friends did, in fact.'

We just got lucky, were her unspoken words. Darren heard them as if she'd said them out loud. He found himself unable to agree.

'He wasn't younger though, was he, Debs? He wasn't eighteen and feeling as bulletproof and invincible as we all thought we were at that age, doing shit like that. Stuart was a grown man; cocky and arrogant by his own admission, and old enough to know better and understand the potential consequences of his actions.

'He had everything to lose, but he did it anyway, and yeah, the price he's paid has been huge, but it's a lot bigger for that poor woman's family. I keep trying to imagine how I feel if someone had done that to you when you were pregnant with Ruby. I'd want to kill the guy, and I dunno if I could ever get past that.'

All credit to the man who'd forgiven Stuart for killing his wife and child.

'Well, the husband forgave him, didn't he?' Debs asked, echoing his thoughts. 'And if he can rise to such a massive challenge, then the rest of the world should be able to as well, and at least try to acknowledge that Stuart and his family have paid a hefty price too. They've lost their family unit, friends, career, home, everything. It's a big enough price to pay, I'd say, unless you believe all that biblical stuff about an eye for an eye.'

'Well of course I don't, and I do agree with you, Debs. I'm the last person to judge, am I not? I'm just saying that he's got his demons and he has to live with them. I'm not saying he doesn't deserve a second chance. More than most people, I understand how much he does, and how important it is. And it somehow feels important to *me*, to help him achieve it, in whatever way I can.'

'I know, and I get it, babe. But I think Teapot Cottage might help them to find the peace they're both searching for.'

Darren hoped his wife was right. Teapot Cottage had a gentle way about it, where the really important things just somehow came back into focus, and what didn't matter receded. It was hard to explain, but Darren and Debby's own stay there had definitely changed their lives for the better, and rumour had it that other tenants had experienced similar revelations, including Adie Raven herself, who had first stayed there in the aftermath of her own turbulent life events, and found peace and new love as a result. Maybe a stay in the cottage would help the Thomsons turn their lives around. They did seem like genuinely decent people who deserved another crack at a good life.

'I really do like those two, Debs, especially Meghan. For a kid who's had her world turned upside down more than once, she has a real sweetness about her that animals seems to respond to really well.'

Debby nodded. 'Yeah, I was thinking that. She's made amazing progress with Astro, and she absolutely *adores* her. She literally lights up when she talks about that horse, and she's so great with Badger, Dolly and even paranoid little Jasper, too. Badger can't get enough of her. She really wants a dog of her own, doesn't she?'

'Yep, and she should have one. If they stay up here, maybe the surgery or the RSPCA can help with that.'

'No, Darren, she shouldn't have the burden of a rescue dog, with all its potential problems. She should have the joy of a brand-new puppy.'

Darren conceded. His wife was right. Meghan did deserve to have a sloppy, silly puppy she could choose a name for and train, who would lick her face and make her laugh out loud with its excitement and naughtiness.

'I can arrange a puppy, certainly. There's always a few pregnant bitches coming to the surgery. I'm sure we could help to get her a lovely puppy, when the time is right.'

Darren had a feeling that there would be a right time. He had the unshakeable conviction that Stuart Thomson would go ahead and buy Beaconsfield Stables, and that he would make a success of it. He also had the feeling that Meghan Thomson would, in her own way, have a profound influence on that business. He couldn't say exactly why, or how, but there was just something about her; a quiet determination, a deep understanding, something he couldn't define. Whatever it was, it would make her an excellent asset to Stuart, as the business came back into its own, and it might actually fulfil her in a way she wouldn't have been expecting.

'Meghan's got Astro on small jumps already. It's only been a couple of weeks, but the progress is fantastic. I think Astro really trusts her. I was watching them tonight. They seem to have a special bond you don't see very often, certainly not that quickly into a relationship. Normally it takes months, sometimes years, for a horse and trainer to truly trust one another.'

'Maybe it's the fact that they've both been a bit lost,' Debby ventured. 'Horses are very spiritual animals, aren't they? Astro was abused and neglected, and Meghan also feels a bit neglected and lost. Maybe Astro's picked up on that, and they've both found a kindred spirit.'

That makes sense, Darren thought to himself as he pulled into their driveway at home. Meghan and Astro certainly had a deep connection. How else would that have developed so quickly if they hadn't both sensed something profound within one another that they could both respond to in a positive way?

Maybe, if Meghan and Stuart did buy Beaconsfield, he could gift the horse to the girl. Astro would need a new home eventually, and who better for her to go to than someone who truly loved and understood her, who gave her the patience and the respect she needed, and who she could love in return?

He hoisted Ruby's car seat out of the Land Rover and carried the sleeping baby inside. As he set her down on the sofa he explained his thoughts to Debby, who just stared at him.

'How weird is that?' she said slowly, half to herself. 'I was just thinking that very same thing, but I didn't mention it because I didn't want to put ideas into your head. What you do with Astro has to be your own decision, but she's a Palomino cross, so you could probably get good money for her, even though I know that's not your main focus.'

'Well, it's not. And since the Ravens aren't charging me for having her there, and Meghan's doing all the work with her, it hardly leaves me out of pocket, does it? Unless you count my time in healing her various wounds from when I first found her, which I don't, by the way.'

Darren shook his head. 'No. I think the way forward might be to gift her to Meghan. She's earning it. They both are, actually, Debs. They're working hard together, so if that's what Meghan would want, I'm not expecting any argument from Astro!'

'I'm sure Meghan would want her. It might be a deal-breaker, too, for helping her make her decision about whether they should buy the stables and move up here?'

Darren shook his head emphatically. 'No, Debs. Think about it. That would feel like bribery. It wouldn't be right or fair. No, Meghan needs to decide what she wants to do without any influence. And if she decides she wants to give it a go up here, she can have the horse, since she'll have the perfect home for her.'

Debby stepped forward and kissed him passionately on the mouth. 'You are a very good man, Darren Davies. A really, *really* good man. And I feel the need to drag you into bed, so I will get our young madam sorted while you attend to these dogs' ablutions, and I'll see you in the boudoir.'

Darren smacked her playfully on the rump as she turned to go. He whistled at Badger, Dolly and Jasper, who needed no second bidding to go outside.

Outside, the sky was littered with stars. So little light pollution filtered into this neck of the woods. Once again he thanked his *own* lucky stars, for the way his life had turned out. He remembered how stunned he'd been, when he'd been offered the opportunity to train as a vet. He remembered how incredulous he was, that anyone would take a chance on him with the history he had. He remembered how rubbish his life was before his chance had come, and he remembered how hard he'd hoped – and still did even now – that Alison Jones, who'd made it all possible, would be proud of him if she could see him here in his new life, and he was open-minded enough to wonder if maybe she somehow could.

Her punt had paid off. He'd owed her that, and he'd delivered, and in the process he'd found his own true heart and what made it sing. You couldn't put a price on that, or on how paying it forward made you feel.

He thought about Tom Findlay, as he often did in quiet moments like this one, and he hoped the young lad was at peace. He no longer beat himself up about Tommy's death. It felt like a lifetime ago, that everything had happened. No less sad, for being distant of course, but not as acute as it was. Tom was gone, and all the good that had unfolded since, in the different lives that had been touched by his passing, well, that was a good enough testament to the fact that he had lived.

The dogs came running back from wherever they'd been in the dark, and Badger deposited a muddy stick at Darren's feet. He looked up hopefully, and Darren chuckled.

'Not tonight, buddy. I'm on a bloody promise and I don't intend to turn it down for you, so get your arses indoors, all of you! Get to bed, so I can do the same. We'll all have a good game of stick-chase in the morning before I go to work.'

Debby was in her pyjamas now, and putting away the pavlova plate as he went back inside. Dolly suddenly started scratching her head and shaking her ears.

'Oh, no! Don't tell me she's got ear mites again!' she cried in dismay. 'They drive her nuts!'

They drive us *all* nuts,' Darren muttered.

Debbie grinned. 'Maybe it's just a brain cell trying to fight its way out.'

'Well, it's not bouncing against another one, is it!'

She laughed out loud and tossed him the bottle of ear drops. He deftly caught it and administered them to Dolly, before tossing it back so Debby could put it back on top of the fridge. She shook some biscuits into the dogs' bowls and topped up their water before kissing them all on the nose. 'Goodnight, gorgeous ones.'

Darren took her outstretched hand and turned off the downstairs lights as they went upstairs to bed. Tomorrow was Friday, which was always an insanely busy day at the practice, and then there would be Saturday morning surgery. After that, he could head over to Beaconsfield to meet Stuart and have a good look around the stables. He felt a surge of excitement. Maybe they were onto something.

It was the last chance he had to think about anything before his wife began, slowly and very surely, to seduce him.

Chapter Eleven

Carlisle didn't seem like a terrible place, although with the reputation the area had for bad weather in the winter, Meghan wasn't sure if it would be any more appealing than her own hometown in the pouring rain. It might look alright in the snow, until it all turned to slush and made walking safely anywhere in town impossible, but how different was that either, from anywhere else? Taunton was just as depressing in the depths of winter. Although the temperatures were probably a bit warmer, what difference did that make, if you still couldn't go anywhere? At least here, with countryside on the doorstep in every direction, the rain felt natural when it fell. It might seem like less of a nuisance.

Yes! Concentrate on the positives!

Since Thursday night, when the Davies' had come over to dinner, Meghan's head had been crammed with all kinds of random thoughts. A sudden concern for the weather; what was that? Probably just all part of the weighing-up process she'd promised her dad she would go into, to try and decide if moving three hundred miles north to a place where it reportedly rained for fifty weeks of the year was sensible or downright insane!

In bald terms like that, of course it wouldn't be. But a business opportunity, which she could one day be a big part of if she chose to, and a school that was as good if not better than the one she was already enrolled at in Taunton; that made full consideration all the more important. There might be a chance here, for her to focus on her schoolwork a little more, and regain some of the momentum she'd lost. A new school scene might help her to refocus on her exams. Whether she succeeded or failed would be her own responsibility, and while she hadn't really cared much about that before, something had changed.

She wasn't sure why she suddenly felt as if she wanted to do a lot better, but she did.

Stuart seemed fairly certain that moving here was the right thing to do, and Meghan didn't want to doubt him. Before everything had crumbled around her, they'd had a pretty decent life. She'd always trusted him, before he'd made that huge mistake, and she truly believed he would never be that stupid again.

Her father was good with money too, she knew that much. He'd been at pains to promise that they would again know some kind of comfort and security after his release. To be fair, he was trying to offer that, with a home and a business that Meghan could work in and one day take over if she chose. And that, to *also* be fair, was an interesting prospect. What if she decided to do more science-based stuff at college, maybe even go to uni?

I could do something in horse sciences, become a trainer, or work with rehabilitation, like Darren! Maybe we even could buy Astro, if Darren would let us.

She shook herself, and told herself off for getting too far ahead of herself. Instead, she turned her attention back to what Carlisle had to offer. She'd looked online and had been pleased to see that most of the chain stores she really liked had a shop in the city. There was also a McDonalds and a couple of Costa coffee shops. That was a pretty good start.

Online shopping was a big thing, of course but, like a lot of her friends, Meghan did enjoy looking around the shops, feeling the clothes, trying things on or smelling different toiletries, and often buying them cheaper online later. It was also a very true thing that even when you didn't feel like going to the shops, there was everything to be said for knowing you could if you wanted to. There would be nothing worse than living in a place where you had to travel for hours just to get to a mall. This was a far cry from that, and it was a fact worth considering.

Aside from that, it was only an hour on the train down to Preston, which was a lot bigger. If she fancied a day shopping, she could easily do that, if her dad would let her go alone. Or maybe she could go with Jayde, or maybe even with Feen or Debby. It occurred to her now, in this line of thinking, that she already had new people in her world that could potentially become good friends. Did the age difference matter? Maybe not so much.

In spite of having always judged herself as being largely irrelevant to the people in her world, there were some who did seem to find her interesting. Debby understood her, and talked to her as if her opinions mattered. She also shared elements of her own life, as if she really believed that Meghan wasn't just some dumb kid who wouldn't understand anything.

She had an idea that Feen Raven-Black kind of 'got' her too, from the brief conversations they'd had, and whenever Darren asked her a question, he really listened to the answer, as if he actually cared what it was. Meghan couldn't remember a time when anyone had done that. Even her teachers had always been impatient for answers, whenever she was required to supply them, and they never seemed to be all that interested in whether she got them right or wrong.

Trudie Sangster had enjoyed having her around too, at the GladRagz boutique, and Adie Raven had invited her to coffee, where she'd got along with everyone. She felt like she kind of fitted in with the people she'd met up here so far. *That* wasn't a bad start, either.

Stuart suggested a bite to eat at Subway, and Meghan was pleased to see a few groups of people her own age hanging around in the streets who all seemed happy enough. Two girls in particular fascinated her. They were about twelve or thirteen, and were almost identically dressed, in white jeans, slouch boots, pink tops and faux leather jackets. They both had blonde hair tied up in messy buns, and they had virtually identical handbags. Clearly best friends, they seemed very happy indeed, wandering the streets, window-shopping, with linked arms and contented smiles. Looking at all these kids who seemed about as normal as kids were anywhere else, being a teenager in Carlisle didn't seem to be a wretched thing at all.

Last night's visit to the Torley Youth Club had been a revelation too. Meghan had texted Jayde, and made her promise to meet her at the door, so she wouldn't have to walk in by herself. She'd taken extra care with her appearance, bringing out the hair straighteners, choosing a dark purple top with gold moons and silver stars on it and a pair of tight but casual black jeans and a plain pair of black ballet flats. She'd taken an hour with her hair and make-up, much to her dad's bafflement, since he'd proclaimed she didn't look any different after all that than she had before she started. He was such a pleb, at times.

True to her promise Jayde had been at the entrance when Meghan arrived. About twenty young people had been hanging around in the hall, aged from around twelve to about seventeen. Jayde had introduced her, and everyone had said hi; some merely mumbling, others showing a bit more enthusiasm. Meghan had then found herself in the middle of an ongoing discussion about the local secondary school, which she'd been wondering about. She hadn't wanted to let anyone know she was thinking of moving up here, but she was very interested in what they all had to say about Lakes Academy. A few kids were waiting for their GCSE results, and one or two were a bit nervous about them. Most seemed to think the school was no worse than any other. Another girl had introduced herself as Renae, and asked Meghan about her own school in Taunton.

'It's ok, I suppose. My friends are there, but some of the teachers are real dicks.'

Everyone laughed at that. One boy piped up 'Yeah, we have dicks here too, but some of the teachers are good sorts. Mr Fraser is great, and so's Mrs Waite. She's an English teacher and she's crazy about books. She gave us a primo reading list last year. I actually read three whole books, one after the other, for the first time in my entire life.'

Renae had asked if Meghan liked dance and drama, and told her there was a great dramatic arts department. 'I do props, you know, finding the stuff for the sets for plays and things,' she explained. 'One time I had to find a roll-top bath, and we had to go around the farms begging for one to borrow for a week. It can be fun, especially if you can act, or if you like art. My boyfriend Jack does the lighting for most of the plays we do. Our dance and drama teacher is Mrs Taylor, and she's kind of old, but she's pretty cool.'

She'd introduced Meghan to Jack. He was a dark-haired boy of about fifteen, who seemed a bit serious, but he had a cheeky grin whenever someone said something funny.

The youth group leader was a guy called Ian, who was in his early twenties, with long curly hair, and wearing a pair of tracksuit bottoms and a t-shirt with a picture of a fighter jet on it. He seemed nice. He was studying for a master's degree in engineering at Lancaster university. He'd set up a projector and run a comedy film for them all to watch on the faraway wall of the hall that doubled as a screen, and he'd marshalled everyone to put the chairs out.

At the end when the lights went up, everyone started packing away the chairs and setting up the trestle tables for the hall to be ready for the farmer's market the following morning. It was part of the deal, for the church allowing the youth group to use the hall. Meghan had been surprised at how quickly everyone had got the hall tidied and set up for the market, without complaint.

As they'd all left, Renae had hugged her, and Meghan had hugged back. It felt nice. Jayde had grinned and put her own arms out and Meghan had stepped into them and hugged her too.

'It was nice to meet you, Meghan,' Renae had offered. 'Maybe you'll come back? We'll be doing something different next week. Ian normally sends us an email to tell us what it is, but you won't be on the list. If you give me your number I can text you and you can see if you fancy it.'

They'd exchanged numbers. Jayde had promised to text her over the weekend too, and Meghan felt pleased to have been so readily accepted into the group. One of the boys (she though his name was Parker) had given her a quiet smile as he was leaving. He'd seemed shy, but he'd told her he hoped she'd come back next week, and he'd melted away into the night on his mountain bike. She supposed a lot of them would have walked or biked to the hall, since it was right in the centre of town, and it wasn't far to most of the residential housing clusters. Apparently, most of kids took the bus to school, which was actually closer to Carlisle than it was to Torley.

Her Dad had been parked up, waiting, and when he'd asked her how it had gone, she'd just shrugged.

'It was fine,' she said, and was noncommittal when he asked her if she'd met any nice kids there. She hadn't wanted to give him too much information. While he still wasn't sure if she was happy, he wouldn't be pressuring her to make a decision on their future plans, and in the car on the way home from youth club she'd still felt a long way from being ready to decide.

*　　*　　*　　*　　*

As they pulled into the car park at Beaconsfield, Meghan felt nervous. The last two times she was here, it had been fun. This time, the reason for coming was different, and she wasn't sure how to react when Lucy came up to her with a beaming, welcoming smile, as if she were an old friend. Meghan didn't want anyone to think this would be a done deal; not yet anyway.

Warwick Ford wasn't far behind his granddaughter, and he greeted Meghan with a nod and a smile, and extended his hand towards Stuart, who shook it warmly. Darren pulled up at that moment, too. Meghan was glad he'd arranged to meet them here. His presence somehow made everything seem less intense. Stuart introduced him to Warwick Ford.

In the yard, four horses were standing around, still with their bridles on, with their saddles sitting on the fence. Lucy had taken three people out that morning and was still in the throes of getting things put away. Meghan would have offered to help, but she was anxious to see the house, so she excused herself and followed Warwick and her father, who were walking in that direction.

Darren slung an arm around her shoulders briefly. 'Hello, young lady. Let's take a look around shall we?' He confessed to her that he'd been really excited to be coming to see Beaconsfield and hadn't got much sleep the night before. Meghan wasn't prepared to admit that she hadn't got much sleep either. She wasn't sure if the fluttery feeling she had in the pit of her stomach was excitement or fear. For now, the less said about it the better.

The house wasn't bad, she decided. It was pretty basic and looked a bit shabby, like nobody had cared about it much for a long time, but it had a nice sunny patio, accessed by a pair of peeling French doors that led off the little dining area next to the kitchen. The living room had an old log burner in it, which would make things cosy in the winter, and a tiny room tucked under the stairs held a toilet and a mini handbasin.

Upstairs were three bedrooms. The two biggest ones had a bathroom between them. Stuart explained that the largest room was big enough to have an en-suite put in it, which would leave the existing bathroom free for her. The idea of having her own bathroom was exciting. At this stage in her life, not having to share one with her father would be the most massive bonus on the planet. She imagined her bedroom repainted, all in white, with one of those bedspreads you could buy online, that had a nature scene on it. She might be able to find one with horses on it.

I'm sure I could, if I looked. I wonder if Dad would let me have a double bed?

The third bedroom was slightly smaller than the other two, but still a good size. Warwick used this room to work on the business, she guessed, noting the small desk with an ageing laptop sitting on it, and a bookshelf groaning under the weight of a collection of bent and buckled lever-arch files that had all seen better days. The bedroom she would undoubtedly be offered overlooked the road, but beyond that, the view across rolling fields to the foothills was stunning.

Could I be happy here? Maybe.

Everything about the house was unexciting, and in dire need of an upgrade, but even Meghan could see how much nicer it could be, if it was done up. The Fords had cared more about their business than their home, that much was obvious, but the house wasn't in bad shape. It just wasn't very homely, which could definitely be changed. The 'warm' woman's touch was missing. Certain ornaments and pictures on the walls had probably once felt welcoming, but Meghan guessed that since Mrs Ford had died, the essence of femininity had gone with her. Men weren't great at making or keeping things cosy, she knew.

An old, dusty vase sat on a little half-moon table on the short landing where the stairs took a turn. It was filled with silk flowers that had probably once looked lovely but were now terminally faded and covered with thick dust. Meghan thought they'd once been purple, or blue. It was hard to tell, now.

A lick of paint here, a bit of new wallpaper there, rip up the *really* bad carpets, and put down some laminate flooring, and that wouldn't be a bad start. Eyeing the old-fashioned Rayburn cooker in the shabby, unloved kitchen, Meghan half thought she'd like to see an Aga in its place, like the ones at Teapot Cottage and at Debby and Darren's place. They were cool. She still didn't know how to use one, but she figured it couldn't be too much of a challenge. If lots of people had them and liked them, they couldn't be *that* hard to get to grips with, could they?

They went back outside to the garden, and as they walked towards a big old barn, Meghan spied a small orchard of apple trees, off to one side.

The barn had real potential, and as her father described his vision to turn it into accommodation for guests, she could see it herself, in her mind's eye. She thought the kitchen that would go in here should also have an Aga; a really big one like Adie Raven's, and one of those massive American fridges with the really cool ice maker in the front of the door. She imagined a romantic fireplace, and sloppy big sofas like the ones the Davies' had.

Warwick and her father spent quite a bit of time discussing the barn, before they all walked along the fence-line towards the stables. As they got to the yard, Meghan could see that Lucy had stowed away all the tack and was now grooming the horses. She looked up and smiled broadly again.

'I'll soon be done, Grandad, and I'll be out of your hair.' She went on to explain that she wouldn't be working this afternoon because she was going shopping for her wedding dress, with her mum and a couple of her friends. Meghan felt a rush of pleasure for Lucy. 'Are you getting married around here?' she enquired.

Lucy nodded. 'Yeah, at the Beeches Hotel. You probably passed it on your way here. It's not until next summer, but there's lots to organise, and I'll feel a lot more like I've got a handle on things if I can at least get my dress sorted.'

Meghan recalled the big, white, elegant old hotel on the main road between Torley and Carlisle. It had looked beautiful, set back from the road, surrounded by tall trees and manicured gardens. There was a lush golf course alongside it, as she recalled, with rolling gentle green slopes, all perfectly mown. The Beeches was *exactly* the kind of place you'd want to have a wedding! She smiled at Lucy and wished her a fun afternoon. It must be so exciting, going shopping for a wedding dress!

The yard still looked scruffy and dilapidated, but better for having been freshly swept out and tidied. Warwick took them into the first stable block, where two opposing rows of five stalls sat empty but ready and waiting for horses to take up residence. The empty, quiet stalls looked and felt a bit forlorn.

The block itself was spotless though. It felt warm, almost cosy, and the narrow windows that ran right across the top of three of the walls brought a gentle, lovely light into the room. Meghan could imagine the stable block *full* of horses, all snorting gently to one another and waiting for human company.

The second block was identical to the first, although it was slightly longer with a big square room at one end. It had once been half-heartedly set up as an office and storage unit, but had long since been abandoned, if the blackened cobwebs and dirty windows were anything to judge by. Warwick explained that originally they were going to use it as the office for the business, but it had proved to be more convenient for his wife to do the paperwork and answer the phone and emails in the house.

Eight horses were in residence in this block, and the smell of them was wonderful. It made Meghan grin from ear to ear. Finnegan, her horse from her previous treks, was in there with the others, and she felt absurdly glad when he recognised her and nickered softly to her. She stroked his beautiful, velvet-soft nose, and kissed it gently. 'Hi, Finny!' she whispered. 'How's it going, fella?'

This block was full of horsey stuff, as well as the beasts themselves. Wall-mounted saddles, bridles, halters and other tack and brushes, were all neatly grouped into separate sets, each with the name of a horse above it. Bales of hay and containers of oats nestled in one corner, and a rack of shelves held a variety of bottles, tubes and jars.

There was plenty of room for everything, and it all appeared to be well organised. The centre area between the two rows of stalls was a generous space, with trenches set into the cobbled floor to drain away excess water from cleaning or hosing horses down if the weather didn't lend itself to doing it outside.

As full as the block was, it was spotless. While Warwick Ford and his granddaughter had limited time or passion for the business itself, their attention to environmental hygiene wasn't in question. They cared deeply about the horses.

Darren spent few minutes with each beast, just quickly checking its eyes and teeth, coat, skin and hooves. When he was done, he said nothing but winked at Meghan, and gave her a slight nod. He then left the group to walk around the back of the second stable block.

After he came back, a few minutes later, they all took a walk along the track that Meghan and Stuart had taken on horseback just a few before. Warwick was explaining that there were several tracks that had been granted right-of-way by the local council and farmers. There were about eight miles of trek-track, all with long-leases in place. By all accounts, the local council was invested in keeping the natural environment preserved for the enjoyment of locals and tourists alike. They were also supportive of business enterprise, so any business that supported their goals was likely to be treated well and encouraged to continue.

Meghan hung back a while, as the three men continued walking and talking. She found a flat rock to sit on and looked out at the views across the valley. This really was a beautiful place.

I suppose we could do a lot worse than live here.

Was she a country girl at heart? She'd never spent enough time in it to really know. *But could I become one? Or would this view, and the reality of living in the middle of nowhere, just drive me mad in the end?*

She thought back to Darren's question at the table the other night, about what she didn't like about city life. All of the things she'd described were all of the things that would be absent, out here; things like crowds and traffic, and the inescapable noise they created. She genuinely did feel frustrated by that stuff. But there was such a thing as a too-radical change.

What if it was *too* quiet here? What if she ended up feeling like she'd made the biggest mistake of her life?

Once the decision was made, there would be no going back. But, on the plus side, she could have a dog, and she might even be able to have Astro. She'd already made a handful of tentative friends in Torley, there was no guarantee that everything would stay the same for long in Taunton anyway, and it was only a train-ride away for Nan and friends to come and visit. The Torley Youth Club was an okay place to hang out, with some nice people, and she was pretty sure her father would never complain about taking her over there and picking her up again on a Friday night. Carlisle seemed ok, as a place to hang out too. There was a movie and ten-pin bowling complex, and everything else she was used to having more or less on tap.

And, as the thought kept nagging at her, she had to confront it. If her friends were true ones they *would* visit. As they all got older and got jobs, even part time ones, they could raise the train or bus fare to get up here if they cared about her, and if they didn't, well … that would be her answer, wouldn't it? Staying in a place she didn't really like, for people who didn't even care, was just stupid. Her nan was the only one she *knew* who actually did, but was that enough to stay in Taunton for, when everything else about the place got on her nerves? The Davies' had kindly offered to take her with them whenever they went down to Devon, and she knew their offer was sincere. She could see her nan just about as often as she wanted.

As she sat there, on her warm rock in the sunshine, Meghan found herself running out of reasons to dig her toes in and refuse to make the move.

Darren came sauntering back. He sat next to her on the rock, and glanced across at her. 'Those two have got their heads together again. They're talking numbers, now, so I figured I'd leave them to it. None of my business really, what they cook up between them.'

She turned to him. 'What do you think? First impressions?'

Darren exhaled slowly. 'First impressions are all good, really. The horses seem to be well looked after, with all the right hygiene rules followed, from what I can see, and the place is clean and tidy. Needs a few licks of paint, mind, but that's no biggie, is it? Scruffy can be made nice, with a bit of vision and elbow grease, and I think your dad has both.'

Meghan inclined her head. 'I'd have my own bathroom, and maybe a puppy.'

He laughed. 'Definitely both, I'd say. Are they deal-breakers?'

She grimaced. 'Could be, if I could bribe Dad. I dunno what to say, really. I don't even know what to *think*, about *any* of this. What do you think of the opportunity for the horse hospital, though? Is there enough space?'

'Not as it stands, but that bit on the far end of Block Two, that they planned to use as an office, is a really good start. It wouldn't be a problem to extend out a bit more to the other side. That could be done in a few weeks, with the right people on it. It's basically just a foundation, concrete blocks and roofing. Your dad and I could line it out ourselves.'

Darren sounded enthusiastic, and she loved how he was talking to her, as if she was an adult, and as if it mattered to him what she thought of his ideas. She trusted him to be honest, and she told him so. He smiled gently, and winked at her.

'Okay Meghan, I will be honest, since you've asked me to be. I do think this is a good proposition for your dad, *and* for you. It's a big change, and a big step, but you know what? A big change and a big step aren't always bad things. Maybe they can be the things that make your life a whole lot better, show you who you really are.'

'Like it did for you, becoming a vet?'

Darren gazed out across the valley, thoughtfully. 'Yep. I had no idea how good my life could be, until I stepped into the great unknown.'

'Were you scared?' *I'm scared*, Meghan thought to herself.

'Absolutely terrified! I was used to having nothing, and *being* nothing. Taking the incredible chance I got, to see if I could be better than nothing? Believe me, that was one of the scariest things I've ever done in my whole life. The fear of failure was paralysing, until I felt things working out, and trusted myself enough to embrace my passion for it. Moving up here, away from the city, was a doddle compared to that.'

Darren shrugged and pulled a face. 'I just asked myself what I had to lose, and the answer was not much. It all comes down to that, really. What have *you* got to lose?' He sighed gently, and looked at her kindly.

'Look, Meghan. For what it's worth, I can see you both here. And I can see you both, and the business, *thriving* here. What this old place needs is new blood, new enthusiasm, and commitment to making it as great again as it once was, and probably even better. Your dad's got all of that ability in spades, but here's the thing, babe: so have *you*, if you put your mind to it.' His voice was quiet, but he sounded truthful.

'You're amazing. I can see the potential in you, and so can your dad. He loves you more than anything else in this world. It's *both* of you he wants this for, not just himself. He's offering you as sound a future as he can muster, if you want it, and he'd sweat blood to provide it. I hardly know him, but I do know that much about him.'

She didn't know what to say. He cocked his head on one side, looked sternly at her, and continued.

'But you know what? This isn't the only option, is it? You can certainly go back to Taunton and figure something else out, and you could both be just as happy doing something completely different, when you both work out what it is. It won't be the end of anyone's world, if you don't go for this. And even if you did, then decided you hated it, you can do whatever you want when you turn eighteen. You're young enough and bright enough to go anywhere, and be or do *anything*. So you could give it the three years or so then scarper if that's what you really wanted to do.' He chuckled and sang, in a high, falsetto voice, 'Bismillah! Nobody will die!'

Meghan doubled up with laughter. She realised that Darren's opinion meant more than anyone else's. Darren Davies believed in Meghan Thomson, he'd said it and he'd shown it, and as unsure as she was of herself, in almost every aspect of her life, she had no cause to doubt *him*. Apart from her nan, she'd never felt anyone's belief in her like this before. Darren's faith in her really did make her feel like anything was possible.

'I guess the other question is, what's the worst that could happen? We hate it, either one of us, and we go bust or give up, and end up back in Taunton where we started.'

'Bismillah! Nobody will die!' Darren sang again.

'That should be our own special code word, yours and mine, for when we're worried or need a reality check about something. When something's really shit, either of us can just say 'Bismillah,' and we can help reassure each other. What do you think?'

'I think that sounds like a great idea. A code word. Very sensible, as a signal that something's not right. But we also need a *reassuring* word; one for when things are all good and we're happy. Choose one for that, too.'

'Whisper'! We should say 'whisper,' because I could become a world-famous horse whisperer one day, and that's a really good thing to be. I'm already learning so much fascinating stuff about horses, through the course I'm doing.'

'Meghan, I meant what I said. You could be anything you wanted. Anything in the world. It's all up for grabs, at your age. If you want a future working in any capacity you choose, with horses or anything else, there's no reason on God's green earth why you can't make it happen. You're clever enough. You just have to want it enough to work hard enough to get it.'

Meghan decided to take her first leap of faith, there on the rock in the lukewarm sunshine, and confide in Darren. She felt *safe* with him, like she could tell him anything, and he'd understand. She confessed to how Astro had filled the huge void she felt she had within herself when they first arrived at Teapot Cottage.

'I don't even know what's wrong with me. I just have what feels like *holes*, big empty spaces inside myself, and I don't know how to talk about them, or even *who* to tell, except for you. Dad would only want to 'fix' me somehow, with all kinds of things I don't want, and nobody else would get it, or me. It's like Astro could see the holes, though, and when I look into her eyes I see hurt and hope in them; a mixture of both. She looks exactly like how I feel, most of the time, but I know that probably just sounds really stupid.'

Darren shook his head emphatically. 'Nope. It doesn't sound stupid at all. In fact, 'holes' is a great way to describe it. Astro *is* hurt, spiritually, and she's trying to trust again. She's desperate to have *her* 'holes' filled. I can see that too.' He shook his head, as if to clear it.

'We felt the same way for a long time, me and Debs, before she got pregnant with Ruby. We'd struggled for years. It's like, you can't have what you always wanted, no matter how hard you try, and the disappointment is killing you, but how do you even start trying to feel better about it, or look to what else might fill the gaps in your soul?'

Meghan gazed at him. 'That's exactly it. Exactly. I always wanted a close family. I didn't want my mum to die, and I didn't want Annabel to be so cold. I wanted my dad to care less about his job and more about his family. I didn't want to feel like I was always on the outside of everything, like everybody's afterthought or something.'

She was surprised to find herself close to tears now, as she confessed her truth. 'But somehow, that's the way it ended up, and I couldn't change anything.' She sniffed, and swallowed hard. 'I don't want things to stay the same, but I don't know how to make them different, and even if I did, how do I know if different would be better? What if it's even worse?'

Darren shrugged. 'You *don't* know. Nobody ever really does! You just have to start by taking a leap of faith, chicken. Ever heard the saying, 'Leap, and the net will appear'? That's what you have to do. Take a leap, and trust the process. Your dad won't let you fall. He's your net, Meghan. He won't be leaving you again, and he won't let anyone hurt you again, but he wants the net to be stronger than just him.

'This,' he gestured around the landscape and back to the stables, 'this is more strength to the net he wants to be for you. That much I know to be true.'

'I guess I'm finding it hard to be such an important factor in the process. It's so weird, that I'm important now. It's a long time since I felt important to *anyone*. I mean, I know Nan cares about me, but she's old, and she has a funny way of showing her love sometimes. A lot of the time she just moans at me, and

I know it's because she cares. If she didn't, she'd just ignore me, and she never does that. Not like my stepmother did.'

'Stu told me that she left you. That must've been really hard.'

'At the time, I didn't think it was hard. I always knew I never mattered to her, and I used to think *that* didn't matter, but now I think it made me angry, that she didn't care about me. I mean, I know I wasn't hers or anything, but I was, like, *nine*, you know? Who dumps a nine-year-old kid, for fuck's sake?'

'Maybe she knew you'd be better off with your nan,' Darren offered. 'Sometimes people just have a shit way of showing it, when they're trying to do something good. It wouldn't have been much fun for you if she had stuck around anyway, would it, by the sound of things?'

'Well, no. You're right, and I know all that, but it's not the fact that Annabel left. It was more that she didn't even *talk* to me about it. No warning, no reasons; she just told me one Saturday morning to pack my stuff up, and she drove me to Nan's and that was the last time I ever saw her. She never even said goodbye properly, or sorry, or *anything*, and I never heard from her again. She just forgot about me, like I'd never existed. And I wonder sometimes, what she would have done if I didn't have Nan. Would she have put me into care, or something?'

'Well, that didn't happen, so I think it might be time to get that part of your past out of your head for good. Put Annabel in a metal dustbin, in your mind, and put the lid on her so tight that it can't come off. That's what I do with people I don't want to think about anymore.

'And promise yourself that you'll never think about her again, because she doesn't deserve your energy. You deserved a lot better than what you got from her, and you *don't* deserve to be tormented by thoughts like that. You were thrown, babe, but here's the thing; you landed safely, and that's all that matters. You landed with family, who love the very bones of you. That's what you need to focus on. Be thankful, if you can find a way, because a lot of kids *do* end up in care, and a lot of those don't do very well in the system.'

Meghan knew he was right. She needed to look at the *upside* of being separated from Annabel, and be grateful for what she had, which was a lot more than some kids got to have. Darren was a diamond. She turned and hugged him hard. He hugged her back.

'You can always talk to me, Meghan. No matter what it is, if you ever need a listening ear, you've got one here. And unless it's something that makes me worry about you, I'll never tell your dad.'

Meghan fought to swallow the lump in her throat. She had never had a big brother, and although Darren was almost as old as her father, she felt like he was a real friend; someone she could confide in, who had seen enough hardship in life to understand what it felt like for someone else. Her dad had endured hardship too, but he was still rebuilding his life. Darren had already rebuilt his. He was successful. He was proof that no matter how shit your life had been, you could turn things around and make it better. She knew it was what Stuart was trying to do too, and for a man who had spent six horrible years in a tiny prison cell, this opportunity must feel like the best in the world.

Darren was a good role model. He 'saw' her, and he treated her with more respect than anyone else had ever shown her. She felt that he genuinely liked her, and she knew he was trying to steer her in a better direction because he cared whether or not she was in a good place. That meant more than he'd probably ever know, unless she could ever find the words to tell him. Maybe one day she would.

She felt like such a freak sometimes, like she didn't fit in anywhere. Her life just felt like one big mess, full of mistakes and uncertainty. Darren must've felt like that too, when his life was in pieces and he couldn't see a way forward. But then he had a chance, and he took it. Stuart had a chance now too, and he wanted to take it, and Meghan had the *same* chance. Darren said he thought it was a good one, and that meant everything. As daunting a prospect as it was, maybe this move to the wop-wops *would* be the key to her own life being better.

She heard Warwick and her father coming back around the hill, their voices carrying on the light breeze. As everyone made their way back to the stables, Meghan turned to looked back at the stunning view. In that moment, she felt something shift, ever-so-slightly, in her chest. Unaware of exactly what it was, she shrugged it off.

It was only later, after everyone had shaken hands again, promised to be in touch very soon, and gone their separate ways, that she realised what it was. It was conviction. It was the beginning of a big *decision*, and when she and Stuart got out of their car at Teapot Cottage to find Astro waiting at the fence, staring with her soulful eyes and nickering a soft but excited welcome, her heart skipped a very big beat. In that moment, she realised she was completely in love with Astro, and Astro was in love with *her*. It was everything. And suddenly, like she suspected it was probably all *supposed* to, everything fell into place.

She turned to her father and said it.

'Okay, Dad, let's do this.'

Chapter Twelve

Bali was hot, and humid. Stuart's shirt clung to him instantly, from the moment he left the air-conditioned airport and joined the throng of people outside, who were waiting for rides and taxis. He'd been assured that someone would be at the airport to meet him, and take him to the resort, which was around three hours west of Denpasar, the capital of the island. He'd booked it because it wasn't far from where Karyn Balik's family lived. The resort looked nice, when he'd found it on the internet, and he was looking forward to getting there after a long and tiring flight. After a few moments of scanning the placards with names on them that were being waved about by the crowd of drivers, he saw his own name and raised a hand. The driver raised one back, and nodded, and beckoned him over.

Within minutes, he was in an air-conditioned van being whisked unnervingly quickly through insanely erratic, dense and deafening traffic. People on scooters, sometimes with a couple of kids balanced precariously on their handlebars or knees, weaved through the melee with a level of confidence that bordered on reckless. Truck and car drivers appeared to be playing 'chicken' as they drove towards one another at speed on the narrow 'main' roads, pulling in or out from behind, just in the nick of time. Tailgating seemed to be the norm, and nobody worried about it.

The system was crazy, but it seemed to work. Everyone simply budged up and made room for everyone else, and apart from the odd honked horn, nobody seemed to have much road rage. *You need nerves of steel and the patience of a saint to drive here,* Stuart thought to himself.

Although he and Annabel had travelled to different places, Indonesia had never been on their list. It wasn't somewhere they'd even thought of, and Stuart was sure that if he hadn't killed a woman with a Balinese family, it would never have entered his head, to come to Bali. Now that he *was* on the island, he decided, he might as well try to appreciate what it had to offer, even though his mission was a heartbreaking one. He had ten days, to find what measure of peace he ever could, before heading home again to start a new chapter in his and Meghan's lives. He was pretty sure he'd made the right decision for them both, in agreeing to buy Beaconsfield Stables, but he hoped that by the time he got to the end of his time in Bali, he would feel a lot more settled about that, as well as a lot of other important things.

After agreeing to take on the business, he and Meghan had finished their holiday at Teapot Cottage, before returning to his mum's place in Taunton, to pack up their belongings. Meghan had returned to school and was spending part of her first semester there. She'd been formally enrolled at Lakes Academy, and would be transferring there as soon as they got possession of the house and business.

The new school had a Work Experience (WE) program, which Meghan was already excited about. Darren had already agreed with David Thornley, his boss at Valley View Veterinary Practice, that if she wanted to, she could do her work experience with him on the farms around Cumbria, when the time came. He would try to plan that week to be doing farm visits, so that he could expose her to as much work as he could, with horses in the area, including working with any who might be in the Beaconsfield horse hospital, which would be a reality by the time she was ready to do her WE.

Before they'd left Torley to go home again, Stuart had talked to Darren a lot, about the accident, and what had happened to Karyn Balik and her unborn baby. In the course of those conversations, it had become clear to him that he would never be at peace until he could achieve at least some degree of self-forgiveness. He'd confessed to being unsure of where to even *start,* in trying to achieve that.

Counselling hadn't really worked. On a rational level he did appreciate that what happened had been a terrible mistake, rather than a vindictive act of intended harm, but he couldn't find a way to make that resonate within himself. To overcome the guilt and shame that deeply overshadowed his ability to live a normal life, a seismic shift was needed. He knew he had to do something more, to achieve that, but he couldn't figure out what it was.

Darren, as wisely as ever, had wondered if Karyn Balik's husband Nengah's letter of forgiveness had in some way made Stuart's anguish worse. He'd asked him what he might do, if Nengah was standing in front of him. What would he say to the man? What would he feel he could offer, or do, to try and make things better?

As he'd struggled to answer the question, an idea had formed in Stuart's head that quickly became the most obvious solution. He suddenly felt compelled to do just that; stand before Nengah, and before Karyn's entire family in fact, and offer his apologies in person. The way he had ended Karyn's life was unfinished business. Once he'd accepted that, the need to resolve it became overwhelming. He wanted, with every fibre of his being, to meet her family and let them know how profoundly sorry he was. He wasn't sure if taking direct, face-to-face responsibility for their torment would help move him forward from his own, but it suddenly became the only thing he could do. If he *didn't* do it, that would only add to his anguish; the wondering, if it might have made a positive difference.

His probation officer had listened, and had generously granted Stuart's wish to travel to Bali, meet with Karyn Balik's family, and offer them his heartfelt apologies. He wanted them to know who he was as a person; not some faceless drunk who hadn't cared a damn about what he'd done, but a man who was genuinely sorry for the devastation he'd caused, who would gladly give his own life to be able to turn back the clock and not have caused it.

He'd approached Nengah about it. Nengah had moved back home to Bali a few years earlier, and he graciously agreed to meet Stuart, and take him to meet Karyn's parents, after paving the way for them to receive him into their home.

So here he was, hurtling through the most insane traffic he'd ever seen, on his way to the resort. He was due to meet Nengah and Karyn's family the day after tomorrow, so he didn't have much time to prepare for being confronted by her parents. The prospect was terrifying. He had no idea what to expect from them, but by the time the van finally drew up outside his resort he'd resolved to dispense with all the excuses and half-baked 'explanations' he'd been trying to offer to *himself* with no success. He needed to be as honest and real as he could be, to a grieving family. He hoped that would be enough.

*   *   *   *   *

The meeting with Karyn's family went a lot better than Stuart had expected. They lived in an incredibly modest village, only about ten minutes' drive from his resort. Luxuries were patently few, but their home was spotless and comfortable, and the dignity the family showed, in the face of such heart-rending loss, left him unable to stop himself from quietly weeping. He sat with Karen's parents and her two brothers, and confessed to what he had done, how the accident had happened, what had happened to his own family as a result, and how much responsibility and regret he felt for his actions.

Karen's dad, Wayan, was Balinese. Her mother, Donna, was Australian. Donna gently took his hand, and quietly explained the cardinal Hindu Dharma values the family lived by, one of which was *'memaafkan'* – the core principle of forgiveness.

'According to the Hindu tradition, a person who cannot forgive will be forever cursed with carrying the trauma and baggage that comes from holding onto the anger of the 'wrong,' with its feelings of resentment, and other unresolved emotions that influence the present and the future,' she'd explained. 'The tenet dictates that forgiveness of the sins of others is the only way to achieve peace within the self.'

Stuart learned that for Hindu people, forgiveness and an absence of anger were two fundamental principles in coming to terms with being wronged by someone. Other principles were patience, truthfulness, reason, and compassion for all beings. All of those principles, as practised correctly within the family, had empowered them to forgive Stuart, especially since he was also clearly suffering as the result of his wrongdoing. He felt their long-established compassion for him as he sat, fighting back the tears, in their home. It humbled him beyond belief.

Karen's father spoke quietly too, in his own native tongue, and Nengah translated for Stuart. According to one of the principles of Karma, Karen was preordained to die when she did. It had been divinely dictated, that her time on earth was over on that day. In other words, he explained, if Stuart hadn't hit her that day, a different fate would have befallen her. As for the unborn baby, Nengah explained, children go straight to heaven, because they have no karmic debt to pay. He'd hastened to reassure Stuart that Karen's and the baby's deaths were not the end; it was just the beginning of a new cycle of life for them. Nengah had confessed, however, that he'd struggled for more than a year to overcome his grief and anger. 'I strayed from my faith for a short time, and I had to find my way back, but I did.'

'And we would not have wanted your innocent family to suffer too, because of your actions,' Donna had offered. 'We are sorry that you went to prison. You've lost much, yourself, yet you have crossed oceans to us, to offer your contrition and repentance. We value that, and we believe that with all you have done you have now paid your karmic debt, over the death of our daughter. We offer you forgiveness, and our wish is that you can now forgive yourself, and be at peace with everything.'

After leaving the family, Stuart went back to the resort. In the safety of his quiet little villa he allowed his tears to fall openly and unchecked for the very first time. While he'd been in prison, he'd *wanted* to cry, many times, but somehow, even during his sessions with the prison psychologist who was always 'holding him' in a 'safe space,' he'd never been able to find a way to let the floodgates open. But, during his time with Karyn Balik's family, surrendering to his grief had felt raw, and real, and cathartic. It was time to let it out, and finally allow the burden of it to start to lift. He cried and cried that night, until he literally ran out of strength to keep crying.

He spent most of his remaining time in Bali doing simple things. He walked for miles along the beach, swam in the surf, had massages, and took the yoga classes offered at the resort. While he was practising his yoga on the beach one morning, he met a local woman, who didn't speak a word of English, but who still seemed to understand that he was on a journey of healing. With her patient, gentle guidance he learned to meditate by retreating into nature. Either on the beach itself, or in the lush green grounds of the resort that faced the open sea, he meditated twice every day; as he watched the sunrise every morning, and the sunset every night.

He watched the fishermen as they went out in the early morning, and came back mid-afternoon with their catch, and he laughed with real delight as he saw the huge welcome they always got from their wives and excited children who were always waiting for them on the beach. He smiled at the young men on their scooters and small motorbikes, parking up on the rocks to sit and chat, and smoke and laugh together. He was wistful when he witnessed the young courting couples that walked, holding hands, while they watched the sun as it set across the water. They were the simplest, most basic elements of local life, going on all around him, but the uncomplicated daily routines gave him a strange sense of comfort.

In the van, on the way back to the airport, he realised that coming to Bali had been the right decision. He'd found a measure of peace on the island that he knew he would never have achieved if he hadn't come. The 'seismic shift' he'd needed had occurred. Bali was a gentle and spiritual place, and he sensed a profound healing within himself.

The forgiveness of Karen Balik's family had moved him deeply. It had come willingly, from a still-sad but endlessly dignified family, and all he could do now was try to fulfil his promise to them all – and to himself – to be the best person he could ever be, going forward.

Chapter Thirteen

Bali looked fantastic, Meghan thought to herself, as she scrolled once again through the website of the resort where her dad had been staying. He had messaged her from Changi airport, in Singapore, to tell her he was on his way home. As reluctant as she was to admit that she'd actually missed him (because, let's face it, that would be *seriously* uncool), she was looking forward to seeing how different he might be when he got back.

Initially, she'd been pretty pissed off that he was going to a tropical island and leaving her behind (again!), but as Darren had pointed out, it wasn't exactly a holiday. Stuart was in torment and he had to make it stop. Confronting the family of the woman he had killed was not going to be a picnic in the park, even though the meeting happened to be taking place on a tropical island. That bit wasn't his fault, to be fair, but it hadn't stopped her from screaming at him, and slamming the door to her bedroom so hard that one of Nan's pictures had fallen off the wall and the glass had broken. It was a horrible picture anyway, but she still felt bad about breaking it. Nan had been quite gracious about it, which somehow made her feel even worse.

And, according to Darren, now that her dad had seen Karyn Balik's family he would still be doing a lot of soul-searching. Having someone else around who might need his attention might mean he didn't get better properly. He had to get through the horrible fog of guilt and shame by himself, without any distractions, and resolve everything on his own terms.

Meghan got it. She would just have preferred it to be somewhere like Beirut, or Afghanistan, or some other place that nobody (in her opinion) would ever want to go to. The fact that Stuart had gone to confront his demons in a luxurious resort on a tropical island was pretty hard to swallow. She *could* have gone with him, She *could* have just floated around in the resort's beautiful infinity pool for ten days and soaked up a bit of sun, flirted with the handsome young waiters, read a couple of books, and stayed out of his way.

But Darren had 'done a number' on her, as he so often did, and swung her around to his way of thinking. As he'd pointed out, she had to be back in school in Taunton, until the purchase of the stables went through and she and Stuart could move north, and Stuart had promised her she could go on the next cultural trip that was being offered by her *new* school. She thought that had been a bit of a bribe, to make himself feel better, but when she'd said as much to Darren, he'd challenged her.

'Maybe it was, but honestly, if you think about it, does that even matter? Your dad isn't in the habit of manipulating you, and that's not what this is, so don't overthink it. Just take it. You'll be going on a cultural education trip, Meghan! It'll be a lot of fun! Isn't it more important that you've got the chance at all, instead of worrying about *how* you got it?'

She would be starting at the new school soon, and she already knew that they took the students to places like Paris, Amsterdam or Brussels, on cultural trips. Knowing she would be allowed to go without question did soothe the sting a little bit, of being deprived of a tropical holiday.

It was exciting, to think about where she might be going. And Darren was right about Stuart needing the time in Bali, too. The location wasn't the major issue. The *mission* was, and if it really had been in Beirut, or even in a tattered tent in the middle of the Sahara desert, that's where he would have gone. She totally understood her dad's need for time to work through his pain and find a way to live with it, better than he'd done until now.

She so often heard him, pacing at night, in his room. There were nights where he didn't seem to get much sleep at all. Meghan wondered if it was the same for everyone who'd done what he had; killed someone without meaning to, and spent years in mental anguish afterwards.

A lot of people *didn't* feel sorry for what they'd done, and that was hard to imagine. But just as many people thought that prison sentences weren't long enough; that people needed to suffer *more* for their mistakes. It probably never occurred to them that prison was only part of the punishment. She wished some of the ones who howled for the death penalty to come back could see what people like her father went through, even after doing their time.

Some wouldn't care. Others, even if they did know, would still insist that a man who'd killed a woman and her unborn baby didn't deserve a 'tropical holiday.' People could be horrible sometimes. Ignorance made them that way, according to Darren, and the more she thought about it, the more she realised he was right about that too.

It was a beautiful resort, that Stuart had gone to. When she'd simmered down enough to bring herself to look at the website, to see where he was, it had taken her breath away.

She looked longingly at the pictures again now. She could imagine him having his breakfast on the patio under the palm trees right at the edge of the beach. She imagined him waking up in his lovely private cottage, in a four-poster bed with the big mosquito net draped across it, and she imagined him swimming in the pool or sitting cross-legged on the beach, before moving into a 'downward-dog' yoga pose.

Him doing yoga! That was pretty funny. At no stage before now, had Meghan ever considered that her father might start sitting with his arms and legs in stupid positions, or that he might turn into some kind of spiritual weirdo while he was away. Religion changed people. She hoped he wouldn't come back spouting a load of Buddhist or Hindu stuff that she wouldn't understand. But, she supposed, if he was happier he'd be easier to live with and maybe the maddening midnight pacing would stop. That would be *great*. He needed to concentrate on the new business, and if sitting with his legs wrapped backwards around his neck would help him do it, well, who was she to argue?

As long as he doesn't expect me to do the same!

Overall, after having a few weeks to get used to the idea, she was now feeling pretty settled about the decision to move north. She hoped the time would fly. She wasn't looking forward to saying goodbye to Nan, or to Hayden, Elise and Amy, but she was *longing* to see Astro again. She missed her so much it was like a physical ache in her chest, but Debby and Darren were great, sending pictures of her all the time, and even a couple of videos. Meghan had recorded a one-way conversation for Astro, for Darren to play to her from his phone, whenever he could. She didn't want the poor horse to think she'd been abandoned again.

While she and her dad had still been at Teapot Cottage, she'd continued to get to know some of the women in the area. She'd worked a couple of Saturdays with Trudie at her boutique, GladRagz, and she'd got to know some of the local customers. Trudie was always happy to introduce her to people, which was nice, and she'd even said there might be more casual days for her at the boutique whenever the need came up, if she wanted them. She didn't have much in the way of nice clothes for teenage girls in her shop, but one afternoon after she'd closed up, they'd spent a fun hour trying on all kinds of stuff. Trudie had made her laugh, as she'd encouraged her to appreciate herself and the good bits about her body, and demonstrated what colours and style of clothes would look nice on her.

She'd also become a 'regular' at the Friday night youth club, where she'd made firm friends with Jayde, Renae and her boyfriend Jack, and a couple of other girls. She'd also gone to the next coffee morning Adie had put on, at Ravensdown House. All the usual people had been there, plus a couple of new faces, and they all made her welcome again.

Feen had spent a lot of time with her that morning, showing her the workshop she'd set up for her jewellery, and her aromatherapy and herbal work, and giving her a tour of the house. Meeting Gavin had been *amazing*, and he was even more of a hunk in real life! Meghan though he was probably the sexiest man she'd ever seen. She didn't know anyone else who had eyes so green and glittery (except for maybe his mother Carla). She'd been tongue-tied at first, at meeting him, but that hadn't lasted long, because he was so *normal!* He wasn't a big-head, like she imagined so many celebrities were. He just talked to her like she was already a friend, and it had been one of the coolest experiences of her life!

I can't be that much of a loser then, can I, if all those people up there want to be my friend?

Hayden had been particularly envious of Meghan meeting Gavin Raven-Black, because he loved rock music. He'd made Meghan promise to introduce Gavin to him when he came to Carlisle to visit her, which he seemed quite keen to do. Amy also said she would come, and Nan promised to come for Christmas, which would be amazing. Meghan vowed to fill the house from floor to ceiling with Christmas decorations, and a really big tree, and when she'd told Stuart he'd laughed and told her to 'knock herself out.'

At Adie's Ravensdown coffee morning Feen had noticed Meghan's pink flamingo backpack, and had been quite excited about it. She'd confessed that she'd developed a passion for a certain brand of handbag after Carla – her mother-in-law – had given her a special one for her wedding day. Meghan's backpack was the same brand, and they'd laughed about it. Feen had remarked that Meghan was probably not yet ready to be snared by anything as 'horribly afflicting' as a handbag addiction, and she was right, but Meghan *had* been impressed when the little woman had shown off her own collection.

Feen had a green 'Apothecary' backpack, another green 'Botanist' handbag, a really pretty yellow 'Flower Shop' one, an amazing blue retro 'Diner' one, a pink glittery 'Fortune Teller' one, a purple 'Halloween' one, and what she said was the brand's entire range of the most gorgeous 'Shakespeare-themed' bags in different colours. The most wonderful piece in her collection was a little bag that Carla had given her as a wedding gift. It was the shape of a toadstool, and it had little doors that opened, and all kinds of beautiful embellishments. The bags *all* had the most amazing detail and colour schemes, but that one really was gorgeous. She said as much, and Feen had laughed, and said that if Meghan was to have her own wedding, she could 'dorrow it for the bay!'

'I blame my mother-in-law for this particular addiction,' she'd laughed again, as she'd put the bags back into their little pink pouches with the brand's logo on them. 'She has a lot to answer for! It's impossible for me *not* to buy bags that represent who I am and what I do, so well. I just can't say no. But believe me, this is *nothing,* compared with what Carla has herself! Her collection goes back to the very beginning of the brand. She has a whole room in her flat dedicated to them, all on show in custom-built floor-to-ceiling class gabinets.'

Meghan had confessed to Feen that she had no idea what her own preferred dress style was.

'I don't even know what looks nice on me. I just wear the same kind of stuff that everyone else does, because even though I find some of it a bit stupid, I think I'd feel even *more* stupid if I looked too different. Trudie has given me a bit of advice, but I'm still not sure how I want to look.'

'Well, come on, then! Let's have a squick quiz through *my* wardrobe, and you can see if there's anything you like in there! Every woman can develop her own style, and if she knows what looks good, she feels good wearing it. I don't let myself overthink it. I find that if I hink too thard about what to wear, it crives me drazy.'

Feen had a vast wardrobe that ran the full length of her and Gavin's big bedroom. She had a lot of retro-style frocks, which were absolutely stunning, and she wore some of the fuller-skirted ones with big petticoats underneath them. She had an orange one that had pictures of black bats all over it, and it made Meghan laugh. Feen said she always wore it to the pub on Hallowe'en.

She'd held a couple of the dresses against herself to give Meghan the idea of what they looked like. They were beautiful. Meghan had, up until that point, envied Feen for being so petite. But she thought again, after Feen had confessed that being a tiny size six was usually more of a problem than a blessing. Most of what she bought, she still needed to have altered to be even smaller, but luckily her friend Josie was handy with a sewing machine.

'I absolutely *adore* vintage dresses, but despite what you might think, I don't often get good genuine ones,' she explained. 'Many are too damaged in different ways, or the colours are awful on me, or they're simply too big or complicated style-wise to have drastically taken in, and still nook lice, but I buy a lot really good stintage *vyle* ones – new ones – from a company I love, called 'Dolly and Dotty.' I get them in size eight, which is their smallest size, then I get Josie to drop them to a six for me. There are other companies that do them, but this is a brand I just love.'

Feen had gone on to tell her that the 1950's style suited most people, and she'd got Meghan to slip one over her own head. It was a full-skirted frock with blackberries and green leaves all over it, and a purple boat-shaped cowl at the neckline. At a 'whopping' size twelve, she didn't have a hope of getting the tiny frock zipped up, but she'd been able to see the general outline, and it did look amazing.

'See? That looks fabulous on you, doesn't it?'

Feen then showed her another one, with a stiletto shoe print scattered all over it. 'This one, I just love, because I'm a shoe freak, but believe me, with midget feet, that's an eternal struggle too! There's a place in London that specialises in shoes for miny or tassive feet, and I spend far too much money there, but you have to have decent shoes with dresses this nice, don't you? Kids' trainers don't usually do the trick, if I'm going out to dinner or to some glitzy after-gig party!'

Meghan loved the dresses, and how they looked on her. The fitted bodices and the full skirts reminded her of movies she'd seen, where the girls and women all wore that type of frock. She'd always thought they looked amazing, but she'd never considered that style for herself. Now that she'd tried one on, she was captivated by the way it made her look and feel. She decided to take a look at 'Dolly and Dotty's' website herself, and maybe see what they had on sale. Feen said their sales were usually pretty good, but you did have to get in early for the best dresses.

A moment of self-doubt washed over her. Suddenly she felt a bit anxious, like she so often did, at a new opportunity.

'It's not too old for me, is it, that style?'

Feen shook her head. 'Hell no, sweetie! These 'rock and rollers,' as I call them, look great on people of *any* age! You could wear them with ballet flats, or plain sneakers, low heels in 'retro' styles, and maybe graduate to higher heels as you get a bit older, if you wanted to. I'd recommend neutral-coloured shoes that will go with most dresses. You know, black, beige or even baby pink.'

Meghan had been profoundly grateful for Feen's insight and suggestions. The tiny woman had such an amazing sense of style.

It made her wonder if maybe she *should* start going out in clothes she felt happy and comfortable in, and know that she looked *nice* in, instead of stuff she wasn't sure about. The school uniform was a great leveller, but the kids at school could be so judgey and mean. It didn't take much for them to stop being your friend if you even just said or *did* something they thought was stupid or weird. They'd tear you to pieces if they saw you in town somewhere in clothes they thought were uncool. But, since she was uncool anyway, maybe it didn't matter what she wore.

After seeing Feen's gorgeous bags, and looking through her funny wardrobe of eclectic and unusual clothes (a lot of which *were* genuine vintage), Meghan had decided to try and do what Feen had done, and cultivate her own style, instead of trying to look like everybody else all the time. That didn't work so well anyway, because although she had a small handful of friends, most of the kids at her school still hated her or, at least, ignored her like she didn't exist.

She was pretty sure that a lot of the reason she was such a misfit at school was to do with her dad. Once someone at school had found out he'd gone to prison, it hadn't taken long for everyone else to find out. Some of what the kids had said about her and Stuart made her angry. She'd reacted badly and started 'acting out,' as the teachers had called it. That probably didn't help win her any nominations for 'Friend Of the Year,' but Meghan didn't care. Most of the kids that riled her were dumb-asses anyway.

When she and Feen had been talking about clothes and fashion, she'd confided that she felt like a fish out of water at school. Feen had sympathised, and explained that she had felt very much the same, growing up. She was an 'oddball' and she'd always known it. But the difference for her was that she'd never *wanted* to be or look like anybody else, because she knew she'd never pull it off.

'I was *always* going to be a frashing crailure at fitting in. It was never going to happen, so I made up my mind about all sorts of things, including wearing what I wanted.' She knew she'd have a hard time from other kids about most of her choices, she'd explained, but she'd made the conscious decision to let it roll over her.

She was different, and she always *had* been. She'd never fitted in at school either, and had been bullied a lot by kids who were scared of her because they thought she was totally off-the-wall. Meghan knew kids at her own school who were a bit different and were shunned by others because of it, and she suddenly felt a bit sorry for them, especially after Feen had confessed to how lonely she'd been growing up. It wasn't her fault that she was kind of crazy, but she had never pretended *not* to be. Right from the start, she said, she'd always known who she was, and had chosen to just be herself.

'The people who wanted to be in my world were, and the ones who didn't understand, or who neated me like a trutcase, didn't belong in my world anyway, so it wasn't as if I lost anything important.'

It kind of made sense, and Feen seemed happy now, with a gorgeous husband and two really sweet little kids. She made beautiful jewellery for a famous clothing designer, and did her 'witchery' work, as her dad Mark had described it. Everything had worked out for her. She was kind of weird, with her lotions and potions, her 'magic' spells and her funny, 'spoony' way of speaking, where she kept switching the first letters on pairs of words, but she was amazing.

Feen was simply herself. What you saw was what you got, and she didn't care what anyone thought of her. Meghan really admired her for that, and wanted very much to be like that too.

She also loved the fact that her other friends were in awe that she could count Feen and Gavin Raven-Black as her friends! She wondered, if she hung out with them more, if she might meet more famous people. Gavin might introduce her to a rock star one day. Maybe she'd end up marrying one, and being as famous as Feen was. It would be pretty cool to have your photo in Hello! magazine, especially if you had some gorgeous, famous hunk's arm around you. And of course you had to be well-dressed for that, didn't you?

Imagine if they invited me to London to stay with them, and one of Gavin's rock-star friends came over, and we fell in love.

The couple of hours she'd spent with Feen, that morning at Ravensdown, had been one of the most fun times of her life. It had felt like a real bonding event. It had changed the way she saw herself, and she'd felt a bit more confident. She wasn't sure whether that had been Feen's intention, but the little woman always seemed to want to make things better, with everyone she met. She was hilarious with her Spoonerism, and she had this funny, mysterious smile all the time, like nothing would ever surprise her, but she was nice with it. She hadn't looked down on Meghan like she was some stupid kid who didn't know anything. She was older, but somehow that didn't seem to matter. She'd felt like a regular friend, while they'd been laughing and 'ooh-ing and aah-ing' over bags, shoes and dresses!

Everyone up in Torley was nice. She hadn't met anyone yet that she didn't like, although Feen's mother-in-law Carla Walton was a bit of a mystery. She was quite a 'sharp-shooter,' as Nan would probably say, and not the sort of person you'd want to get on the wrong side of. But she made people laugh, because she often took the piss out of herself, and that was something most people wouldn't do. She was sarcastic about other people too, but not in a mean way. She was always rolling her eyes at people, but she nearly always did it with a smile. Meghan had the idea that if Carla liked someone they'd be okay but, if she didn't, they'd know about it.

Now that the decision to move to Carlisle had been made, and the purchase of Beaconsfield Stables was going through, she was keen to get underway with the next phase of her life. She was excited now, and she had a funny feeling that she and her father would do well 'up north.' She would soon be reunited with Astro too, and *nothing* was more important than that.

Chapter Fourteen

Stuart stoked up the log burner in the living room and threw a couple more small logs into it. In the past couple of weeks, the weather had turned significantly colder. Autumn was biting hard now, and winter would soon be up on them. He straightened up, stretched his back, and eyed the kitchen clock with irritation, as its hands drew ever-closer to ten o'clock.

It wasn't like Warwick to be late for work. Eight thirty was the agreed start time, and Stuart had been up, dressed, breakfasted and ready to go from half past seven! He'd tried twice already to ring Warwick, but the calls went straight to voicemail. He supposed that something must've come up, but he was miffed that Warwick hadn't thought to give him the head's up. It was Monday, they'd taken the weekend off, and Stuart was champing at the bit to get restarted. He'd assumed that Warwick would be too.

He'd exchanged contracts on the stables a few weeks earlier, and had been awarded the planning permission for the barn conversion just a few days later. He'd hedged his bets and got the application in very early, even before he'd known for sure that the sale would go through without a hitch, and the timing couldn't have been better. The local council had been super-efficient. It had taken less than three months for the green light to come through.

No time had been wasted on making a good start. Warwick was now staying with his daughter Stephanie, and both men were keen to get the barn finished as soon as possible, so that Warwick could move into it. The abrupt change in the weather was a big tap on the shoulder to remind them there was no time to lose. They were losing the light a little earlier each evening now. They had to press on and throw every available hour at the project.

A truckload of timber had recently been delivered, along with the truly sublime find of enough used, lichen-covered slate tiles to do the entire roof and restore some character to it. They'd come at quite a cost. New tiles, ironically, would have cost a lot less but Stuart's desire to keep the old structure as authentic as possible had won the toss. He told himself, quite a few times, that the quality would be appreciated long after the eye-watering cost had eventually been absorbed and forgotten.

Warwick had already strengthened the barn's foundations and put a damp course through. That in itself had been a full week's work, but it was such a great thing to have ticked off their list. The structural survey had shown no major damage or structural weakness to be addressed, but there was still a massive amount of work to be done and with the go-ahead given, they were going for it, full speed ahead.

Stuart frowned and looked at the clock again. He debated whether to go out by himself and make a start, but wasn't sure what to be getting on with, as he was more or less the builder's labourer on the job, taking direction from Warwick, who knew precisely in what order everything should be done. As frustrating and annoying as it was, there wasn't much he could realistically do but wait.

He decided to brew another pot of coffee, and was just pouring himself a cup when he heard a car draw up at the house. It was Lucy.

Slightly panicked, Stuart forced himself to think. She wasn't meant to be here today, was she? They didn't have any treks booked, did they? They were always closed on Mondays and Tuesdays.

Have I missed something here?

He threw the door open to let Lucy come into the house. She brushed past him with her head down, muttering a faint 'thank you' as she went. It was only after she got into the kitchen and turned to face him that he could see her puffy, red-rimmed eyes. She looked like she'd been crying for a week.

'Lucy! Are you alright? What's happened?' He was instantly alarmed.

Lucy shook her head. She just stared at him, and blurted out, in a flat, lifeless tone; 'Grandad died.'

He gaped at her. *What? Warwick's dead? No! That can't be right! Surely there has to be some mistake?*

'What? I don't understand. What happened? Tell me!' Shocked, Stuart stood speechless, starting at poor Lucy. She sat down heavily at the table and took a deep, shuddering breath.

'Heart attack. They think it happened in his sleep. Mum went to wake him this morning, just before she was due to leave for work. She was concerned he'd be late for work himself. He's normally up really early – well before the rest of us actually – but this morning he wasn't, so she went to get him. She found him dead in bed. He was already cold.'

Stuart suddenly felt chilled to the bone too. 'Oh my God. Lucy, oh, God, I'm so sorry!' Horrified, he watched Lucy's face crumple as she started to cry in earnest.

'He won't be at my wedding now. And I'll never see him, or hug him, ever again.'

'Oh, Lucy! I'm so sorry! So, so sorry, for your loss.'

Stuart was at a complete loss himself, for what else to say. He could hardly believe what he'd heard. He wasn't great with crying women at the best of times, but bereavement was another thing entirely. Having lost his first wife, he understood exactly how bereft Lucy and the rest of Warwick's family must be feeling, but he had no idea what to offer in the way of comfort. A mug of coffee seemed so paltry, but he offered it anyway and she took it gratefully. He vaguely wondered if she'd even had any breakfast this morning. It somehow didn't feel quite appropriate to hug her, so he sat down at the table, picked up her hand, and gently squeezed it.

'It's terrible news Lucy, the absolute worst, and I understand how much you could have done without having to come up here so early after, to let me know, but I'm really glad you did. I appreciate it very much.'

Lucy nodded, sniffing wetly. Stuart tore off a sheet of kitchen roll and handed it to her, and she blew her nose into it.

'It didn't seem right to tell you over the phone. I left as soon as the doctor did, after he'd arranged the ambulance to come and take Grandad from the house. And I wanted to come here anyway, to be honest. It was my first reaction. I just wanted to be where his spirit is, and I think it's still here. It hasn't been long enough for it to have gone anywhere else, really, if that makes sense?'

Stuart nodded. 'It makes *perfect* sense. I get that, totally. Poor Warwick! I really liked him, Lucy, and I'll miss him. He was a good, fair man with a heart of gold, and he adored his family.'

Lucy gave him a watery smile. 'Yeah, he did. He liked you too. He said he was glad it was you he'd sold to. He felt that you'd resurrect Grandma's dream and keep it alive, better than anyone else would. And he was really enjoying working on the barn. He was excited about that, and about moving into it for a while. It was the happiest I'd seen him in years! Lucy sniffed hard.

'He had plans to learn beekeeping! Did he tell you that? This place; his whole life was here. The business was Grandma's dream, not his. He loved this place too, but he wanted something different, something to call his own for the rest of his days. He had everything to look forward to, and he almost got to have it.'

Lucy's voice hitched, and she started to cry again. 'I'm sorry. I don't want to fall apart on you, really I don't, but I wanted to tell you face to face, and it's just really, really hard.'

Stuart found himself struggling with the lump in his throat. Warwick Ford had literally changed his and Meghan's lives, and now he wasn't going to get to realise his *own* dreams. It was only a few weeks since he'd been living right here, in this house, all excited and reassured, with a whole new phase of his life to look forward to. Now it was all gone. Warwick himself was gone, forever. Stuart felt immensely sad.

Lucy cleared her throat. She was still weeping, but was managing to speak again without being overwhelmed. She sniffed again and sighed heavily.

'Stuart, we may have a favour to ask of you. Grandma's ashes were scattered up here on the land, at her request, after she died. Unless Grandad's will stipulates anything different, we'd like to scatter his ashes up here too, if you'd allow us that? Nothing's been decided yet, of course. It's still too soon.

But if he hasn't specified anywhere, that he wants something else, I do think he'd want his ashes to be with Grandma's. What do you think?'

Stuart's own voice was husky with emotion now. He didn't even try to clear his throat.

'Of course, Lucy. Meghan and I, we'd be absolutely *honoured* to have that happen. We can even hold the wake here, if you like. Maybe put a marquee up, in the ring, get the horses out, and have a send-off party for him.'

Lucy nodded and smiled sadly. 'I think he'd love that. It's so kind of you to offer. I'll let Mum know all of that. She's still in shock. My brother Oliver is on his way over, but Mum's only got a neighbour with her, so I'd better be getting back. We've all the arrangements to make, and everything. Say hi to Meghan for me.' She rose to leave, and Stuart opened the door for her.

'I will, I'll let her know what's happened. She'll be devastated too. She was quite fond of Warwick, I think. And Lucy; if you want to, if it helps, you can come up here and spend as much time as you want or need, whenever you want. Your Mum too. This was her home for a long time too, wasn't it? Our place is your place, as the saying goes, whenever you want to use it.'

Lucy nodded miserably, then stopped in her tracks. 'By the way, please do let me continue with the trekking days as planned. I'd really appreciate the chance to keep busy. It might be enough to stop me from going mad with grief. I might have to skip a day, though, depending on when the funeral is, but I guess you'd want to go to that, anyway?'

Stuart nodded. 'Of course, but only if you're sure. We'd close for the day if it clashed, that goes without saying. There's only two small weekend treks booked in at the moment. Meghan and I would have to try and manage them on our own, but I think we could. I only want you here if you really do want to be, of course. Your personal life, and your family; they're a lot more important right now. I can contact the riders and reschedule the dates, quite easily, if my confidence deserts me. They're locals, so they'd understand.'

Lucy shook her head at him briefly. 'I'll be here.'

She mumbled her thanks, and left. He didn't watch her as she got into her car and drove away. Instead, he found himself stumbling back to the kitchen table, sitting abruptly and pouring another cup of coffee. Tears pricked his eyes, and his hands were shaking.

Warwick *dead*? Christ, he was only in his seventies! He was full of life, full of hopes and dreams, great ideas, and so much more! He still had too much to do in the world, and too much more still to offer it, to be so suddenly gone. Once again, the random brutality of life being cut unexpectedly short took Stuart's breath away. He felt crushed. As his own disbelieving silence settled around him, all he could hear was the ticking of the kitchen clock.

He scrambled to collect his scattered thoughts. Warwick's untimely death wasn't just a devastating blow for the poor man's family and friends. It was also a major disruption to the newly acquired stables in the *practical* sense. As much as it pained him to even be thinking about it, the situation had to be confronted. The guide Stuart had been relying on the most, to advise him until he found his own feet in a business he didn't know nearly enough about, was suddenly gone with no warning.

So, what now? How should he proceed from here? Quickly he dialled Darren's number, hoping his friend wouldn't be in surgery. His luck held. Darren answered on the third ring. He was on his way back to the practice after a farm visit. He couldn't believe it either, that Warwick had died.

'Jesus, are you kidding? The poor old sod! He was just about to start enjoying his retirement!'

'I know. I'm shocked out of my head. And I know it's the worst time to even be saying it, but...'

Darren cut in swiftly. 'But it's left you in a pickle, and you have to figure out – pronto – what *you're* going to do.'

'Exactly. It feels so bloody insensitive to even be *talking* about all that right now. The man's dead, Darren. But I really *am* fairly and squarely in the shit right now, and I can't afford to be in limbo for long. I don't have a bank balance to cope with that.'

'It's not insensitive, Stu. Your reality's just done a complete one-eighty. As the saying goes, life goes on, and you have to be practical. Every penny you've got is riding on the success of this new venture. You should grieve for your friend, but you don't have the luxury of taking time to put everything on hold while you do that.'

'Yes. That's it, in a nutshell.'

Darren's quick appraisal of Stuart's new circumstances relieved him. He really did need to get going quickly on alternative plans to go forward, with both the barn and with the stables.

Darren promised to make a few calls over the next couple of days, to his contacts in the area, to see if there were any available sole-trader carpenters and builders who might work for a lower hourly rate than the big firms.

'I'll call Mark Raven too, over at Ravendsown. He's lived here for decades. If anyone knows who's who around these parts, and who might be looking for a chance to use their skills, there's a fair chance it'll be him, or his brother-in-law Bob Shalloe. It's quite a community, as you know. If the locals get their heads together, you never know what they might come up with. I'll swing by after work, too.'

Stuart wanted to tell Meghan about Warwick, but it would have to wait until after school. He sent her a text. *Nothing to worry about, brat, but I'm going to pick you up from school today. Don't get the bus. Wait for me at the school gate.*

OK came the immediate reply. He didn't allow himself to dwell on why his daughter was able to use her mobile phone in what was, presumably, the middle of a lesson. He knew better than to ask.

Meghan would be upset too, to hear Stuart's sad news. She liked Warwick, and he'd helped alongside Lucy to show her what was involved in organising the different equipment for the horses, and how to 'tack them up' properly with their halters, bits, bridles and saddles. He'd also explained a lot to her about hygiene, and about horse behaviour and what some of it means. She'd learned a lot of that already in her studies over the summer while they'd been staying at Teapot Cottage, but it was good for her to have her learning validated by someone as knowledgeable as Warwick, and to see in practical terms what she'd only really learned on paper. Losing Warwick was a big destabiliser for her as well, so soon after moving up here and starting the daunting process of getting settled.

Meghan had slotted quite well, so far, into her new school. She missed her friends back home in Taunton, who'd been understandably surprised and dismayed when they found out she was moving away. There had been a lot of video calling, and sometimes it was upsetting, but other times reassuring. For the most part, her friends though her new life might be pretty cool. She'd already made tentative arrangements to have them up to stay at different times, and Stuart's mother was coming for Christmas, which would help a lot.

Meghan's new school friends sounded nice enough, too. It was GCSE year, and they all seemed to be taking it seriously, which was having a positive influence on her. She was keeping her head above water, balancing school and homework with training Astro (who Darren had relocated to Beaconsfield as soon as they'd moved in) and helping tend to the other horses. She'd also helped out on a couple of Saturdays over in Torley at the GladRagz Boutique, when Trudie Sangster had been left in the lurch by her regular part-timer.

As far as learning the ropes with the stables and the existing horses was concerned, Lucy could still be of real help, going forward, although Stuart wondered how much time she might realistically have, with her uni studies, planning her wedding, and now of course she'd have to grieve for her grandfather and support her Mum through that process as well. It might become too difficult emotionally too, for her to keep coming to the stables, with the ghost of Warwick everywhere she looked.

He had to be prepared for the fact that it might be too much for her now, to be of help to him. He could barely afford to employ her, but he'd have to pay *someone* to guide him, even if it was only for a few weeks. Being thrown in at the deep end wasn't the end of the world, but it was a long way from ideal. Warwick's death amounted to a serious shockwave across Stuart's fledgling business, and he had little choice now but to get up to speed a lot quicker, whichever way he could. The luxury of learning the ropes at a relaxed pace was no longer an option.

He thought back to Debby Davies' idea, which she'd floated in the pre-purchase discussions they all had one night over dinner at Teapot Cottage, about getting a 'Woofer' type of person. Woofers were seasonal workers who gained experience on organic farms in return for food and lodging. He didn't qualify as an organic farm but the basic premise of getting a carpenter who would work in return for food, lodging and free horse riding *might* work. It meant they would have to live in the house, though, and he wasn't sure how appropriate that might be for a teenage daughter to suddenly be sharing a house and a bathroom with some random stranger after every other adjustment she'd had to make lately. That wouldn't be fair at all.

Stuart found himself fretting about it all, but he brought himself up short. *Come on, man! Think! Think laterally. Stop focussing on the obstacle, and find a solution that works.*

Firing up his laptop, he logged onto eBay and looked for caravans for sale. If he could get something nice and comfortable at a price he could manage, it might serve as lodgings for someone who was willing to work, and he would of course cook their meals. It would be more logical to offer something like that, so that Meghan didn't have to deal with a stranger in her new home, as an added stressor.

His budget was utterly miniscule for extras like this, but he reasoned that it was a justifiable expense to get something halfway decent because if he couldn't find anyone to help finish the barn, or if he was faced with paying thousands for the labour to get it kitted out and finished, in line with the current design, he could offer caravan accommodation to stable guests instead. That could still add value to people's horse-riding experience and provide some extra income to the business.

His head was crammed with questions and different alternatives, but one thing he knew for certain was that he wanted to finish the barn. The house needed a lot of work doing to it as well, but they could keep living in it the way it was until the spring. It wasn't uncomfortable, just a little old fashioned and scruffy.

This far into autumn, there were some fairly decent caravans on offer at reasonable prices. It was reassuring to know that he could have that as an option, after checking with the local authority to establish that he could indeed allow someone to stay in it on a temporary basis, who was working on construction. He put a 'watch' on a few nice ones, while he continued to mull things over.

He went for a walk around the property, to get some much-needed fresh air, and to simply connect with nature, as if Warwick's spirit might be out there. He found himself talking out loud to his dead friend.

'I can't believe you're gone, Warwick! I can't believe I won't see you again. I know you're with Susan now, and that must be brilliant, but you'll be so missed here! What are we all going to do without you?'

The lump in his throat was huge. He didn't even try to force back the tears when they came. The old horse Finnegan came ambling up to him and whinnied at him softly. Stuart reached up and softly stroked his velvety nose.

'Well, don't worry, Warwick. I'll make this place work again, like it did before. I'll finish everything, I promise, one way or another. If it's the last thing I do, I'll make you and Susan proud.'

Stuart got himself back under control, and headed back to the house. He sat at the dining table and drew up several lists of what he needed to do and get for the barn. The first instruction to himself was to draw up a list of what building materials would still be needed for the barn to be completed, but he wasn't confident.

Building materials had been Warwick's domain. They'd already discussed it all, and Stuart knew Warwick had already started a very comprehensive notebook with various details about what was needed. Now wasn't the time to worry Lucy or her mother about that notebook, but he'd need to get hold of it soon, since he didn't have the faintest idea himself of what would be needed. Warwick had known all of it, right down to the size of the nails they needed for certain jobs.

Maybe Darren could swing by and pick it up, on his way up here later, if Warwick's daughter Stephanie didn't mind. Under the circumstances it seemed spectacularly insensitive to even be asking but, as Darren had said, certain things had to carry on, especially where large sums of money were involved. He just had to hope that Stephanie and Lucy would understand, and forgive him for his unintended but necessary crassness.

Everything Stuart could think of, from taps to curtains, went onto his lists. He even went as far as jotting down what needed to go into the cupboards for guests to use. Surprisingly, it was quite a cathartic and enormously helpful process, and by the time he was due to go and pick Meghan up from school he felt he had most considerations covered.

As he got into his car, to go and collect Meghan, he braced himself for the unhappy job of telling her that one of their new friends – a really critical one – had unexpectedly upped and died.

Breaking news like that was simply a matter of saying it, as gently as possible, and letting it sink in. He knew that, but as Meghan opened the passenger door, and said, 'Hi, Dad' so cheerfully, he felt the weight of his task very keenly.

'Can we give my friend Renae a ride home?'

Stuart shook his head. 'Not today. Sorry sweetheart. We need to talk. She'll have to get the bus.'

He could see the school bus arriving just ahead of him on the other side of the street, to pick up the babbling gaggle of kids who were waiting. A hard flash of annoyance crossed Meghan's face and she turned to shrug expressively at her friend. Poor Renae just nodded, smiled, and turned away to go and catch the bus.

'Rude! How hard would it have been to have just taken her home? It's on our way! For God's sake, Dad! That was so embarrassing! Why bother to come and pick me up if you couldn't pick Renae up too? You do know that we have to drive past her house to get home, right?'

Meghan's face was mutinous. Stuart had embarrassed her in front of her friend, and he appreciated that, but he wasn't in the mood for histrionics, and he told her so.

'Pull your head in, kiddo, and get in the bloody car. The world doesn't revolve around you and your friends,' he said shortly, and then sucked his breath in and braced himself as

Meghan threw herself onto the passenger seat and slammed the car door in protest. She heaved a heavy sigh, but he didn't rise to the bait. Instead, he continued to look forward, out through the car's windscreen.

'Warwick died. Last night, in his sleep. I found out this morning and I wanted to pick you up so I could tell you, and I thought maybe we could go for a pizza or something while you wrap your head around it, because it's horrible news, and I'm struggling with it myself. Obviously, it wouldn't have been appropriate for Renae to be in the car for this.'

Meghan gaped at him, all thoughts of her friend forgotten. 'What? *Warwick* died? *Our* Warwick?'

'Yes, our Warwick. They think it was a heart attack.'

Tears sprang to Meghan's eyes. 'No way! No! I don't believe that. Are you sure? Sure it was him, I mean? That's so horrible. Poor Warwick. And poor Lucy! She was really close to him. How did you find out? Did someone call you?'

Stuart went on to explain that Lucy had come to the stables to let him know.

'Would you like to go for a pizza? I didn't feel like anything at lunchtime, and now I'm starving. All I've had since breakfast is coffee, while I tried to get my head around this, and I've probably had far too much of that, and not enough food.'

He suspected that the jittery, unfocussed feeling he was experiencing might be down to the three pots of coffee he'd drunk during the morning, on the back of the devastating news. He glanced over at his daughter who was sitting looking straight ahead, with a deep furrow in her forehead. She was, like him, struggling to make sense of such an unexpected development.

'I really liked Warwick, Dad. He was a kind old man, and he was so excited about working on the barn with you. I guess that won't be getting done now, will it? And what about the stables?'

Stuart tried to reassure her, as best he could, that it would be business as usual. They parked up at the Pizza Hut restaurant, and were quickly shown to a table. After they placed their orders, he continued.

'I have to find a carpenter, but if I can't get someone affordable locally I'll have to look elsewhere.'

He told Meghan about the idea of trying to get someone who would work for food and rent. She didn't seem very enthusiastic about the idea of a new person on site, but as Stuart pointed out, he had no chance of doing it by himself and the barn needed to be finished before the coming winter, which didn't leave a lot of time.

As she chewed her food, thoughtfully, Meghan suggested that it might negate the need for a caravan if they could find a female carpenter.

'I wouldn't have a problem sharing the house with another woman, if she was nice.' Stuart looked at her, baffled, but she just shrugged, sighed theatrically, and rolled her eyes. She rolled them at him so often, he was surprised they ever stayed where they were supposed to, in her head.

'Female carpenters are out there, Dad. Women are doing all kinds of so-called 'male-dominated' jobs these days.' She held up her fingers in quotation marks.

'Some of them are even running their own all-female companies like window cleaning, fixing cars, and stuff. We're all being encouraged to go for whatever we want to do. Gender doesn't even come into it anymore.'

She heaved a heavy sigh of exasperation. 'Look, you need to wise up, Dad. You guys don't get to have sole charge of the big-pants jobs anymore. It's the 21st century! Women are taking over. Engineers, builders, fighter pilots, HGV truckers, surgeons, you name it. They're all out there. Women are smashing men to bits in the big jobs. You worked with female lawyers, and barristers, didn't you? So what's so bizarre about getting a female builder?' She arched her eyebrows at him, in a demanding expression.

Stuart held up his hands in mock surrender. There was certainly a lot of sense in Meghan's logic, and he did appreciate that it was no longer a man's world when it came to the disciplines that had traditionally always been more gender specific when he'd been growing up. He didn't have a problem with any of it, but he wasn't entirely sure they could get someone at *all*, let alone a woman, and he said so.

Meghan just shrugged at him again. 'Well, you won't know if you don't look, will you? By the way, should we get a card of something, for Lucy and her family? A sympathy card? And maybe some flowers, or a wreath, or something?'

'Yeah, that's a good idea, a card at least. I've offered to let them have the wake, you know, the party after the funeral, up at the stables.'

Meghan frowned. 'It seems weird to have a party when someone dies, don't you think? I mean, I know it's meant to be a celebration of their life and everything, but wouldn't you really just be too sad to enjoy yourself? Wouldn't it be a bit like going through the motions, or something? I think it seems... I dunno, kind of *inappropriate*? Disrespectful?'

Stuart shook his head. 'No, it's actually quite the opposite. You'd be surprised. I've been to a few wakes, and they're nearly always very happy affairs. It's a kind of closure, a kind of reminder at the end of a tough time of grieving, to be thankful that you had them in your life.'

'I suppose so.' Meghan didn't seem entirely convinced, but Stuart wondered if maybe she would be more so after Warwick's wake, wherever it was held. She'd been too little to remember much about when her mother died, and she hadn't lost anyone else, apart from her grandfather, whose funeral had been a bit dry, even for the adults who'd gone to it. It wasn't surprising that the various functions of a funeral process escaped her.

Back at the house, Meghan went straight outside to spend some time with Astro. The horse would no doubt help her get her head together about Warwick. Stuart thought she'd taken the news about his death surprisingly well. It was sad, of course, but in Meghan's egocentric young world it would really only amount to a blip on the landscape. He just hoped he could shield her from whatever hardships might ensue, financial or otherwise, as a result of it. Their future suddenly seem a lot less straightforward, in the short-term at least, than it had just twenty-four hours earlier.

Stuart sat down at his laptop again. This time he Googled 'female carpenters.' To his surprise, there were quite a few listings, with one company in particular advertising an all-trade, all-female workforce.

He checked his watch. It was after five thirty and he doubted whether anyone would answer the phone, but he rang the number anyway, figuring he could at least leave a message for someone to ring him back tomorrow. He wasn't expecting the bright, cheerful voice that answered his call on the fourth ring.

'Sisters In The Trades, this Kelly, how may I help you?'

'Oh! Hi. Sorry, I didn't realise you'd still be there. I was planning on just leaving a message.'

'No, the office is manned until six. How can I help?'

Stuart cleared his throat, briefly outlined his circumstances, and then went on to discuss his specific requirements. Kelly listened intently, asking relevant questions about the location and scale of the job, his budget and timeframe, and other pertinent information. When he'd finished explaining, she sounded regretful.

'Well, I don't want to pour cold water on your ideas, but I do have to say, right off the bat, that the nearest female carpenter to you on our books lives a hundred miles away, in Edinburgh! That's not very commutable, and most of our staff like to go home at night!' She gave a short laugh.

'I have to be honest, Mr Thomson. I don't think I can help you with someone who might want to come and stay onsite. Can I ask you why you're keen to have a woman, rather than a man?'

Stuart explained to her about Meghan, and how much upheaval she'd already had. 'She's at a funny age too, and I just don't want her to have to deal with having a strange guy in the house, after everything she's already had to get her head around. She could cope with having a woman around here, I think, but putting up with a man might be a bit too much to ask of her, right now.'

He then went on to tell Kelly a bit more detail about the plans he'd had with his friend who had unexpectedly died, and the position it had left him in. He also explained his initial idea of trying to find someone who would come and work in exchange for board. He admitted that his budget was tight, but he could run to a caravan to offer to someone who was prepared to come and stay on site.

At that point he'd given up thinking Kelly or her company could be of any help but, as he confessed, he just wanted to float the idea out loud, with someone who might just be qualified enough to tell him if it was a workable idea or an idealistic and stupid one.

Kelly wasn't immediately dismissive, as he'd feared.

'Well, I think maybe it *could* work. The first problem is that most tradespeople – and that includes carpenters – are already busy and booked up well in advance. Your chances of getting someone decent to come and complete your job before winter might be pretty slim.

'You have to get the roof on, that's the really important thing. Get the building watertight and then if you have to wait until spring, you might get someone to do it then, if you book them now.' The line went quiet for a minute. Stuart wondered if Kelly was even still there. Eventually she cleared her throat and spoke again.

'Actually, I have an idea. I can't tell you what it is right away, but let me make a phone call and I'll ring you back.'

She took Stuart's number and rang off. He looked at the phone, confused. Kelly had rung off quite abruptly. Had he said something to put her off? She said she was going to make a call. Maybe she had an idea that could help him. Or maybe it was just her way of getting rid of him quickly. Maybe she thought he was a bit dodgy, and she wouldn't ring back at all. A deep sense of defeat suddenly washed over him like a tidal wave. Maybe it was all going to prove to be hopeless.

Kelly didn't call him back for almost twenty minutes, but when she did, she had a proposal for him that left him virtually speechless.

One of her employees, who was a carpenter by trade, had taken an indefinite leave of absence from her job. In the course of conversation, it transpired that this woman, who was thirty-eight years old, had been in an abusive relationship for almost four years, and had finally found the courage to leave her husband. It was a messy business that had gone to court, and her husband was almost certainly going to prison, but was currently out on bail. The woman had left the relationship with nothing but a mass of bruises and broken bones, and she was still trying to work a lot of things out for her future.

Her ex was awaiting trial, and she was lying pretty low, because he'd flouted his restraining order a couple of times and was continuing to harass her whenever he could find out where she was. She'd been living in a refuge for a long time but Kelly thought she could perhaps use an out-of-the-way place like Stuart's as a bit of a bolt-hole while she got her longer-term plans together. Kelly stressed most emphatically that this was purely an idea, that the woman in question, who she called Yvonne, would need to know a lot more about Stuart and about the situation he was in, but Kelly had already spoken to her, and Yvonne had apparently expressed an initial, tentative interest.

Kelly went on to say that the caravan idea would be more appropriate for Yvonne than staying in the house with a man she didn't know.

'She's not afraid of men, let's make that clear. She just has big trust issues, as you might expect, and she really needs a private space to call her own. It wouldn't be appropriate to put her in a house with a male stranger, and I'm sure you understand the vulnerability there, as you mentioned yourself that you wouldn't want the same for your daughter.'

Kelly added that Yvonne's work was exemplary, the agency had several references from happy clients, and Yvonne might just be the ideal candidate, being able to come and stay for the duration, and commit fully to the work.

'This would fall outside of SITT's jurisdiction. It would be an arrangement purely between the two of you. And I do think you'd have to pay her something, even just as pocket money. She has nothing. She left home with nothing but her dog and the shirt on her back. Rebuilding her independence would have to include budgeting even a nominal amount of money she could call her own again.

'So, as a first reaction, what do you think? And you need to think about the dog too, because that would be a deal breaker. If she couldn't bring her dog, she wouldn't come. End of story. I know that for a fact.'

Stuart suddenly had a lot of questions. Was Yvonne physically capable of undertaking the work? A lot of it was heavy, and while he could certainly do the bulk of the lifting himself, he needed to know that any carpenter, male or female, would be robust enough to do what amounted to labouring work with heavy timber, and concrete, bricks and slate tiles too.

He also wanted to know if there was any likelihood that the woman would want to go back to her ex, and whether she would be committed enough to keep her whereabouts a secret for Stuart, Meghan and the horses' safety. The last thing he wanted was for some violent bloke to show up here, shouting the odds and threatening God-knows what.

Kelly assured him that Yvonne was time-served and competent, and that what she lacked in brute strength, she more than made up for in speed, attention to detail and practical approaches to what needed to be done.

'She was one of my best chippies until she had to leave. As far as I'm concerned she's still one of my staff. Her job will be waiting for her whenever she wants to come back, and as long as they can send her scumbag husband away for a decent stretch, she's got every chance. As for going back to him? She's come too far for that. She wants a fresh start, and she wouldn't jeopardise that.'

Stuart decided it was worth at least a telephone chat with Yvonne, and he said as much to Kelly, who said she would give Yvonne his number, so that she could make an anonymous call to him. He agreed to let that happen, and as they finished the conversation, Darren's Land Rover pulled into the yard. It was perfect timing.

Darren gave him a quick man-hug. 'Sorry I'm a bit late. I was over at Poplar Farm, up on Navigation Way. It's a goats milk and cheese business they've got going up there. Anyway, one of the goats had got out onto the road and was hit by a car. Not a good outcome, but that's how it goes sometimes, poor little sod. How are you doing?'

Stuart reached into the fridge, pulled out a can of beer and waved it at Darren, who nodded. 'Yep, go on then, I could use one right now, and maybe you could too?'

'Yeah. Some days really are enough to drive you to drink. I'll have a rare can too, just to raise a glass to poor old Warwick, God rest him.'

'Here's to Warwick!' Darren tore the tab off his can and raised it.

'So, where've you got to, with making alternative arrangements? Anywhere, or nowhere? I have to confess I've drawn a bit of a blank. I've made a few calls, asked around the people I know up here, but everyone I talked to, the story's the bloody same. They're all jammed solid with work, some until the end of next summer! Bob Shalloe, over at Bracefields Farm is going to ask further afield. He knows a lot of people. Word of mouth might unearth something.'

Stuart gestured for Darren to sit.

'Well, there's been a bit of a development, as it happens. I'm not sure if it'll fly, but maybe.'

He went on to tell Darren about the conversation he'd had with Kelly from Sisters In The Trades.

'It was Meghan who floated the idea of a female builder, so I did a bit of digging, and this was the result. Same deal, everyone's rammed, and they haven't got anyone within a hundred miles who could come, even if they did have time. Most have families they want to go home to at night, and that's fair enough.'

Darren pulled an easy-osey face at Stuart. 'But this woman; the one you've just told me about? She might be just what you need. You've got an ideal set up here, for anyone who doesn't want to be found for a while. And if she's competent, she could be a real help to you. In the absence of any other timely alternatives, that might offer a way forward, I mean. The last think you need is to get desperate and end up with some cowboy builder who'd do more harm than good around here.'

'Do I really want a traumatized woman around the place, though? What impact might that have on Meghan?'

Darren considered this for a moment, and the shrugged. 'It's a fair question of course, but Stu, I reckon you just have to hear her out. Give her a chance to at least give you an impression. Until you do, it's just all thoughts in your head, and they can be as good or as bad as you want them to be, but either way it doesn't give her – or you – a decent chance to make an informed choice, does it?'

'I just can't afford to make a big mistake, mate, financially or otherwise.'

'I know.' Darren drained his beer, pulled another face, and looked contemplatively at Stuart. 'But it can't hurt to hear this woman out, can it? And you know your gut well enough to trust it. If alarm bells are ringing, listen to them. You know how to read people, and you know how to ask the right questions to complete your picture. You used to do it for a living. If she's likely to be a nightmare, it won't take you long to suss that out. But, if she's not, this might be a way forward for you.'

He stood to go. As he headed towards the door Meghan came barrelling through it.

'Hi, Darren! I just saw your Land Rover. Dad, you should have told me Darren was here.' Her voice was reproachful. She turned to him. 'Warwick died, did Dad tell you? Bismillah,' she added, half under her breath.

'Yeah. It's why I'm here, to check on you both. Poor Warwick. It's really sad, isn't it? He was one of the good guys. Anyway, I'll be over again at the weekend, so I'll see you both then? Give me a ring if you have any other ideas, and I'll do the same. Catch you later.'

He saw himself out, and as he did so, Stuart pulled out a chair for Meghan. 'I'm glad you're here. I want to run an idea by you.'

*　　*　　*　　*　　*

The call on Stuart's mobile came up as 'number withheld.'

'Hello, is that Stuart? This is Yvonne. From S.I.T.T. Sisters In The Trades?'

'Oh, hi Yvonne, thanks for calling. I've been looking forward to having a chat with you.'

'Kelly said you might have a position that could work for me, in my current circumstances?' She had a soft Birmingham accent, and her voice was gentle and very measured. Her lack of confidence was palpable, even over the phone.

'Yeah, maybe. I have a proposition that could potentially be of benefit to both of us. But how do you want to do this? Do you want to tell me about yourself first, or ask me about myself first? We can go with whichever way feels most comfortable for you.'

Yvonne took a deep breath and started filling him in on her situation, after ascertaining that Kelly had told him very little.

'They think he'll go to jail for long time, because his previous girlfriend has now come forward too, to testify about his violent behaviour. It's going to help a lot, but the trial isn't for at least a couple more months yet, and he's out on bail. I need to get out of town for a while, because I'm sick of having to look over my shoulder every time I go anywhere. Restraining orders don't mean much to him.'

Yvonne went on to explain that she wanted to leave the refuge she was staying in, but needed to go somewhere her ex wouldn't think to look for her.

'I'm worried he'll find me wherever I go, around here.' Her voice went quieter.

'It's making me a nervous wreck. I'm not sleeping properly and I don't know what to do with myself. Everywhere I could go next, after I leave the refuge, he already knows about. Being where he wouldn't think to look, and having a project to get my teeth into, until all of this gets resolved, well, it might just stop me from going completely crazy.'

'Would you ever go back? If he asked you, and promised to change, would you go back?' Stuart had to ask. 'I know it's really none of my business, but I have a teenage daughter who's been through a lot, and she doesn't need any more upheaval.'

Yvonne chuckled lightly. 'It's a fair question, under the circumstances, and I'm happy to answer it. No, I wouldn't go back. For the first few months, I did consider it, I can't lie. I was pretty fragile back then, and I believed him when he said I wasn't worth anything, that nobody else would ever want me, or my skills. He always convinced me to go back, in the past, because I had nowhere else to go, where I or the people I was with could be safe.'

She took a deep breath. 'But it's been almost a year now, and I've managed to move on a lot. I'd never go back now, in a *million* years. I've been in the refuge for long enough to learn a lot about myself, and him, and what my life *could* look like. They're helping me a lot. So is Kelly, by keeping me on and continuing to offer me work,' she added. 'But I can't stay in town, so that limits my options. So, tell me about this opportunity. Tell me what I need to know.'

Stuart filled her in about the current situation and the terms under which Warwick Ford had intended to support him with the stables, and explained that Warwick had unexpectedly died. He told her about the caravan he could make available, and the fact that there were horses on site that would always provide solid, non-human company if required. He also added that her dog would be welcome, as long as it didn't worry the horses. Yvonne reassured him that it wouldn't.

She told him that she preferred to spend her leisure time by herself, that she didn't want male company, and that she loved carpentry work. She told him that she loved gardening and animals too, and preferred them to people, and she was honest enough to admit that she slept with a knife under her pillow. She also confessed that she expected to be in counselling for at least another year, but she could carry on with that by phone.

The conversation lasted for a good half-hour, after which they planned to meet at the weekend in a cafe in Preston, which was roughly a halfway point for them both.

As he finally rang off the call, Stuart felt hopeful. He took as many photos and videos of the stables, house, barn and land as he could, to show to Yvonne, so she could make a more informed choice, and he also captured the images of a couple of the caravans he was watching, to show her as well, to see if either of them would be to her liking. As Saturday rolled around, and he and Meghan set off to meet her, Stuart found himself praying that they would all like one another, and that a way forward might be possible, for the barn.

Chapter Fifteen

The woman they met was a complete surprise to Meghan. She'd been expecting Yvonne to be heavy-set and less than attractive, but on entering the cafe she had to laugh at her own preconceived notions about what a female builder might look like!

Yvonne was no thick-necked wrestler with bulging muscles and a crew cut. She was very pretty; tall and slim, with a curly, jaw-length mop of very dark brown hair, that framed her lightly freckled face. Her brown eyes were warm, if slightly wary, and her mouth was generous, even if her smile was less so. She had beautiful teeth, and her gorgeous, coffee-coloured skin had a satiny sheen to it. She shook Meghan's hand strongly, which gave a hint of her carpentry capabilities, and as she sat back down and started pouring tea from a pot into three waiting cups, the muscles in her hands were clearly evident. Her nails were short, clean and well-kept. Competent, capable hands, Meghan decided.

After the introductions and pleasantries were dispensed with, Yvonne and Stuart had a good talk about the barn itself, what needed to be done, and the expectations and promises around the job. He showed her the different photos and videos he'd taken, to give her a better idea of what was needed and she seemed confident that it wasn't going to be outside her remit. It sounded as though she was quite keen to give it a go, but Meghan knew that her father hadn't yet told her about his own history, about the accident and prison and everything. She knew that he was planning to do so now, at this meeting. Her heart was in her mouth as his words came.

'Yvonne, before you make a decision, there's some stuff I need to tell you that I haven't mentioned before. I wanted to wait until we were face to face, because I wanted you to get an idea of me – of *us*,' he gestured towards Meghan, 'before you made a decision based on what I'm about to tell you.'

Yvonne looked instantly wary.

Stuart took a deep breath. He talked briefly about the loss of Meghan's mother, and his second wife, and then launched into the whole sorry story about his accident, his time in prison, the loss of his previous career. He ended by telling Yvonne about the abrupt and devastating loss of Warwick Ford, and how much of a tailspin it had thrown them into at the newly acquired stables, off the back of everything else. He didn't need to spell out, at the end of all that, how radically his and Meghan's lives had been changed by everything that had happened. It all spoke for itself.

Throughout, Yvonne sat listening but completely devoid of expression. As Stuart's story finally came to an end and he ran out of steam, she still sat there saying nothing. Stuart, for his part, had nowhere else to take the tale, and an awkward silence hung over the table. Meghan leaned forward, desperate to break it.

'Yvonne, we can't pretend to be something we're not. Just like you, we've had our lives upended, and had to rebuild them, and it's been really, really tough. But Dad's a good man. He made a stupid, deadly mistake, but he's paid for it with almost everything he had, and he's trying to rebuild our lives, and he can help you rebuild yours too, if you let him. And you can help us. Maybe we can *all* get on our feet again by helping each other.'

Even to her own ears, it sounded cheesy, and too much like an over-simplification of what might be too big a deal for Yvonne to get her head around. While most people understood Stuart's circumstances and didn't condemn him for his actions from more than half a decade ago, not everyone was so accepting. How would a woman who'd been horribly abused by a monster of a man reconcile the actions of another who'd robbed a different woman of her and her unborn baby's lives, through his own selfish actions?

Yvonne blinked several times, then looked first at Meghan and then at her Dad. 'Well, that's quite a story, and a lot to admit. I guess you have your demons?'

Stuart gave her a tight-lipped smile. 'Like you wouldn't believe. There isn't a day that goes by that I don't regret the accident. There never will be. But I have done a lot of work on myself to come to terms with it all, including meeting face to face with the dead woman's family. I just want to make a better life, especially for Meghan. None of what happened was her fault.'

He went on to describe how lost he'd been, over how to move forward in life, even at the point of release from prison, and how the chance encounter with Warwick Ford had shown him what his and Meghan's future could look like.

'So I grabbed the opportunity with both hands. Before that happened, I'd felt so dead, so defeated, inside. I really didn't see myself ever looking forward to anything, ever again, but then this opportunity came up. It's my second chance, but now that Warwick's just up and died on me, it's thrown such a big spanner in the works, I don't know whether I'm coming or going anymore! I need real help, and even admitting that is really difficult.'

Yvonne nodded slowly. 'I know what it's like to feel defeated. And how hard it is, to ask for help. It took me *years* to work up the courage. I made a big mistake myself, getting involved with my ex in the first place. I was not in a good situation when I met him. My self-esteem was on the floor, at that point. I was vulnerable, needing validation as a woman, I suppose, and then I met my husband. It was all lovely at first, but everything changed as soon as the honeymoon was over. I hadn't seen that coming at *all*. The terrible meanness in him.

'It was probably always there, but I just didn't see it, and even when I started to, I stayed, because part of me still thought I didn't deserve anything better than the kind of man he was. By the time I realised how wrong I was about that, I was trapped, and I didn't know how to get out. Not for ages. So I know what it's like to hate yourself.'

'The difference between you and me was that I made conscious choices that ended in tragedy for someone else.'

Yvonne smiled softly at Stuart. 'But it wasn't just a tragedy for her and her family, was it? It was a tragedy for yours too.'

Meghan suddenly found herself weeping. She was horrified, and tried to stop, but the silent tears just kept coming. 'Oh, God! I'm so sorry. I don't mean to cry, really I don't!'

Yvonne handed her one of the paper napkins that had come with the pot of tea, and touched her hand lightly.

'It's okay, Meghan. You're still healing. I understand that. I'll probably still be crying for years myself, if I'm honest. They're big wounds to recover from, aren't they? And it's surprising, what can set us off. Sometimes a random thing can happen, something that isn't even really connected, like a song or a memory, and it'll have me in a heap. Why would you be any different? Looking back doesn't always hurt but sometimes it just unexpectedly does. All part of the process, I guess.' She shrugged helplessly at Meghan and Stuart.

Meghan managed to recover herself a little but her face still flamed with embarrassment. What a cringe!

'Thanks, Yvonne, for getting it. Most times I'm fine, but you're right, weird things happen, and off I go, having to pull myself back together again. But I'm really proud of my Dad, for how *he's* started pulling things back together. I hate what he did, but there's so much more to us than our mistakes. We just need the chance to prove it.' Meghan was getting a better hold of herself, now.

Keep focussing on the positives.

She looked down as Stuart grabbed her hand and gave it a squeeze. She squeezed back, and suddenly she realised that if this woman, this Yvonne, didn't want to be a part of their lives, of rebuilding the barn and helping them get back on their feet, it didn't matter. If she didn't want to help, there would be someone else who would. It was just a case of finding them. They didn't need anyone in their lives who didn't want to be there. She felt the need to say that, so she did.

'This isn't an ambush. If you don't want to come, that's cool. Really, it is. If we're all not right for each other, that's the way it is. We have to be right for each other, or this wouldn't work, would it? So it's better to figure that out now, than for us to have someone come and then go again because they decide they don't *really* want to be in our lives.'

Yvonne stared at her, and she felt her stomach drop a little.

Oh fuck. Poor Dad. I think I've blown it.

'Wow. Well, gosh, Meghan! That's quite a big statement!' Yvonne sounded astonished. Meghan stuck to her guns, though.

'Don't get me wrong. We'd love to have you, wouldn't we, Dad?' She looked enquiringly at her father, who simply nodded and started into his cup. 'But only if you want to come! It's all too big a deal. It's too important to mess about with, for any of us. We've all been through enough.'

She watched Stuart put his elbows on the table and drop his head into his hands. He sighed heavily and rubbed his eyes. All of a sudden he looked exhausted. But he backed her up.

'Meghan's right, Yvonne. We're here in front of you, warts and all, and we haven't left anything out of our story. It's totally fine if you'd rather not take this up. There'd be no hard feelings, please believe that. But whoever comes to help us has to be on the same page, with no resentment or distaste.'

Yvonne put her own elbows on the table. Meghan stifled a grin.

Nan would have a fit if she could see us all! She's such a stickler for table manners!

Yvonne looked levelly at Stuart. 'I'm not judging. And I'm not saying no, because I can see how important this is, and I can't deny it would help me a lot too. But I need bit of time, to think about everything.' It was clear that she was choosing her words very carefully.

'Your accident, it shouldn't matter. I know that. And it probably doesn't. But you've only just laid this on me, and I have to make sure I really *do* feel that way, before I can make a commitment to coming and living on your land, and working with you. I made a false error of judgement once before, remember, and that nearly cost me my life. I just can't make any more mistakes that put me back in a horrible headspace I've had to fight like hell to get out of.'

Meghan understood. She nodded at Yvonne, and so did Stuart. They waited for her to speak again.

'I don't expect to be long in making a decision. But I want some time to think about it. Is it ok if I take tomorrow, and let you know by Monday morning?'

As they all left the cafe, Yvonne shook their hands again. 'Thank you for being so honest. That in itself means a lot. You're both brave, and smart, and even if this proposal goes nowhere, I hope you make a good go of things, and I'm sure you will. You don't give up easily, and I like that. I'll be in touch.'

On the drive back to Carlisle, they didn't talk much. Stuart was deep in thought and it unsettled Meghan.

'Dad, I'm sorry if I scared her away; if I've blown this for you. Truly. I didn't want that, of all things! I just felt like I had to tell her it wasn't going to be the end of the world for us, if she didn't want to come. I guess I didn't want her to think she was our only option, even if she is. If people think you're desperate, they end up with all the power over you, you know?'

'Sweetheart, I do know, and it's fine. But you probably did her a favour too, in letting her know that. Would *you* want to be under pressure to say yes to something if you didn't really want to? I think she's been through enough, and I think this has to be less about not giving someone power, and more about being kind to them when they need it.

'I actually thought it was very mature of you, to say what you did, especially to say that we weren't trying to ambush her, by waiting until we met, before telling her about some of the past. That showed good insight, brat! I'm proud of you for that.'

'What will we do if she doesn't want to come?'

'She'll come if it's meant to be, Meggie. If she doesn't, it *wasn't* meant to be, and we'll figure something else out. There'll be another solution. As Darren would say, 'nobody will die.'

On Monday morning, as Meghan was heading out the door to catch the bus to school, Stuart's mobile rang. There on the kitchen table, she could see it was a 'number withheld' call.

Instinctively, she knew it was Yvonne. She stopped and put down her school bag. Her father grabbed the phone and took the call. Meghan watched him closely, for any signs that would reveal what Yvonne had decided. He looked up at her, pointed at the clock on the wall, and glared at her.

She ignored him. Go catch the bus to school? No chance! This was too important to miss. Stuart's face was inscrutable as he listened to his phone. Meghan started to fidget. It was becoming unbearable. She was desperate to know what the woman had decided. Would she come, or not?

Stuart turned his back on Meghan and walked into the garden, which irritated her intensely. What was so secret about this conversation that she couldn't be allowed to hear it? Her father's face continued to offer no clue as to what decisions were being made. Meghan felt like screaming. Eventually he ended the call and came back into the kitchen.

'Well? Dad? *What?* What did she say?'

'She's agreed to come and work with us. She arrives next Sunday afternoon, which gives me precisely one week to buy and get delivered a decent caravan for her to live in. And she is bringing her dog with her. That was the deal-breaker, and since you've clearly now missed the bloody bus, I'm going to have to run you to school.'

He sounded unmistakably cross, but he softened his criticism with a smile, as Meghan broke into a happy-dance and said 'Yay!' He was happy again. If Yvonne was a good enough carpenter, his plan to finish the barn before winter was totally on again. What a rollercoaster of a week it had been, since Warwick died.

'That's great. Do I *have* to go to school today? Can't I just help you instead, to look for caravans and stuff? Maybe tell the school I've got period cramps or something?'

'Nice try, brat, but no. Finding a caravan is something I can do on my own, and you have exams to prepare for, in case you'd forgotten.'

'How could I forget, with you banging on about it every five minutes? By the way, Mrs Taylor wants to have a word with you, when you've got time. Sorry, I forgot to tell you on Friday.'

Her dad looked completely confused. 'Who's Mrs Taylor?'

Meghan rolled her eyes at him. God, he could be such a dick, sometimes! He only ever remembered half of what she ever told him, and it was usually the unimportant half.

'She's the dance and drama teacher at school. She's also the careers advisor. I've been telling you about her for weeks! You met her, remember? When we went on open day, before I started?'

'Oh, you mean that blonde lady with the gorgeous cheekbones and the twinkly eyes? She was rather lovely, as I remember.'

Meghan cringed. 'Dad! For God's *sake!* Don't get any stupid ideas. She's happily married, with a grown-up son and a grandkid.'

'How do you know that?'

'Duh! Because she has pictures of them all in her office! I think she probably has about twenty cats, as well. Dad, that's not the point! She wants to talk to you!'

'Okay, okay! I've got the message. Should I be worried?'

Meghan shrugged. 'I dunno. Call her and find out.'

Stuart pulled a face at her. 'Okay, I'll call her. Better still, I'll pop in and see her when I drop you off, if she's around. Now get your backpack, and let's get going!'

Meghan got into the car and slammed the door. *Great,* she thought. *If Dad actually fancies Mrs Taylor, I'll never live it down for the rest of my whole life. If he wanted to find the best way in the world to embarrass the crap out of me, this would be the way to do it; making desperate puppy eyes at a respectable married woman.*

As the car swung out of the driveway and onto Redemption Road, she heaved a great sigh and muttered; 'you'd better not flirt with her, Dad. If I find out you've flirted with her, I'll strangle you in your sleep, and that's a promise.'

Chapter Sixteen

Stuart dropped Meghan at the kerb, and then went to find a parking space. He wasn't sure what to expect, or if Mrs Taylor would even be around, but he may as well take the opportunity to have a face-to-face meeting with her, if she was.

It had nothing to do with 'fancying' the woman, as Meghan was so terrified he might. That was pretty ridiculous. The last thing on his mind was romance with *anybody*, let alone a married grandmother, and someone at his daughter's school, to boot! Meghan was over-dramatizing his comments, and reading far more into them than she should, but that was fairly typical, he supposed. Almost everything was a drama to a fourteen-year-old girl, wasn't it? Meghan and her mates made such a monstrous fuss over so many things, he wondered how they even managed to *survive* their own dramas!

No, there was more than enough going on in his life already, thanks very much, without adding a romantic complication. He hoped it would happen one day, of course, because he was only forty-seven, and the prospect of being on his own for the rest of his life was a pretty bleak one. But whoever 'she' was, when (if?) she eventually turned up, she would have to be someone very special. After being widowed and then divorced, he wouldn't be jumping into the first opportunity that presented itself, and he figured a few might pop up. He supposed that despite his 'shady' past, he could still be considered a bit of a catch for someone, but he felt a million miles away from being able to think about meeting anyone new. Meghan was way off base, to think otherwise.

At the reception desk, he asked if Mrs Taylor was around, and he was shown how to find her office, down towards the end of the corridor. He hoped she was free and could spare him a few minutes.

He was in luck. She was sitting behind her computer looking vaguely harassed, but she smiled when he knocked on her door and peered around it. She motioned for him to come in, and shook her head at her computer.

'All I need this morning is a computer that won't boot up. I guess whoever was in here on Friday afternoon, and using it, didn't shut it down properly. It happens all the time, because it's a shared office, but this is the last thing I need today with a million bits of research to do before the seminar I have to give to the Year elevens this afternoon. But what can I do for you, Mr…?'

Stuart proffered his hand. 'Thomson. Stuart. I'm Meghan's dad. She said you wanted to have a chat with me, and I thought since I had to drop her in this morning I may as well seize the moment, so to speak. I do prefer a face-to-face meeting than a phone call wherever possible, if I'm honest.'

'Me too,' she smiled. 'Have a seat, Mr Thomson.'

'You can call me Stuart.'

'Okay, then you can call me Kim. Well, there's nothing to be too concerned about, but you need to know that Meghan's not *quite* where she should be, in terms of preparation for her GCSE's. She has been applying herself as best she can, from what I understand, but we are aware that she's had a lot to come to terms with, and that's probably all had an impact on her concentration and her confidence. She has quite a lot of work to do, I'm afraid, to successfully pass her exams.'

Stuart was confused. 'Sorry, but wouldn't it normally be one of her teachers that talked to me about this stuff? I thought your role was more focussed on suitability for career opportunities?'

Kim nodded. 'Normally, yes, but I've already had a few conversations with Meghan about what she wants to do. She's dropped in to see me a couple of times, and after meeting with her teachers we agreed that I might be the better person to talk to you, about her prospects.'

'Prospects? Prospects for what?' Stuart had no idea where this conversation was going.

'Meghan has told me she wants to explore the idea of doing a business degree, later on. She also wants to work with horses professionally, but she's not sure in what capacity. She has some half-formed ideas in her head, and we've talked about a few things, including psychology or even veterinary practice.' Kim paused for a beat or two before continuing.

'I do have to say though, that the amount of work she would have to do, to train as a vet, may be a little challenging for her.'

'Are you saying she's not clever enough?' Stuart didn't want to sound combative, but he was starting to lose patience with the fact that the conversation didn't seem to be going in the best direction.

Kim smiled, and shook her head. 'No. I'm not saying she's not clever. I think she really is, and more than she knows, but I do wonder if her talents might be better suited to working with horses in a different way. There are other choices. With your permission, and hers of course, I'd like to spend a little more time with her, in determining where her best aptitudes lie.'

Kim went on to say that Meghan could work in horse rehabilitation, fostering and rehoming. Careers in training, brokerage, psychology and a host of other options might be available to her too, but the range of options would depend on how well she could do academically.

'That's very important. Meghan has a certain vulnerability about her, and while that's not a bad thing at all, it may or may not change. She might 'toughen up,' or she may always be a sweet and sensitive soul. In either case, certain pathways of working with horses would suit her more or less well, and if her grades could come up, she would have a wider range of choices that could suit her vocation, if you see what I mean.'

Stuart did. Kim Taylor wanted to make sure that Meghan ended up on a career path that was the right one for *her*, and she wanted to ensure that the study pathway she chose now would set her up to take full advantage of the choices on offer when the time came.

'Okay, so what happens next? I've been on at her about her studies, but she's a typical teen who intermittently hates me and truly believes that everything that comes out of my mouth is horse-shit. Oops! Sorry. I didn't mean to say that. I learned a few bad habits during my time behind bars, and swearing was unfortunately one of them.'

Kim was laughing. 'No offence taken. And you're right. Parents aren't always the best people to be trying to get their kids to do better. I could never get my son to listen to me, and I'm fascinated to see whether he will be able to get his daughter to listen to *him*, when its important. But let me offer you something, now.'

She sat back in her chair and looked at him speculatively for a few seconds, before continuing.

'My job here at the school is a mixed bag. I do one day a week as a Careers Advisor. Three days a week, I teach dance and drama. You're lucky to have found me on 'Careers' day, as I call Mondays. I'd love to do this fulltime, actually, because I think the students could certainly do with more readily available careers guidance and advice, but sadly there's just no budget for it.'

Kim went on to explain that even her one day a week was a bit of an experiment for the school, to see how much benefit it could realistically offer, because some of the kids were still at the stage where they were changing their minds every five minutes about what they wanted to do.

'But I do have a few committed students with very clear ideas, that I'm encouraged to tutor. It's done during school time, during an elective or less critical core subject, so they don't miss out on anything too important, and the gains from one-to-one tutoring have made a huge difference, to confidence *and* academic results. I would love to tutor Meghan, and I could do it on a Thursday morning, from ten until twelve.'

Kim explained that the school had organised her proposed tutorship of Meghan to fit around her existing timetable. 'The Thursday classes she would miss would be her Art, and her Geography. Both are important, of course, but they are less so, in regard to the grades she needs in other subjects that will matter more; things like the sciences, maths and English.

'And it's not forever,' Kim added. 'She can go back to her other subjects later on, when she's pulled up her grades a little, found a bit more confidence, and feels she can give the full curriculum a bit more commitment'

Stuart was astonished. It seemed that the school really cared about students who needed extra tuition or showed aptitude or desire to follow certain career pathways. He'd already heard somewhere that Lakes Academy had a reputation for piloting beneficial schemes, but Kim Taylor's offer was extraordinary. He thought Meghan would be a fool not to take it.

He said as much to Kim, but added, somewhat ruefully; 'Convincing her might take some doing. She's not the most compliant kid on the block, I have to say. Anything I might recommend is always treated with the utmost suspicion, and then usually roundly ridiculed and rejected as complete and utter lunacy.'

Kim grinned at him. 'I think I can probably convince her to do this. As I said, we've had a few chats already. I'm keen to work with her, and I will tell her that. I think with a bit more confidence, and a few improved grades, she might surprise us all. I have a feeling that young lady is going places, and nothing would please me more than to help her on her way.'

Stuart stood up and offered his hand to Kim. 'Thank you. And thank everyone else involved for me too, would you, please? This is an amazing opportunity. I really hope we can get her to take it.'

As he walked to the door, he felt compelled to offer Kim a compliment. 'Please don't think I'm trying to flirt with you, because I am categorically *not*. But I do have to say that I think you have the loveliest cheekbones.'

She smiled widely, and her eyes twinkled. 'Well, thank you. I get them from my mum, God rest her, and I will just take what you've said for what it is; a lovely compliment.'

'Okay then, but please don't ever tell my daughter I said that to you. She would never speak to me again, and would probably threaten to slash her own wrists over the unbearable mortification. What must it be like, I wonder, to be almost permanently paralysed by your own outrage?'

'Ah, teenage girls! Don't we just love them, with all their drama? I must've been like that once, but I really don't remember, and it's probably just as well!'

Kim proffered her hand again. 'I'll be having a chat with Meghan again, probably later this morning, and we'll be in touch again after that. If she goes for it, the school will write to you, outlining the arrangement as discussed, and we'll take it from there.'

She looked at him and smiled. 'By the way, in the interests of repaying a nice compliment, let *me* just say that I'm so pleased you've decided to make a go of running a new business in this area. It's a lot different from your previous career, before everything got so horribly turned upside down.'

'Well, thank you for that. There's still a lot of judgment out there, but at least there isn't any in here. I appreciate it.'

Kim's eyes twinkled again. She really was *very* pretty. 'Everyone makes mistakes, and everyone deserves a second chance. Imagine what sort of world we'd have, if they didn't get it?'

She looked back at her computer, and pulled a face at it.

'I hope that thing has woken up by now, otherwise I'm going to be in hot water later. There's nothing worse than standing in front of a class full of teenagers who instinctively seem to smell blood when you don't know your stuff!'

'Good luck with that,' Stuart grinned and left the office.

His thoughts bounced around in his head, as he drove home to Beaconsfield. Kim Taylor's kind offer this morning had carried with it the implication that if Meghan didn't pull her socks up, she wouldn't be able to pull her *grades* up, at least not to anything that would enable her to do what she now seemed to be hoping for; to have some kind of career with horses.

It infuriated Stuart deeply, that she'd been so ambivalent about her study. She was a really bright kid, and it was gratifying that the school had identified that, and were wanting to catch her before she fell into the academic abyss, like so many students he'd heard about, who showed promise but never amounted to anything. He didn't want that for Meghan. But the school's attention meant she was still in with a good chance to turn things around and, like Kim Taylor, he wanted her to have the best of choices when the time came.

It was a bit of a reality check for him too, that the playing field of education wasn't as level as it should be. The size of the academic mountain some kids had to climb was pretty big, even when they knew where they wanted to go. For some, if they didn't get support, they wouldn't make it.

He'd never found learning hard. At uni, he'd *partied* hard, and he'd always known he was clever enough to not have to slog away as diligently as some of his friends did, to get the all-important grades. The learning and the knowledge came easily to him. While others were freaking out towards the end of the year, at the seemingly impossible feat of having to remember the necessary two hundred criminal cases in preparation for the Criminal Law exam, or nailing the finer points of whether defamation was slander or libel in the Torts exam, Stuart had 'breezed' it all.

He'd seen how worried some students were, and he'd known that some found studying harder than others. But, while intelligence was one thing, the application of it was quite another, and he thought Mrs Taylor had been right when she talked about the importance of confidence. He'd always had plenty of confidence and swagger. There hadn't been a single moment, all through law school, when he'd even had the vaguest *thought* that he wouldn't come out with top grades. He'd taken his own intelligence for granted.

But he wondered now, for the first time, if Meghan felt intimidated by his expectations, and by his own assurances that studying was a piece of cake. Worrying that she'd never measure up would surely kill her confidence stone dead. Maybe she just wasn't as much of a 'chip off the old block' as he wanted her to be. Maybe he needed to shut up about being frustrated, quit banging on about how easy it 'should' be, and accept that just because studying had been easy for *him*, that didn't mean Meghan would find it the same. He'd done incredibly well academically, but he had to stop expecting it to be inevitable that she would too. And maybe it wasn't that she didn't care. Maybe she just wasn't as capable as he expected her to be, although Kim Taylor *had* suggested otherwise. Perhaps in the end, his daughter simply had to find her passion for whatever it was she'd go on to be great at. For him, it had been law. For her, it would be something different. Once she'd figured it out, she'd probably fly as high as a kite with whatever she took on. She just needed help to get there.

The only clear thing he did know, about any of it, was that he needed to change tack and concentrate instead on supporting Meghan more, no matter what career she might want to choose, or no matter what she had to do to get there. They'd had fun doing that Equine Management Diploma together, hadn't they? Maybe they could build on that shared dedication. He needed to actively foster *her* dedication, instead of simply complaining about the lack of it. Helping her to identify her desired pathways, and studying with her if necessary, to keep her on track, was a collaborative and positive approach that might work a whole lot better.

At fourteen-going-on-fifteen, girls were pretty fickle about a lot of things. But Meghan's affinity with horses was real, and so was her passion for *them*. Stuart had the feeling that if she couldn't have a career working with them the way she wanted to, in ways that were still forming as ideas in her head, she'd never stop regretting it.

*   *   *   *   *

Four hours later, he'd managed to buy a very nice, spacious caravan online. It was eight years old and had belonged to a family from new, and it came with a full-sized awning, a fixed bed, a compact but well-appointed kitchenette, and an equally well-furnished little bathroom. The seller had also thrown in a microwave oven, a TV, and a wall-mounted docking station and speakers. The online sale site had shown a comprehensive video, and he'd had a chat on the phone with the owner, and everything seemed okay. After transferring the funds and arranging to have it delivered later in the week, all he had to do was clear a space for it in the yard, and find a long-enough extension cable to hook up the power, in time for its arrival.

He sat back in his chair, aware that he was still feeling a bit unsettled. It certainly had been a rollercoaster of a week, and he was still trying to get to grips with Warwick Ford's untimely death and the unexpected turn his life had taken as a result. On the one hand, he was looking forward to restarting the work on the barn. On the other, he was full of apprehension, at having invited a complete stranger with a very sad and complicated history into his and Meghan's lives. They'd already had more than enough complications, and they really didn't need any more.

Offering Yvonne a contract didn't feel like the *wrong* thing to do, but getting used to having a strange woman around was certainly going to change the dynamics, at least until they all got to know one another better. Having a dog around the place would be a nice thing, he supposed, as long as it didn't worry the horses, or bark all night. Yvonne had assured him that her golden retriever 'Chase' was well behaved, so he had to take that on trust.

As to the work itself, well, it would be interesting to see what Yvonne's skillset really was. As a qualified carpenter, she would at least understand the basics of what was required. But Stuart wondered if she might also lend a little creative flair to the building process. They might end up with something even nicer than what he already had in his mind.

Ah well, he thought to himself. *At worst, I hope, I'll get what I ask for. At best, I may end up with something even better.*

Chapter Seventeen

'I think you and Chase should have everything you need, here, Yvonne. Teapot Cottage is as well-equipped as I've been able to make it, but if there's anything else you need, please just come on up to the farmhouse, and ask.'

Adie glanced over at the dog her newest guest had brought with her. 'He's lovely. I have a soft spot for retrievers. I've met quite a few, and never a bad one. They have such gentle natures, don't they?'

Yvonne nodded. 'They do. Chase has been my rock, through the worst of times. I owe him everything. I don't know how much Stuart told you before booking me in here, but I've had a lot of upheaval, and the one constant has been this dog. I couldn't have got through everything without him.'

Adie offered a gentle smile. 'Stuart didn't say much, actually, only that your caravan was delayed by a week because the delivery people let him down at the last minute and you needed somewhere to stay in the meantime. I'm just glad the cottage wasn't already booked, so it was free for you to come. He also mentioned that we weren't to let anyone know that you were staying here, and if there were any enquiries from anywhere, we had to deny that you were here. Please be reassured that we will guard your privacy, absolutely.'

She was surprised when Yvonne's eyes filled with tears, and she quickly put a light hand on her arm.

'Gosh, I'm sorry, Yvonne! I don't want to pry. Your life is none of my business. All I want is for you to feel safe and comfortable here. I understand that this is an unexpected hiccup for you. It must be frustrating, to have to delay starting work for a week, when you'd all got yourselves geared up for it. Stuart was hopping mad about the caravan delay, but more for *your* sake than his own. He did say that another week won't make too much of a difference to the work, in the overall scheme of things. I think they're still reeling a bit from the death of Warwick Ford, to be honest. It was a shock to everyone, and dust like that needs time to settle.'

'It's not that, Mrs Raven. I don't mind the delay either. It gives me more time to get mentally focussed on the new job. This has all come together very quickly, and I'm still running to catch myself.' She took a deep breath.

'No, it's just the kindness, you know, of him looking out for me. He doesn't even really know me, not yet, and he's covering my back. It deserves an explanation for you, at least in part.'

Adie shook her head emphatically. 'Yvonne no, it really doesn't. You don't owe me anything at all. As I said, your business is none of mine, so please think nothing more of it. I will agree with you, though. Stuart is a very kind man, but he's been through a few fires, and I think that's taught him that people taking care of one another is more important than anything else.'

'Well, I've managed to break free from an abusive marriage, and I'm still waiting for it all to go to court. My ex-husband's on bail, and that's why I'm up here, kind of in hiding, while I take the chance to earn some money and independence at the same time.' She looked apologetic.

'People being nice to me still feels unexpected, even after the months I spent at a refuge, where everyone was *ridiculously* kind. I still sometimes catch my breath, when someone shows they care.'

Adie was horrified. She blinked, several times. 'Oh, God, Yvonne! How awful. I'm so sorry you had to go through that!'

Yvonne nodded, and sat at the kitchen table. She bit her lower lip, and looked around. 'This cottage is beautiful. So cosy. I can already see I won't want to leave, when the time comes!'

Adie grinned. 'It's a very special little place. Almost everyone who comes here rebooks to come back, at some stage. It's a bit of a magnet for the heart and soul, at least that's what a lot of people say.'

She set the teapot down on the table and got the milk out of the fridge, and pulled some cups from the cupboard.

'Well, as you don't plan to go anywhere, you should have a nice quiet week.'

'I feel very spoiled. This was completely unexpected. I'm still pinching myself, about all of it. A big part of me doesn't feel I deserve *any* of this.'

'What? A job, and a place to live? People around you who care? That's what *everyone* deserves.'

'The basics of life, right?'

'Absolutely! And, you know, being in a coercive environment where your needs are ignored or trivialised, and you're forced to comply with the demands of a horrible person is a hard thing to overcome. For what it's worth, I admire you for leaving. That took guts.'

Yvonne leaned back in her chair, and confessed that the decision to come to Beaconsfield had been the hardest she'd ever made in her life – harder than leaving her husband in the first place.

She seemed to want to talk, and that was nothing new to Adie. Teapot Cottage had the effect of loosening people's tongues. These quiet, gentle walls somehow gave them the courage to speak their truth, and it was always a privilege to hear the stories of people who were struggling to overcome difficult and sometimes even catastrophic circumstances. Offloading their anguish was just something that people seemed compelled to do here.

'What gave you the courage to finally leave?' Adie kept her voice as soft as possible.

Yvonne responded to her question without hesitating. 'The last beating, the one where Chase had been terrified too. That was the one that showed me what the future was going to look like. In short, there wasn't going to be one. Keith would kill me. He'd said it many times. And he'd also said, that in spite of the fact that he loved Chase himself, he'd happily kill him too, just to piss me off. The worst of it was, I knew he meant it. He'd kill me, but he'd let me have the agony first, of watching him kill the only real friend I had left, right in front of me. He'd long-since lost any sense of reason or compassion.'

She went on to say that the refuge offered a twice-weekly group sharing session that took place downstairs in a communal room. She couldn't make herself go, for a long time, and she couldn't even confide much in her key worker at first. But, after she found the courage to join in the sessions, she found that sharing her story helped her to come to terms with it.

'I was finally able to accept that the problem wasn't me, or anything I'd ever said or done, and that was important, because by the time I showed up at that place, I felt completely worthless and useless. I felt that everything that had happened to me had been my own fault; that I'd *deserved* to be abused!'

Yvonne went on to explain that through therapy she realised that the only mistake she'd made was to have trusted him in the first place. 'But they even had to show me how to forgive myself for that, because the person he'd managed to convince me he was, when I first met him, didn't really exist. He was the classic 'textbook abuser,' manipulating me into feeling like I'd *made* him like he was.'

'Sadly, some men are very clever, and manipulative, Yvonne. They manage to hide the worst of themselves in plain sight, sometimes. None of us can blame ourselves for that. That's on *them.*'

She handed a roll of kitchen towel to Yvonne who tore a piece off it and blew her nose.

'Keith was always so remorseful after every event. Sometimes he even cried, when he realised how hurt I was. It was always the same. He'd say he didn't know what was wrong with him or why he got so mad at me that he lashed out without thinking, and he'd promise never to do it again, but always pointing out that I had a responsibility too, to not make him angry or upset!'

Yvonne shook her head. 'I swallowed it all, because all I wanted was my lovely man back, you know? Sometimes, I'd suggested he get help, and he'd smile, and nod, and tell me he would. At first, I believed that too. I believed he really wanted to be better, and would find the support he needed.'

But, she explained, when things escalated to the terrifying level of almost nightly rape, cutting off the phone and confiscating her bank cards, she knew she was kidding herself. When it got to the point where she stopped seeing even random glimpses of the man Keith used to be, that's when she knew that the life she'd once been so keen to imagine, so keen to embrace, was never going to happen. She was trapped.

'He started telling me that I was nothing, and I may as well be dead because nobody cared whether I lived or died. In the beginning I knew he was wrong. But over time, towards the end, I came to believe that too, along with everything else I'd been gullible enough to fall for.

'He was a racist too, as it turned out. He'd started off saying he loved my dark eyes and skin, but the names he started called me, towards the end? That was when I knew that every nice thing he'd ever said had been a lie. He thought I was worse than nothing, and I ended up believing it myself.'

'He isolated you very thoroughly, didn't he?'

'Yes, he did. It's what they do, Mrs Raven. And I was so defeated, I had no emotional strength left to do anything for myself. But the threat of my dog being killed; that's what finally got through the mush that my brain had turned into. That was the moment things turned on their head. He'd underestimated the power of my love for Chase.

'I did come to appreciate the irony, eventually, that what he thought of as just another form of psychological torture and control turned out to be the thing that finally gave me the strength to leave him!'

He'd gone to work that morning, and Yvonne had played the wounded, helpless victim, lying on the bed crying as he left, after another night of being brutalised and half strangled.

'I still had bruises fading on my face and my upper left arm, along with a bunch of new ones. I managed to convince him that I wasn't capable of going anywhere. After he left, I got up, pulled out the bag beneath the bed that I'd packed the day before, hitched the lead to Chase's collar dog, and left the house. It hurt like hell, but I walked a mile and a half to the police station, and I told them everything.'

Her husband had been charged and bailed, and she was worried, because although the courts had imposed a restraining order, it wouldn't count for much if he thought he could get her alone.

'I can't relax until he's behind bars, which seems like a sure enough thing, now that one of his previous partners has also come forward with her own account of how violent was with her too. He splashed her with petrol and threatened to set fire to her, out on their front lawn. Neighbours called the police, who went out with dogs to their house, and they dragged him away. He did time for that, but I met him after the fact. I never knew anything about it.'

She shook her head, slowly. 'It helped, actually, to learn about that, because it was solid proof that the way he was had nothing to do with me. He was the crazy one! But I do still wonder how long it might be before I can hear a door slam, or a plate being banged on a table, without jumping out of my skin, and feeling the dread in the pit of my stomach, about what might happen next.'

'The main thing is that you are free, or at least you will be, when he's put away.'

'Yeah, that day can't come soon enough. In the meantime, I just have to keep my head down and keep making progress as best I can. You won't say anything, to anyone, will you, Mrs Raven?'

'What? God, no! Never in a million *years!* But please call me Adie. I know too much about you for you to have to stand on ceremony with me. I'm Adie to my friends, and to the people I care about.'

'Okay, Adie, then. And thank you for listening. I don't tell many people my story, but somehow if felt safe to tell *you*. I don't know why that is. And thank you for letting me stay here, in this gorgeous little house. I feel like its hugging me! Stuart said he would be sorting the bill out with you himself, for my stay here. Is that right?'

'Yes, and it's already taken care of. You just relax in here, enjoy the view, the tub, the 'vibe', and there's a bookshelf full of books and DVD's if you want something to read or watch. It's turned into quite an eclectic collection, because some guests who come bring stuff that they very kindly leave behind.'

Adie also explained about the basket of takeaway menus in the bookshelf too. 'Most people deliver to here. We're only about eight minutes' drive from the town, actually, and the ones that come will take card payments, except for the Flaming Wok; the Chinese. They always want cash, so you need to remember that, if you want to order from there.'

As she let herself out through the back door, Adie was deep in thought. It had been emotional, hearing Yvonne's story.

Evil is alive and well in the world, she thought to herself grimly, as she made her way back to Ravensdown House. *There are people out there that shouldn't be allowed to walk the earth. I hope they lock that man up for a very long time.*

Yvonne's courage had been immense, in managing to walk away from her thug of a husband. It must still be terrifying, having to hide until the matter went to court, because that monster was insane enough to violate a restraining order; because hurting or killing her mattered more to him than the repercussions. It was unimaginable, how anyone could think that way. He *had* to be mentally deranged. There was no other explanation.

She found Feen in her workshop, putting the last of a new jewellery order together for her 'boss,' the Italian dress designer Gina Giordano, who was also Adie's daughter in law, married to her daughter Ruth.

Feen made beautiful necklaces, bracelets, earrings and brooches from flowers and plants encased in clear resin, set against sterling silver. Her pieces were utterly gorgeous, and very limited edition. She never made more than a handful in the same style, and she made some lines exclusively for GinGio, Gina's clothing company. She worked on four collections per year, and the work kept her busy for most of it, designing, coming up with prototypes, and working on other lines as well, to sell from her own website.

She looked shrewdly at Adie. 'Are you okay? You seem a bit distracted. Something happen at Teapot?'

Adie shrugged, and then grinned. She was well-used to Feen's uncanny knack for picking up on the vibrations of others, particularly when they were less than calm and serene. She wasn't surprised that Feen had picked up on the vibe from her visit to the cottage.

'Just settling the new tenant in. She has quite a story, and I won't tell you what it is, but it *is* unsettling, yes. It's awful, actually, but I think there might be some light at the end of the tunnel for her. I hope so, anyway.'

'Yes, she is very wounded, and she still has a rifficult doad to travel for a while. She's one of the special ones that get drawn here.'

'You're right, as usual. She's fragile, and hurting, and struggling with a lot of things, but she has already found enough courage to open up a little. Will everything be alright in the end, d'you think?' Adie was always hopeful for any nuggets Feen could provide, with her insight.

'Eventually it will,' Feen said simply. 'There are a few more shocks in store for her yet, and it's not terribly clear to me what they are, but everything will work out in the end. In the meantime, you don't have to worry about our safety. Nobody is going to come looking for her here.'

Adie nodded gently, feeling reassured that Yvonne would, as most of her tenants did, move on and carry on with her life.

*　*　*　*　*

After cleaning Teapot Cottage, Adie closed the front door and started walking back to Ravensdown House. She was thrilled that Yvonne had enjoyed her week there so much. She'd come up to Ravensdown House earlier in the morning, to say goodbye. The caravan had now arrived at Beaconsfield, and was ready for her to move into. Stuart had been to collect her and Chase, and her two small suitcases that contained everything she had left in the world. She'd been nervous but excited, and profoundly grateful for the unexpected hiccup that had allowed her some much-needed breathing space.

She'd told Adie that the week had allowed her real time to reflect on her own journey and, in some strange way she couldn't describe, she felt a lot stronger, and more sure about her future. She was prepared now, for whatever came next, and was feeling a lot more positive about all of it.

Adie understood that completely, and she chuckled to herself now. What happened with the caravan hadn't been Stuart's fault. The delivery people had suffered a setback of their own, which couldn't have been foreseen, and it had caused a week's delay. But it was incredibly funny how such random things seemed to occur, that drove people who were recovering from trauma and in need of healing, to the door of Teapot Cottage!

Yvonne had accepted the change of plan with good grace, and had – some might say predictably – found herself in a much better place in her own head, about what was happening in her life. She was no longer as timid or as apprehensive as she had been when she'd arrived, about the new phase of her 'fresh start.' After a week of quiet, solitary contemplation, it seemed that a few things had fallen into place for her, and she was clearly looking forward to getting on with the job at Beaconsfield.

The cottage had worked its magic, again.

Chapter Eighteen

As anxious as he'd initially been to get going on the barn at Beaconsfield, Stuart knew that Yvonne could not have started work before the caravan was in place. It wasn't fair to expect her to stay in the house, with no notice, after he'd promised her she'd have her own space. He had already arranged her journey to Carlisle on the train, before the delay had occurred, so he needed to find somewhere appropriate for her to stay.

There were B & B's close to Beaconsfield, but he figured that a week at Teapot Cottage, as frustrating and expensive as that would be for him, made more sense. A little personal time wouldn't go amiss for Yvonne, in a quiet, gentle, out-of-the-way place, where she only had herself to think about. It would give her more time to adjust, and get fully focussed on the work that needed doing. Once it began, there wouldn't be much respite from it.

She was very chatty in the car, on the way back to Beaconsfield, and she'd happily confirmed his thoughts. She *had* relished the experience of being on her own, and being able to please herself for the first time in years. If she didn't want to get up early, she didn't. If she wanted to take her morning coffee back to bed, she did. Whenever she'd felt like getting into the lovely little hot tub at the back of the cottage, she'd done that too, whether it was midnight, six in the morning, or two in the afternoon. She'd eaten when she felt like it, and even did some yoga on the bedroom floor, safe in the knowledge that nobody would come barging in. When she hadn't been doing any of that, or out exploring the local walking trails with Chase, she'd spent most of her time sitting in one of the window seats, drinking tea and staring down into the valley.

'The view from those windows is mesmerising, isn't it? I sat there for *hours*, some days. It was amazing how wonderful it was; just doing nothing! Navel-gazing, but somehow in a *good* way, for a change. I feel like some of my demons have left me! That sounds a bit strange, doesn't it?'

Stuart laughed. 'Not at all. I felt the same way, when I stayed there through the summer with Meghan. We weren't in a great place, separately or together, but being there changed everything. Meggie fell in love with a horse, of all crazy things, and I found my future, and hopefully hers too, if she wants it. We also met some great people who I already trust with my life, which is no small thing, either. Teapot Cottage is a pretty special little place. I'm glad you've enjoyed your stay there.'

Yvonne said she'd slept like a baby at the cottage, too. 'Oftentimes, even though I was getting a full eight hours' peaceful sleep every night – for the first time in *years*, I might add – I'd sit in the window with a book or a magazine and somehow manage to doze off *again*, and I'd wake up just as the sun was setting or when the book I was reading finally slid off my lap and onto the floor with a thump that woke me up.'

'It's only when you take time out that you realise how exhausted you are just generally, by life,' Stuart observed, as the guided the car onto the main road towards Carlisle.

'That's so true! I had no idea how tired and depleted I really was! This week by myself, in such a peaceful place, has mended me better than anything else, at least until now. I actually feel like I finally have some energy to throw at the barn project. Don't get me wrong – the mind was always willing, but now I have some physical energy too. I really can't thank you enough.'

She talked about how much she was looking forward to starting the job, and she admitted to Stuart that in the last couple of days, she'd started thinking differently about her ex-husband. Even though the dreaded court case was still months away, she was no longer so afraid of facing him in court. She felt stronger, and less intimidated by the process of reclaiming her life.

'I'm still uneasy, I can't deny that, but I'm not terrified, like I was when I first got on the train to come to Carlisle. I imagined him hiding around every pillar and corner, waiting to leap out at me, screaming, with his fists flying in my face. The bad dreams I've been having are still happening, some nights, but they've lost their intensity. Now, I'm escaping more often, and more quickly. Even in my *dreams* I've got more strength!'

Stuart nodded. What she was saying made more sense than she realised.

'I hope you like the caravan. It's quite modern, and comfortable. It's certainly spacious enough, I think, for you and Chase. He's lovely, by the way. We'll be happy to have him around.'

When Yvonne had first got off the train with Chase, the lollopy, soft-as-butter dog had greeted Stuart and Meghan like long-lost friends, and had made them both laugh with delight. Chase was a happy hound who would be good fun to have around the place, especially for Meghan, who had already made no bones about wanting a puppy. This might be a good chance for Stuart to see how she interacted with someone else's dog, before they committed to having one of their own.

Stuart had positioned the caravan with its biggest window facing the trees, away from where anyone could see in, to offer maximum privacy. Meghan had scattered some pretty pink cushions in it, and a fluffy pink and grey crocheted throw. She'd found them in a charity shop in the city, along with a couple of little scented candles in jars, which she'd put on the shelf beside the TV. She'd also put a small glass vase on the bench in the kitchenette with deep purple and mauve tulips in it. She had done a nice job of making the caravan homely. It looked as welcoming as it probably ever could.

Yvonne had already seen the photos and video of the barn's 'bare bones,' and the plans Stuart had drawn up with Warwick. Seeing it for real was likely to still be something of a shock for her, and he hoped she was ready. It needed a hell of a lot of work. It was all completely doable, although it wasn't going to be a quick job. He assured her that he'd be on hand to do any of the heavy lifting. He was a willing labourer, and all she needed to do was tell him what to do and he'd cheerfully get on with it.

Her reaction, when she saw the state of the barn, wasn't as bad as he'd feared. Her estimate at this stage was two months, if everything they needed was on hand. If they had to wait for supplies, that could push out their timeline a lot. Stuart prayed it wouldn't happen.

At best, the project could be finished in time for Christmas. At worst, it might run to February. Keith's court case wouldn't be until then at the earliest, according to Yvonne's solicitor, and Stuart reassured her that it would be no problem to him or to Meghan if she was still here over the holiday.

She seemed to be a bit ambivalent about the festive season, like she was about a lot of other things, but he knew that she couldn't safely go to her mum's for Christmas, which was the only place she'd probably *want* to go. She was also clearly still at the stage where nothing affected her much either way, good or bad, happy or sad, but her stay at Teapot Cottage had been lovely, and had helped her journey towards recovery. Stuart hoped she could continue at Beaconsfield to build on the progress she'd made. It would be nice to see her happy.

Apparently, according to counsellors who treated people suffering from trauma, the weird, flatline 'numbness' they so often felt was normal, and would wear off in time as they continued to work their way through it and started to rebuild their lives. Yvonne had already told him that her counsellor thought coming here might be good for her. Doing some work, having space to breathe, learning to sleep properly again, appreciating nature; all these things might help her to put the shattered pieces of herself back together at a pace that didn't feel rushed or in keeping with anyone else's expectations.

It made sense. He'd chuckled to himself, when she'd confessed that on some level she'd been hoping her counsellor would have tried to talk her *out* of coming here, that she'd say it was a bad idea or would slow her recovery. That way, the excuse would be there at the ready, to refuse this rather unusual and no doubt massively daunting offer.

He totally got that. Sometimes staying in your self-protective cocoon often did feel like the better option. He'd had enough counselling himself, in prison, to understand the process of recovery. It hadn't been particularly effective for him, but he wondered if that might have been because most of the work done with inmates was geared more to enabling them to be managed more effectively *within* the prison system, rather than setting them up to cope better in the real world once they'd left it.

Despite its best intentions, His Majesty's Prison and Probation Service fell woefully short of providing a proper rehabilitative infrastructure on the outside that gave released inmates a decent chance at staying out. The hard reality for most of them was going back to the same situations that had driven them inside in the first place. The revolving door was constantly in motion and Stuart saw the same guys coming back, time and time again, with depressing regularity. As a trained 'Listener,' he knew how frustrating and demoralising it was for them, having so little support to improve their lot in life. They felt powerless, and ignored. Society had big expectations of them, but offered very little support to help them get there.

Stuart doubted whether Yvonne's husband would get anything positive from being in prison, when he eventually got sent down. Being in the system had worked for Stuart, and it had worked for Darren Davies, but only because they were determined *themselves*, to make things better. It had nothing to do with the meagre, inadequate resources on offer to them on release. Darren had observed too, a few conversations ago, how many people the prison system managed to fail, compared with the handful who ended up with better lives because of it.

He and Stuart both knew that they'd managed to succeed in *spite* of being banged up, rather than because of it. The irresponsible choices both men had made had cost other people their lives and devastated too many families. That was a very big incentive to them both, as intelligent men with conscience, to try and be better people, and it was their own inherent drive and initiative that enabled them to do it. Not everyone was made the same way, however, and the so-called 'rehabilitative' arm of the prison service simply didn't have the resources to take that into account or do much about it.

Yvonne finished her inspection of the barn, and seemed satisfied that the work was all achievable. She talked about the some of the jobs she'd previously done, for Sisters In The Trades. They'd been a great firm to work for, and she missed her friends there, fellow tradeswomen who were absolutely 'storming it,' in a so-called man's world.

She chuckled, lightly. 'My parents and my brother all thought I was mad, wanting to be a carpenter. They had other plans for me. I got good grades at school, and Mum had grand hopes of me having a wonderful career as an interpreter, after she saw my marks for French and German. I had a bit of a knack for learning languages.'

But it wasn't to be. Yvonne was clever, but she wasn't academic. University held no appeal for her. Nor was she a big 'go-getter.' She just wanted to make things with her hands; big things, important, lasting things that would live on, long after she'd gone from the world. She'd enrolled on woodwork and metalwork electives at school and had finally found her 'ecological niche' in construction. One apprenticeship later, and here she was – a qualified carpenter.

'Mum eventually came to accept it, saying if I was happy, that was all that mattered.' She went on to explain that her Dad had died before she'd completed her apprenticeship. 'If he'd still been alive, he'd have been as proud as punch. If he'd still been alive, I wouldn't have ended up enduring four years at the hands of a wife-beating maniac! He'd have torn Keith limb from limb with his bare hands.'

Stuart understood that too. His brother Colin lived in Australia, and he hadn't seen him for years, but if anyone ever attacked him, he'd be straight on a plane over there, to hunt the bastard down and beat the living shit out of him.

Yvonne asked about the wi-fi, and Stuart confirmed that it was fine, thanks to a booster he'd set up in the caravan. She pulled a face. 'I don't plan to spend much time online, but I've set up a social media account in a different name. I don't have any friends on it, and I don't want to make any, but it means I can keep an eye on Keith's profile. He hasn't thought to make it private. He's always posting or sharing something, or checking in somewhere.

'It's kind of reassuring in a way,' she went on to explain. 'It's not that I expect him to post that he's found out where I am and is on his way to kill me and bury me six feet under. But, knowing that tonight he's probably going to announce that he's sitting with his mate in a pub somewhere with no intention of doing anything other than stuffing his face with steak and chips and 'getting bladdered,' it means I can relax a bit.'

Stuart hauled Yvonne's suitcases out of the boot and took them into the caravan. Chase was already out and bounding around the yard, and Stuart grinned as the dog stopped, sniffed around, then cocked his leg against a nearby gate. 'Looks like he's already making his mark!'

He unlocked the caravan door, and gave the key to Yvonne with a flourish. 'This is your key. I have a spare that I'll keep in the house, on a hook behind the back door, just in case this one gets lost or damaged. This is your space, and yours alone. Neither myself nor Meghan will ever come into it uninvited, unless it's on fire or something.' He looked around, making sure there was nothing important he'd forgotten.

'So I'll leave you to get unpacked and settled. The wi-fi code is on a piece of paper on the table. We normally eat around seven, and Meghan's cooking tonight, It's just a spag bol with some garlic bread, if that's ok? I never even thought to ask you if you're vegetarian!'

Yvonne laughed 'I'm not a huge red meat fan, to be honest. I mostly stick to fish, chicken and veg, but I do have meat occasionally, so spag bol sounds great.'

The conversation over dinner was light and convivial. Meghan told Yvonne all about Astro, and Stuart loved how she came alive when she talked about the horse, like someone had literally turned a light on inside her. They also talked a fair bit about dogs, with Meghan again steering the conversation, saying that she was hoping to get a puppy soon, and wondering if she could spend some time with Yvonne's dog while they were both here.

'It might be nice for Chase, to have someone else who can spend a little time with him while we're busy working,' she offered, and Yvonne agreed. Stuart offered to show her the horses as soon as there was some free time, if she wanted.

'D'you ride, Yvonne?' he asked.

She shook her head. 'No, I'm afraid not. I was raised in the city, never got the opportunity to meet any horses. They scare me, to be honest. They're so big and powerful. I'd have no idea how to handle one.'

Meghan very kindly offered to teach her. 'It might help with your confidence,' she explained. 'I know it really helped with mine. Somehow, sitting on a horse, and being in control of it, I started feeling like I could control everything *else* in my life. It probably sounds stupid, but when I met Astro I just started feeling better about *everything*. I dunno what happened really, or what she did, but my whole life changed.' She looked self-conscious, and a bit embarrassed, but she continued quietly. 'It wasn't that great before then, especially when Dad was in prison. I was pretty messed up by everything that happened. I felt kind of *frozen*.'

Yvonne nodded slowly and put down her fork. 'It doesn't sound stupid at all, Meghan. I believe that animals are a great healers. Chase's love and loyalty is what saved *my* sanity. I'm sure about that.' She took a deep breath and went quiet for a moment, and Stuart gently cleared his throat.

'Please know that we don't expect you to tell us anything at all about your life, or what it's been like. We'd be happy to listen, of course, but you don't owe us any explanations. If you never want to say a single word about the past, that's completely fine.'

She nodded her acknowledgement to him and carried on. 'Thanks. I think it's good that people have at least some idea of where I'm at, in my head, with it all. I'll always answer people's questions, because it helps them to understand why I'm like I am, sometimes; you know, a bit on edge or mistrustful. Maybe even a bit paranoid, at times.

'My world had become a very small place. I'd been systematically isolated from everyone I knew. Chase was all I had left. When I realised that he was in danger too, that my ex was willing to kill him just to hurt me more, I knew I couldn't put him at risk. But it wasn't enough to just let him go to a new home where he wouldn't be in danger, and for me to stay behind. He deserved to be protected, but I finally woke up and realised I did too.'

After Yvonne had shared a little more of her story, an awkward silence settled over the table, but Meghan, bless her, decided that she'd be the one to break it.

'Well, I'm glad you're here with us, and Chase too. I think this was fate; you were *meant* to come here, and stay with us, and I also think Chase and Astro should meet. They're both amazing animals, and I think they'll be good friends. Let's introduce them tomorrow.'

Yvonne nodded and smiled, then took advantage of a lull in the conversation to make her excuses and turn in for the night. 'This has been a lovely welcome. But I think I need an early night before starting tomorrow, so shall we get these dishes done?'

Stuart waved her away. 'As friends of mine recently said to me; guests don't do dishes, and tonight you're our guest. Friends and colleagues do wash up though, so you can start from tomorrow.'

She gave him a warm smile. 'Thank you! That's very kind. So shall I see you in the morning then, at the barn?'

'Well, you'll want breakfast, won't you?' Stuart raised his eyebrows at her.

'Oh! Yes, of course. Sorry! Only, there's food in the fridge, so I thought it was up to me to organise my own.'

Stuart grinned at her. 'That's stuff for snacking. Of course, if you'd rather ....'

'Oh no! Breakfast with you guys will be great. So, what time?'

Meghan spoke up first. 'I catch the bus to school so I head out about ten past eight, so any time from seven thirty would work, if the plan is for us to all eat together, right Dad?'

Stuart nodded. 'Yep, seven thirty will be fine. All this week, is it okay if we can make a start at eight, break for lunch at twelve thirty for half an hour, then work until around six? It's long days, but there's a lot to get done, and we can do fewer hours when we're closer to being on schedule. We can grab a cuppa whenever we like, all the fixings will be in the barn, but can we keep working while we drink it, and maybe next week we can button back a bit?'

Yvonne gave him the thumbs up. 'Sounds good. Hit the ground running. Best way, I think. So have a great night, and thanks again Meghan, for a lovely meal. And I hope me sharing some of my story hasn't put too much of a downer on things. Since I'm staying with you, it's probably a good thing that you know at least some of what happened to me, even if it's not very pleasant. I'd rather you know, and ask me whatever you need to, than we try to work together in some kind of weird silence, wondering, or being too guarded or nervous to talk about the circumstances.'

Stuart nodded. 'Agreed. It's a terrible thing, what you've been through. We'll support you in whatever way we can, to get past all this, and rebuild your life.'

Meghan nodded, resolutely. 'Of course we will. I'm sorry you've had to go through what you have. It's cruel, and unfair, but you're here now, and you're safe, Yvonne. You *and* Chase.'

Stuart stood and walked her to the door. 'Sing out if you need anything. And of course if you fancy a walk around the property, just go ahead. I do it myself most nights, usually later than this, just before going to bed. I find a few lungfuls of fresh air help me sleep a bit better. You might find the same. Goodnight Yvonne, and once again, welcome to our little slice of paradise. See you in the morning.'

By the time Stuart went out for his late-night stroll, the night had turned chilly. Far in the distance, an owl hooted plaintively, almost as if to ask; 'is anybody out there?'

We're here. Stuart sent what he fancied might be a telepathic message to the solitary bird. *We all know what it's like to wonder if there's anybody listening. But we're all here, little owl. You're not all alone in the dark tonight.*

He hoped the darkness wouldn't be too unnerving for Yvonne. This place was a fair way from where light pollution could affect it. The sky was as black as coal, but crystal clear and littered with millions of stars. As he watched, a shooting star streaked across the sky above him. It felt like a promise, somehow; a good omen that things were about to get better for them all.

Chapter Nineteen

'What was it like at the refuge, Yvonne? You don't have to tell me, if you don't want to. It's okay if you don't.' Meghan shrugged, as she poured milk onto her breakfast cereal.

She glanced over at her father, to see what his reaction was. He'd been fairly quiet since he and Yvonne had sat down for breakfast. She figured he was probably just tired. They'd made good progress on the barn in the last couple of weeks, but they *both* looked tired. Maybe they should take a day off.

Stuart's face remained impassive, but he cleared his throat. 'Yvonne, as I said when you first arrived here, you never have to tell us anything. We respect your privacy absolutely. Refuges are sacred spaces, and there are very good reasons for why most people don't know what they do, or even where they are.'

Meghan nodded. 'Dad's right. It's not an expectation. It really is fine if you don't want to talk about it. I'm just interested in how they help people, that's all. It's a different world than anything I know.'

Yvonne bit her bottom lip and thought for a moment, as if she was trying to decide whether to answer.

Meghan shrugged, and continued to try to explain. 'I'd like to understand more, because I think I want to go into some kind of vocational career, with horses who can help people recover from trauma. I don't know exactly what I can do yet, but I feel like I'm kind of leaning towards wanting to do something like that, you know, for a career or something.'

'Well, I think it's good to be curious about what goes on in the world. Domestic violence is something far too many people still don't know or want to talk about. It's a terrible, corrosive thing, and many women don't want to share their experiences of it, but I've learned that if stories *are* shared, they can help to prevent a lot of *other* women from ever ending up in such terrible circumstances.'

Meghan held the teapot up, and Yvonne nodded, and smiled. 'Yes please. Refuges are good places. They serve as a temporary safe homes to broken women. I accepted the police's offer to take me to one, because it was important that I could go somewhere my husband wouldn't find me.'

Yvonne bit her bottom lip, before continuing. 'I had no idea what to expect, when I first arrived there. I found myself in this kind of bubble, where I didn't know a single soul, and very few of the women I met there talked or asked much about anything. That was pretty strange, to start with, when you think that nobody who's there wants to say much about themselves or their circumstances, or ask you about yours, but everyone still has to trust each other with their safety!

'The rules of being allowed to stay included not telling anyone where it is, of course, or who's in there, to protect the everyone's anonymity. I couldn't even tell my mum where I was or the names of anyone I might've made friends with. I didn't make any, as it turns out. It really wasn't that kind of place; not for me, anyway.'

Meghan felt a pang of compassion. 'Gosh, it must've felt pretty lonely, if nobody really talked, and you couldn't contact the people who cared about you.'

'It didn't feel lonely, to be honest. I was cut off from everyone on the outside, but I actually appreciated the opportunity to be alone with my thoughts for once, without having to worry about what my face might be saying, you know? My ex was always demanding to know what I was thinking. Coming up with something convincing all the time, to keep the pressure off; it was exhausting, so it was nice to not have that.'

Yvonne carried on describing what the refuge itself was like. 'The staff there were amazing. Very sensitive and kind. They welcomed me, and they very quickly identified what I needed. They reassured me that they would do whatever was necessary to keep me safe, and they helped me build the infrastructure to become independent again. They put Chase into safe foster care for me, too, while I got sorted out. That was important to me.

'A *lot* of the women didn't talk. Don't get me wrong; they weren't unfriendly, but many did keep to themselves. We all understood what we'd all gone through, but many of us weren't ready to listen to anyone else's story or talk about our own. That came later, through familiarity and trust but, again, only for some of us. A lot of women came and went without ever saying much to anyone about anything.

'I had an IDVA worker; that's an Independent Domestic Violence Advocate. Her name was Maura. She was my key worker, in effect. She sorted out my housing benefit so I could pay to stay at the refuge. She organised a new bank account for me, and part of her role was to enable me to communicate with my mum, which meant everything.'

Yvonne went on to explain that her ex had stopped her from contacting her mother or her friends. She was afraid to contact her mum directly, because doing so could put her in direct danger.

'He used to follow her, to see where she went. He was probably hoping she would lead him straight to me. If she genuinely didn't know where I was, it was safer for us *both*. He's not above hurting someone, to get what he wants.'

Meghan couldn't imagine how it must feel; to be cut off from all your friends and family by someone who'd could hurt or kill your mother, or your friends, just to get back at you for leaving them. That was some kind of crazy. So was threatening to kill a dog you loved yourself.

Yvonne said that she had made the decision to revert to her maiden name, which Meghan *did* understand, and Maura had helped her with the paperwork. Yvonne couldn't go back to her job for a while, but Maura helped to make sure she would be able to, when she'd got some of her independence back.

Meghan wondered. Men who hurt women; are they happy, being what they are? Does their brutality make them feel better, or worse? Do they start to hate themselves more, or love themselves more, for their ability to control someone else? She asked Yvonne, who thought about it for a minute.

'You know, those are really good questions. I've never thought about that. And I don't have the answers, but there's probably some research on it, somewhere.'

She smiled gently and rose from the table, saying she needed to go back to the caravan and clean her teeth before starting work.

Mehan pulled a face at her father, as he stifled a yawn and passed a hand over his face. 'You guys should take some time out. You've been working your butts off and you look knackered, Dad. Yvonne does too, but don't tell her I said that.'

'Already ahead of you, brat. We've decided to have today off. Going to get a few more supplies from the DIY superstore, and Yvonne needs a few personal bits and pieces. We can pick you up after school if you like, and go for a pizza. Sound good?'

'Yeah, that would be cool!'

'You've been quiet the last few days, Meggie. Everything alright? Anything you want to share, or ask about?'

Meghan nodded. 'Yeah, everything's okay. I do want to talk to you sometime soon about my ideas, Dad. You know, for careers and all that? I think I might be okay with the GCSE exams. I'm feeling better about them, now I've got help from Mrs Taylor, and I think I want to go on and do A levels after that, then go to university.'

'You do know you probably need five decent GCSE grades, to be eligible for A Levels? D'you think you can get there?'

Stuart braced himself for the backlash. Meghan was so sensitive at times, she would probably see his innocent question as a far more loaded one; a patronising attempt to insinuate that he didn't think she had it in her. But he blinked a couple of times, when all she did was shrug, and grin at him instead.

'Yeah, I think so. I've been enjoying the tutoring from Mrs Taylor. She makes it interesting, and she never makes me feel like I'm stupid or something, when I don't get what she's explaining, the first time she says it.'

'Well, that's a good start. You've only done a couple of weeks with her, though. Are you sure it's not just a novelty that might wear off? I don't mean to suggest anything by that, just that it's still early days, you know?'

Meghan nodded. 'Yeah. But there's stuff that's already kind of falling into place in my head, Dad. Like learning so much with Astro, and being so close with her and the other horses now too, and all this stuff with Yvonne, and what she's been through.' She took a deep breath, and carried on.

'Dad, I think I want to do something with horses and people, you know, like psychology or something? I've been reading about a thing called equine therapy, where horses are trained to help people heal from trauma. The process includes horse-based activities or a horse-based environment, to help with things like anxiety and depression, dementia, PTSD, and stuff like that. It's good for people in recovery from addictions, brain injuries, and even genetic syndromes like Down's and stuff, too.'

Stuart was gobsmacked. 'Ok, so who are you *really*, and what have you done with my wayward gargoyle daughter, who looks exactly like you, by the way?'

Meghan laughed. 'C'mon Dad! I'm serious. Learning about the horses, and being with them, has changed *me* so much. It's changed how I feel about *everything*. And learning about what happened to Yvonne, and how domestic violence affects people's self-esteem and everything? Well, I think I want to do something to bring all that together, somehow. To make people better, you know?'

Stuart did know. He was vaguely familiar with the concept of Equine Assisted Therapy. EAP was experiential; it used the dynamic power and innate empathy of horses to encourage participants to learn about themselves and others by taking part in activities with the animals. It helped them get to grips with their feelings, reactions, and behaviours. The benefits of interacting with animals, for people who were suffering in different ways, were well documented. The fact that Meghan wanted to be involved somehow, was amazing to him. He felt a sudden rush of pride so strong it brought tears to his eyes.

'Wow! That's fantastic. I've been meaning to ask, actually, if you've been uncomfortable about any of what Yvonne has told us. Some of what she's talked about was pretty hairy stuff, but I guess you've dealt with it okay, if this proposed career choice is the outcome?'

'Yeah, it was horrible to hear, but all its made me want to do is help her, and other people like her. I've already talked to Mrs Taylor about it all, and she wants to have another chat with you, whenever it suits, to talk about the study pathway. There's no rush, Dad. But I think I'm leaning towards doing science-based A-Levels, then going to uni, and maybe studying psychology or something.'

Stuart nodded, mulling over what she was saying. 'I think there will be quite a few potential avenues, and like a lot of students who do their broader papers and then start to work towards specialisation and narrow things down a bit, the choices will open up for you to consider as you go along.

'That's really exciting. I felt it myself, at uni, after I'd done most of my core papers. I discovered that whatever 'legal' door I looked through didn't just open into a single room of specialism. All of the rooms have more doors off them. To me, that was the most thrilling part of considering a career. The choices you'll have, and even carving a new niche for yourself that nobody else is doing, is an amazing prospect.'

'That's what Mrs Taylor said. A lot of students change their mind about the specialisms, the more they learn. Like, they think they're going one way, then something changes and they learn something else that gets them more excited about what's behind a *different* door, I guess.'

'That's exactly it. When the penny starts to drop, it's a great moment in any student's life. I'm proud of you, brat. I like your line of thinking, and I'll certainly talk to Kim Taylor again, very soon. Now, you'd better get a rattle on, or you'll miss the bloody bus, and I really *don't* have time to take you to school today! Please believe that.'

Meghan glanced quickly at the clock then downed the last of her orange juice and picked up her toast. As she ran out the door, she called back;

'Have fun shopping! See you after school!'

She really couldn't see what might be fun about shopping at a DIY store. She'd been into the one in town with Stuart a few times, but it was the most boring place on the planet, in her opinion. Other kids said the same thing; their parents almost went into *convulsions* of delight, at the thought of shopping for bathrooms, kitchens, nails and lightbulbs. It was embarrassing, and totally weird, how interesting some people found that.

*　*　*　*　*

Autumn rolled relentlessly on, with ever-increasing cold, and everything started to appear in the shops, for Christmas. Heavily-decorated trees went up, and strings of baubles and fairy lights began to take centre stage in Carlisle. Meghan already had a shopping list, of what she wanted to get for her family and friends, and Trudie at GladRagz had given her enough Saturday work to have boosted her budget a lot. She had also babysat for Debby and Darren a couple of times, and they always insisted on giving her thirty pounds, which was a lot of money. Stuart had thought it was outrageous, but Darren was always adamant that it was the best money they spent, on a night out.

Meghan wanted to buy Stuart a saddle. She could only afford a second hand one, but she wanted to get something nice, and of good quality. There were one or two on eBay, and some people on Marketplace had them too, but her problem was how to get one of those without her dad cottoning on to what she was up to. Most times, if you bought something on Marketplace, you had to go and collect it. She figured she could probably ask her 'big brother' Darren. He didn't know anything much about riding, but she was fairly confident that he would be able to help her find a really nice saddle, and hide it too, if it came to that. Maybe she could get it engraved with Stuart's initials. She figured he would like that.

She'd talked with Jayde and Renae about going Christmas shopping in early December, on a day out together. They planned to ask their parents if they could take the train down to Preston for the day. There was a lot more choice down there, for one thing, and Meghan hadn't been yet. It would be nice to see the shops, and all the Christmas lights. Nan was coming up to stay for Christmas too, so there was plenty to look forward to.

The familiar sound of an engine starting up snapped her out of her daydream, and her heart sank. Shit! The bus was going! Even as she was running now, towards the bus stop, she saw that she didn't have a hope of reaching it in time. It was already pulling away. She could count on one hand, with fingers to spare, how many times she'd missed catching it home from school. She'd been close, a couple of times, but the driver had always spotted her dashing up from behind, and held on for her.

Not today. A guy who'd stopped her in the street to ask directions had stolen all of the precious minutes from her that she needed, to comfortably make it to the bus stop before the whine of the diesel engine told her she was too late. Frustratingly, the guy hadn't understood most of what she was trying to tell him. He'd kept asking her to repeat herself. The time it took to get through to him was all the time it took to ensure she'd missed her bus, and would have to call her Dad to come and pick her up.

Great. He'll be bloody furious!

Meghan figured she may as well walk into town to wait for him there. She decided to send him a text instead of calling. That way, by the time he got to her, he might have calmed down.

With her attention on her phone, and her mind composing the grovelling text she intended to send him, she didn't notice the white van pulling up behind her. By the time she heard it and looked up, she was already being dragged towards it. One filthy hand covered her mouth to prevent her from screaming, and the other pulled her roughly into the back. Everything happened in the blink of an eye. The man she instantly recognised as the one who'd stopped her to ask her for directions landed on top of her. In a split second, he'd turned and yanked the door closed behind him. He released his hold over Meghan's mouth and she opened it to scream, but she immediately stopped as he produced a Stanley knife and held it in front of her face.

'Shut your trap, bitch, or I'll open it so wide you'll never get it shut again.' His voice was vicious, more like a snarl.

Meghan shrank back, as far as the filthy floor of the van would allow. 'W-w-what do you w-want?' She stammered.

'Ah! Now there's a good question! What do we want?' He laughed harshly then raised his head and yelled at someone, presumably the driver of the van.

'What do we want, Pete? A little bit of fun, maybe? Should we have some fun with this one, mate? I bet she bucks like a bronco. I bet she'd lap it all up and beg for more.' He licked his lips and kept raising his eyebrows at her. She felt a sharp stab of fear. She stared at him, noting his heavy five-o'clock shadow, his small, neat teeth, and his half-crazy eyes.

Details. I have to remember details. Everything. Face, voice, body shape, smell, clothing, tattoos, rings, details. I need to remember. Details.

She tried to concentrate on details, but she was terrified. Was she going to be raped and murdered buy this random stranger? And he *was* a stranger. She'd never seen him before in her life. And what about the driver? What did they want from her? Her mind scrambled to make sense of what was happening.

I've heard about this. I've read about it. Girls being bundled into cars, driven to remote places, raped and strangled, and their bodies sometimes never found. Or worse, being trafficked out of the country to God knows where, as sex slaves. I hope someone saw. Maybe someone saw, and they've already called the police. Maybe the police are on their way.

'D-did you *make* me miss my bus? D-did you *plan* to abduct me?'

The man pulled a leery face at her. 'Oh, who's a clever girl then?'

Meghan found her courage. 'It w-won't work. Someone will have s-seen what you did. The police will find us, any minute now. And I've already texted my dad.'

A sudden, stinging slap across her face made her gasp with pain. Her bottom lip had split wide open. She could feel it beginning to swell, and she swallowed the blood that pooled in her mouth. She shrank back, as the man pushed his hand up her skirt.

'Pete!' he hollered. 'Keep driving, man. I'm gonna have myself a big slice of fun back here with this hot little bitch. You can have her after, if there's anything left!' He was grinning and licking his lips again. He moved to pull her panties down. Instinctively she screamed and cringed away from him. He grabbed her hand and shoved it into his crotch as he rolled on top of her. 'Feel what I've got for ya!'

Meghan struggled, tried to knee him in the balls just as her Dad had always told her she should if a man tried to attack her, but it didn't work. She screamed again, as loudly as she could, then stopped as his fist landed with a sickening crunch halfway between her nose and her left eye. The white-hot pain blinded her to everything else around her. She struggled for breath as he struggled to get his fingers inside her panties. She tried not to pass out, tried to keep concentrating on details. The van then came to an abrupt, screeching stop. Both Meghan and her attacker found themselves sliding around, as the brakes were jammed on. She hit the back of her head on a wheel arch and gasped in pain. The man looked up in surprise. 'What the fuck? I said keep driving, Pete!'

The back door of the van opened, and a pair of hands pulled the man roughly off Meghan. Presumably, it was the driver, the man she knew was called Pete.

'Keith, don't! Don't rape this kid. That wasn't the deal.'

The man Meghan now knew as Keith, inched up to Pete and laughed in his face. 'Oh, come on, you fucking killjoy! It's a bloody nice little sweetener, don't you think? A tasty, sweet bit of cherry?' He rubbed his crotch suggestively and grinned crazily at Meghan. 'Or maybe there is no cherry! Maybe that's long gone. Maybe you're a horny little slut who still couldn't get enough of me if I banged you all day long. Maybe you'd just keep screaming for more.'

Pete, who was as thick-set and heavy as Keith, and who would easily have been a match for him, shook his head.

'Stop being a prick, Keith. She's just a kid! We came here to find your missus. That's it. That's all we do. Anything else, and you're on your own. You keep trying to do this, I'll dump you right here and drive away, and you can find your own way back to fucking Birmingham. It's bastard-bloody wrong mate, and you know it.'

He pushed Keith away from him and glanced over at Meghan then quickly looked away. He didn't say another word, and his face was grim. He clearly didn't want to get involved any further. She knew there was no point in trying to appeal to him.

Keith rubbed his face with a dirty hand, clearly weighing up Pete's ultimatum. He looked again at Meghan, licked his lips again, and looked her up and down. His shoulders slumped.

'Oh, have it your way, you boring twat,' he mumbled. 'But she's seen our faces, mate.'

'I don't give a fuck. You find out what you want to know, and that's the end of it. Nothing more. I mean it, Keith.'

Keith turned back towards Meghan and put his face right up against hers. She could smell his breath. It stank of stale beer and rancid cigarette smoke. She fought the impulse to gag. 'Where's Caroline?' he snarled.

Meghan blinked at him. *Caroline? Who the hell is Caroline?*

She had no idea what he was talking about. 'I d-don't know who you m-mean. I don't know any Caroline. You've got the wrong p-person.'

Keith frowned at her. 'Oh, come on, now! Sure you know her! You know her well enough to have pizza with her. Nice little family photo I've got, of that. Very cosy.' His voice took a vicious tone. 'And I want to know who the fucker is, that was with you – your daddy maybe? Is the guy in the picture your daddy? Is that who the slag is fucking? Maybe if I carve your face up real nice, maybe you'll remember.'

Meghan was crying hard now. 'I don't know anybody called Caroline, and my dad isn't seeing anyone!'

Keith smashed his knee into Meghan's belly. She screamed in pain and drew herself into a tight ball, to try and ease the agony. Her breath came in ragged gasps as she tried to comprehend what was happening. She struggled not to faint. Keith reached over and pulled her hair so hard she thought it would come out of her scalp.

'You're lying, you dirty little bitch. Now tell me where they are, or I'll turn your pretty face into a jigsaw puzzle.' He brought the Stanley knife close to her face. Suddenly, with no warning, he literally screamed. 'I'm not kidding!'

Meghan flinched hard, then scrabbled backwards, to try and put some distance between the knife and her face. She was terrified, and utterly confused. Keith leaned closer and she felt the first prick of the blade against her cheek. She felt the blood oozing down her face in a hot, sticky trail, and wondered how bad the cut was.

'Really,' she sobbed. 'I d-don't know any Caroline. I s-swear.'

Keith let go of Meghan's hair and fumbled in his pocket for his mobile phone. He flicked through it with his spare hand, while the other still held the knife to her cheek. He scrolled through until he found what he wanted and showed it to her. It was, unmistakably, a photograph of her and Stuart, in Pizza Hut in Carlisle, with their carpenter Yvonne.

'What? *Her*? I know her, b-but her name's not Caroline!'

Meghan's mind was completely fogged and uncomprehending. Then, slowly, it dawned on her. This must be Yvonne's ex, and her name – clearly – wasn't Yvonne. It was Caroline. Keith lunged forward again, dropping his phone and pulling Meghan's hair again so hard it made her cry out with pain.

'Her name is Caroline. I don't know what she's told you, but I need to know where she is. Right. Fucking. Now.' His voice was suddenly very quiet and very deadly. She couldn't stop shaking. 'I *will* carve your face into a roadmap in the next thirty seconds, if you don't tell me where she is.'

Meghan could hardly breathe. She didn't want to betray Yvonne, but she had no choice. 'W-we live at B-beaconsfield Stables. Yvonne w-works for my dad. She's rebuilding our barn.'

Keith smiled, slyly. 'Yvonne! Well, well, well. How interesting is that... Well, thank you very much, kitten. I'm glad we could see eye to eye. Shame I can't give you the hours of manly attention you'd really love right now, but I've got places to be, people to see. You know how it is.'

He licked the blood from the side of her face, from bottom to top, and she shuddered. He whispered, his vile breath making her choke, 'I'm a very busy boy. But how about a rain-check? Maybe I can come back sometime, and munch on your juicy little muff, make you squirm a little.'

He got up from on top of Meghan and backed out of the van. He hauled her out by the collar of her shirt, and dumped her on the ground, where she lay motionless and shaking, too afraid to move. She gasped for breath as she kept her head down, barely noticing the slamming of the van's doors. The sound of it pulling away was the first thing her mind managed to properly register. She waited until she was sure it was gone before uncurling her body and slowly getting to her hands and knees. She vomited hard, into the road. Her face stung, and the dull ache in her belly had spread to her lower back. She lifted her head and looked around.

She was in a place she didn't recognise. As she shakily got to her feet, she realised it was a backroad that didn't look like it saw much traffic. It might be hours before anyone else drove up here. She put a hand to her face and felt the wound on her cheek. To her fingers, it seemed small. She hoped it would be. Limping to the side of the road, she sat down and scrabbled for her phone which was, thankfully, still in the inside pocket of her blazer. Shakily she pressed Stuart's number, and wailed when it went straight to voicemail.

'You've reached Stuart Thomson at Beaconsfield Stables. I'm sorry I can't take your call right now. Please leave your name, number and a brief message, and I'll get back to you as soon as I can.'

She promptly burst into tears. 'Daddy, it's Meghan. I don't know where I am, but I've b-been attacked by s-someone who is looking for Yvonne.' Meghan wasn't aware of how hard she was crying. 'Daddy, I'm hurt, and s-someone is coming for Yvonne. A man called Keith. I had to tell him where she was. He was going to c-cut me and maybe even k-kill me. I'm s-so sorry, Daddy.'

She stared out into the middle distance for a moment, then looked down at her phone. Refocusing, she found Darren Davies' number. Mercifully, he answered. She sobbed into the phone, 'Bismillah. Bismillah. Bismillah.' She was so relieved, she started sobbing uncontrollably as she tried to tell him what had happened, and the fact that she was trying to reach her father and couldn't.

Darren's voice was calm and reassuring. 'Ok, babe. Okay. Just listen to me, now. If you can get the internet, look up your coordinates on your map and text them to me. Then ring me straight back. I'm coming to get you.' Darren's voice was kind but authoritative. It helped Meghan to focus.

She managed to get enough of an internet signal to work out where she was, and she quickly texted Darren. He rang her back immediately. It sounded as if he was already in his Land Rover.

'I know where you are, Meghan. You're out on Deliverance Road, out the back of Foster's Reach. Stay exactly where you are. I'll be there in less than ten minutes.'

Despite it being the longest ten minutes of Meghan's life, Darren was as good as his word. As soon as he reached her, he leapt out of his Land Rover and ran across to where she was sitting, on the ground not far from where she'd been dragged from the van. He couldn't conceal his horror from her. She was still crying, but this time with relief, as he pulled her up off the road and into a big warm hug. It hurt, but it felt really, really good. She was safe now. Darren would never let anything happen to her. He led her to the Land Rover and helped her to get inside.

'Okay. It's okay, baby. I'm here now. You're okay. Let's get you into the Landy, and we can get you to the hospital.'

Meghan shook her head. 'No. We have to get to the stables. The man, Keith, he's on his way there. He's going to hurt Yvonne, and Dad. We have to stop him.'

Darren glanced over at her as he threw the Land Rover into gear and set off. He rang the police on his hands-free, and reported the incident, adding that he thought the perpetrators were on their way to Beaconsfield Stables and he was on his way there himself. The police confirmed they would meet him there.

As he drove, he asked Meghan to tell him everything she could remember, right from the minute she'd first been accosted in the street by the man who asked for directions. She could see his jaw setting harder as she spoke, relaying everything about her encounter. She'd never seen him so angry. He looked literally murderous. He never took his eyes off the road, but he reached over and took her hand and squeezed it.

'You've remembered a lot of detail. That's good. Now you've told me, I can remember it too. It will be useful later. Are you hurt anywhere else?'

'Just my stomach. He put his knee into my stomach really hard, and he was going to rape me, but his friend stopped him. Is my nose broken?'

Darren nodded grimly. 'Yes, it might be. But we'll find out for sure. I know you're probably desperate to wash your face, but don't, at least not until the police have taken a look at it.'

It seemed like a long way to the stables, and when they eventually pulled into the car park, the white van was already there.

'Oh, no!'

Darren leapt from the Land Rover. 'Stay here, Meghan. Don't move. No matter what happens, no matter what you hear or see, promise me – *promise me* – you'll stay in this vehicle, okay? Don't get out. Not for anything.'

She couldn't answer, but he was already running towards the barn, and she clambered down from the passenger seat and ran after him. He didn't notice, and she didn't know what he'd have done if he had, but she followed him anyway. She wasn't able to run properly because of the pain in her belly, but she was more worried about her father, and about Darren, to care.

As Darren rounded the corner of the stable block and the barn came into sight, Meghan saw him come to a sudden stop. He then began to creep forward, stealthily, towards the barn door. Meghan could hear the screaming sound of her father's table saw, and her blood ran cold. She could also hear shouting and she came up behind Darren who turned, realising that she'd ignored his order that she stay in the Land Rover. He frowned and shook his head at her, then put his finger to his lips and turned away from her, holding a hand behind him as if to push her back.

Out of the corner of her eye she could see a man running along the fence line, back the way they'd come, back towards where the white van was parked. She saw that it was Pete, the driver, but before she had time to understand what he was doing, more shouting made her turn back towards the barn.

Darren had picked up a three-foot long piece of timber and was again creeping silently towards the barn's open door. The table saw hadn't stopped for a second, and she wondered if that meant there was nothing wrong at all in there. But, as Darren stepped into the barn, and Meghan followed, she could see Yvonne slumped over a sawhorse just inside the entrance. She appeared to be unconscious, with blood seeping from a heavy, deep cut above her right eye. Meghan's breath hitched in her throat.

Darren suddenly stopped, and stared straight ahead. Meghan could see Keith stealthily approaching her father from behind, holding a heavy length of timber, similar to the one Darren was holding, high above his head. To Meghan's horror, Stuart was completely oblivious. He had his back to everything, working the saw with his heavy-duty ear protectors on. The noise of the machine meant he'd probably heard nothing of what had happened behind him. Clearly, Keith was lining up to bash his head in with the piece of wood.

'Dad!' Meghan screamed involuntarily behind Darren, just as he lunged forward. As he did so, Keith caught the movement from the corner of his eye and swung around, and aimed his lump of wood at him instead. Darren managed to dodge it, before dealing a swift, precise blow to the side of Keith's face. The man went down in a crumpled heap, hitting his head on the sharp edge of a pallet of stone slabs as he went. His lifeless eyes stared up at the ceiling as the table saw whined to a stop.

Stuart turned, aghast. His mouth hung open in disbelief, at the sights before him; Yvonne, unconscious and bleeding, Meghan bloodied and wild-eyed, Darren Davies standing stock still as if in deep shock and holding a hunk of four-by-two, and a man he'd never seen before in his life lying dead at his feet. All of a sudden, after all the chaotic noise, you could have heard a pin drop in the barn. Meghan felt the tears pouring down her cheeks as the approaching sirens grew louder, and the sound of slamming doors and mumbled voices reached her ears. As she slowly sank to the floor, a sharp wailing noise entered her consciousness, and it took her a moment to realise it was herself that she could hear.

Suddenly the barn was full of people, all talking at once. Four paramedics swarmed over Yvonne and Meghan after it was quickly established that Keith was a lost cause.

A couple of police officers, a man and a woman, were talking to Stuart. Meghan heard someone say that more were on the way and a SOCO team (whatever that was) was coming to assess the timeline of what had happened, gather evidence, and remove the body and the van for forensic analysis, and the female officer would stay with Meghan. The officers quickly shepherded everyone out of the barn, and one started to wind police tape across the entrance to stop anyone from going back in.

He then informed a colleague that he had already apprehended Pete as he'd tried to hightail it from the stables after he'd seen what he thought was Keith murdering Yvonne. He was currently handcuffed and sitting in the back of one of the squad cars, and would be taken to the station for further questioning. Put on the spot, Pete had confessed to thinking Keith had already killed Yvonne and was about to kill Stuart. It was why he was running in the opposite direction from the barn. He'd said he wanted no part of murder.

The police told Darren they would interview him later. Stuart wasn't of much help to them, it seemed, as he hadn't seen or heard a thing prior to Darren disabling Keith, but they also wanted a statement from him, nonetheless.

Meghan's nose did appear to be broken, and her left eye socket fractured. She would need to go to the hospital for x-rays to confirm everything, and to have a stitch put into her cheek, but she didn't want to do it right away. She just wanted to be with her Dad, and with Darren. She felt completely numb as Yvonne, who was still unconscious, was put into another of the ambulances and taken away and the last one of the three drove off empty. Nobody was available to go with Yvonne, but the police assured everyone that they would report on any progress, as soon as they could. The piece of wood that Keith had been intending to use on Stuart already had Yvonne's blood on it. It seemed fairly clear that he'd delivered the wound that had rendered her unconscious.

It also was mentioned, but Meghan wasn't sure who by, that Darren would likely escape without charge. He'd undoubtedly saved Stuart's life, and it already seemed obvious that his blow to Keith wasn't heavy enough to have been fatal. It was the way the man had fallen, hitting his head on the corner of a heavy pallet of slabs, that had killed him. Under all apparent circumstances, Darren's actions in trying to protect Stuart, and himself when Keith had turned on him instead, would likely be classed as self-defence.

The policewoman put her arm around Meghan's shoulders. 'Shall we go into the house? I dunno about you, but I'm freezing, and I could use a cup of tea.' She led Meghan to the house and sat her at the kitchen table. 'You don't mind if I make us a drink, do you?'

Meghan shook her head as she tried – and failed – to stop herself from shaking. The policewoman made the tea, then ran a little water into it from the cold tap. 'Here, that should be just warm now, not too painful for you to drink.' She was very kind, and a bit 'mumsy.'

'Did he rape you?' she asked bluntly. Meghan shook her head.

'He tried,' she mumbled through her swollen lip. 'I resisted, but it wasn't much help. That other guy, Pete? He stopped him. If it wasn't for that, he would've.' She was crying again now.

Her dad came into the kitchen, followed quickly by Darren, who had Chase on a short lead. He'd rescued the dog from the caravan. 'He was barking his prunes off,' Darren explained quietly to the policewoman. 'Panicking, wondering what's happened to his mum. I thought I should bring him in.'

'Good idea,' the policewoman said simply.

Both men looked utterly shocked. Stuart reached his daughter in two swift strides and gathered her into his arms. He buried his face in her hair. He was crying. 'Sweetheart, I'm so sorry! I'm so sorry for what's happened to you. We need to get you to the hospital, to get you seen to.'

She hugged him hard, not knowing what to say. She looked over his shoulder at Darren, who had tears in his own eyes. He just nodded at her, unsmiling, and then he gave her one of his trademark winks, one of those that always said the same thing; 'it's gonna be okay.'

The policewoman handed both men a mug of tea each, and they all sat down at the table. Stuart wouldn't let go of Meghan's hand. Her left eye was closing rapidly now, and when she put her hand to it, it felt like a tender, soft, squishy tennis ball growing on her face. She struggled to breathe through her nose, and her back and stomach felt like they were on fire. She knew she needed to go to the hospital, to get properly checked out. She was terrified of being scarred and injured for life. The sooner they could get there, the sooner she would know for sure, one way or the other.

She looked across at Darren. He looked half dazed, still, as if he couldn't believe what he'd done in the barn. Meghan could hardly believe it herself. She knew that the image, of an evil man preparing to murder her dad, and Darren managing to stop him, would be a long time leaving her mind, if it ever did at all.

The policewoman was brisk. 'Alright gentlemen, please stop staring at the table. It doesn't have any answers or ideas. But I do. One of you needs to take this young lady to the hospital, pronto. They are expecting her, imminently, so you need to get going. I will wait here for SOCO to arrive and for my colleague to come back and get me. I'll hold the fort, don't you worry about that. Dr Davies, have you already been told that we'll need to speak to you formally tomorrow?'

'Er, yeah. That's fine. Do I need to come to the station, or will you come to my work?'

'Best come to the station. We'll ring you first thing with an appointment time. Mr Thomson, we'll need to speak to you and Meghan tomorrow as well. Same deal. We'll phone you with a time to come out to you. You don't need to come to the station. Now go! Get this lass to the hospital.'

Meghan turned to her father. 'I want to get changed first, and get a shower.'

The policewoman shook her head. 'Sorry love, you can take a change of clothes with you to the hospital and you can possibly have a shower there after they've examined you. But they need to take your clothes, and swabs of your skin, before you can do any of that.'

'But I've told you. He didn't rape me.'

Stuart gasped and put his hands to the sides of his head, and Darren looked at her in anguish.

'I'm telling you the truth. He didn't.'

'I know love,' the policewoman smiled at her gently. 'But we'll still want whatever evidence we can get.'

'But why? He's dead. What difference does it make?'

'It's just to tie everything in together, so there's no loose ends, and so we can get you the right help, medically and emotionally. There's victim counselling, stuff like that.'

Meghan snapped at her. 'Don't call me a victim! I'm not a victim!'

'Okay, love, that's fair enough. I'm sorry. Please, forgive me. It's just that we have a procedure to follow, for everyone's sake, so please just let us do it. It won't take long, and then you can have your shower and your fresh clothes.'

'Dad, I need to go and see Astro.'

Stuart turned to her. 'What, *now?* Can't it wait until you get back?'

'No, Dad. I need to see her before we go.'

The policewoman looked confused. 'Who, or what, is Astro?'

Darren spoke up. 'One of the horses here. Her best friend.' He looked over at Stuart. 'I'll take her. Five minutes Meghan, that's all, ok? Then after you get home you can spend as much time as you want with her.'

He stood up and held his hand out. She took it gratefully and allowed him to walk her out into the chilly early evening. He put his arm around her gently as they walked.

The horses were still out, and as they approached, they all lifted their heads to look at her. All nine of them stood stock still, staring, until she got to the ring. She just stood there, crying, as they all came up to her as a group, whinnying gently as they surrounded her. Astro stepped closer, blew softy into Meghan's battered face, and put her soft nose gently into the side of her neck. Meghan reached up and put her arms around her. The other horses all touched her with their noses too, blowing cool, soft air onto her and nickering softly. She could feel their love, their concern, and she stumbled a little when Finnegan pressed the full length of his head gently into the small of her back. She realised he was offering her intuitive healing and she steadied herself while he gently nudged her with his nose.

'Astro!' she sobbed quietly into the horse's mane. 'Astro.'

Surrounded by her quiet, solid friends, she felt calmer, more centred. Most people didn't understand the healing power of horses, she knew that. But here it was; equine balm on open wounds, the most soothing salve imaginable. She whispered to them.

'I'll be home soon. We can all be together again as soon as I get back.' She kissed all nine of their noses, marvelling that some of them were letting her do it for the very first time. These creatures knew what her need was, and they all stood ready to meet it. Astro snorted gently into her face again.

'I know, girl. I know. Thank you, baby. I'll see you soon.' Instinctively the horses broke apart, giving Meghan passage back to the side of the ring. They watched her with calm, serious faces as she walked away, still offering their love and healing.

She was astonished, on returning to where Darren was standing, to see that his eyes were glistening with unshed tears. She just looked at him and closed her eyes.

'Thank you for saving my Dad's life.'

'Meghan, I'm sorry you had to see...'

'No, it's okay. He got what he deserved, that man. I'm glad you got to him before he hurt Dad. I don't think I'd survive it, if anything happened to him.'

'I don't think *he'd* survive it if anything worse had happened to *you*! Today's hit him very hard. It's hit us *all* very hard. You the most.'

'Are you going to be okay? Legally, I mean?'

Darren agave her another of his trademark winks but, again, it came without its usual smile. 'Yeah. I'll be fine, babe. They seem to think it's a cut-and-dried case of self-defence, and all I did was give him a glancing blow. They already know that. It wouldn't have been enough to kill him; maybe not even to knock him out. It was the way he fell that finished him off.

'So listen, your Dad's going to take you to the hospital, and I'm going to head home for the day. I'll see if I can get Debs to come home early from work. We'll check in with you guys, later tonight, and we'll come back over if you want us to. No problem.'

They walked back to the house, where Stuart was waiting, now with his jacket on. 'Right? Ready? Let's go.' He held a coat out to Meghan and she shrugged her way into it. Her face was throbbing and it felt like it was on fire.

'My backpack was in the van, Dad. I don't know if it's still there. But I want to take fresh clothes, so I need something to put them in.'

Stuart took his own backpack off the hook behind the front door, and handed it to her. She took it and went upstairs to get a clean pair of jeans, fresh underwear and a jumper.

As they walked towards the car park, Stuart put his arm around Meghan. When they reached their cars, he turned to Darren.

'I can't thank you enough for today, for stopping that monster, and for what you did for Meghan. I'll *never* be able to thank you enough.'

Darren closed his eyes and shook his head. 'No thanks needed, Stu. It's what any good mate would do for another. And this young lady?' He gestured at Meghan. 'She's like my little sister, and a bloke would fight to the fucking death for his little sister, wouldn't he? It's just what you do.'

Stuart hugged him hard. 'I'm glad you've got my back, mate.'

In the car, on the way to the hospital, he spoke quietly. 'I'm so sorry I didn't pick up the phone when you rang me, from out there. I just didn't hear it! I wish with all my heart that I could have picked it up. The thought of you out there, with those monsters...'

'Dad, it's okay. Darren came, and we got here in time to save you. That's what matters. I wasn't on my own for long.'

'I'm your dad, Meghan, and it's my job to protect you. I didn't do that today. I let you down, in not picking up the phone. I should always pick up the phone.'

'Dad, you didn't let me down! I heard it for myself, how noisy that saw was! You couldn't hear *anything* over that. You couldn't even hear Yvonne being bashed unconscious right behind you, or me screaming when I could see what was going to happen! How could you have heard a phone ringing on the workbench?'

'Well, I'm going to use the vibrate function from now on, and I'm going to keep it in my pocket at all times, so I'll never miss it ringing, *ever* again.' He glanced in his rearview mirror and changed lanes as the approach to the hospital came into sight. 'Maybe we could check on Yvonne while we're here.'

'Why? It's all because of her that this has happened. If she hadn't come here, we wouldn't have had today. It's all her fault, everything that's happened. I don't want to see her. I just want her to go away and never come back. Her name's not Yvonne, either, by the way. Its Caroline.'

'What? Well, ok, I guess we'll get to the bottom of that, at some stage. But you need to remember Meghan, that what you endured today from that man; that's what she had to endure too, only for a lot longer and it was probably even worse. She wanted to get away from that. She would never have intentionally brought trouble to our door. She wouldn't have wanted that.'

'Well maybe it wasn't intentional, but he still found out she was here, didn't he?'

Stuart shook his head. 'I don't know how he even found that out. Yvonne – or should I say, Caroline? She swore that she'd never tell a soul. Her own mother didn't even know she was here, Meggie. *Nobody* knew where she was, and I would stake my own life on her not telling anyone. I don't know how he could have worked it out.'

Meghan started to cry again. 'He had a photo of us all in Pizza Hut. It was my school uniform that led him to the school, to wait for me. He thought you were having a relationship.'

'Dad, I didn't want to tell him where you were. Please believe me, I didn't want to. But he told me he was going to cut me up. He held a knife in my face and said he would turn it into a roadmap. I believed him, and I thought he was going to rape me too, and then kill me. I'm so sorry, Daddy.'

Stuart briefly closed his eyes. 'No, you did the right thing. Honestly, you did! There was no choice for you. There's nothing to be sorry for.' He looked at her as he pulled into a parking space. 'What else did he say to you. How else did he threaten you?'

Meghan felt uncomfortable. She didn't want to tell her father the acutely embarrassing details about what Keith had threatened to do to her. It was disgusting, what he'd talked about. The memory of it, and of his rancid breath on her face, made her want to throw up again. Luckily, there was nothing except a cup of tea left in her stomach to vomit back.

Tears pricked her eyes again as she mumbled. 'Nothing Dad. It was nothing.'

I'm gonna have myself a big slice of fun back here with this hot little bitch.

She shook her head, as if to clear it. After they'd reported to the desk as expected and been ushered through to a treatment bay, she vowed that while she would tell them what her injuries were and how she got them, she would never tell a single living human being what had been said to her in the back of that filthy van.

Chapter Twenty-one

'He certainly was a nasty piece of work,' the sergeant concluded, at the end of his summary. 'I doubt many people will mourn his passing. Certainly not the women he's hurt in the past, I'd wager.'

Stuart was sickened by what he'd been told about his daughter's abductor. Keith Brockett really had been the worst kind of animal. The fact that poor Meghan had ended up at the mercy of someone like that was pretty tough to come to terms with. What kind of monster beats and threatens to rape an innocent fourteen-year-old girl? Stuart thanked the angels who had prevented Meghan from being violated in the worst possible way. He was even grateful to Brockett's accomplice, Pete Higgins, who clearly had at least enough moral conscience to stop Brockett from doing that. Listening to Meghan's anguished voicemail message on his phone was utterly heartbreaking.

After he'd been reassured that his daughter was in capable hands, Stuart went in search of his carpenter. He found her in a ward just one floor up from the A & E department. She'd been admitted and was now conscious. The police were about to interview her, so Stuart wasn't allowed to see her. He left a message, to say that he'd be back in the morning, but if she was being released she just had to call him to come and collect her. He also asked the nursing staff to let her know that Chase was being well looked after. She wouldn't know any of what had happened to Meghan yet, or that Keith Brockett was dead, although he was sure she'd be told that particular pertinent nugget as soon as she was *compos mentis* enough to understand it.

Would she feel sad, or relieved? With victims of abuse, it was hard to predict. Stuart imagined that she'd probably feel a little of both. At any rate, she'd be utterly horrified when she found out the events that had led to Brockett's demise.

He didn't know how he felt about her now; whether he wanted her to stay and finish the barn, even if *she* did. Poor Meghan had suffered enough. How would she feel about having a constant, unrelenting reminder around, of what she'd had to endure?

He wouldn't know the answers for a while yet. He spoke for a few minutes to the police officers waiting to interview 'Yvonne,' whose real name was in fact Caroline Swift, and he gave permission for them to access Meghan's medical notes once she'd been treated.

He owned a massive debt of gratitude to Darren. Not only had his new friend saved his life, he may well also have saved Caroline's. Most importantly of all, he was there for Meghan when she needed someone more than she ever had before, traumatized, terrified, injured, and left shaking and bleeding at the roadside, miles from anywhere. He had to swallow down the lump in his throat when he thought about what she'd had to endure in the back of that van. She wouldn't talk to him about what had been said to her, and he did kind of understand why she might not want to, but he hoped she would be able to talk to *somebody*, and soon.

As he made his way back to the A & E department, he heard his name called and he turned around to see Debby walking quickly towards him, her face frozen in disbelief. She was wearing street clothes instead of her nurse's uniform. She immediately threw her arms around him.

'Oh, my God, Stuart! Darren called me. He told me everything. I've just bailed on my shift early, to head home. It's almost unbelievable, all this! Is Meghan okay? Are *you* okay?'

'Yeah, I'm alright. I think Meghan's alright. She's being checked over now. Pretty roughed up and very upset, but a lot of it looks superficial, physically at least. As to her emotional state, well I don't know. It might be too soon to say, Debs. There's a lot to process.'

Debby grimaced. 'Yes, there is. I'll come down with you now and say hi to her, before I head off. Do you have everything you need?'

Stuart nodded. 'I think so. Might be takeaways tonight though. I don't really feel like cooking. If Meghan wants to eat anything at all, it can be her choice.'

'Good idea. I hope you can get her to eat something. And she'll need to sleep, for as long as she can. I'll see if they'll give her a mild sedative to take for a couple of days, just so she can get some good rest and her body can start to heal.'

Meghan's examination was nearly finished. Debby went behind the curtain and Stuart could hear her reassuring his daughter. Everything went quiet, and then the doctor and other nurse who were attending to her left. Only Debby remained. Stuart could hear Meghan crying softly, and it tore him apart.

If you weren't already dead, you monstrous son of a bitch, I'd fucking kill you myself.

All he wanted to do was make Meghan's pain go away. He wished, in that moment, that he could turn back the clock; that they'd never met Caroline Swift. As much as he had no idea how to feel about her right now, he certainly didn't blame her for one second, for not wanting to be known by anyone as Caroline Brockett!

After a time, another nurse appeared, and Debby stepped back out. Clearly, they were taking great care not to leave Meghan on her own. Debby squeezed Stuart's arm.

'They're pretty much done. She's going to have a quick shower and then you can take her home. She'll be given a couple of mild sleeping tablets, for the next couple of nights.' She sighed, deeply, as if she'd hauled it all the way up from the bottom of her feet.

'We're having takeaways too. I think Darren could do with some serious stodge tonight and I pretty much feel the same. To hell with it. I'm breaking all my own rules. We'll call you later on tonight, Stu, and we'll come over if you want us to.'

'Is Darren okay? He seemed it, but what he did was a hell of a thing. He's been through a lot today, too.'

Debby nodded, shortly. 'He's fine, Stu. He needs to process everything too, and we'll probably talk about it a lot tonight, to help get it settled in his own head, but he's mostly just glad you and Meghan are okay. I'd hate to think what state he'd be in if you weren't; if he hadn't got to you in time. But he did, and you're both safe, and that's all that matters. Take care.' She kissed him on the cheek and left.

Stuart hovered as close as he could to Meghan's treatment bay. He wanted to be the first person she saw when she came out. When she finally did, she looked a lot better. She'd had a quick shower and was wearing a clean pair of jeans and a jumper. Her hair hung damply around her swollen face. She looked small and very young.

Her face had been cleaned up a lot. Her left eye was still bulging and swollen shut and her split lip looked swollen and painful too, but with the encrusted blood cleared away neither looked so bad. Her cheek had a small stitch in it, where Brockett's Stanley knife had punctured the skin, but the nurse informed him that they expected everything to heal well, and not leave any scars. They'd done an ultrasound of Meghan's abdomen, and happily had found nothing sinister, but she would have a lot of painful bruising for a week or so, and Stuart was advised to keep her off school.

'You might want to go see the Head, and explain in person, rather than over the phone. A sexually motivated attack needs to be very sensitively handled. A good conversation will help clarify for you *and* for Meghan, how the school will deal with this and support her as she recovers.'

'Is PTSD likely to be an issue?'

The nurse nodded. 'Yeah, maybe. There could be a bit of emotional upheaval. It's fairly common after an assault like this. That's why it's important to put the school in the picture so they can watch out for any behaviour that might indicate Meghan's struggling.

'They see her for more waking hours than you do, remember. They'll notice her interactions, her performance in her classes, all the stuff that can indicate changes that might need to be addressed before they become more problematic. But, there again, she may be absolutely fine. A lot of young women in this situation do bounce back surprisingly well, with no major after-effects. It's worth keeping an eye on her, for sure, but try not to worry too much. Let her talk if she wants to, in the next day or two, but don't press her if she doesn't.'

Meghan stayed quiet on the way home. Stuart didn't make too much effort to engage her in conversation. She had a lot to process. He told her that he was there if she wanted to talk, but he promised he wouldn't pressure her.

'Sweetheart, I love you so much, and I'm so very, very proud of you; so much it makes me want to cry. I don't know whether I've ever even said that to you before today. If I haven't, I'm sorry. But I've *always* been proud, of the way you've handled *everything*, especially since my accident. I know how tough it's been, and how horrible, and you never deserved any of it. I never wanted any of that for you, but I've ended up throwing so much at you. The way you've coped with everything, and the beautiful young woman you're turning into; I'm so proud I can hardly fucking breathe.'

Meghan was reflective for a minute. 'Thanks Dad, and I'm really proud of you too. It takes guts to do what you've done, you know, start a new life and everything? Life can be so cruel. So horrible. We can't control what happens out there. We just have to make the best life we can in our own world, don't we, with the horses, and our friends?'

They picked up a Chinese takeaway on the way home, which Stuart put in the warming oven of their newly-refurbished Rayburn, while they went to get the horses in for the night. It was dark outside now, and the night air was chilly. Stuart was comforted to see how the animals all converged around Meghan when they saw her approach them. They'd definitely been waiting for her to come back. He was humbled, listening to them, as they all did their equine best to actually talk to her. She spent plenty of time with them, and especially with Astro, before and after locking them up.

The policewoman had brought Chase's bed into the kitchen, along with his food and water bowls, both of which were full to overflowing. She'd clearly done whatever she could to make the dog comfortable. Although very brisk and businesslike, she had a warm and caring heart, and a gentle smile.

The SOCO team would be back tomorrow morning first thing, to finish up, and then the tape would be taken down and Stuart could go back to the rebuild.

That bloody barn! The project's jinxed. If I didn't already have so much invested in it, I'd scrap it altogether and demolish the damn thing. Nothing but trouble from start to fucking finish.

Warwick Ford hadn't died on the property, but he may as well have. The shock wouldn't have been any greater. The barn project should have been his. That's what it was intended as – his project and his *home* – but he'd tragically died before they'd even really got started. Now someone else was dead too, albeit someone who probably deserved to be, but it didn't make the thought of the barn any more palatable.

Stuart came to the conclusion that if Yvonne, or Caroline, or whoever the hell she really was didn't want to continue, or if he or Meghan decided they didn't want her to, then it probably wasn't meant to be. He'd write off the losses, heavy as they were, and put an end to all thoughts of offering it as accommodation to paying guests. It simply didn't feel like the project he'd wanted it to be, anymore. The joy and the anticipation were gone. All Stuart felt now was a dull sense of obligation to seeing it through because they'd already spent so much on it.

Would he regain his optimism if they could make good progress on it and get it completed as intended before the spring? Maybe, but right now he couldn't imagine feeling better about it. He was seriously starting to doubt if it was worth the heavy price being paid, because who knew what else might go wrong? Could they *face* anything else?

After they had eaten, Meghan said she was going upstairs to bed. Stuart reminded her to take her sedative. She pulled a face but complied. Impulsively he pulled her into his arms and gave her a tight hug. 'Ow, piss off, Dad! Stop!' But she didn't pull away. Instead, she hugged him back. He fought back tears as he let her go, and he swallowed hard.

'See you in the morning, brat. Stay in bed for as long as you want.'

A small, tired smile played across her lips as she said a virtually inaudible 'goodnight.' When she'd gone upstairs Stuart finally allowed his pent-up tears to fall, there in the quiet kitchen, with nobody around to see.

His own sleep was fitful. He woke several times, and he wondered how Meghan was sleeping. The door to her bedroom was firmly shut, as it always was, but he opened it quietly, just a little, to check on her.

She was sound asleep. Her dark brown hair fanned across her pillow, and her face was still. Her breathing was rhythmic and slow. She was sleeping with her nightlight on, and he wasn't sure whether it was something she always did, or whether it was just tonight. Satisfied that she was peaceful, he closed the door again and tiptoed back to bed. It was going to be a long night.

He must have got *some* sleep, however, because he woke with a jolt, and a long pale shaft of watery sunlight was bouncing off the mirror on the opposite wall. It made the room feel brighter than it should have been at a quarter to eight on a late autumn morning. The beauty of living here was that you didn't even have to shut your curtains at night. Doing so did help to keep the heat in, but if he wanted to go to sleep in moonlight and wake up with the sun, he really could. Their nearest neighbour was almost a quarter of a mile away.

He heard the shower in the bathroom along the hall. Meghan was up, which was a good sign. Pre-empting her, he hastily threw on some track pants, a jumper and some slippers, and ran downstairs to get the coffee on. Since she wasn't going to school today, he figured she would probably want to spend the day with the horses. Maybe they could go for a ride later, just the two of them, if she felt up to that. Fresh air, time in nature, time with the horses, and maybe even taking the exuberant, affable Chase for a decent walk, all these things were healing activities.

He needed to phone the school, and he was on the phone to the Head as Meghan came into the kitchen. The Head didn't question why Stuart wanted to see him urgently. Instead, he simply cleared space in his diary for a nine thirty appointment.

As soon as they'd sat down to breakfast, of poached eggs on toast and fresh coffee, Stuart's phone was ringing again. It was Yvonne, or Caroline, to say she was being discharged and wondered if he would pick her up. She didn't say or ask anything else, and Stuart was glad. The last thing he wanted was to get into a heavy conversation over the phone about what had happened, especially in front of his daughter.

'I'll be there around ten. I have an appointment first, then I'll head straight over.'

He grinned humourlessly at Meghan. 'Busy morning for me, brat. I have to go out just after nine, to talk to your Head Teacher. Then I'm picking our bloody carpenter up from the hospital. She's being discharged.'

Meghan's face showed no emotion. Instead, she looked down at Chase, who had come and placed his nose on her knee. She patted the big shaggy retriever and bent down to kiss his nose. He gently licked her swollen eye, and she didn't stop him.

Stuart cleared his throat. 'Meggie; Yvonne, or should I say Caroline, is coming back today, so we have to talk about whether we want her to stay or go. We need to make a decision very soon, particularly if it's the latter.'

'Yeah, I know.' She didn't look up. He pressed on.

'I'm sorry we don't have more time, to make that choice. It feels like pressure, I know, but think it's vital that we do what feels right for us, and only after we both agree on what that is. I'd like to know what *you* think about it.'

She took some time to reply, speaking very quietly when she did. 'Well, I know he's not coming back. He can't hurt us anymore. He can't hurt *her* anymore. It's over for *all* of us. If she wants to stay, I don't mind.'

Stuart stared at her, astonished. He'd been expecting her to declare that she wanted Caroline out, with no preamble, given how hostile she'd been feeling towards her the night before. 'Are you sure that's how you really feel?'

Meghan nodded slowly. 'What you said in the car, yesterday? About her having to live with so much of his abuse? I can't imagine how anyone could put up with that for so long and still say sane. I thought I was going to go crazy in that van, and after what happened in the barn, yesterday. The battered women syndrome, and the whole dependency thing? I've read about it. I know how it works, for those women, and how hard it gets for them to leave. I know what happens to a lot of the ones who don't.

'But she *did* manage to leave, didn't she, Dad? She got out. Maybe she feels stronger now, and maybe if we throw her out she'll go back to feeling like nobody cares, and she's not worth anything. She might end up with someone *else* who hurts her, and maybe she won't ever be brave enough to leave again. Maybe she'll die because of the next asshole she ends up with.'

Stuart privately thought that those were a lot of maybes! But Meghan was right. It did sometimes take unimaginable courage, to save yourself.

'I've thought about it, Dad. She's lucky she survived yesterday. Maybe he thought he'd killed her, and maybe he would have gone back and finished her off after he was done with you, if she'd started to wake up or something. We'll never know. But you need the barn finished and she needs a job, so it's okay with me if you keep her on. You're the one who has to work with her though, so you have to feel okay about it too.'

Stuart blew his breath out through pursed lips, and shrugged. 'Wow! Okay. That's a pretty mature level of insight, Meghan, and it makes a lot of sense. It's really up to her then, I guess. If she doesn't want to stay, we can't stop her from going. I wouldn't even try, because I don't want anyone here who doesn't want to be, like you said from the very beginning. But if she would stay, I'd be okay with it too.'

Meghan shrugged at him. 'So I guess what we're saying is that we don't want her to stay but we don't want her to go. We're on the fence, and it's up to her.'

He mulled this observation over for a moment or two. 'Actually, no, that's not quite right. I think I really *do* want her to stay. I got given a big second chance, remember, with a lot of encouragement from Darren, after he'd been given a massive one from someone else. Maybe it's our turn, or should I say *my* turn, to pay it forward and be part of changing someone else's ruined life for the better. I know Darren would support that.'

'But he'd understand just as well if you didn't do it, Dad, and he'd still support you. If you told her to go, I mean, or just let her.'

'Yeah, you're right, he would. And get you, playing devil's advocate! But everyone deserves another bite of the apple, don't they? I'm going to offer Caroline the chance to stay, if she wants it. Not just to get the barn done, but to show some faith in her, so she can see that the world can be a good place, that not everyone will just sit in judgement or refuse to try and help. It doesn't feel right, somehow, to just write her off. It's not her fault Brockett came here. It was a freakish coincidence, and they happen sometimes.'

He looked up at the sound of tyres on the driveway. The SOCO team was back to finish up in the barn. He checked the clock, it was already just after nine. 'Are you going to be okay here on your own, while I run into town? I'll tell these guys to stay well away from the house. I don't think they need to come in here.'

Meghan eyed the van as it pulled up. 'Yeah, that's fine. I'll probably be out with Astro anyway. Get going if you want. I can get the horses out.'

'Thanks, brat. Maybe we could go for a ride this afternoon? If you're feeling up to it? Maybe take Finny and Sesame out?'

She nodded, distractedly. Stuart picked up his jacket, mobile phone and car keys.

'It looks cold out there,' he observed as he watched the SOCO team coming to the back door, all huddled up in warm coats. 'Wrap up warm, and don't stay out there if you start to feel chilled. You're still suffering from shock, so keep an eye on how you're feeling, okay? And remember the police are coming to take a statement from you at four o'clock, as arranged. I plan to be back by lunchtime anyway, at the very latest.'

'Dad, are you going to tell the Head everything?' Meghan's voice sounded small.

'Yes, sweetheart. I have to, I think. But it's all in the strictest confidence, and I'll tell you all about the conversation later. Every detail. I promise.'

She didn't smile, but she gave him the thumbs up. He met the SOCO team on the path and one of them gave him Meghan's backpack, that they'd found in the back of Brockett's van. It had a little blood on it. Stuart decided he would treat her to a new one, and put this one in the bin.

His meeting with the Head teacher at Meghan's school went well enough. The Head had been outraged and horrified at what had happened. Stuart left feeling reassured, though, that Meghan would be well supervised, covertly in most cases, to see if she was in need of extra support.

It was her choice about what she wanted to tell her peers, and Stuart would talk to her about the potential consequences of telling the truth or being economical with it, so she would be prepared for whatever happened. Some kids were surprisingly cruel, even to other kids who were victims of trauma and crime, but the Head thought that most, particularly the girls, would rally round Meghan. Some of the boys would show themselves as being protective too. She hadn't been at the school very long, but she already had some nice friends who would support her.

Stuart pulled into the drop-off area at the hospital, and quickly texted Caroline to let her know he was outside. Within about twenty seconds she was on her way out. Her head was heavily bandaged and she looked exhausted. As she got into the car she glanced sideways at him. 'Thank you for picking me up, and first please let me explain why I didn't give you my real name.'

Stuart shook his head as he pulled away from the kerb. 'You don't have to. I get it.'

'Well, I'm Caroline Swift, but most people call me Caro. You can do that from now on, if you want.'

He nodded, but kept his eyes on the road. 'How are you feeling?'

She looked out the window, away from him, fixing her eyes on the road ahead. 'I'm okay. How is Meghan?'

'I'm not sure how much you know.'

'I know all of it. Stuart. The police told me everything last night, from what Pete Higgins has told them.'

Apparently Higgins had sung like a canary to the police, in a bid to keep the heat off himself. Stuart wasn't surprised but, he reasoned, at least the bastard was doing the right thing now by telling everything he knew. As the driver of the van, he'd be charged as an accomplice to an abduction, at the very least. The police had also found a witness who had noticed a man matching Brockett's description detaining Meghan in the street on the pretext of asking directions. CCTV had corroborated that, as well as providing the evidence of him bundling her into the back of the van that Higgins was driving. In driving Brockett to Beaconsfield, Higgins would likely be implicated in his attempt to murder Stuart and Caroline, too. He could sing all he wanted, and Stuart was grateful for it, but the idiot wasn't going to get off scot-free. Nobody had any evidence of a gun being held to his head. Everything the stupid man did had been a choice.

Stuart never took his eyes from the road. 'So how did Brockett know you were here?'

'The worst, most bizarre kind of rotten luck, as it happens,' she responded. 'A workmate of his was up here on holiday. He happened to see me with you and Meghan in the Pizza Hut in Carlisle. It must've been that day we went into town for more nails and hinges, and we picked Meghan up and went there. He wasn't sure it was me, but he took a photo anyway, and he showed it to Keith after he got back to Birmingham.'

Stuart pulled into the local McDonalds as Caroline continued with the story. Meghan's school uniform in the photo Keith had was enough for him to track down which school she was at. According to Higgins, they'd waited for quite a few days for their chance to distract her, make her miss her bus, then abduct her to get her to tell them where Caroline was. It had all been a very calculated plan. Higgins confirmed that Brockett had intended to kill Caroline *and* Stuart, as he'd believed them to be a couple.

They found a quiet booth at one end of the restaurant. Neither he nor Caroline was particularly hungry, but they had a breakfast meal anyway. It was always easier to talk over food, and far more comfortable if you had something in your stomach. Stuart told her everything he knew about Meghan's ordeal in the van with Brockett, and added that it was Pete Higgins who'd stopped his daughter from being raped.

Caroline's eyes filled with tears. 'Oh my God, poor Meghan. Pete's not such a fine upstanding character himself, to be fair, but he's just weak, and easily led. He's not mean, like Keith. I don't know him all that well, but I never thought he was violent, at least not in the way Keith was. I used to wonder if Pete would always go along with whatever Keith wanted, because he so often did when it came to other stuff, but I'm glad to know he had enough principles to stand against him over that.'

'Me too. Apparently, he spilled his guts pretty quickly once they had him in custody, which was to be expected I suppose. If you blame a dead guy for everything, there's not much in the way of counterattack, is there?'

She shook her head and stared into her coffee. 'No, there's not. Pete's going down though, I imagine, once the police have finished gathering all the evidence. He also had no tax or MOT on the van, and there were fourteen outstanding other traffic violations.'

'Christ,' Stuart muttered. 'He hasn't helped himself much, has he?'

'No, but he's helping the police. It's his account that's giving them a picture of everything that happened. Of course, with Keith dead, there's nowhere for this to go now for anyone else *but* Pete. It's not looking good for him. Not that I really care.'

Stuart looked at her curiously. 'So how do you feel about the fact that your husband's dead?'

She looked at him squarely. 'Ex-husband. Honestly? I'm feeling lots of things. Mad, sad, glad. Mostly glad, now that we've talked, because I knew he was a horrible person, but I never thought he was capable of behaving in such a disgusting way to a young, impressionable girl. Pete told the police what Keith had done to Meghan in the van, and the fact that he beat her, and cut her face. They told me all of it. I think they wanted to leave me in no doubt about what had happened and how horrifying it was. I'm just so glad, that he can never hurt another woman again.'

She gazed out to the middle distance and carried on. 'Part of me does feel sad though, because I once saw him very

differently. I saw the person he *wanted* me to see, the one I
thought he was actually capable of being. The one I believed in.
I was wrong, but the life I wanted to have with him, and once
imagined we *could* have, that's what I'm sad for.'

She looked at him miserably, and he could see the anguish
in her eyes. 'If you want me to leave, I completely understand.
For Meghan's sake, I do think it's probably better if I just go.'

'What do you *want* to do, Caroline? If you had the choice, if
it was all up to you, what would *you* decide, and why? And it's
not a trick question, by the way. I just want the truth. Under the
circumstances, I think I deserve that.'

She thought for a moment, then she gave him a very light,
tentative smile.

'A big part of me is so ashamed, that you've both had to
experience the worst of my reality with him, I just want to
crawl away so you never have to see me again.'

She sat up and straightened her shoulders. 'But, if the choice
was all mine, I'd want to stay. I'd want to complete what I
started, not just for you as a client I made a promise to, but for
myself, to *prove* to myself that I'm really free of his shadow,
that I can do something worthwhile. I'd want the job to carry on
being what it was always supposed to be – a fresh start, my
foundation for getting on my feet again. Putting him behind me.
But I don't expect you to feel that's appropriate at all anymore,
especially not for Meghan.'

Stuart let out a long slow breath. 'Meghan and I have talked
it over, and we'd both like you to stay and finish the work.'

She gaped at him. 'Are you sure? I mean, *really?*'

He shrugged and grinned sheepishly. 'Well, since the truth
is all that matters now, let me just say that *I* want you to stay,
Meghan doesn't *mind* if you do, and that's the accurate nutshell
version of the discussions we've had.'

She laughed a little. 'Well, thank you for the honesty.
Meghan doesn't mind. Well, that's a whole lot more than I even
dared to hope for, under the circumstances, so I'll take it. But
it's incredibly generous of both of you. I can hardly believe it!'

'Caroline, you know about my past. Someone recently
helped me to take a very big second chance when I needed one
in my own smashed up life, that they paid forward after

someone helped *them* get back on their feet. We've all done things we wish
we'd never done. We'd all turn back the clock if we could, to avoid the pain we've caused to others that they didn't deserve.

'A lot of people don't get a decent second chance. My friend did, the one who saved our lives as a matter of fact, and then *I* got one, thanks to *him*. Maybe *your* big second chance is coming from *me*, and perhaps one day you can pay it forward too, and offer a second chance to someone else who needs a break in life. Maybe we all can, one by one, in some form or another, make the world a happier place for someone else.'

Caroline's dark brown eyes shone with unshed tears. 'Thank you. And I think this *is* my big chance to turn my life around.' She chewed her bottom lip thoughtfully. 'D'you think Meghan would talk to me, about what happened to her?'

'I doubt it.' Stuart cringed at his own bluntness, but he had to be honest.

'She is going to be having some counselling, that's for sure, but whether she'd talk to *you*, I really don't know. I suspect not. You're probably too close to it all. She'll need someone objective, at least to start with, but we'll see. Maybe in time she'd see the value of talking to someone else who actually knew Brockett. Put it this way, you can't offer. If she approaches you, then fine. But she can't feel like you expect her to open up to you, under the circumstances. That would be completely unfair.'

Caroline agreed. 'That's fine, Stuart. I'll be there for her if she does want to talk. Sometimes it helps to talk to someone else who's been through it, that's all. I know that to be true. But if she *never* wants to talk about it with me, that's okay too.'

'How's your head? Do you want to take the rest of this week off, and start again next Monday?'

Caroline shook her head. 'No. I'm fine. I do have a headache, but I can work with it on the lighter stuff we can do right now, as long as I don't go up any ladders or scaffolding for a bit. If I can keep my feet firmly on the ground, and stop for a break if I need one, I'm happy to continue.'

'Well, take today at least, and we can start back tomorrow, and see how that goes. All going well, is it okay of we can plan to work through the weekend?'

She nodded again as they headed out to the car to head for home. 'Yeah, that's absolutely fine.'

So, the work on the barn would continue. Stuart didn't know how to feel about it, but it made economic and practical sense to carry on and finish what he'd started. Hopefully, there would be no further drama. Now, more than ever, he was driven by the need to have the project completed. Drawing a line under this part of the new plan for their lives, as wretched as it currently felt, couldn't come soon enough.

ONE YEAR LATER

Meghan zipped up her red quilted puffer jacket, fished her black beanie hat out of one of its pockets, and pulled it onto her head. She only ever wore this jacket (or her red waistcoat on warmer days) for training or exercise sessions. Astro knew that a red 'top' meant business. She also knew that when Meghan *wasn't* wearing red, things would be a lot more relaxed; they would just be hanging out together and having fun. This was an exercise morning, but they were pretty fun mostly, too. She and Astro worked well together, and it *never* felt like a chore and a bore.

She blew into her hands and rubbed them, before putting on her gloves and winding her scarf across her nose and chin, and back around her neck. It never took her long to warm up, when she worked with Astro, but she didn't want to start off with a numb face and fingers.

It was really cold this morning. After a week of warmish sunshine, the weather had done an abrupt U-turn as it so often did across Cumbria. Since she and Stuart had moved up here, just over a year ago, she'd found the unpredictability of the elements to be her biggest challenge. Sometimes they literally had four seasons in one day! It was taking some getting used to, but Meghan felt she was finally figuring out how to cope with the constant changes in temperature. As Nan had said, the secret was 'layers' of clothing, an umbrella and a bobble hat in one side pocket of her backpack, and sunnies and sunscreen in the other!

Moving up here hadn't been as disruptive as she'd expected. She'd slotted in fairly well at her new school, and now had friends there who seemed solid. She saw some of them on the weekends too. She worked every other Saturday over in Torley, at GladRagz Boutique, and she would have a quick lunch break with Jayde after the Farmers Market finished at one o'clock. On the alternate Saturday afternoons, Jayde would come over on the bus after finishing at the market, and sometimes Renae would come with her. They would meet a few of the other kids from Lakes, and hang out in the city centre; mostly at Costa, if the weather was bad, or in front of the Crown and Mitre hotel where there were usually plenty of seats, if it was warm enough to be outside. They'd normally all get a burger and chips or a Subway sandwich before her friends caught the bus back to Torley.

They were mostly good kids, who didn't say mean stuff to make her feel bad about herself. She wasn't the only one who had a raft of acne across her chin and forehead, and she certainly wasn't the only girl who worried about her boobs being too tiny! After *that* particular cringing confession, Renae had 'felt her pain,' and had actually dragged her off to the department store to buy a couple of very well-padded bras! That had been hilarious; giggling in the fitting room like a couple of ten-year-olds.

The kids she was hanging out with all had stuff they felt a bit weird or self-conscious about, but nobody made a big deal about it. Apart from moaning about their parents, or friends they'd fallen out with, and complaining about the amount of homework they always got for the weekend, they seemed to cope okay with most things. Somehow, stuff that had bothered Meghan and so many of the kids she knew down in Taunton didn't seem to be such big issues for the ones up here.

She knew that a lot of the angst she'd felt down south was a direct result of how she'd been *herself,* with people. She'd been hostile and resentful, and suspicious of virtually everything anyone said to her. She'd been angry, confused and scared about a lot of things, especially facing the future with a father she felt she didn't know anymore. Knowing he was about to be released had put a lot of pressure on her. She hadn't been sure what might be expected of her, or what she could or should expect of *him.*

Her insecurities had been huge, and they'd spilled over into every area of her life. The proposed holiday to the Lake District had left her more uncertain than ever, about the future, but it had worked out better than either of them could ever have foreseen. Within a day of arriving, she'd met Astro! She'd also met Jayde, and Renae, and other people who'd accepted her without struggle, and she'd felt so much better about everything. Although the decision about moving to the other end of the country had been a tough one to make, once she *had* decided, everything fell neatly and easily into place in ways that still astonished her.

She'd had a few therapy sessions with a woman called Dawn Mott, a counsellor in Carlisle, after her traumatic attack by Keith Brockett and his attempt to kill her dad. She'd been surprised to discover that opening up to someone who didn't know or judge her was incredibly helpful. The experience had helped her to come to terms with a lot of other stuff that had been dragging her down too, like how she *really* felt about her stepmother dumping her with no warning. Her latent anger around Annabel's abrupt desertion had been significant; it had driven her a lot more that she'd understood, or been prepared for.

She had come through what had happened with Brockett pretty well too, thanks to the solid support she'd been given. She felt that although a lot of people knew about the attack, they were the *right* people to know about it; people like her dad, Caroline, Darren and Debby, the Head at school, and the friends she knew she could trust. That was the most important thing of all; that the people who knew were the kind who could and *did* help her to process it and put it behind her, without it causing the kind of trauma she would otherwise have struggled to overcome.

It hadn't been easy, to accept what Brockett had done, and there had been quite a few sleepless nights and bouts of tearfulness, but mercifully it hadn't left her feeling like the world was an unsafe place, or that all men were bastards, or anything else that would have unfairly coloured her view of life. She had good people to thank for that. Good people, and a beautiful horse who understood *everything*.

It's amazing how well you can do, and how far you can fly, when people believe in you and help you to believe in yourself.

In talking things through with her counsellor it had also become important to Meghan to understand how her friendships functioned, and what needed to change, for her to keep them on an even keel. She also needed to make the best of the chances that came up, to make new ones that would last and be meaningful. That meant taking a good look at herself from other people's perspective, so she decided to start by asking the ones who she felt knew her best. It was scary, asking for that type of feedback, *especially* from people who knew her well, but she really wanted to do it. As she'd said to Dawn; 'if I don't know what's broken, how can I fix it?'

On her first trip back down to Taunton, after the move, she'd invited Hayden and Amy out for a coffee to talk about it. They had both been supportive, but candid; saying she had a bit of an 'attitude' that probably wasn't going to help her succeed in life. It had been tough, hearing their perspective on how she'd been behaving, but she trusted them, and she'd managed to stay true to the promise she'd made to herself, that she wouldn't kick off at the criticism. They'd all been friends for long enough to have seen the best and worst of one another. Hayden and Amy knew her as well as anyone did, so she valued their input, even though bits of it were pretty hard to hear.

Amy even said that she was intimidated by her at times, when she was 'in one of her strops,' as Amy had called it. It had surprised Meghan badly, that her closest friend was sometimes almost scared of her and didn't know how to talk to her. Hayden had said that even if he didn't know her as a friend, and just fancied her instead, he'd never have asked her out on a date because she seemed too 'complicated' and easily upset. But after the get-together they'd both hugged her hard and told her how much they cared, and how important it was to them, that she was happy.

Her other friend Elise hadn't been at her coffee-meet with Amy and Hayden. Meghan had chosen not to invite her. Elise had been a little different, a little aloof, after her return from New Zealand. The dynamics of that friendship had changed; subtly but certainly, with Elise not saying much about how the kiwi winter had worked out, and gravitating towards some of the more 'sophisticated' girls, in the new school year. It had left Meghan feeling glad she hadn't made the choice to stay in Somerset based on the value of her friendship with Elise.

Amy had been to stay at Beaconsfield for a fortnight, though the summer holidays, and that had been wonderful for her as well as for Meghan. Amy had met Jayde, Renae and a couple of

Meghan's other friends from Lakes Academy. Everyone had got along, and there were plans for Amy to come again. With Lucy's help, Meghan had taught her to ride, and they were all keen to do more trekking when she came back. Lucy's wedding had taken place while Amy had been here and she'd generously invited both girls, and Stuart too, to the evening reception party at the Beeches. It had been an amazing night.

Meghan's fortnightly Saturday job, working for Trudie Sangster in the GladRagz boutique, meant she had to be quite strict with her timetabling of working with Astro, to fit everything in. Occasionally she found the bus ride over to the boutique to be a bit of a pain, especially when the weather was terrible, or when she would rather have been doing something with her friends or even just spending more time with Astro. But the money really helped, and since Trudie had started leaving her to 'cash-up,' put the day's takings and the till roll in the safe and close the shop at the end of Saturday trading, she felt the responsibility was a privilege. She didn't want to let Trudie down.

Working in the boutique was fun anyway. Even when the shop was really busy, with fussy, demanding or dithering customers, it never felt much like work. Sometimes, if things were really quiet, Trudie would drag the catalogues out and they'd make a coffee and sit poring and giggling over different styles and trends. Meghan would sometimes try on the hats, shoes and sunglasses in the shop, and she trusted Trudie totally, to tell her what suited her and what didn't.

With Trudie's help (and Feen's, when she was about), she'd learned to develop her own dress style; a kind of funky but youthful 'vintage vibe' that really suited her, and that most of her friends thought was pretty cool. Parker Truman, one of the boys she'd met at the youth club when she'd first started going there, and who she also met regularly at puppy training school with her new dog Bingo, had said she looked like a sweet but sassy girl from the 1950's that everyone wanted to go out with. Meghan took that as the best compliment she'd ever been given. Parker was sweet too. He had become a good friend.

She greeted Astro now, with the usual cuddle and polo mint, and the horse whinnied softly at her. This was Meghan's favourite time of day. No matter what the hour or the weather, or no matter what the temptations ever were for other things to do, nothing compared with the joy she felt at spending time with Astro.

She'd learned a raft of highly effective training techniques that were based on positive reinforcement. Rewarding Astro well for learning desired behaviours had helped to cement the all-important trust the horse needed to have in Meghan, as her trainer, for her rehabilitation to be complete. Through patience, appropriate reward and a determination never to use aversive stimuli that could put Astro under stress, Meghan had made incredible progress with her. Her genuine desire to train the horse in the correct and most supportive way was only half of the reason for the success, though.

She had found a real affinity, not just with Astro but with *all* of the horses. She just somehow knew, instinctively, how to approach them and gain their trust. She had a good bond with them all now, and they were unfailingly compliant. Stuart often complained that she had more success than he did, with getting some of them to toe the line, even with things like getting into a horse box or coming in from an afternoon of foraging. While he saw their reluctance to do what they were told as a frustration at times, Meghan saw it as a challenge to be gently overcome.

Her bond with Astro was deep and strong. The horse didn't really need rewards anymore, to be compliant. She would simply do as Meghan asked her, out of love and obedience, but Meghan never wavered in her reinforcement strategies. It was her way of communicating to Astro that she would never let her down, that her treatment would always be consistent and reliable.

One of her favourite moments, that had started to occur a lot more often, was Astro communicating with *her*, by putting her nose into Meghan's neck, just above her shoulder, and blowing softly. The little snorts were Astro's way of showing love and trust. Meghan always rewarded that love with some of her own. She would put her arms around Astro's neck and simply hold her gently, and let Astro's eyelashes skim her cheek.

And the beautiful, gentle horse was hers, now! In the run-up to her fifteenth birthday, which had fallen on a Sunday, she hadn't been able to understand why her father had been acting like a moron. He'd been like a cat on a hot tin roof for days beforehand. He'd told her they were going to have a special breakfast, and she'd happily agreed to that, but Suart had been nervous, and jumpy, unable to sit still, and he kept randomly giggling to himself, which was incredibly unnerving. He was behaving like such a weirdo that Meghan had wondered whether he was having some bizarre male equivalent of the menopause. She'd even made a mental note to talk to Trudie about it, since Trudie was menopausal herself and could probably say whether men suffered with it too, and whether fidgeting and uncontrollably bursting into stupid giggles was part of it.

She'd also had no idea why Darren and Debby had more or less invited themselves over for her birthday breakfast, at the very last minute. It wasn't like them at all, to muscle their way into someone else's orbit like that. But when they'd shown up with Ruby and all three of their mad excitable dogs, and sat in the newly built conservatory, they were giggling stupidly too. Meghan had given up on trying to figure out what was wrong with them all.

Stuart had produced a spectacular stack of fluffy pancakes with bacon, blueberries and maple syrup, a platter of rich, creamy scrambled eggs, a pot of coffee, a pitcher of freshly squeezed orange juice and a chilled bottle of good quality champagne. He'd opened the champagne and had made a big show of serving Meghan first.

Debby had declined a glass, and had quietly announced that she was pregnant again! Meghan had been thrilled for her and Darren, and she'd said so, thinking that was the big 'reveal' they'd all been laughing like hyenas about, and how nice it was that they wanted her and Stuart to be among the first to know. It was massively exciting for them to be having a second baby, so soon after facing the horrible prospect of never having any kids at all. She knew how special it, was for her and her dad, to have been among the first to find out.

But then, Stuart and Debby had started openly laughing and drumming their fingers on the table. The minute they stopped, Darren had stood up and said; 'Happy Fifteenth Birthday, babe,' and with an elaborate flourish, he'd presented Meghan with an envelope. When she'd opened it, she'd been stunned to find the ownership documents for Astro, which were in her name, she had promptly burst into tears. In that moment, she'd been more overwhelmed and stuck for words than she'd ever been in her life.

Darren hadn't said anything for many months prior to that, about Astro's future. Meghan had always known that he wanted the horse to have a new home eventually, but she had never, in her wildest dreams, imagined he might gift Astro to *her*. She'd secretly hoped to one day be able to buy Astro from him, but she had never managed to work up the courage to ask him how much he might want for her. Horses varied so much in price, depending on so many things, like temperament, size, breed, breeding potential, training. Astro was part palomino and, as Mrs Raven had said at the start, she was a valuable horse. The last thing Meghan wanted was to ask Darren what Astro's 'price tag' was, and be crushed at the thought of never being able to afford her.

Darren and Debby weren't rich people, and the money they could have got for Astro would have been helpful to them, especially with a new baby on the way. Darren had often said that the money wasn't the primary consideration; that Astro's welfare was more important than what anyone might be prepared to pay for her. But, if someone came along and dangled a few thousand in front of them, would they find it so easy to turn that down? As someone once had sad, 'everything is for sale if the price is right.'

She'd been riddled with doubt, about her future with Astro, but she was always too afraid to push the point. All she knew was that if she and Astro had to part, it would be the worst thing that ever happened to her; worse than her mum dying, worse than her dad going to prison, worse than Annabel dumping her, and worse than Keith Brockett trying to rape her, and kill her father.

Losing Astro would be worse than all of those other horrible things combined, and she'd never allowed herself to think too much about it. Instinctively, she knew that to do that would send her spinning back to a dark place that she wouldn't know how to get out of. She'd just had to hope that Darren, Debby, and Stuart knew it; well enough not to break her heart. She'd had to trust the universe; that fate would not have brought her and Astro together if they weren't meant to *stay* together. And now, fate had delivered her most cherished dream. It had come full circle for her.

It had been a year of highs and lows, but mostly highs. Life was a long, long way from being what it had been just over a year ago. Back then, she and her father had been full of doubt, and fear for the future, and what it might hold. Now, they were as far ahead of that as they could ever have imagined. They'd leapt, and the net had appeared. Stuart had wanted to provide some security, and he'd done it. His vision, and his belief in them both, had brought them here, to this amazing life. Meghan pinched herself again, as she did quite often, just to be sure that it wasn't all some fanciful dream.

As she led Astro out of the stable now, and into the ring, she turned and hugged the horse tightly again, and offered her gratitude once more.

Beautiful girl, I will never let you go. We belong to one another now, and nothing can change that. I will love you until my dying day.

*   *   *   *   *

As he leaned against the corner of the newly-christened Karen Balik Equine Clinic, Stuart was in a reflective mood. He grinned to himself, thinking back over the first full year and a bit, at Beaconsfield, and how it had passed in an absolute blur of study and work. For a lot of the time, both he and Meghan had struggled to work out which way was up, as the stables progressed and they slotted into life in the Lake District. But, he had to admit, almost everything had fallen almost unbelievably neatly into place.

The extension at the back of the first stable block had been completed within the first four months and Darren Davies had lost little time in kitting it out as a horse hospital. It was already a well-known and respected facility in the area, and Darren was regularly ministering to sick and injured horses in there. He was juggling that, and his demanding work at the practice, and being a father to toddler Ruby and a brand-new baby son Thomas. In another example of the kind of serendipity that constantly seemed to occur, Debby had given birth in October; a year to the very day that Stuart had picked up the keys as the proud new owner of Beaconsfield Stables and Trekking.

Getting Meghan settled at Lakes Academy had also been astonishingly easy, helped significantly by the fact that she already had one or two new friends there. She was well on track now, after completing her GCSE exams with respectable grades, thanks to solid support and tutoring from the amazing Kim Taylor, and she was already looking towards her A levels. Stuart was immensely proud of how hard she had worked. She wasn't sixteen yet, but she already appeared to be firmly on track for what she wanted to do, careerwise, and she didn't seem to be missing her life in Taunton much at all.

That was probably helped by the fact that his mother had been to stay a few times. 'Nan' had come for Christmas last year, and that had been a lot of fun. Meghan had decorated the house beautifully, and on Christmas morning she had presented Stuart with a gorgeous antique, hand-tooled, black leather saddle. She had oiled and polished it until it gleamed. It was beautiful. Her thoughtfulness, over that, had made him want to weep.

Meghan had also managed to get back to Taunton a few times to see her friends, and plans were also afoot for his mother to come again this Christmas. At least this time the poor woman wouldn't have to live with the endless drilling, sawing, hammering and banging that had been going on around the place last year! Stuart and his carpenter, Caro, had busted their arses right up until the night before Christmas Eve, working on the barn. Nobody could hear themselves think, with all that going on. Caro had booked Teapot Cottage for Christmas week, and she'd got her own mum to come up and stay with her there for the holiday. The week off had been very much appreciated by all.

Meghan had only had a few serious wobbles since she'd been up here, where she'd questioned the decision to move. There were times, especially over the first few months, when she really had missed her old life. In the aftermath of her attack by Keith Brockett, she had understandably expressed a very deep urge to bolt back to Taunton, to be with her nan and her more established friends, Hayden and Amy.

Debby Davies had proved to be a staunch support to them both during that rocky time, when the old 'monster Meghan' had been hovering constantly around the fringes of their life, and threatening to return with full force. On more than one occasion Debby had steadied the ship in the face of a burgeoning, tornado-sized tantrum, with her pragmatic, sensitive approach. She somehow had the knack of calming Meghan down, whereas every time Stuart tried, he only ever seemed to make matters worse. His daughter was a door-slammer, and there were times when he doubted if any of the doors in the house would actually stay on their hinges.

A short involvement that had turned a bit sour, with a young lad she'd met at youth club, hadn't helped. The boy's name was Riley Jenks, and he'd seemed like a nice enough boy, to begin with. Stuart had been as nervous as a cat on a hot tin roof, about his pretty teenage daughter hanging around with boys, and that hadn't changed much, over the past year. He knew it was an inevitable part of her maturing, but he wasn't so old that he couldn't remember the shameless sexual goals of most sixteen-year-old boys, which kept him in a constant state of near-hyperventilation, whenever she left the house.

Meghan had long since had the conversations with Nan, about sex, and about pressure from boys. Stuart had made a point of having 'the dreaded chat' with her again, and she'd looked at him with a scorn that had made him cringe, at the time. As conversations went, it was hard to say who had been the most embarrassed, but certain things had to be said, certain promises had to be made, and once they'd settled on the boundaries, and the open-door policy of communication about anything worrying from either side, everything went back to being about as normal as it could be, given the circumstances. It didn't stop Stuart from fretting hard, but he trusted Meghan, and he knew she trusted him. It was the best he could hope for, wasn't it?

The Jenks boy hadn't lasted long. He'd been respectful enough, and according to Meghan he'd never pressured her too much to go further than she wanted to. She'd also admitted, with the most violent bright-red blush Stuart had ever seen on *anybody*, that she was a lot further from ready to take that step than she initially believed she might have been. He'd hastened to reassure her that waiting was just fine, in spite of what her friends might be doing, and when the right boy came along and made her feel differently, they could have another chat about it then.

This revelation had come after Jenks had started pulling away from her, and preferring the affections of a different girl who apparently *didn't* keep resisting his efforts to pull her into bed. Meghan had been disproportionally upset, and Stuart had to fight the overriding temptation to go and find the boy and knock his teeth out.

But again, Debby Davies had put things into perspective, pointing out that a fifteen-year-old girl who doesn't want to have sex with a sixteen-year-old boy is nearly always going to end up being thrown over for one who does, because that's just what happens in the teenage world.

'It's devastating, because it knocks a young woman's confidence and forces her to question the validity of her own moral code,' Debby explained. She'd talked to Meghan too, and shared some of her own wisdom and her own experiences. So did Feen Raven, who had also become a good friend. Having grown up without a mother herself, at a difficult developmental stage, Feen identified closely with Meghan.

Both women were wonderful with her. They were older, but they both related well to her, and they'd become more than just mentors. They were good mates, who unfailingly rallied around her at her most vulnerable times. Feen's father, Mark Raven – ever the blunt pragmatist – had occasionally been a wise sounding board for Stuart too. He'd also raised a daughter alone, after her mother had died, and gone through the horrific early teens.

'Teenage lasses? Ecky frickin' pecky, man! There'll be times when yer won't know whether yer Arthur or bloody Martha, wit' young 'un. Wi' Feen, it were often a case o' ten different types of shyte on't same day. She came right in the end, like, but there were times when I thought ride were never gonna stop or I'd go barkin' bloody mad before it did.'

Stuart was immensely grateful that so many people were so kind, and took such a loving interest in his daughter. Darren treated her like a cherished little sister, and the bond they shared was something Stuart had eventually managed to swallow his envy about, and was now just profoundly grateful for.

Luckily, the timing of the whole 'Riley Jenks falling-apart' malarkey had been perfect, with Amy coming to stay, and giving Meghan something different to dwell on, namely teaching her friend to ride and taking a couple of the horses out with Lucy who very generously gave her time to the girls twice. By the time Amy had gone home again, Riley Jenks (or Riley Jerk, as they'd both started calling him), had been consigned to the annals of unfortunate history and Meghan's bruised heart had recovered and been stronger for the incident.

Stuart was quietly proud of how resilient his daughter was proving to be, on every level. She was a very different person from the one who had first come to the Lake District in resentful silence, not so very long ago; barbed and belligerent, and sneering at every attempt Stuart had made to get to know her better.

To say it had all been plain sailing emotionally, even in spite of the changes, would have been a lie. Meghan still had her moments, and there had been plenty of days when Stuart still wondered *himself* if they'd done the right thing, especially when the money was trickling away like water through a sieve, with nothing coming in to provide any kind of counterbalance. He could hardly blame his daughter for having her doubts as well, and acting out when she felt unsure of herself.

But, more often than not, Meghan had simply been too busy to give in to the urge to kick off about something. She was very involved at the stables, especially with Astro, and she had ongoing part time work with Trudie Sangster at Gladragz, and a few other days during the school holidays. Thanks to Debby and a few of her colleagues at the hospital, she now had a few regular babysitting jobs too. Stuart sometimes wondered if his daughter was making more money than he was!

The ability to earn a bit of her own cash had given Meghan a sense of responsibility, opportunities to make new friends, and enough funds to be able to meet some of her school mates for coffee, movies, bowling and the like, at weekends. She was managing to save a little too, and Stuart knew that she appreciated having her own money, so she didn't have to ask him to bankroll her every time she needed or wanted something. As Debby put it, with no Mum or Nan around, a girl needed to be able to buy her own tampons on her own terms!

Financially, things were still incredibly tight. They'd spent pretty much everything Stuart had been able to get his hands on initially, including all of Darren's fifteen thousand, but the horse hospital was always busy, with one horse or another recovering from illness or surgery. Darren was every bit as grateful for the space as Stuart was for the investment.

He'd needed to ask a couple of friends for small loans, but there hadn't been any heavy discussions. 'No problem,' was the response from both of the friends he'd approached, and they'd been happy to lend on the 'pay me back when you can' basis. Those sums weren't huge, but they'd kept the food on the table during the exceptionally lean times, and it wouldn't be long now before the stables would start turning a modest profit and he could work on paying them back.

Stuart still had a few contacts from his old life, people who'd been happy enough to hear from him to willingly pledge their support for his new venture. One old friend had generously created a wonderful new website and linked social media pages, which had helped to boost the profile of the business.

The campaign locally launched, to get Beaconsfield back on the radar, had included a two-page spread in the local paper, and a full page in the Lancashire Evening Post, along with flyers placed in the hotels, B & B houses and tourist information centres across the Lake District.

He'd come clean with the local community, in talking about his past, and naming the hospital annexe after Karen Balik had turned out to be a good strategy. A few trolls had vented their spleens on social media, in response to Stuart's confession about his terrible mistake, and a few of the kids at Meghan's school had given her a bit of a hard time, but most people had acknowledged his honesty with positive responses.

Dedicating his new horse hospital to his victim had made it more meaningful, not just for himself but also for the woman he'd killed, so that her name would never be forgotten.

The Karen Balik Equine Clinic had been named such after Stuart had contacted Karen's husband, Nengah, to request his blessing. Nengah had been very happy that the new stable hospital would be named after Karen. He affirmed that she would be thrilled. He countered Stuart's offer of visiting the stables at any time he wished to, with a 'maybe.'

Stuart suspected that really meant no thank you, but the man was too polite to say that. He'd probably moved on a lot himself, after all these years, and maybe he wanted to keep the past (including Stuart) behind him. But, if Nengah ever changed his mind, he'd always be welcome, and Stuart had made sure he knew it, before he'd ended the conversation.

Enquiries were coming in regularly now, as word spread that Beaconsfield was under new management. They were taking a few spring bookings already, for the following year, including a pretty decent one from a primary school in Lancaster. Easter was already booked up, and they'd had to buy a few new horses, to be ready.

The stables had been spruced up and given a new coat of paint, but since they were in good shape to start with, Stuart hadn't needed to do much more. The grazing fields' fencing had needed repairs, for the beasts to be secure while they grazed, played and browsed the surrounding trees, but Caro Swift had lent a hand with that, before she finally left in mid-February.

He couldn't fault any of Caro's work. In spite of the fact that her headaches were still problematic at times, after her ex-husband's attack, she'd pushed through and stayed until the end of the job. The project had run into mid-February but, incredibly, it hadn't gone over budget. Stuart mostly put that down to a guy called Eddie Flynn, a local retired carpenter who Stuart had hired by word of mouth, to help them with the finishing off. Eddie was something of a pack-rat; always on the lookout for a bargain, and always hoping to do things on the cheap without compromising on the quality. He'd taken Stuart and Caro to a couple of very interesting reclamation yards, where they'd found a few treasures that had helped kit the building out to a high standard, at much less than the materials would have cost to buy new.

Eddie had also introduced him to the joys of social media selling sites that offered every conceivable thing people could ever want, from ripped-out fitted kitchens to curtains, radios to roll-top baths, and lengths of timber to leftover rolls of ready-lawn. Some stuff was new, other stuff was used, some was free, the rest was mostly cheap as chips, and Stuart had so far managed to get everything he needed for the barn's bathrooms and kitchen at a fraction of what it would otherwise have cost. He was constantly amazed, and secretly delighted, at how many DIY and refurbishment projects people had simply given up on ever completing. They often sold their unwanted stuff for next to nothing, or they actually gave it away.

Someone had given him a brand-new shower system for free, complete with screen, shower head, solid stone tray, and taps, that they'd bought for a second-bathroom project they never got around to completing before they sold their house. Someone else had given him a huge, double-door fridge freezer, the 'American' kind, that Meghan had talked about, with an ice-maker and water dispenser in the doors. They said it was too big for their new fitted kitchen, and nobody had wanted to buy it, so they were offering it for free to anyone who could save them the drama of having to dispose of it themselves. There wasn't a single thing wrong with it, and Stuart had been absolutely thrilled to see how well it had it cleaned up, and slotted perfectly into the barn's new kitchen.

He'd caught the bargain bug from Eddie; he was turning into a bit of a steal-of-a-deal hunter himself. He'd often laughed at his own excitement, when he'd spied something on a website that they could potentially use in the barn.

At one time, he would never have considered buying *anything* second hand. He'd never have dreamt of even attending a car boot sale, let alone haggling at one over the price of something! At one time, he'd thought all that to be little more than pitiable entertainment for the miserly, penniless and pathetic. But, thanks to Eddie's enthusiasm and encouragement, he and Meghan had joined the bargain-hunting ranks after drawing up the full inventory of what they'd need to furnish and kit out the newly completed barn. They started going treasure hunting at a variety of field-based flea markets and car boot sales for what they needed, and Stuart had been *gobsmacked* at how much fun it had been!

Once the barn was finished, they had turned their attention to the house itself, and were slowly making it more modern and comfortable too, with various internet and car-boot finds.

Meghan had also picked up a fair few bargains for herself at car boots, including a couple of pairs of good jeans and some pretty tops, and truly baffling quantities of makeup and beauty products at knockdown prices. Stuart knew he'd never understand why she needed so much of that stuff, like a 'job lot' of twenty-five boxes that each contained four pairs of false eyelashes, and enough bottles of a certain type of conditioner to last her into the middle of the next decade, but since she was using her own money, he wasn't going to complain. As long as she was happy, that was all that mattered. When they'd had a long bout of rain and the car boot sales had been cancelled for a full fortnight, they'd actually spent those Sundays wandering around their own property, in a kind of half-daze, wondering what to do with themselves!

Meghan also finally got to have her longed-for puppy; a lovely black and tan collie-cross. She'd called him Bingo.

It had been hard for Stuart not to spill the beans to Meghan about the fact that Darren had planned to give Astro to her on her fifteenth birthday. He'd somehow managed, through Herculean effort (and jogging dozens of solitary laps around the stables to help him keep his nerves in check), to hold his tongue. Sitting on that surprise was the hardest thing he'd ever had to do.

Meghan had passed her online diploma course in Horse Management with a distinction, and she'd continued to work with and cherish Astro from the moment Darren had brought her across to Beaconsfield, once they'd moved in. The pair were best friends, and true soulmates. It was Astro that had led Meghan to deciding on her career path, and she was very passionate about that, as well as Astro herself. The horse trusted her like she didn't trust anyone else and Stuart knew how utterly devastating it would be, for both Meghan *and* the horse, to be parted.

He'd talked to Darren about it, had offered to buy Astro himself, and Darren had confirmed that he would consider it, 'when the time was right.' Stuart knew that he probably wanted to wait until Meghan was fully settled, and quietly watch how the next few months panned out, before making a decision about ownership.

He couldn't argue. He knew how much Astro's welfare had mattered to Darren, but he was certain that Astro wasn't just a novelty to Meghan. Their relationship was far more meaningful and profound than that. Darren knew it too, but the dedicated vet wanted to be careful to a fault, so the matter wasn't discussed any further, until he approached Stuart again, at the end of winter.

As usual, he didn't beat around the bush. 'As you know, I've been keeping an eye on Meghan's progress with Astro, and thinking about the chat we had about it last year. I agree, and I always have, that she should have first dibs. It would be so unfair to not let her have the horse after all this, so I'm going to give Astro to her as a fifteenth birthday gift from me and Debs, if that's ok with you, and if you genuinely think it's what she'd want.'

Stuart had been humbled almost to the point of tears. Was there no end to the kindness of these people? He'd swallowed the lump in his throat and nodded. When he'd spoken, his voice had been choked. 'I know she'd love that, more than anything. And I know she'd take care of Astro until her own dying day. But let me pay you, something at least.'

Darren had shaken his head. 'No, mate. Meghan's more than earned that horse. Taking money would seem wrong. You guys are like family to us. Astro's family too, to us all, isn't she? So, can we settle on that, then? I can get the papers done anytime, so just say yes and we can get it all done legally.'

Stuart had offered to handle the legal side of the transfer, but Darren insisted on doing it himself. Then he'd insisted on coming over with Debby, on Meghan's birthday, to give her the ownership papers. Stuart had known, beyond all doubt, that it would be the happiest day of his daughter's life, and it was.

The love and trust both had for one another was something to behold. Not for the first time, or the thousandth, Stuart gave silent thanks to the universe for so lovingly and sensitively connecting these two extraordinary beings. Astro had reached something deep within his daughter, at a time when she'd been really troubled, and the horse's quiet love had healed her. It wasn't something he could describe or truly quantify, but Darren himself had said several times that the trust Astro had developed so quickly with Meghan was uncanny, and a rare thing to witness.

The patience she unfailingly showed was incredible, giving Astro time and space to get to know the other tame horses at the stables and showing her how well the stable horses were treated and cared for, and how they accepted taking riders. She was incredibly sensitive with Astro, particularly when the poor creature went into season, for about one week in every five, where she would often be uncharacteristically grumpy and flighty during any attempts to work with her. Meghan reduced the amount of time spent training or exercising in those weeks, and gave Astro enormous amounts of reassurance and loving contact. She also put the quiet and solid gelding Finnegan out with her, and the two seemed to get along well, to the point where they had already started playing together.

Darren was particularly impressed by that. 'If this girl really does want to have a career with horses, as a trainer or a psychologist, she'll be bloody brilliant. She has a real gift.'

As Stuart continued his reflection, he conceded that all in all, in spite of its ups and downs, it had been a pretty good year. There were some regular bookings now, from schools and a couple of local charities, for riding lessons.

There had been another interesting development in his life too. Without much warning, it seemed that he might just be in the throes of starting a 'love life'! He'd just met a woman who'd been a friend of one of his customers, Minty Cartwright, who had stayed at Teapot Cottage. She'd spent a week at Stuart's barn as a stopgap, after a stay at the cottage, while she waited for it to be available again.

Minty had agreed to take part in a trek, while she was staying at Stuart's, but she'd fallen from her horse and suffered a broken shoulder. Stuart had gone to check on her after her return to Torley, and to return an earring she'd left behind, and it was there at Teapot Cottage that he'd met her friend who was staying there with her; Fiona Winterson. He'd been instantly attracted to Fiona, but he knew that things would be very slow to develop. She had a complicated story, including a very serious cancer that she was fighting with every ounce of her strength.

Stuart was absolutely fine about taking things slowly, as Fiona had a lot of surgery and treatment to get through, and she wanted to concentrate on getting through that before committing to anything else. She'd made it clear that she wasn't looking for a relationship, because she had no idea how quickly her cancer would progress, and she was currently down in her home city of Bristol, having treatment. But they spoke on the phone every day, sometimes more than once, and sometimes for more than an hour at a time, and they'd started getting to know one another quite well.

He understood the implications of getting too attached to someone who might die sooner rather than later, and he'd already been through the devastation of losing his first wife Wendy to a brain haemorrhage. On one level he sensed that getting involved with Fiona was something he needed like a hole in the head, but there was something about her that drew him in. He *wanted* to support her through her illness, whatever it might mean for him in the long term. It was another way of 'paying it forward,' he supposed. Only time would tell, if a relationship would develop, but Stuart was hopeful that it might.

So, with everything that was happening in his and Meghan's world, he felt that they were moving along at a fair pace, towards security and stability. In many ways it was hard to believe that just eighteen months ago, he had no idea what he was going to do with the rest of his life, and security had felt like a far-off dream. But, here he was, with a business he enjoyed that was heading in the right direction, and with good prospects for Meghan's future too. She'd found her *own* niche, and was thriving in a way he once never dreamed could be possible.

Regrettably, Caro Swift hadn't kept in touch after she'd left Beaconsfield. They'd been on excellent terms when she left but, as she explained, while she'd always be grateful for the opportunity she'd had with the Thomsons, there was still an 'overhang' attached to it from her life with Keith Brockett. She simply needed to make a fresh start without it, and Stuart understood that completely. When she'd left, after making absolutely certain that Meghan was as well-adjusted as she could be after Brockett's attack, Caro was going back to Birmingham, and to her job with Sisters In The Trades.

After waving her off, with every good wish for a wonderful life, Stuart had felt a profound sense of gratitude, not just for having had Caro's input with what had turned out to be a beautiful barn conversion, but also for the opportunity she'd given *them*, to help her get back on her feet. Her new-found confidence was a wonderful thing. She'd been profoundly grateful for her opportunity with the Thomsons, and she'd solemnly promised to find a way to continue in the spirit of what had been offered to her, and 'pay the kindness forward.'

It was all Stuart could ask for, and he was quietly convinced that Caro *would* find a way to do it. She was just that kind of person. She recognised and valued support, and she wanted the world to be a better place. After being an 'underdog' herself, she had vowed to help another one, somewhere down the line.

Like ripples in a pond, goodness had a way of filtering out, Throw a pebble of kindness into the water, and the effect could be profound. Turning someone's shitty life into a better one, one person at a time, really could make the world a better place.

He looked up as Meghan came around the corner from the courtyard. She'd been putting the horses away.

'What are you doing out here, with no coat on, Dad? It's bloody freezing! You'll catch your death of cold.'

He laughed at her concern. Sometimes she sounded just like his mother. He told her so, and she playfully punched him on the arm.

'Ow! Leave off, brat. That one hurt. Just because you're nearly as tall as me now, it doesn't give you the right to hit me harder than you used to when you were knee high.'

'Oh, for God's sake, Dad; toughen up! That was just a tap. Don't tell me you're going soft in your old age? And you can stop calling me a brat any time you like. I'm nearly sixteen, now. I think you should start calling me Meg.'

'Oh, is that right? You want to be all grown up, now? Well, okay, but know this, young lady; even if you were a *hundred* and sixteen, you'd still be my brat.'

She rolled her eyes. 'Don't be such an idiot, Dad. That would make you, what, a hundred and forty-eight?'

'Somewhere around that, I guess, and I'd be a pretty bad-tempered old bastard at that, wouldn't I? Much worse than I am now!'

'You're not so bad now. Most of the time.'

'I'll take that. So not everything I say or do, or don't say or don't do, is wrong? Can I have that in writing please?'

'If you insist, since you're such a cretin and I have to humour you so much. But I do have to say one thing...'

'Oh, and what's that? Should I put a helmet and a flak jacket on, before you do?'

'No, Dad. I just have to say, that while you get far too many things wrong and probably always will because you're a man, and my dad, and all kinds of other seriously uncool things, this wasn't one of them.' She swept her hand across the house, barn and stables. 'This was hell of a job to get right, and you did it.'

'We both did it, Meggie, or should I say *Meg*, since you're so grown up and sophisticated now. We *both* pulled this together, and you've done a hell of a job too! We make a pretty good team, don't we, for a couple of erstwhile screw-ups?'

'Yeah, we do. And I didn't mean it when I said you're uncool as a dad. I actually think you're the coolest dad on the planet. I'm sorry for all the times I was mean to you. That letter I wrote, and everything? I didn't mean to be so horrible. I think I was just so pissed off about everything that was wrong in my life, and I didn't know how to handle it. I think I hated you for a while, but it wasn't for long. I hope you know that.'

'I do, and it's okay, sweetheart. I hated *myself* for a lot longer, and I think it's always harder to forgive ourselves than it is to forgive anyone else. But we have to, or we can't move on. I've finally forgiven myself now, for what I did, and I hope you have too.'

He felt her slip an arm around his waist, and he slipped one back, around hers. She laid her head on his shoulder.

'Have you ever wondered if we live on Redemption Road for a reason, Dad? It seems like fate took us to Teapot Cottage, and to Astro, which led us to here. It all feels really special, and connected somehow, and after everything we went through, maybe the name of the road is part of it.'

'Yeah, I *have* wondered about that. It does seem kind of funny; the idea of being 'delivered from sin,' as the definition goes.'

You've never been a sinner, in the real sense. You're actually one of the good guys, Dad. Good people sometimes do bad stuff, and it's like, you did some bad stuff, but you've more than made up for it. It's not just your own life you've turned around. You've helped a lot of people do *good* stuff, like me, and Caro with her new life, and Darren with his horse hospital. And, maybe even Fiona. Maybe you'll make a big difference to her life too. You're my hero, Dad.'

'Can I have *that* in writing, too?'

'What do *you* think? I have a reputation to think about, and you don't get to blow it by waving soppy confessions around.'

'Well, how about this; I promise I won't kick off if you call me a *superhero*, instead of just a hero. Heroes are boring. Superheroes are a little bit special, and I'd like to be that, to you.'

'You already are, you dingbat. You're my own personal Superman. But I do have to say one thing…

'If you ever put your underpants on over your trousers, I will strangle you in your sleep, and that's a promise.'

Note from the Author:

If you enjoyed *Ruin, Reins and Redemption,* or any of my other books, I'd love you to leave a review on Amazon.
It would mean so much to me!

www.anniecookwriter.com

Facebook: Annie Cook Writer
Instagram: anniecookwriter

Birmingham and Solihull Women's Aid do a magnificent job of helping women in crisis. If you would like to support their cause, you can do so here:
https://bswaid.org/get-involved/

And for fabulous retro clothing, find: DollyandDotty.co.uk

Acknowledgements

Thanks go to:

My rock; my husband, Kerry Purvis, for giving me the time and space to be creative. I couldn't write a single thing without his unwavering support and belief in everything I do.

Rondy Ginawan, my wonderful friend in Bali who took time out of running his hugely successful business there, to talk to me about the Hindu faith and its principles. He is the kindest man, who makes time for everyone, in whatever way he can.

Cheltenham Equine Vets, for their invaluable advice on horse health and management.

Sally Dennis, from Birmingham and Solihull Women's Aid, for taking the time to talk to me about the support that amazing place provides to women in domestic crisis.

My beautiful friends Dawn Walter, Deborah Rayner, Karen Gidall, Katherine McDiarmid and Lisa Raats, for the incredible brainstorming process that got me to here.

Aisha Jamal, for her work in designing the cover for this book.

Gwen Morrison and her team at PublishNation for the work involved in getting this book to market.

Dolly and Dotty retro clothing store; one of my favourite clothing retailers, for allowing me to use their brand name as an example of just how fabulously a woman can cultivate her own retro style.

To my fans and supporters across the world, whose excitement and encouragement means everything to me.

The Power of Notes and Spells
A Teapot Cottage Tale (#2)

**Every woman dreams of finding the love of her life.
But what do you do when yours brings baggage that
can hurt you and your family?**

Feen Raven is often described as more than just a little bit barmy. The young 'white witch' has finally found her soulmate, but old family wounds are opened again when she finds out who he's involved with.

Gavin Black is on an unhappy errand that forces him to reconnect with his estranged mother. All he wants is to claim what's his and go home again, without any complications.

Carla Walton can't let go of a grudge. After a lifetime of pushing everyone away, she is isolated, bitter, and blaming everyone else for her problems. She wants to be left alone so she can keep ignoring her demons.

But Teapot Cottage, with its mysterious ability to heal the broken-hearted, always has a more complicated agenda for people who don't want to rake up the past. Pretty soon, Gavin, Feen and Carla come to question everything they think they do and don't want in life.

Will love and a little bit of magic help them find a way forward? Or will old family fractures be too hard to heal?

Come to the Lake District, to a gentle place where a beautiful blend of music and magic can heal the hardest hearts.

A Moral Swerve

Nobody comes home expecting to find intruders -
But what would you do if you did?

Alison Jones is single, lives alone, and doesn't have a lot of self-awareness. But, after coming home to find burglars in her house, she does a terrible thing without thinking, and is forced to confront some ugly truths about herself.

Darren Davies is a petty thief, stuck in the revolving door between small-time crime and prison. After he makes the biggest mistake of his life, he is compelled to re-evaluate the path his life is taking, and deal with the demons that drive him.

When Darren and Alison's lives intersect, they each find themselves on a soul-searing journey, as they struggle to come to terms with the catastrophic impact of their acts and omissions. After stumbling through the wreckage, the future for them both becomes crystal clear, but it's not what either of them expected.

As one door opens and another slams shut, choices expand and diminish.

At the crossroads of Beginnings and Endings,
who decides to go where?

WHEN IT'S MEANT TO HAPPEN
A Teapot Cottage Tale (#3)

**Having a baby is something most women
dream of and plan for. But what does it mean if you can't
make it happen, no matter how hard you try?**

Debby Davies longs for a family of her own. She is desperate to have a baby with the husband she adores, but fruitless years of trying to conceive have left her feeling like a failure. It's starting to make her crazy, that she can't seem to achieve the one thing she always felt destined to do.

Darren Davies is at his wits' end with his wife. Her simmering resentment is changing her in ways that really scare him, and the horrible way her parents treat him is starting to take its toll. He's beginning to question whether their marriage can survive what feels like a never-ending series of storms.

As their doubts take hold, that their love can survive, they know they're in the last chance saloon. But Teapot Cottage, with its mystical ability to pour balm on battered souls, has plans for Debby and Darren that show them what's possible in ways they could never have imagined.

Can they stay together and face a very different future from the one they had planned, or will they find the challenges too great, and go their separate ways?

Run away from home for a while! Come to the Lake District, to a place where miracles can happen, with the help of a little bit of magic!